Tales from Ballyhornet

Sarah's Gate

VALERIE MAHER

Brookland Press

First published

by

Brookland Press
16 Roseville Crescent
Randalstown
Co. Antrim
BT41 2LY
Tel: Antrim 472696

ISBN 1 902013 00 X

Typeset by December Publications

Printed by Colourbooks Ltd

Cover illustration by Rowel Friers

All characters and events in this novel are entirely fictitious and bear no relation to any real person or actual happening. Any resemblance to real characters or to actual events is entirely accidental.

Dedicated

to

Dorothy and Jack

Also by Valerie Maher

WALLS OF GLASS

by

Pretani Press

An autobiography of the author's own life

Contents

1

Saturday, 24 February 1996

The city of Belfast and the smaller towns and villages that surround it had been draped with a blanket of snow the previous night. Silently it had dusted the houses sheltering the sleeping inhabitants of the estate as they tried to find sweet oblivion from their worries brought on by the lack of money, and all that goes with it.

The grey early-morning sky made the trees silhouetted against it appear almost spooky, their lifeless branches resembling the gnarled limbs of blind lepers begging for help.

The sun played hide-and-seek between the clouds that hovered menacingly over the small estate on the outskirts of Belfast. It had now turned the night-white snow to dirty slush. The same clouds hung over most of Northern Ireland, Ballyhornet just somehow or other appeared more forlorn. God must have been having a kip when the estate was being built and forgot to give it a heart. It was too late to give it a transplant now that the rest of its innards were falling apart.

It was indeed a grey day. If you had a brain at all you would have stayed under the duvet, cocooned like an unborn child in the womb and dreaming of the impossible. Dreams of the government handing out holidays to Barbados for those on the dole. The streets there would be multi-coloured. The people would sway to the music of Bob Marley, and the women would be beautiful, even if their beauty had been enhanced by the effects of a couple of tokes of the auld wacky backy that would most likely be easily available on this particular island.

In Ballyhornet the streets all looked the same, dull and lifeless and devoid of women blessed with beauty; apart from the young, whose faces had not yet been scarred by the wrinkles brought on with worry about where the next cheque would come from to pay the bills, groceries, catalogue payments and drink for the auld lad at the weekend. It would take more than a few puffs of Acupulco Gold to put a rosy hue on the female population here.

People referred to it as being a bastard of an estate. No shops, no community centre, no atmosphere, no jobs, no hope. Just a pile of bricks and mortar put together for those who wanted to escape the hustle and bustle of the city. Ironically, the city of Belfast was now an escape from the life of the estate, black taxis shuttling to and fro to keep up with those in search of life outside Ballyhornet, men heading for the pubs that offered the lure of sex and alcoholic oblivion.

In the early hours of the morning when the snow had been unsullied Ballyhornet had looked almost picturesque. Now hamburger boxes, chip papers and beer tins from Friday night's drunkenness littered the streets. The snow on the roofs around the chimney pots had been melted by the heat from fires and grey smoke was billowing towards the sky as if it had an empathy with the clouds. Water had started to drip from eaves, and a film of condensation coated the windows as the residents boiled their kettles for a first brew of coffee or tea to warm their hearts or lubricate arthritic joints.

A magpie hopped from one leg to the other on the branch of a leafless tree as if performing some bizarre ritualistic dance, perhaps a Snow Dance. Its beady eyes were trained on the green van parked at the kerb, a van more commonly known as the "green wine gum" by the customers, since it was so old and weather-beaten it resembled a green wine gum that had been well and truly masticated by a toothless hag. It belonged to the vegetable seller who called each Monday, Wednesday and Saturday mornings with the housewives of the estate thus saving them the walk to and from the shops, that were a good mile away. Most had little choice, as the family car was usually driven by the man of the house, and the man of the house was almost certainly in bed until lunch-time either nursing a hangover or out of sheer boredom. The smell of more snow still hung in the air this morning and the less the housewives had to carry back through the cold, with the snow blattering them in the face, the better would be their thankless task.

The back doors were latched on to the sides of the van, partly to stop the wind from blowing them to and fro, and partly to let the customers see what was on offer. Ernie, the owner of this mobile wreck stood beside it, hunched over and blowing into his cupped hands in a vain effort to get a bit of circulation back into his frozen fingers. He had been contemplating getting rid of it for quite a while now and the cold that was playing havoc with his extremities had made up his mind for him until he reminded himself that the money he would receive on the dole would not keep him up in the style of life to which he had been used. His annual holiday in the sun would have to be abandoned, the withdrawal symptoms if he ditched his smoking habit of forty a day would be painful, as would be giving up his weekend bottle of malt whiskey. The fact that his smoker's plugher might clear up if he did give up the fags was not a sufficient incentive to give up the "dirty, filthy habit", as his wife called it, and he doubted very much if the lack of money would put a stop to his weekend tipple. Anyway, he was on tenterhooks twenty-four hours a day. His nerves were shattered as he was doing the double and he could not be too careful. All strangers were potential snoopers and he had to keep reminding himself to be ready with a good story if approached unexpectedly by a nosy stranger.

A muffled crunch in the snow heralded the approach of someone or something towards the van. It sounded menacing and the hairs on the back of his neck stood upright. Ernie had been robbed that many times over the years he automatically pulled his money bag over his head to hand over to whoever was about to lighten him of his morning's takings.

That's it, thought Ernie, his body sagging in defeat. The bloody van goes! Tae hell wi' holidays, fegs an' whiskey, whoever it is can have the friggin' lot, lock, stock an' barrel, fer I'm pissed aff an' friggin' freezin' this very mornin' without gettin' robbed again.

He heard a loud click! click! and froze. Holy Jaysus! Whoever it is has a bloody gun, he thought, as his legs buckled beneath him. His life flashed before his eyes and he started praying out loud. "Lord, I've worked this estate all through the Troubles, twenty odd effin' bloody years. I have been subjected to the occasional hiding, but never have I luked down the gun barrel." With eyes upturned he pleaded, "Please, God, spare me the bullet. Let him bate hells bells outa me, but don't let the bastard put out me lights."

"Hae ye a light fer this feg Ernie? This flamin' lighter is buggered, no flint or else run outa fuel. I think I'll get meself wan o' those wee disposables, this bloody Zippo gulps the petrol like an' auld banger."

Peggy, the one with a face that would look more at home carved out on the side of Mount Rushmore along with the Presidents of the United States, was standing with a shopping bag hanging over her scrawny arm knocking seven bells out of her lighter against the palm of her spade-like hand in an effort to get the fuel to the wick.

Ernie recognised the gruff voice that sounded as if it was coming out of the boots of a weary and bronchitic navvy, and relaxed. Turning on the spot, he cursed Peggy in and out of hell for scaring seven shades of crap out of him.

"Aye, I've a light all right, I'll light ye across that road wi' th' back aff me haun for creepin' up on me wi' thon size nine feet aff yours – bloody 'Big fut' wudn't be in it. Give us a light! Christ knows I cud have sworn that wuz a gun bein' cocked. I know th' flamin' ceasefire has ended but I wuz prayin' they wud leave bloody vegetable men alone. After all ye have till ate."

He lit Peggy's cigarette with the tip of his own that was almost down to a butt, dropped it on the ground (no need to stamp it out as the slush drowned it) and gave Peggy a look that would have withered the nose cone of Concorde.

Peggy's cheeks that had turned purple and almost collapsed with the effort of sucking on Ernie's butt, in her bid to get her cigarette lit, now returned to their normal shade of ash grey and she guldered, "Ah, shut up, ye daft auld eejit!"

This gave her a fit of the smoker's cough that most of Ballyhornet suffered from. As her eyes watered with the effort she spluttered, "Who th' hell wud want to bump you aff? God knows thur's nat much ye cud do wi' a beg af carrots an' motley fruit. If ye sold the lot it wudn'd pay fer a piddle in a railway piss house." She wiped the tears from her eyes with a piece of toilet roll, then proceeded to wipe a "dewdrop" off the end of her nose before it fell on the cigarette that she had stuck in between her lips for safety.

Ernie turned on Peggy with vehemence, his untimely shock giving way to bad temper, and hollered, "I'll have ye know my life's savin's are in that van."

Peggy was taken aback at Ernie's unexpected verbal attack, and she composed herself by inhaling deeply on her cigarette before pouncing. She poked him in the chest with her bony finger: "Get stuffed! Life's savin's me arsehole! If I know you Ernie Flaherty, ye'll have money in every bank an' orifice in Ulster, an I'm nat talkin' money that rattles, I'm thinkin' af th' kind that folds wi' th' numbers five, twenty, fifty an' a hundred printed on the corners."

A humongous inflamed zit, threatening to explode from Peggy's manly chin, made Ernie baulk. He ducked like a boxer avoiding a right hook, hitting the front of his head on the side of his van as he did so. He rubbed his temple and cursed: "Hell roast ye, nye me flamin' nut will bate like blazes all day wi' th' pain." He cursed her again in and out of hell as he nursed his head.

"What's wrang wi' ye! Are yer bloody nerves bad or somethin'? Bobbin' about like a flea-ridden auld cat. Will ye stan' at pace fer yer makin' me head light." She bent down to see if he looked concussed, for he was wobbling about like a buoy at sea.

Ernie blushed to the roots of his bright ginger hair, and with a flustered wave of his right arm tried to avoid staring Peggy in the eye, for he was not only embarrassed at making a fool of himself, he was also aware of his substantial funds that he tried to hide from his wife. "It's all right fer you. I'm a Taig among Prods in this estate. I nearly shat meself when ye sneaked up on me like that. Sneakin' up on people! Especially at this time when everyone in th' country is beggin' fer a bita pace."

"Ach, stop yer nyamerin' an' moanin' for Chrissakes, yer nat th' only Fenian in this estate. There are more Catholic families in here than ye think, an' nat one a' them gets on the way you do. But then of coorse they are so busy tryin' to make ends meet they have no time to worry about the bloody eejits who have nathin' better to do than blow us all inta kingdom come. Nye, get yer finger out for I'm bloody freezin' standin' here. Freeze the goolies aff the Statue af Liberty, that's if it wuz a man af coorse. But before ye start yakkin' I know it isn't, so don't go rabbitin' on about it."

"Thurs nat much hate about th' day right enough, is there Peggy?" said he, trying to change the subject, as he knew Peggy spoke the truth. "A few months in th' Australian sun wid nat go amiss this time o' th' year all the while. Wud ye agree wi' me?"

"Aye I wud, Ernie," Peggy answered. "But do ye nat think Australia is a bit on th' far side?"

"The further away from this God forsaken place the better, if ye ask me. By the luk af yersel' ye cud do wi' a bit af the auld sun. Yer like death warmed up."

Peggy threw him a dirty look, and pulled the collar of her long woollen cardigan up over her ears and started to perform a little dance in a vain attempt to get some heat into her huge feet. She had come out of the house in her husband's carpet slippers without reverence for the snow and it gave no mercy in return.

"Well, seein' as ye mention it, I suppose a few weeks in a warmer climate wud nat go amiss, a wee bit af a tan might just make me that wee bit more attractive!" She patted her hair and batted her eyelids at Ernie.

His heart dropped to the pit of his stomach at the idea of Peggy fancying him. Surely she's jokin? I hope to hell sh' hasn't set her eyes on me for I'm nat that desperate, he thought. On th' other haun, maybe she sees herself in a different light than the rest aff us – a dark light. He tittered to himself as his brain ran riot. He pictured Peggy stripped naked, the light of a flickering candle playing havoc with her zit, and his titter caught in his throat when she spewed forth another prize winning statement.

"A week tucked up in bed wi' Tom Cruise wud do me rightly, Ernie. God, thon man wud get yer engine warmed up wi' just a luk of them lovely, sexy eyes af his."

Ernie had a vision of Peggy and Tom Cruise together and his mind boggled. "If you stood fernenst Tom Cruise he wud need a ladder till reach yer bake till kiss it. Th' maun's about a fut shorter than ye, fer Christ's sake."

"Well, he cud staun on a bucket. I'm nat that proud. An' anyway, when yer lyin' down size doesn't matter, as Dudley Moore might have said to Bo Derek."

"A case af nat the size but what ye do wi' it then, Peggy? Then af coorse ye wud probably have till catch him first, thon wee legs af his might go like the divil when he realizes the damage ye cud do wi' thon hauns af yours if ye caught him. A fondle wi' those roun' th' family jewels cud lave 'im damaged fer life."

Peggy threw a stare of disgust in Ernie's direction. He watched in amazement as she closed her eyes and trembled with imagined passion. He pictured Tom Cruise racing through the streets holding up his breeks as Peggy begged him to bed her and his mind boggled. He glanced at Peggy, who was hyperventilating by now, and grabbed a paper bag should she need to breathe into it to help stem an attack of the panics. He had heard about this on a television programme and he hoped he could put it to use some day. He watched in amazement as her eyelids opened and her eyes turned backwards in her head and braced himself in case he would have to catch her if she fainted with lust.

The thought of this hunk of masculinity embracing and pulling her body towards his almost had Peggy in a sexual frenzy, or as her husband Rab would have joked "Her grillicks ached an' her oxters quivered." Her vision of Tom Cruise in Dracula filled her with unabandoned passion and even Ernie was in mortal danger of being raped on the spot. Her sexual appetite was insatiable: if it wore trousers and buttoned its coat to the right it was fair game. She could almost feel the film star's lips on hers and she groaned as they became one in her mind. The cold had left her now as she became more engrossed in her fantasy. She rolled the sleeves of her cardigan up and fanned her face with her purse to cool down as she had taken a hot flush. Her breathing became so heavy Ernie thought she was going into an asthma attack and he stepped back in alarm. In doing so he hit the van and sent a few vegetables rolling out of it.

Peggy was brought back to reality when an onion landed on her big toe and she cursed Ernie for intruding into her fantasy world. "Damn ye, Ernie, will ye nat handle yer onions more carefully."

Ernie laughed and Peggy wriggled on the spot, as if trying to suppress the urge to go to the toilet. She blushed and took a long draw of her cigarette, wiped away an imaginary bit of ash from her cardigan and asked Ernie for a few pounds of the afore mentioned vegetable.

"Aye all right, but leave my onions out af this Peggy, I can handle me onions any way I like. The day I can't take care af me onions will be my problem an' nat yours."

He rummaged in the sack of carrots until he found a large one and proceeded to wave it under Peggy's nose.

"Wud this one suffice yer needs?" he cajoled, as he knew Peggy would get a kick out of anything that resembled a phallic symbol.

"Get away a' this, ye auld eejit," giggled Peggy. "Stop play actin an' give us a stone af them Egyptian spuds as well, an' less af th' bloody twaddle."

"Your th' one that's play actin', Peggy. For a minute thur I had visions aff ye rapin' me on th' spot." He cocked his head to one side. "Here, have ye bloody Royalty comin' fer dinner? Them Egyption spuds are forty-five pence a poun' this time af th' year."

"Holy Jaysus! Did King Tut grow them in his back yard, or did ye travel 'til Egypt to pick them yerself?" Peggy almost fainted as she totted up how much fourteen pounds of these potatoes would cost and a bottle of gin flashed before her eyes. "Do you realise I cud get plastered fer th' price of them spuds? Give me th' chape wans, fer Christs sake. I'll cut th' black bits aff. That auld lad af min' can nyeuk a few fram that snattery farmer he knows if he wants till ate like a gent, an' throw in a couple af carrots as well, an' stap yer auld dirty talk ...!"

"Dirty talk! Sure ye thrive on it, Peg. I see it's stew the day again by the luk af things." He tilted his head to the side and asked, "Do ye ever vary yer diet?"

"How do ye know I'm makin' stew?" Peggy inquired indignantly out of the side of her mouth for fear the neighbours would hear, as if she would be jailed for daring to even contemplate making stew for the dinner. If truth be known, she felt a trifle guilty as she made stew more times than enough as it was both quick and cheap.

"Holy God! It wudn't take a degree to work that out. If I had a poun' af mince beef on me I cud have made it for ye, I wud have had all th' ingredients."

"Aye, thur's no flies on you, Ernie." She laughed out loud now as she had got the drift of Ernie's wit. She slapped him so hard on the back he lost his footing and landed head first in a bag of parsnips.

"Haule on thur, Peggy," cried Ernie as he dusted himself down and regained his composure. "Ye have a right hook on ye like Frank Bruno, it cud flur a heavyweight boxer wi' one swipe."

"Have a titter af wit, will ye. The way yer carryin' on the neighbours will think we're havin' an affair with all this pushin' an' shovin' in broad daylight." She twittered about like a pubescent teenager and once more patted her lank greasy hair with her free hand.

Ernie baulked at the very idea of the woman even imagining having an affair with himself. He emptied the carrots into her shopping bag, lightened her purse of a few pounds and tried to bid her goodbye, for he knew Peggy would keep a man gabbling for hours if she were given half a chance.

The curtains on some of the houses were drawn slightly to the side by nosy neighbours who had heard the din. Peggy gripped her large canvas bag full of vegetables and cocked her nose in the air.

"Wud ye luk at them auld gather ups gazin' out like farmer Brown's cows. Ye wud think butter wudn't melt in their gubs. I cud tell ye a thing or two about some af them'ns, only it wud be like the arse af th' pot callin' the kettle black."

"At layste yer honest," Ernie answered in her defence. "I have to admire ye for that. There's no round edges on ye. They are as sharp as yer wit, Peggy. Everythin's in black an' white, nat coloured or faded roun' th' edges."

"Well, there's no back durs in me, Ernie, if that's what ye mean. I say what's on me mind an' get it over an done with. I can't be accused of bein' two-faced like some people I cud mention." She cocked her head towards the pensioners' flats as she made this last remark. "Take that auld doll over thur, fer instance. She luks that oule she must huv wore peat moss fer nappies when she wuz born."

"Where dae ye get the sayin's from?" asked Ernie quizzically "When did they wear peat moss on their bums?"

"Ach, they put peat moss on the weans backsides before nappies an' such were invented. It wuz either that or let the wee crathurs widdle all over ye."

"I thought ye grew things in peat. Vegetables an' the like," replied Ernie. "Well now, ye learn somethin' every day, Peggy. Here am I thinkin' how well me onions luk when all along they have been grown in muck awash wi' pee from years af widdlin' weans."

Peggy tut-tutted and poked Ernie in the ribs. "That's moss peat, nat peat moss, ye stupid get."

Ernie scratched his head as he thought about the difference between the two. All of a sudden the answer hit him with a jolt and he prided

Peggy on her intelligence. "You're nat just a pretty face after all." He had to stifle a snigger, for she had a face that could have stopped a bus at fifty paces. If Peggy had been around when the Vikings landed in their long boats they would have stuck to pillaging and put rape on hold.

"Aye, I'm better lukin' than that prune-faced Sarah Cruickshank. Gate, gate, gate, that's all she can talk about. Poor Elsie, imagine havin' a mother like that livin' opposite ye, the crathur must be feelin' suicidal. If it wasn't fer her wee jaunts up t' me an' my auld lad's house at the weekend, even though it's only a few durs up, she wud go doo-lally."

She tut-tutted once again, shook her head from side to side and sighed before bidding Ernie goodbye. Turning on her heels she plodded and skidded through the slush towards her home.

The magpie stood on one leg and craked its neck at the glitter of the tray on the weighing scales, its beady eyes taking in all they could. Its mate flew from the other side of the tree, landed on the same branch and sidled towards her partner. At a time when being faithful in marriage didn't amount to a hill of beans, the magpie remained loyal to its mate for life. The two birds sat motionless as they watched Peggy amble unsteadily up the street to her house. If she had seen them she would have saluted them and spat on the ground for good luck, but she was too busy trying to keep her balance through the melting snow without taking in the scenery.

Ernie climbed back into his van and beeped his horn three times, a sign he was going to drive further up the street. A strangled wheeze escaped from the engine when he turned the key in the ignition and he sighed with relief when the engine started to purr. If Ernie's van had been human it would be on disability living allowance it was that knackered.

An upstairs window opened in one of the houses and a bedraggled, unshaven male thrust his head through the opening.

"Will ye fuck up or I'll stick that horn up yer arse sideways. Can a man nat get lyin' in of a Saturday mornin' wi'out arseholes like you creatin' a fuckin' din."

Ernie stuck two fingers through his open window. "It's lucky for some that can get a lie-in any mornin', never min' a Saturday." He felt scundered at the sight of the man in his dirty string vest. The same auld lad hadn't a days work in him. He honked his horn for six seconds non-stop for badness. That lazy old bastard lay in every morning and Ernie couldn't care two diddely squats if he annoyed him for he was a scrounger of the first degree.

He would have taken the death rattle off a dying man and come back for the shroud.

The man's wife appeared at the front door and proceeded to hurl a barrage of insults in Ernie's direction. "Did ye hear what my maun said. He taule ye to fuck aff, can ye nat understaun' English?"

"Ah get away ina this, woman," laughed Ernie. "Ye have a gub on ye that wud stap a train, take that luk aff yer bake before th' devil claps eyes on ye or he'll use ye as a gargoyle when ye snuff it. An' by the way, I can spake better English than you!"

"Did you hear what that skitter said, Billy?" She shouted up the stairs. "I'm affronted I am! Did you know the butcher in the shopping centre thinks I'm a fine lukin' woman fer me age."

"Belt up woman! Yer as bad as that bloody horn af his. Yer gob blasts away fram mornin' till night. It wud ... it wud shatter glass. Put a sock in it fer Christ's sake."

Ernie knew that to the butcher in the shopping centre, a woman was just another bit of meat to play around with. "Ah get away wi' ye, woman. It was no compliment, believe me. Sure that horny auld geezer wud jump on a cracked baule!"

Her husband had the last word. "I have to agree wi' the man, an' apart from him bein' over-sexed he uses a white stick an' he owns a labrador! Does that nat tell ye somethin'?"

The bedroom window slammed shut at the same time as the front door, which almost came off its hinges it was slammed that hard.

Ernie put his boot on the accelerator and his van backfired. The noise startled the magpies on the tree, they left their perch in a flurry of black wings and loosened snow and headed toward quieter territory.

2

"*Clart!*" retorted Sarah Cruickshank, as she fixed the net on her living room window. She had been nebbing out the window of her flat as usual and had not been disappointed in what she saw.

"Dirty big gop, good for nothin' other than scrubbin' out toilets. That one should be neutered!. Wud ye luk at the pockle's of that big glipe, what th' hell men see in 'er is a mystery. To hell an' she falls on her arse for that's where her brains are."

She let the curtain fall back into place, and pottered towards her chair and plopped herself down, her spindly legs went up and down like pistons as she positioned her skinny feet into her extra wide carpet slippers. Her bunion had been throbbing for weeks and it was making her more bad tempered than usual, although it didn't take much to put our Sarah into a bad mood.

"Don't go casting aspersions about what you don't understand, mother. You know nothing about the woman apart from what you conjure up in that over fertile and over aged brain of yours."

Elsie Friars glared at Sarah in disgust and adjusted her glasses so they sat snugly on the bridge of her nose. She held the *Sun* newspaper slightly to the left of herself so as the weak winter sun that shone through her mother's netted window in the small living room would be an aid to her ailing eyesight.

"I know plenty, our Elsie. I wasn't born yesterday ye know. Men would go with anythin' that wore a skirt, put a beg over her head an' after half a bottle of whiskey no man would say no. Although, God knows, they would have to be desperate. The woman doesn't even know what soap or deodorant's for, never min' how to use it. Disinfectant and bleach must never be on her shoppin' list. Her house must be piggin' inta the bargain."

"Her house is not dirty. Rab cleans it as well as Peggy. Rab was in the army you know, anyone who's been in the army is very meticulous about their hygiene," retorted Elsie. She removed her glasses and squinted at her mother, huffing like a bull in a rage at the same time. Without her glasses Elsie was almost blind, and at times she looked on it as a blessing. If she took her glasses off, her mother was nothing other than a blur, which suited her down to the ground as the sight of her made her feel ill. Her mother's bitterness showed itself in her screwed-up face and her wizened body resembled a dried-up corpse at times. Elsie often wondered what held it together apart from sinew and bone.

"Aye, meticulous and shifty," replied Sarah, puckering her lips after she made this much thought out observation. "In for a whiplash claim an' he can turn that neck of his full circle. If ye ask me he's nothin' other than a crook."

"I'm not asking you anything, ma. Rab would run to the ends of the earth for anyone, including you, and you know it. His legs are run off him over the head of that flamin' gate of yours."

"He's the dregs of humanity!" snapped Sarah.

"God forgive ye, ma. He's a human being. He has feelings like everyone else. Everyone apart from yourself, who has feelings for no-one. At least he doesn't go running people down all the time. You have to give a bit of lee-way now an' then ye know. I'm the one who has to pick up the pieces when you blow your top, ma, an' that's becoming a regular occurrence these days."

Elsie turned the page of her newspaper. She replaced her glasses but had lost the thread of what she had been reading. She folded the newspaper and threw it onto the floor with a sigh. Trying to read in Sarah's company was futile.

"You're puttin' me into an early grave, do ye know that?" screeched Sarah.

"An early grave! Good heavens, ma, you're nearly in your nineties. If anyone's goin' to an early grave it will be Rab. He's barely turned fifty an' he has a bad heart an' lungs, and before you say it he never smoked or drank in his life."

"Neither did yer da, an' he died at seventy. An' I am not old, I'm mature!"

"If you're mature, ma, I'm an infant. An' there's a hell of a difference between fifty an' seventy!" rebuked Elsie. "And another thing. My da didn't suffer like Rab. He died in his sleep. He probably didn't know a thing about it."

Sarah reneged. "Well I suppose he's not too bad." She huffed for a few seconds as she thought about Peggy. "But that Peggy one is nothin' other than a trollop!" She then got up from her chair and started dusting with a rag that she kept in her apron pocket, then she began fidgeting with the ornaments, a sure sign that she had lost the argument.

Elsie rested her elbow on her knee to steady her right arm. Her frayed nerves had her shaking to the marrow, as Sarah had done nothing other than bad mouth the world and it's wife for the past two hours. She had been up since the crack of dawn attending to Sarah's needs, delivering her newspaper and gathering up her bits and pieces that needed to be washed, for Sarah didn't have a washing machine. A phone call had got her up an hour earlier that day. Sarah had rung at half seven to inform her of the previous night's snowfall and that the end of the world must be coming as the street looked so dead. Would she come over and keep her company? Elsie felt so tired and peeved off she wished the end of the world *was* nigh so she could have a few hour's extra kip of a morning. Sure the flaming estate looked dead every morning, why was today so different? No, it was only an excuse to get her over early, an extra hour of listening to Sarah's incessant bitching about how every person in the news was either a degenerate, a thief or a scoundrel. According to Sarah every female in show business must have had more nips and tucks and face-lifts than hot dinners.

"I'd have had my own face lifted only it would have dropped again at the price," Sarah informed her daughter, who was now ready for screaming, her nerves were that jangled.

Elsie squinted out of the corner of her eye at Sarah and thought to herself, it would take Harland and Wolff shipyard workers to do the scaffolding, your face is that dropped.

Sarah had taken two *Pro-plus* earlier on in the morning. They gave her energy and her mouth was now firing on all cylinders. The extra caffeine had the effect of a lubricant on her tongue.

She glared at her daughter who had once again lifted the newspaper in another bid to read.

"As for the nude model on the third page of that newspaper yer lookin' at, don't they realise breasts are fer feedin' youngsters an' not fer the titillation of randy auld gets. Standin' there without a runion on, ye wid think sex had only been invented." Sarah's face puckered up in disgust as she tried to pry the newspaper away from Elsie's hands as if she were a dirty old man caught in the act of some sexual deviancy.

"Catch yourself on, give me back my newspaper," snapped Elsie. "You must have had your moments, for you had more than your allocated share of two-point-four children in your lifetime. I'm sure you felt a flutter when you rode on the pillion of your dearly intended. Don't tell me you just sat and held hands astride his bike an' picked daisies in the woods at the end of the day."

The look of disgust turned to one of horror at Elsie's insinuations.

"Don't you dare accuse me of gettin' up to shenanigans or of being over-sexed. Anyway, my husband had a job, remember."

"What has a job got to do with it?" asked Elsie in amazement. "Does a job entitle one to more nookie than those who are unemployed?"

Elsie changed position. She plumped up a cushion, and tucking her legs up under herself, laid her head down on the cushion hoping the softness would ease the headache she could feel starting at the back of her neck. Sarah rambled on. She had no sympathy for others in pain, even though she herself moaned about every ailment imaginable, from constipation to the nipping ulcer on her ankle. An ulcer the size of a pinhead. This gave her something in common with the Queen Mother, who supposedly suffers from the same malady. So either she felt an empathy or else she felt entitled to lord it in front of her neighbours, who were fed up with the hoity-toity voice she put on when riled.

"People who are unemployed should not have children!" Sarah hit the arm of her chair with her fist and her eyeballs nearly shot out of her head. "They should abstain from all that auld carry-on, put their energy where it's needed. Years ago they would be trampin' the streets in shoes worn to the uppers with a piece tucked under their oxters in search of work, instead of cafufflin' about between the sheets."

"God, would you listen to it. Past her three score years and ten and talkin' about sex. And just exactly what would your answer be to the thousands of unemployed in Ireland who felt the urge to engage in a little bit of the other?" And you mean lunch, not a piece. A piece of what?

Sarah glared at Elsie in utter horror. "The other" was not in her vocabulary, in fact anything referring to the act of sex was not "nice talk".

"A piece of my mind ye sarky know all." A remedy for the unemployed not having children came to mind. "The women should have all taken away after having two youngsters, or else the men should all be castrated!" This was Sarah's way of referring to a hysterectomy. She hirpled over to the window and pulled back the lace curtain. She started tut-tutting and with a beckoning of her index finger called Elsie over to witness the antics that were going on across the road.

Two teenagers were engaged in a romantic embrace in the doorway of a house opposite the flats.

"Now that's what puts bad thoughts into the young, standin' there birdlin' in broad daylight, kissin' and feelin' each others bums. They get it from their parents, ye know. Did you know that child's mother lets that young lad stay th' night? He must sleep with that wee hussy, for the rest of the youngsters take up the other rooms along with all the other degenerates who call with their carry-outs from the off licence. It's only eleven in the mornin'. He must have stayed th' night and now he's goin' home to his own house to lie in his pit for the rest of the day an' scrounge off his parents. Bloody vampires, stay up all night, then sleep all day. Sure ye would know they are vampires: their necks are covered in bites. The next thing ye will see is thon mother of hers wheelin' the pram up the street while that wee tramp lies in bed snatterin' all day. The youngen's aren't content till they have a buggie or some other contraption wi' a chile gurnin' in it. The mothers an' fathers have no shame in today's society. They probably flaunt their animalistic antics in front of their weans instead of keepin' it behind closed doors like me an' my husband did. Ach, an-nee an' an-nee, what's the world comin' to?"

She collapsed into her armchair and wiped her forehead with the corner of her apron. Her speech on the depravity of the teenagers of today had left her exhausted. She asked Elsie to put the kettle on for a cup of tea as her throat felt dry.

For a moment Elsie hoped her talking had tired her out. She might have a wee doze and give her ears a rest.

"Not a bit of wonder your throat's dry. That was near enough as long as President Clinton's and the mayor's speech put together at Christmas, and that was as big a waste of time as you trying to persuade the young to abstain from sex. Your husband was my father in case you've forgotten, so come down from your high horse and let me read this paper in peace. Birdlin! Where the hell did you get that expression from? You must have a very fruitful imagination, not to mention disgusting. Now who's talkin' sex? And, by the way, it is not animalistic as you so eloquently put it". Elsie said the word in a sarcastic tone which annoyed Sarah even more.

"*It is*!" Sarah yelled back, her voice taking on a new resonance. She sounded almost hysterical, like a DUP politician held captive at a Sinn Fein conference. "There should have been other ways to have weans."

"What other way can you have children? They don't appear from the blue, you know. The last time that happened there was a bright star in the east while the shepherds watched their flocks by night."

"Don't mock religion, our Elsie." Sarah yapped back. "Anyway, ye could adopt a child if ye were that desperate. God knows there are enough orphans in the world." Her toothless mouth screwed up like a button hole.

Elsie laughed at her mother's logic. "And just where do you think the children come from that are up for adoption? And you're the one that runs down religion, not me. So remember that in future, if you don't mind."

Sarah's screwed up mouth relaxed and started to flap and spit with temper. "From under-educated natives that know no better. The heat makes them do "*it*" or "*the other*", as you might say. I'm sure I don't know where you got that language from, ye girl ye. Marrying below yourself I suppose. An' I don't run down religion. I just don't believe all that much in it. Not when you look at the state of the world."

"Then all the children would be coloured and that would be another fault in your eyes. Sex is not only to have children, you know."

Elsie could have bitten her tongue off for she knew she had risked provoking her mother even further, but decided to go for gold. "It is an expression of one's love for another. And excuse me, I did not marry below myself, my father did that. And don't blame God for the state of the world. Human beings did that." Elsie prepared herself for a rollicking with this last remark but was surprised at her mother's response.

Sarah looked flustered and shifted uneasily in her chair, picking up imaginary bits of fluff with her fingers, and started wringing the corner of her apron, for she knew this last remark to be true.

"Ah give over. Talkin' nonsense ye are, an' at your age. I hope you an' thon husband of yours have givin up all that auld kissin' an' cuddlin'," she said sheepishly.

Elsie sighed to herself, I've done it again, I've hurt her feelings, now my conscience will be up the left all day. As for sex, well, she had long given up nights spent in unabandoned passion but given the right man, one wouldn't know what erotic behaviour and wanton lust might emerge from her dormant female desires.

At the age of eighty-nine Sarah had the eyesight of a hawk, the tongue of a lizard, and ears that could have heard a fly fart in mid flight. Elsie was fifty-seven, she needed glasses, but was as quiet as a mouse, in the company of everyone except her mother. She brought out the worst in Elsie. She was not going to come up for breath now she was on a roll and had started on the Royal family.

"Take the Queen, for example. She won't stand no nonsense, she rules thon family of hers with a rod of iron. Charlie boy has to do what he's told, Diana has no say in the matter. I bet those two boys of theirs would have been the last even if they hadn't have split up. I can't see the Queen being held down with a pack of grandchildren."

Elsie giggled at the scene that flashed before her eyes. The thought of the Queen baby-sitting in curlers, carpet-slippers and sweating cobs as she told William and Harry to keep one's royal mucky mitts off one's family heirlooms in case one wanted a right royal hiding round one's shell-like lug-holes was enough to send the most dour of persons into a fit.

"I don't know what's so funny, our Elsie. After all she's human. She has to pee an' pass wind like the rest of us." She wagged her finger at Elsie who was by now taking as much notice as an eskimo inspecting an air-cooling unit, as she had heard the same story a hundred times before.

"Do you know? I pity thon poor woman. She must be astray in the mind. What, with running the country, that's if you could call it a country now – it's more like a zoo full of animals if ye ask me."

She realised Elsie wasn't listening to her and slapped her on the ear to get her attention. "Will you look at me when I'm talkin' till ye, ye have a habit of ignoring me these days. No time for th' old, I suppose?"

Elsie rubbed her ear, pulled the newspaper up to hide her face and mouthed the words, "By Christ I've better things to look at!", then bit down hard on the boiled sweet she had been sucking in an attempt to help drown out the old woman's incessant bantering with the crunch.

"Of course, I don't think she need worry about Edward, he's too busy making tea in that flamin' theatre company he works for. What will his Royal emblem be – a Tetley tea bag? His da should have made him stay in the Marines. A good kick up the arse would have put the life back into him."

She reminded Elsie that she had not put on the kettle as she pondered on this last remark. "As for Andrew an' Fergie, well, her head must be turned with th' antics they get up to. Then again it's sex talkin'. All the Dukes of York were fly men. What do ye think he gets up to with all them sailors when his boat docks? He's a man just like the rest of them – a girl in every port."

Princess Anne was on the point of getting a tongue-lashing when Sarah spotted a trail of dust on the mantelpiece. Once again she eased herself out of her chair and hirpled towards the kitchen for a duster to vent her frustrations with a bit of polishing.

"Ye could clean this auld flat till ye were blue in the face and it would look no better," she remarked with a bitter tone to her voice. She was thinking of better days when she could boast to all and sundry about her life in a bungalow in a posh area.

Christ! Is she never goin' to give up rabbiting, thought Elsie as she lifted her head from the newspaper that she was once more attempting to read. For a brief moment she glanced at Sarah who was now feverishly polishing a brass candle stick. She visualised the brass object thumping the daylights out of her mother. That would shut her up once and for all. Why the hell had she not even thought of replacing her mothers *Pro-Plus* with *Valium,* maybe even popped a dozen or so into her tea. At least it would have shut her up for a few hours. She had a gut feeling her mother would live to see her out the door feet first in a wooden overcoat and shuddered at the thought of not having a few years' respite to herself without the old moan bending her ear night and day. She was quickly brought to her senses at the thought of spending the rest of her life in jail for murder or attempted poisoning and decided it was not a good idea after all. Sarah had no intentions of letting the grim reaper carry her off without a fight. She fed herself on porridge, with Acacia honey as a substitute for sugar. She would often remark, "Honey is more healthy for body an' the soul." She followed this with a more than adequate supply of wheat-bran toasted bread liberally plastered with whiskey-flavoured orange marmalade.

"A good breakfast gets th' auld bowels workin' in the mornin'.

Once yer cleaned out in the nether regions the rest af the body plus the mind works better."

Her observation must have been spot on as she had a brain that worked at the speed of light. The honey had her buzzing like a bee while the whiskey in her marmalade had her drunk with her own importance. Her body, which now had a dowager's hump and was shrunken with age, still had the strength to swipe the odd back-hander round the ear of anyone who got in her way.

Why, you might be tempted to ask, was Elsie wearing her mother's glasses if Sarah's eyesight was keener than that of a hawk. The answer is simple. Sarah had obtained a pair of reading glasses as a visual aid to snobbery in Castle Court shopping centre on a day trip to Belfast. She had been watching Dame Edna Everage on the television one night, and out of nothing other than sheer ignorance she decided that if a pair of spectacles could help wield a little more power over the lower classes they were definitely an asset to one's outward demeanour. In fact she had gone as far as getting a pair similar to Dame Edna's, which only made her look like a gremlin when she wore them on her shrunken head. Thank God she didn't multiply when she splashed water on herself or Elsie would be completely away in the head with miniature Sarahs hopping about all over the place.

"It's all I've got is the television, not like thon auld gather-up up th' stairs who sits in pubs all night an' would drink out of a shitty reg. She needs a good slap up the bake, spendin' all her money on drink an' not a bite in the house. No wonder she looks like a herrin' with stays on, an' the face the colour of clay. As for that wee crathur next door that's knee high to a fairy, how the hell he got into the Parachute Regiment is a mystery."

She put the candlestick back on the mantelpiece with a thump, turned round and started on Elsie all over again. "See thon wee legs of his, they must have got buried up his arse when he hit the groun' wrong. Five feet nothin' in 'is hob-nail boots he is.

Do you ever see his tartles hangin' out on th' washin' line?

Woollen underpants darned at the bum. Imagine! Darnin' yer drawers in this day an' age, makes me sick to the stomach it does. Dirt and filth dregged up to know no better. Yer father would turn in 'is grave if he knew where I was livin'." Mind you, this would have been no mean trick as he had been cremated twenty years earlier, his ashes having been scattered in the wind.

"For God's sake, ma, give over gabblin'. My head's splittin', squintin' at this newspaper without listening to your mouth goin' a mile a minute. Why aren't you watchin' the television anyway? It's not like you to miss a trick on the box."

"There's nothin' on only bloody children's nonsense, either that or sport. Saturday mornin' is a lot of old b..." She was going to say "bollox" but bit her tongue. She didn't want to lower herself to the language of the other people who lived in the flats. Walls have ears. No, she had to keep some semblance of politeness, even if it killed her.

Elsie's finances did not stretch to the luxury of spectacles.

Her husband, Bert, had been on the dole for the better part of a decade after he had accepted voluntary redundancy at the car factory. Sure he could always do the double in times of dire need. He didn't stop to think. Half of the males in the Ballyhornet estate had thrown their heads back and decided life on the dole would be more rewarding than slogging your guts out or dying of monotony at the end of an assembly line of car parts. Wee jobs on the side were hard to come by now. The dull rows of street upon street of terrace houses of the estate were littered with men scratching their arses and smoking fag ends in front of the television. Each wondered what odd job would save his hide and pay for the weekend's drinking spree, plus a wee flutter on the gee-gees, a go at the football pools and a few quid on the lottery to get the adrenalin going.

If they got five numbers up plus the bonus number, a wee win of a quarter of a million would suffice very nicely.

Poor Elsie, life had not been kind to her. Apart from watching the likes of *Coronation Street* and *Eastenders* and whatever other soap operas the television could spew forth her only other activities were traipsing to the local shops for groceries or visiting close friends. A trip to Belfast was a luxury she could ill afford on Bert's dole money, never mind a holiday. She dreamed of a holiday to Tenerife. A visit to Marks & Spencers was a treat. The sight of flowered toilet rolls and lace-trimmed duvet covers conjured up visions of romantic bedrooms and bathrooms fit for a male Chippendale, and not Bert, whose toes turned up whenever sex entered his mind. This danger signal sent Elsie to the confines of her bathroom for shelter until his ardour cooled.

Elsie was tired to the marrow running to her mother's every whim and fancy without having to lie back and think of Ulster. Anyway, her body had lost it's nubile appearance, middle-age spread had hit her with a vengeance and her stomach got in the way of negotiating the joys of sex.

Bert had tried to talk her into trying out new positions in order to get round this obstacle, but Elsie was having none of it. Anything other than the missionary position was out of the question. No way was he going to creep up from behind like a dog. So she would slap him on a most sensitive part of his anatomy with the back of her hand at night and tell him on no uncertain terms to bugger off. He had informed her on one occasion that this was the way to find her "G" spot and she had told him to find a quiet spot instead and take himself in hand! He had huffed for a fortnight and fell into a fit of depression for a few months before resigning himself to the fact that he was no longer regarded as a virile partner by his wife.

Having to go through life with a name that conjured up visions of a maiden aunt was penance enough, without the added insult of letting a man haw and paw her now she was in the menopause.

She had suffered enough indignities in her lifetime. As a child she had a lazy eye and had to wear an ugly-eye patch for years. Her hair was neither blonde nor brown, it was mousey, as her mother often described it. On a Friday night Sarah added insult to injury with her "de-nitting" regime.

"Elsie Cruickshank! Get thon mousy napper of yours over this newspaper till ye get de-loused, and none aff yer moanin' or I'll flay ye till ye know nobody."

Elsie would obey without argument rather than risk the buckle-end of the belt. Sarah loved Friday nights. Being a bit of a battle-axe she could take her bad temper out on a good weekend, when head lice were rampant for some unknown reason. She did this to all six of her children. But Elsie suffered the most because she lacked the golden tresses that adorned her brother's and sister's heads much to her mother's chagrin. Sarah would scrape the fine tooth comb over Elsie's scalp until her head stung as if a horde of wasps had embedded their poisonous barbs in every square inch.

She would then fling Elsie to bed after a bowl of porridge and mutter, "I can't see the flamin lice in yer damned hair. The bloody things are as dirty lookin' as the hair they are stickin' to."

So Elsie had to endure the de-lousing ritual until no further lice fell onto the newspaper to be squashed between her mother's thumbnails, accompanied by the cry, "Die, ye buggers, do ye hear me ... Die!" She had a habit of talking to anything that moved, even head lice. She also had a field day with blue bottles and flies. The sight of Sarah running round the house with a rolled-up newspaper swatting, swearing and sweating in the confines of her whale-boned corsets in an effort to rid her home of these pests was a novelty not to be missed, except by her husband and children, who felt ashamed when visitors were around. They used to stare at their mother as if she were mental, then look at the family with pity written on their faces. Sticky, brown, fly paper catchers hung from the ceilings of the house like party streamers. They were covered with dead or dying flies and Elsie's father, who was over six foot tall, was forever walking into them face first. This only added to the mayhem in the Cruickshank household of a Friday night as he tried to prise them off his face and out of his hair. While Sarah swore at the nits he swore at Sarah.

"For Christ sake, woman, will you remove these bolloxing flies' graveyards, for it's like walking through the second attack of the Black Plague."

In order to escape into a world of make-believe Elsie spent the better part of her childhood feeding birds and stray dogs, especially mangy ones infested with fleas. As she herself had felt unloved in her early life and knew what it felt like to be deloused, she felt an empathy with them. She took pity on all of God's creatures of the non-human variety and became the patron saint to all the local animals in need of care. Her favourite was a one-eyed cat called Pirate, Pirate being the obvious choice of name for a moggy with this disability.

It did not end with animals. When she was six years old she gave her last Kali sucker to an under-privileged child, as she felt unworthy of having such luxuries, forgetting that she herself was also under privileged, and more than slightly unloved. She grew up feeling guilty at having anything new and accepted other peoples cast offs as punishment.

Her gentleness gave her a serenity that showed on her face, and she became a very pretty girl. She had a good facial bone structure, high cheek-bones and heart-shaped face and, before mother nature had robbed her of her twenty-one inch waist with child bearing in later life, she had a figure to die for. Most of the local males had an eye for Elsie at one time or other, but her mother had left her with a legacy of feeling inferior and she spurned their advances, thinking that they were only poking fun at her expense when they wolf whistled in her direction.

But fate always wins in the end. At the age of twenty she met Albert Friars, her ticket to freedom. She felt safe with Bert, at least no one would rob her of his affection. He had a kindly disposition and he showered her with a love she had been denied as a child. A year later they married. No church bells rang out loud, no long black limousines for the bride and groom and family. Just a quiet affair. Elsie and Bert plus two witnesses in a small country church. The only other person present was the Minister, who married them with a look of bewilderment at the lack of guests, not to mention parents. Elsie felt she deserved nothing better, and got on with making the best of her big day. They had a nice dinner in a restaurant, then went back to Bert's parent's house to spend their honeymoon in the back bedroom. Getting married was not going to make her parents love her all of a sudden, so why go to the bother of make believe for the benefit of two people who wouldn't care less if she eloped in the middle of the night with a seven-foot-tall gorilla, as long as it didn't cost them anything.

Thirty-one years and four children plus six grandchildren later, she was reduced to the level of wearing borrowed spectacles, occupying a working kitchen with two odd taps on the sink, and not even enough room to swing a mouse round, never mind the proverbial cat. Ironically she now danced to the tune of her mother's every demand, whilst pondering on the meaning of life, how humans were created and where they went in the hereafter. When some religious boffin came up with another theory, Elsie would muse on their newly-found beliefs with enthusiasm for weeks. She changed religion every other month in her search for the perfect answer to the mystery of life. At one stage she had gone into hospital for an operation as Methodist and came out a Jehovah's Witness a week later. The twenty-odd years of the Troubles had left her with a belief in the existence of spacemen. According to her, they had put us on earth to watch us destroy each other as an experiment. Four-foot-tall grey men were really our rulers. Now that peace had once more been shattered in Ulster, she was convinced a craft from outer space was going to make a landing in the not too distant future and redeem us from this awful planet and take us back to their fold.

When Sarah's husband passed on to better pastures, she sold her precious bungalow and moved to Ballyhornet to be near Elsie. The other two, Helen and Isobel, had managed to escape this misfortune by buying houses in areas that did not cater for pensioners, while her three sons had gone one better and emigrated: clever thinking, although unfair on Elsie, who couldn't say no to a flea-ridden tramp in need of succour, never mind the person who had given her life, albeit a hard one.

The sun disappeared behind a snow cloud, plunging the tiny living room into premature darkness. Elsie removed the spectacles and replaced them with extra care in their blue velvet-covered case for fear they would get scraped, thus giving her mother ammunition for another argument. She sat up straight on the settee and rubbed her tired eyes.

"I'm away over home to make Bert his lunch, ma. Do you need anything from the shops this afternoon?"

Elsie sighed after voicing this last remark as the thought of walking over to the shops on a cold, snowy February afternoon did not cheer her at all. She usually went in the morning but today she felt tired and tetchy and had left it until later in the hope that her energy would take a turn for the better.

"It killed him, ye know." Sarah was staring at a photograph of a young man standing beside an aspidistra plant. The photograph was brown with age and looked out of place beside Sarah's collection of brightly-framed colour snaps of her many grandchildren. Apart from the odd bunch of artificial flowers, her small living room resembled a shrine to a family blessed with fertility. Children's faces adorned every nook and cranny. No Royal Doulton or Ainsley china, just a motley array of seaside ornaments and cheap photographic frames.

It depressed Elsie, who always held the idea that the old should have something to show for their lives, even if it was only the luxury of a nice china tea-set or the odd bit of cut glass. She stifled the urge to scream with frustration for she knew this old ploy of Sarahs. The old photograph trick was only another way of getting her to stay a little longer. Her self-inflicted loneliness, born out of bad temper and jealousy of her neighbours, made her appear pitiful when viewed in the context of her frail exterior. Elsie was gullible when off guard, but today she was not only tired and tetchy. Bert had told her earlier on of his decision to get all his teeth pulled, as they were giving him jip. Christ Almighty! Elsie didn't feel all that romantic towards her husband at the best of times, but this was the last straw. So Elsie was not in the mood to play riddles of what killed who, and why.

"What killed him? For God's sake ma, I didn't even know the man." She hunched forwards and, holding her head in her hands, shook it from side to side and felt like yelling until Sarah came up with the gem.

"Seein' thon man gettin' killed by a bull. Threw him up in the air it did like an auld rag doll, it's bloody horns rammed him straight in the bum, and wiggled him about till the lights were shook out af him. Then it flung him six foot in the air," Sarah indicated his fate by shoving her right thumb in the air.

Elsie's eyes lit up for she enjoyed a good gory story. She sat back in the settee in anticipation of a good old tale of blood and guts and maybe the added titbit of the ghost of the deceased making an appearance, proving that life after death did indeed exist.

"Aye, he couldn't eat nor sleep fer months, his heart gave in as he peddled past the scene on his bike. Willy John Fitzpatrick, a cousin of yer da's he was, one minute full of health and vigour, the next, dead as a doornail wi' fright."

"You mean to say the shock killed him? I never thought you could die of shock. Sure his parents must have been devastated."

"Nat at all, they were long dead."

Elsie's eyes lit up even further. "Are you telling me he was an orphan? He looks very young in the photo." The idea of having an orphan in the family at one time had brightened her day, a little tit-bit such as that would be cause for an afternoon's conversation.

"An orphan! Good God woman, his parents died when he was in his seventies."

"His seventies! In the name of all that's holy, what age was *he* when he died?"

"A hundred an' one." Sarah answered with a wistful look as if he had been a mere slip of a lad.

"A hundred and one! It was about time he kicked the bucket. In the name of heaven, the man died of old age. Ma, if you make bones as old as his you'll be doin' all right."

"There was a few years left in th' auld boy mind ye, he was still ridin' his bike to work."

"Ridin' his bike! Ridin' his bike, ye say. A hundred and one and still ridin' his bike. And still workin! Lay off it, ma, me head's splitten'. I'm in no mood for fairy tales."

Sarah replaced the framed photograph on the shelf, and heched and peched her way towards the bathroom, still muttering and moaning. "Are ye tryin' to tell me I should do away with myself, seein' as I've outlived me three-score-an'-ten years. Ye might as well put me in the wheelie bin and throw me on th' rubbish tip and be done wi' it."

Elsie had offended her by giving the impression a hundred-and-one was too long for any human being to live to. As she herself intended to outlive the century her dowager's hump was up in defiance.

Elsie never swore in her life but at this moment in time she could have taken on the mouth of a fish-wife. She silently effed her mother in and out of hell, then asked God for forgiveness. She felt a tinge of sadness as she watched her mother falter at the door to the bathroom and a lump came to her throat. After all was said and done, she *was* old. Someday she herself would be old, with any luck, and how would she feel? Maybe her mother was just crabbit with old age and afraid of death. After all, who wouldn't be? The lump in her throat had risen to the point were her tears were almost ready to boil over and she swallowed deeply to stop them. But her sadness was to be short-lived. The sound of Sarah piddling into the toilet bowl disgusted Elsie. She had told her off more times than enough for not shutting the bathroom door when there were people in the flat. Every last drip echoed from the confines of the small primrose painted room and Elsie winced as she overheard her mother pass wind while squeezing out the last drop.

She grimaced and hissed loudly. "For goodness sake will you get a grip on yourself ma, that's disgustin'."

Sarah giggled and shouted out to her daughter to have a titter of wit. "Don't tell me you're like a hen an' ye don't pee yourself." She recited,

"Here I sit, broken hearted, paid a penny an' only farted."

Elsie shouted back, "You didn't grow old gracefully ma, you grew disgracefully old."

"Ah give me head pace." Sarah hissed as she emerged a few moments later and stomped unsteadily into the kitchen, stopping now and then to hitch up her knickers and yank her stockings up, twisting the top of them round her finger and then tucking in the slack. Lifting her shopping list off the kitchen table she hobbled into the living room. As she passed Elsie she giggled again at the look on her daughter's face and remarked in clipped tones, "Well ye can't hold what's nat in yer haun, as the sailor said to the prostitute."

"Now who's talkin' filth and sex?" said Elsie waving her finger at Sarah as if she were reprimanding a child.

"Don't you waggle yer finger at me or I'll slap ye round the lugs. Ye might be bigger than me but, by Jaysus, ye lack the wisdom I have. Remember this, bought wit's the best of wit, an' I've been shoppin' longer than you."

As Sarah turned her back to fetch her purse, Elsie noticed her mother's dress had got caught up in her knickers, another annoying habit that often embarrassed Elsie. She was ready to give her mother another talking to, but she held her tongue. After all, who wants to be treated like a child when you have lived a lifetime. Her spindly legs were dangling from beneath a pair of long pink thermal knickers, which made her appear even more pitiful and child-like. For a brief moment she felt like apologising for being so harsh, until Sarah spun round and glared at her.

"I never wanted to grow old. Mark my words, young Elsie, someday you will be saying the same."

"Young Elsie." These words amused her. Fifty-seven years' old and she was "young Elsie". But she realised that at the age of eighty-nine, fifty-seven would appear to be young. Her mother was right, she might be saying the same words in years to come. She turned her mother round and pulled her skirt down but pretended she was dusting her down rather than embarrass her.

"Stop yer pattin' an' fiddlin', will ye!" scolded Sarah, who hated to be touched. Touching was a sign of endearment and Sarah hated anything to do with outward feelings of affection or sentiment. "If ye have to haw an' paw at me, rub me feet. Me bunions are killin' me."

Elsie almost vomited, she couldn't bear the sight of feet, never mind touch the wretched things. "That reminds me, mother. I've inherited the family bunion as well as the varicose veins. I don't think it's a bit fair that I should have been afflicted with all the bad traits in the family. I even inherited my fathers skinny legs and bony knees."

Sarah glared at Elsie as if she used her late husbands name in vain. "Your father had good legs, he wore a kilt at one time." She lifted a photograph of her late husband off the top of the china cabinet, one that had been taken when he played the bagpipes for the Orange Lodge, and stared at it with glazed eyes.

"Yer da wud have put Andy Stewart to shame, made him look like a puny Englishman he did. As for yer veins, well, ye got those from havin' weans and runnin' after thon thing ye married, just think yourself lucky ye didn't inherit his piles or ye wouldn't be able to sit, for they turned skeptic an' he was in utter agony for years before he got them removed."

"You mean septic, ma."

"I know what I mean so don't try to belittle me!" Sarah shrugged her shoulders in anger and once more drew her mouth up into a button in anger, she wasn't amused at being told how to pronounce her words. "After all his piles might have been a bit skeptic, they might have had doubts about peepin' out of his bum if they had an idea they were goin' till be chopped off." She laughed inwardly at this brainwave. Her mind could still work in a comic manner. She made a "Mona Lisa" smile before replacing the photograph of her departed husband back on the shelf.

"And where do the bunions originate from? Ye can't deny it's heredity for all the women on your side of the family are full of bloody bunions and corns. Their feet look like buzzards claws."

"Ah get away, ye ..." Sarah had been caught in mid speech. A key turned in the lock of the front door and Sarah lost her thread of backchat. In walked Bert enveloped in a cloud of cigarette smoke. The last of the bull dog breed. A pit bull terrier would have been proud to own a pair of hind legs like Bert's, They wouldn't have stood a chance of stopping a pig in an entry. The little bit of hair that stuck out like a yard brush at the back of his head was pure white, a platinum frame for a bright-red portrait painting. His face had turned almost puce with the biting winter wind.

"Hey, Elsie, what about me lunch? Me belly's waving at me throat through lack af nourishment. I'm that hungry I cud ate a dog that has scabbies." Bert was almost having an attack of the rickets. "What have ye got for me lunch anyway? I hope it's nat bloody boiled eggs again, fer I'm beginning tae cluck." He said flapping his arms like a bird.

"The cheek of him, sits all mornin' lookin' at the television, he does. He'd starve to death before he'd make himself a bite to eat. The only exercise he gets is playin' bowls or eatin'. I wish the bloody man would get on '*his*' bike, for I'm scundered, an' stop flappin' ye look like a bloody hen"

"See what I mean, our Elsie? Ye'd have been better aff marryin' for money, I was goin' till say rather than looks, only that wud have been an exaggeration. God knows ye have nothin' goin' for ye."

Elsie felt as if she were in a rut. The urge to run away from life had often crossed her mind. But where in God's great waiting room for eternity could she run to. So she persevered with her dull existence in the hope a knight in shining armour would charge up her street and carry her of to his castle in never-never land. Either that or Reg Holdsworth out of *Coronation Street*. Elsie was a Reg Holdsworth groupie, a unique breed of women who fantasized about childhood romances that never actually took off because of interfering mothers. Had her mother not interfered when she was courting Bert, if she had not twittered on about losing half of Elsie's wages by getting married, she might have waited a few years before jumping into marriage and parenthood and her legs would have been varicose free.

"Where's your shopping list? I hope to God you haven't put down any of those giant bottles of *Coca-Cola* and bottles of *Domestos*. They're a flamin' weight to cart over from the shops. I see you have put down another box of cling film. What are you doin' with it, wrapping dead bodies up for the bin men to take away, or maybe to keep them fresh so you can suck out their blood? You could be a vampire, ye know, seeing as you don't like looking in the mirror."

It was true. Sarah didn't like looking in the mirror. it reminded her of her age.

"Never you mind what I want it for. Just get it an' shut up."

"Thank you, mother. There's one thing about you, you're polite to a fault," answered Elsie sarcastically. She shoved her mother's grocery list in the pocket of her winter-weight anorak and headed out the door. As she was about to close it behind her she stopped in her tracks and gave

Sarah a warning. "Don't go ringing me every five minutes this evening, for I'll be out. We're going up to Rab and Peggy's tonight for a couple of hours. Just in case you think I've run off without giving notice in writing."

"Oh aye! Take yerself aff up to thon two headcases, the nymphomaniac an' her side kick. That'll cheer ye up no end. I have come across rough people in my time but they are two of the coorsest Christians to ever get married in a church."

"Did you hear her, Bert? Eighty-nine years of age and a tongue on her like a fishwife. Would you call Peggy a nymphomaniac?"

"An understatement in any language" Bert replied.

"Speak up, man, and stop staring like a trout, for God's sake! And as for you, mother, I was under the impression anything to do with sex was a dirty word. How do you know what a nymphomaniac is anyway?"

"I'm not *that* bloody stupid. God knows it wudn't take a degree to work out what that one was." She poked Elsie on the shoulder and warned her to mind it didn't rub off on her, turning into a nymphomaniac, that is.

Bert silently prayed it would, but he was a man of few words and kept his thoughts to himself, a bit like John Wayne with an Ulster dialect.

"Elsie's alright, she ..." he made a feeble effort to stand up for his wife, but Sarah would have none of it.

"Keep yer neb out of it, what the hell wud a gabshite like you know anyway!" Sarah was not too fond of Bert; only for him she could have Elsie all to herself, an unpaid scivvy.

"Don't you dare call Bert a gabshite!" Elsie reprimanded her mother and then shouted back in self defence. "I'm the only one here who has the right to call Bert by that name. If you had 've called my da a gabshite your ass would have been makin' buttons with fright in a bid for shelter."

"If you weren't over fifty I'd wash yer mouth out with soap for talkin' to me in that tone of voice, my girl." Sarah's face screwed up like a pound of tripe that had been put through a mangle and she was ready to start another verbal attack on her daughter when Elsie girded her loins in defiance and yelled back.

"It's better than sitting listening to verbal diarrhoea for that's all that ever comes out of your mouth." This made Elsie feel guilty again and she could have bitten her tongue once more.

"Elsie, ye shudn't talk back to yer ma like that. After all she reared ye," scolded Bert.

"Have you foot and mouth disease? By God you don't say much but when you do you put your foot in your gob. Now she will think she can run rings round me."

Sarah pockled towards the sideboard and lifted a photograph of her late husband. "See thon man, yer father. He worked all the hours God gave him to keep a decent roof over yer head. If he knew you talked to me like that he'd come back an' haunt ye!"

"Give over grippin' for heaven's sake. He only worked all those hours to get out of the house and your way. If he's going to haunt anyone, it will be you!" Elsie pushed Bert out the front door of the flat and slammed it behind them. The door was immediately opened again by Sarah whose face was now scarlet with rage.

"Don't forget to ram the bolt home on that flamin' gate after ye! I didn't spend six months wasting my breath to get the damned thing on. Bloody youngsters! You can't keep them out. They pee in the hallway for badness an' write obscenities all over the walls. You wouldn't believe a wee lad of about eight exposed his wee man to me the other day for telling him to clear aff, the wee skitter. Where did he learn that, will ye tell me? Imagine! Having to live cheek by jowl with a pack of mongrels who would be better off livin' in doghouses. When I was young ye would have been bate till ye knew nobody for being cheeky to yer elders. Now their mothers give them a slap on the back an' get them a violent video to watch, so they'll know how till bate ye right. An' another thing. What if a burglar tries to get in while I'm here on me own an' your up there with fannycock an' her auld lad?"

"For God sake get back into your flat and catch yourself on. He'd need trauma treatment for a start. The sight of your bad-tempered gob would send him into a shock so deep he'd need electric shock treatment to bring him out of it."

"And don't forget to leave over me groceries before takin' yourself out for the night. I haven't a bite in the house," Sarah yelled as an afterthought. She had to get the last word in. "I suppose I could boil two eggs an' beat them up in a cup for me lunch. Sure no-one gives a tinker's damn if I have to live on eggs!"

Bert calmly closed the gate and lit another cigarette. Nothing flustered Elsie's husband, not even the threat of World War Three would be cause to bring one drop of sweat to his brow. If the world was to end on a

Friday, Bert's only worry would be missing his bowls match on the Saturday. Elsie, on the other hand, was ready for the asylum. She left her mother to cool off. She knew that by the time she returned from the shops Sarah would have forgotten the whole incident. She had to, for Elsie was the only person fool enough to listen to the targe of Ballyhornet.

Sarah yelled. "Ye forgot to put the kettle on for me. No time for them that's ready for the knacker's yard. It won't be long before I'm kicking up the daisies anyway, I can feel meself goin' downhill fast."

"There's not a graveyard with corpses that are hard of hearin' that would have ye," hissed Elsie as she trundled through the snow with her shopping bag on wheels in tow. It crossed her mind that they would most likely be the only set of wheels in her life from now on. Not enough money for cars on the dole, not in this life anyway.

Bert followed closely behind, muttering something about boiled eggs and sore teeth. "What's that your mutterin' about?" inquired Elsie.

"Nathin', nathin' at all," he pulled on his cigarette. "I'll just keep me trap shut, sure anything fer a quiet life." He rubbed his jaw and wished it was Monday morning!

3

Pip Dunlop, the son of Shaun and Jacinta, who lived beside Bert and Elsie Friars, was on the verge of descending the stairs of number six Hetherington Green. At the same time Bert and Elsie were getting ready to leave number four to visit Rab and Peggy, who lived at number ten. These terraced houses were thrown up by builders who cared not a jot for people's privacy, and Pip could hear Elsie giving Bert hell for not standing up for himself when her mother had called him a gabshite earlier in the day.

"There's more back bone in a tea-leaf than there is in your body, do you know that? Thirty-six years married to the same man and not once have I heard you say boo to a goose never mind stand up for your wife."

There was no reply from Bert, who went through life at two speeds, dead slow and stop. He didn't believe in wasting energy arguing. It was better kept for a game of bowls or the off chance of a bit of 'the other' cropping up.

Pip stopped on the second step and put his ear to the wall for a bit of an eariwig, blessed himself by making an exaggerated sign of the cross before uttering out aloud, "Thank Christ I'm nat in a hurry to get married if that's what yer reduced to, a neggin' woman doin' yer head in from mornin' till night."

"Are you talkin' about me, big lad?" His sister, Siobhan, had been plastering her face with make-up in the bedroom for a night out with her new boyfriend and had peered round the corner of her bedroom door with an indignant expression. "I don't neg. Ask Jimmy, the fella I'm datin' the night. He says my voice is like the tinkle of an angel's harp."

"Fuck me, listen to Tinkerbelle. Voice like the tinkle of an angel's harp me balls! More like th' clap of a navvie's arse in full fart. Get yer ears cleaned out, I'm nat talkin' about you, it's thon eejits next door. They wud get on yer tits the way they neg each other."

"Watch yer language, ye shitehawk." His da had heard the din from the kitchen and had decided to have his say in the matter.

"I hate that word 'shitehawk'. What the hell is a 'shitehawk' anyway? For Christ's sake da let me know and put me out of me misery will ye," implored Pip. "And who's the one usin' the bad language? If me memory serves me well I learnt it at me father's knee."

"It's a hawk that shits, just like yerself," answered his da. His head was turned by the antics of his brood, every last one of them was a shitehawk. He had lost interest in the whole damned lot of his offspring after the judge had put two of them on probation for being drunk and disorderly while in charge of an alsatian in the shopping centre, for the third time in a month.

"I presume yer talkin' about me there? Seein' as I gat the blame of bein' yer da. Fer all I know it cud have been the coalman!"

"It cud have been, da, it's nat the first time I saw me ma get an extra beg af nutty slack fer nathin'."

"It's a pity none af yes was till the bank manager. I cud be doin' with an overdraught."

"One man wuz enough fer me till handle, Shaun Dunlop. And I'd be pleased if the two af yes wud stap cursin'," interrupted Jacinta. "An' keep yer voices down. I don't want the street knowin' our business."

Pip prised his ear from the wall and started his descent all over again. He flicked a piece of lint off his perfectly ironed jeans, fixed the rollneck on his chunky-knit cotton sweater and flexed what little muscle he had. The heady aroma of *Drakna Noir* aftershave was overpowering. Shaun, who was by now on his way up the stairs with the *Belfast Telegraph* under his arm for a stint on the toilet, had to hold his breath for fear of getting an instant hit of the heebie-jeebies from the fragrance that was forming a cloud over his beloved son's head.

"Jesus wept! Ye smell like a whore's boudoir. Where are ye fartin' aff to tonight?" His father tried in vain to clear the air by waving a newspaper too and fro. "An' what's with th' aftershave anyway? You've no beard to shave, there's more hair on a gnat's arse than there is on yer chin."

"There's more hair on my upper lip than there is on your head, da. Do ye pay full price to get that cut?" Pip rubbed his da's head with his elbow and quipped, "I bet he's out more on furniture polish tryin' to get a shine on that dome than hair gel."

"Clear off, ye wee runt, I had hair until you came along. Apart from wearing the patience of a saint, ye wore the hair aff me head wi' worry. Another thing. Take a tip. Stay away from that auld woolly woofter up the street. The one wi' a head of hair you'd think his ma had knit wi' poodle wool an' enough hairs on his chest to make a welcome mat, or you'll have his tail wagglin'. He smells just the way you do an' if ye dropped a tenner ye wud kick it from here to Dublin before picking it up to get out of bending down in front of him."

"Come on, da, don't worry yer wee head. I promise nat to steal yer boyfriend, honest I won't. So don't be jealous," chided Pip.

"Clear aff, ye wee shitehawk. The only thing that's bent in me are me ribs an' me skull."

"See, you've said it again, that word. I'll forgive ye if ye givus a kiss, an' I won't tell the neighbours about the women's silk underwear ye wear under yer over-alls."

The *Belfast Telegraph* hit Pip so hard on the head it tore in half. "Now see what you've done, how the hell am I goin' to read that?"

"Ye can read bits af the news, sure that's all ye get anyway, the bits that aren't true," remarked Pip. "There's a *Men Only* magazine under me bed da. If ye like, ye can have the loan of it for a five spot."

"Bugger aff."

Jacinta could not abide Shaun's cursing and chastised him with a yell from the kitchen, where she was up to her neck in dirty dishes. He blushed at the idea of a grown man like himself being told off and skulked up the rest of the stairs with his head bent while Pip laughed. Shaun hit out at him, missed and hit the wall, and cursed.

"I told you once an' 'll not tell ye again, stap yer cursin'." Jacinta was fit to be tied at all the bad talk. She vented her anger by giving the cooker a good scrub with a scouring pad.

Shaun and Jacinta Dunlop had christened their last born Philip in the hope a good Protestant name – they were Catholic – would open doors to all sorts of employment. The Shipyard, or maybe behind the counter in the dole office, instead of standing begging at the front of it. Only it would take another lot of years plus a hell of a lot of peace talks and job boosts before that happened. She got down every night on her knees and prayed for peace but God must had cotton wool in his ears for the natives had been getting very restless lately.

They had four other children, two girls and two boys, Mary, Siobhan, Kevin and Declan, not forgetting their alsatian dog, called Moses. Good Catholic names but not a job between them. Not that they did too much job hunting. They popped their heads round the door of the job centre every other week to save face. If they were offered a job the shock would kill them, according to Shaun.

He worked twelve hours a day as a house renovator. In fact he put his hand to anything. A jack of all trades but master of none.

At the age of fifty-seven Shaun was worn out working long hours in order to keep his brood in the luxury they had got used to. Jacinta was also tired of her job, working part-time in the local hospital as a cleaner. All they had to show for it was a third-hand BMW car that sat outside in the lay-by. Shaun had it shining to perfection. It was his pride and joy.

They had big ideas for the scrapins of the pot of the family but had been badly disappointed. Pip was as big a waster as the rest of their brood. Jacinta had him at the age of thirty-eight and her nerves had been ravaged ever since. Philip had been shortened to Pip by all who knew him as he was inclined to give one the pip with his constant borrowing.

"Hey, da! Before I go, give us the keys of yer BMW." Pip's tone on the stairs had turned from cursing to begging.

"Piss off! That car stays stationary while I'm in the house. I told ye before, yer nat, an' I repeat, nat over my dead body puttin' yer backside on the drivin' seat aff that car!" Shaun had stopped two stairs short from the bathroom door at the sheer cheek of his son.

"I don't want the car, just the keys. They impress the broads at the pub."

Shaun stepped back in amazement, nearly falling down the stairs in doing so.

"How in God's name can a set of car keys impress the girls? Eh? Tell me that?" He held on to the bannister rail for support he was that taken aback at Pip's words, then sat on the stairs for a few moments and rubbed his head as he tried to get his thoughts together.

"I nonchalantly play with them at the bar, it never fails when it comes to pullin' the birds. They see the key ring an' think I'm loaded."

"So ye have done this before, borrow my keys that is. And without my knowledge? Ye wee sh..."

"Don't say it, da, or I will have to slap the head aff ye," joked Pip, who by now was in mortal danger of being slapped round the head himself.

Shaun got up from his seat on the stairs and made for the top. Reaching the bathroom he held onto the wall with his arms spreadeagled, and beat his head on the bathroom door in defeat.

It was no use, he could stand at the top of the stairs all night arguing until he was blue in the face. His son was an insistent little git who would winge until you felt the urge to commit suicide.

"They are on the mantelpiece. Lose them an' my boot will bury itself that far up yer backside you'll need micro-surgery to get it removed."

Pip jumped the last few stairs in one fell swoop and yelled,

"Good on ye, da. Yer nat a bad auld sport. Just fer that I'll tell auld woolly head ye still love him."

He stopped for a few seconds in the hall for one last look in the mirror.

"My God, yer a handsome sonofabitch. I'm goin' till slay 'em tonight." Not a hair out of place, cut in the poet style, parted in the middle and draped over the eyes. His blonde highlights were shining from the hair spray he had borrowed from his sisters. The only imperfection was the bump on the bridge of his nose, an unwanted legacy from a pub fracas. His nose had been on the receiving end of a fist that was attached to the arm attached to the torso of a six-foot-six muscle-bound bouncer. A reminder not to get involved with someone else's girl, especially a bouncer's who resembled King Kong. Not to worry. A broken neb was worth a few thousand quid in damages. He had put a claim in for being battered by a crowd after getting two shifty witnesses to give evidence. His case was up in a few month's time. After pocketing the proceeds he would get it fixed, but not until then. He intended looking a sorry sight in front of the judge.

He sleeked the back of his hair with an open hand and kissed his reflection, as if sampling his own virility. A worried look came over his face and he felt the inside pocket of his jacket.

"Mustn't forget the old *Mates*. A packet of three should be sufficient. Take precautions, an' never give a girl yer real name. Two important rules in the mating game. Can't be too careful in this day an' age. Ye never know what ye might pick up other than a girl something not so easy to get rid of. Too chancy to go steeplechasing without an overcoat these days!"

A taxi had pulled up outside the front door. It bumped its horn three times.

"Cheerio, folks. And mum, don't go gettin' me da all worked up inta a sexual frenzy the night. The shock might kill him, an' I don't want him to pop it before his policies mature. See ye later, petal. Don't wait up. Ye need yer beauty sleep fer auld baldy there to keep his love alight for ye."

Ye say that every night thought Jacinta. Th' awful thing is, ye mean it, ye always turn up. She went back to her dishes and prayed to God that he would come back without a bullet in his head. The other two sons lay on the floor watching *Blind Date* while Moses lay on the settee.

Typical, thought Jacinta. The dog's got more sense than the lot of them put together.

Pip closed the door behind him and sauntered down the driveway as if he were Hugh Grant. He had seen the film *Four Weddings and a Funeral* and saw himself as the fella in the big picture. All the girls were fawning over this new poetic look, and he was determined to take advantage. Maybe a filly called Devine would carry on with him where she left off with auld Hugh. He opened the door of the waiting taxi and slid in beside the driver.

"Take us to the Starlight, my good man," a touch of the Hugh Grant upper-crust lingo had now crept into his vocabulary. "An' if you would be so kind as to drop me off about fifty yards from it I would be ever so grateful." An added protection for the old car-key caper. No-one would see him drive up in a taxi and spoil his chances of clicking for the night.

The taxi driver smiled in amusement and added, "Wud ye take the marlies out of yer gub, son. Ye sound like one of them university glipes."

"Thank you Jeeves. I will give you a small but given-from-the-heart gift for being so observative. Now kindly get a move on before the horses need fed. An I learnt all I know from the university of life, an I didn't have to sit any exam"

"Eejit," replied the taxi driver. "What did ye have for yer tea? Pickled brains!"

"If ye don't stap bein' so cocky mate it'll be pickled bollox! Nye, it doesn't take brains till work that one out. So watch it lovey. The last one that talked till me in that tone is lyin' in the Royal with his head in plaster."

"Is that right, big lad? Jaysus I'm quakin' in me seat." The driver put his foot down, much to Pips annoyance. Pip hit the dashboard with the palm of his hand. "Stap here, mate! Any nearer an' they'll see me gettin' out."

The driver skidded to a halt. "Aye alright. Keep yer wig on."

The ride was that short the engine didn't have time to warm up, Two pounds less for a gormless eejit on the dole. The name Philip had not as yet managed to gain him employment. Still, he had only hit his twentieth year, time enough for something so mundane as work.

Pip extracted himself from the taxi, handed the driver two one pound coins and told him to keep the change.

"Bastard!"

"Gat it in one," replied Pip. He gave the bonnet a hard thump and the driver sped off into the night.

The Starlight was really a working men's club, a modern building that doubled as a rave venue at the weekends. The men of the area were none too pleased about this arrangement, but as hardly any of them worked, the name didn't really fit the image. Bodies intertwined and lunged back and forth to the rhythm of the rave music, while the video backdrop of the dishevelled pop group looked as if they were all afflicted with St Vitus's Dance. The arms of the frenzied dancers flayed frantically in the air, as if hitting out in karate chops or practising shadow boxing. No wallflowers here. Nobody knew who they were dancing with anyway. A second or third party went unnoticed. In fact, you could have taken yourself by the hand and danced with yourself and no-one would have batted an eyelid. Pip's eyes scanned the crowd, his brain taking photographs like a camera for bits of spare crumpet and anyone who would be good for a tap if the finances ran low. Not any old wench. It had to be a chick with a bit of class, something that would look good attached to his arm in front of the mates.

Jaysus, I've seen better behind the paddocks at the Balmoral Agricultural Show, thought Pip as he eyed the talent that was on offer.

Nat a one over th' age af sixteen. Probably under-aged, under-sexed, over-drugged an' all covered in acne. He ambled over to the bar trying to look sexy, not an easy task in the crowd jostling him. Before he sat down he hitched his trouser leg at the knee and plonked a hip on the revolving stool.

He swung round towards the bar, spied the barman, cupped his hands round his mouth and yelled, "*Give us a pint of harp, Joe, an' no bloody wisecracks fer I'm in no mood the night. The bastards took money out of my dole this week to help pay off the loan I got for a new bed.*" It was the only way you could be heard over the racket.

"*Haule on there will ye. I'm run aff me feet fer Chrissakes. It would take a bloody pair of roller skates to help me serve at this speed,*" Joe, the barman, shouted back. "*This effen lot must be taken somethin' other than paracetamol fer they're meetin' themselves comin' back.*"

A quizzical expression creeped over his dour looking face. "*What's this bed business. Sure yer still at home. Ye have a flamin' bed!*"

"*That's nat what I told the dole. I told them I was homeless an' they got in touch with the Housing Executive. The fuckers gave me a flea-ridden flat an' I told them I needed a bed to sleep on. I asked for a hundred but th' stuffed-up bastards only sent me a cheque fer fifty quid. I shud have asked fer two. I might have known they'd cut it by half. Miserable bastards.*"

"*What did ye do with it?*" enquired Joe.

"*What the fuck do ye think I done with it? I cashed it, turned it into liquid an' poured it down me throat!*"

Joe pointed at the crowd with a nod of the head. "*At least ye didn't spend it on drugs like this lot.*"

"*Aye, yer friggin' right there, Joe. I'm effin' high enough without resorting to chemicals. Anyway, I like to keep me wits about me. It wud take an accountant to keep track af the money I owe.*"

He eyed the eejits on the dance floor and came to the conclusion that drink was almost history in haunts such as this. An "E" tab and a tank of water was more fun to these clampets. Pip felt a dunt in his back. For a split second he thought it was one of the sweaty ravers flaying his arms about and turned his head to the side, for that was about all he could move in the crush of bodies, to give whoever it was a bit of verbal abuse.

"*Hey mucker! Watch who yer effin' hittin' wi' thon bony elbows.*"

"*Shut yer fat gub. It's only me, ye big drip.*" Sharon Kirk, Rab's daughter, pushed her way towards the bar and grabbed Pip's arm with a grip that made him winch with pain.

"*Buy us a drink will ye? I'm boracic the night,*" pleaded Sharon.

"*So what else is new? Frig off! Does yer ma know yer here tonight? Anyway, I don't want to be arrested. Yer nat even fifteen.*"

She wasn't Pip's type for a start, all freckles and zits. You would have sworn she had been sunbathing through a cheese grater.

She also resembled a string bean, no arse or tits. He slapped his da's car keys on to the bar.

"*Don't tell me yer still at that auld game, borrowin' yer da's keys,*" Sharon shouted.

Pip flicked her on the ear with his index finger. "*Look, I told ye to clear aff. Yer crampin' me style. Go find some headbanger still at nursery school or I'll tell yer da ye were here an he'll knock ye inta next week.*"

"*Me ma an' da won't care anyway. Them two next door to yousens are up te' night fer a drink. Me ma will be that pissed she won't even know I'm out af the house.*"

"*Ah, but your da will know. He can't drink wi' the medication he's on.*"

She grabbed Pip's car keys and dropped them on the floor. As he bent down to pick them up she spied someone more to her liking hanging around the toilet doorway.

"*Stuff yer drink anyway. Who needs it? Hugh over there has somethin' more interestin' than drink. An' ye only need one of them.*"

"*If yiv no money fer drink, ye can't afford drugs, ye stupid bitch,*" spat Pip.

Pip wasn't a bad lad. A bit-scatter brained, but he knew drugs were the road to nowhere. He had a few puffs of dope now and then to heighten his sex drive, but he was not on the "doves" or "the pink panthers". They gave a man the equivalent of brewer's drop.

"*There's ways an' means,*" quipped Sharon as she rubbed Pip's bum and licked her lips provocatively.

"*Christ, but ye'r an ugly wee doll. Why don't ye use somethin' on those flamin' lumps on yer bake? Anyway, that gouger will be up in court sooner than he realises,*" Pip answered, pushing her out of his way as if she smelt of pig manure. "*Now he's out af jail he can't go gun runnin' an' plantin' bombs for th' boys so he's turned to sellin' shit for th' bastards.*"

"*Get stuffed Dunlop!*" hissed Sharon, showering Pip with spit in the process.

"*I said clear aff!*" Pip scowled right in her face, as he wiped her spit off his face with the back of his hand.

"*God, yer ma keeps ye lovely while yer da's in jail,*" jibbed Sharon before she stomped off in the direction of Hugh, the bringer of happiness in the form of a pill that often brought despair at the end of the day.

His attention was drawn to a sexy bit of stuff sitting on a bar stool at the other end of the bar, a stranger in town, fodder for the auld car-key trick. She didn't look drugged so she must be out for a man. He gave Joe another shout to hurry up with his drink. This one was some pup, all lips, legs and lycra plus platinum blonde hair down to her waist. A bit tarty looking, but then again good material for practising on.

Joe was changing the spirit bottles on the optics, pulling pints of beer, cleaning out the ashtrays and running round in circles. In fact he was in danger of disappearing up his rectum. Beads of sweat dripped off his forehead, a *Berkeley Blue* dangled from his lips that were also wet from a trail of sweat that lay in the crevice of his upper lip and nose. He was not a happy man and it showed.

His aims in life were to own a nice little taverna in Spain and to get rid of his fat-arsed wife, only his fat-arsed wife had visions of lying soaking up the sun while Joe poured out the sangria and pulled in the pesetas. Still, he would be in the sun and out of this God forsaken hole. The worry lines on his forehead had almost disappeared as he got lost in his little dream world and they appeared as quickly as they had left when Pip once again yelled over the bar, "*For God's sake, Joe, get yer finger out. There's a bit of stuff askin' for it over there. Put yer arse in a cramp an' give us that pint before she takes aff.*"

"*Patience is a virtue,*" answered Joe as he chucked his cigarette on the floor and stubbed it out with the ball of his foot.

"*Aye, an' a slow coach is a pain in th' arse,*" quipped Pip, as he kept a watch on his prey.

"*Hey, gorgeous what are ye drinkin'?*" Pip went straight for the jugular, no point in wasting time with small talk.

The sexy bit of stuff looked down her nose at Pip as if he was an object that had flown out of someone's nose after a sneeze.

"*What's it to you, Flash Harry? Does the contents of my glass turn ye on or somethin'?*" She threw her head back and her golden tresses fell away from her face.

She wasn't bad looking mind. He felt embarrassed now. A wrong word at a time like this could spoil it all. He told her it was the contents of her dress that turned him on, that her body was like a Greek goddess's and should be worshipped by thousands and covered with the best of raiment.

"*God, yer an auld charmer. Did ye go to finishing school to learn that chat up line.*" She looked him up and down and turned him inside out with her eyes before asking sardonically, "*Do ye still want to buy me a drink?*"

"*Well, I did ask, if ye can remember as far back as three seconds,*" he answered, just as sarcastically. "*Even a bloody goldfish is capable af that.*"

"*Well, I'm only answerin*!" She took a second look at Pip and thought he didn't seem too bad considering what else was on offer.

"*If yer that keen I'll have a double screwdriver.*"

Pip wondered if this was a *double entendre*. Well, she did use the word "screw". The pulse on the side of his temple beat to the rhythm of the music in anticipation of a night of unabandoned passion. He added up the price of the drink and his mathematics just about broke even with the few pounds he had in his wallet.

"*Hey Joe, give the lady one of them screw jobbies, will ye?*"

Joe winked. A few of those, a drive home in a taxi and the screw would come later. Lucky bastard, he thought to himself. A picture of his wife had flashed before his eyes. It would take more than a few screwdrivers to give me the Dutch courage to make passionate love to that one, he thought. He pictured his wife struggling out of her full-length corset and wondered how so much flesh could fit into so little material. When he had met her she had been a slip of a thing, now her skin was not only marked by the lines of the corset that had been stretched to the limit, but her belly hung low in folds. Before she spilled into her nightie she would scratch her cellulite-pocked behind and spray herself with *Elizabeth Taylor's White Diamonds* perfume. As if that was not enough to quell the passion of any hot-blooded male, she would proceed to pluck the hairs off her chin with an eyebrow plucker and trim her nose hair with a pair of nail clippers. And to think he used to be the envy of his mates as he walked the streets with his arm round her waspish waist, a bonny wee lass who could have raised Lazarus from the dead with a flutter of her eyelashes. He shook his head and shot a pitiful gaze at Pip. God help ye lad, yer brains are in yer trousers, he thought. Make the most of yer youth, for it's only a matter af time before you'll have nothin' left but dreams an' a wife with facial hair an' an arse that's dropped to th' balls of her legs.

"*What's yer handle? I like to know the name of me broad before I whisk her off her feet with lust.*"

An eejit with a baby's dummy teat stuck in his mouth and a pair of white gloves on danced past. The flickering lights gave him the appearance of something out of a silent movie. A female in a pink tu-tu and hobnailed boots followed. The sweat was dripping off their brows and their eyes were almost turned back in their heads. Pip swallowed a large gulp of his lager and wondered who looked the most idiotic, the Al Jolson lookalike or the prima ballerina in navvie's boots.

Thank God I've passed that stage he thought.

"*Maureen*" answered lips, legs and lycra. "*An' before I get carried away with the drink I like to at least know the name of the man who bought me it.*"

Pip played for time, he unearthed a hanky from his trouser pocket and blew his nose to give him time to think up a fictitious name.

"*Eh ... It's Paul, Paul O'Leary.*"

"*Did ye have to think about it? For it took ye long enough to say it.*" Maureen was a Protestant. She wondered if O'Leary was a Catholic name. Her da would take a buckle in his eye if he had gotten wind of his daughter dating a Catholic, him being a member of the Orange Lodge.

"*I had a wee touch of amnesia for a split second,*" Pip answered sheepishly, thinking he had been rumbled. He threw the car keys onto the bar to distract her attention until he gathered his thoughts.

Maureen's eyes lit up at the BMW insignia on the key-ring. He must be flush. Maybe he's in business, or his da's wealthy. Either way, he was worth a quicky. Good for a few nights out on the town and with a bit of luck he might set her up in a flat of her own and keep her as a mistress. Our Maureen was no fool. Sure what the hell if he was a Catholic, a wealthy Taig was better than a Prod on the dole.

"*Are you a left futter?*" she enquired, inwardly hoping he would say no.

"*I'm a human bein',*" replied Pip as quick as a flash. He didn't believe in religious discrimination where sex was concerned. Sure a prick has no conscience.

"*I see ye drive,*" she made herself comfortable on the bar stool, and thrust out her ample bosom, straining the fastener of her *Wonderbra* to breaking point in the process. Pip's eyes almost fell out onto her cleavage.

Maureen emptied the contents of her glass down her throat and nearly choked in the process.

"*Ye must be flush! What do ye work at?*" Her eyes were sitting out like organ stops by now, and it wasn't with the drink, or the effects of almost choking on her drink.

"*I have me own business,*" lied Pip. "*Double glazing.*" That was a joke for a start. The nearest he got to double glazing was downing two glasses of lager one after the other.

"*I hear ye can make a mint at that game.*" She wiggled on her stool, her black miniskirt rode up a few inches in doing so, almost making Pip spill his beer at the sight. Not only was her cleavage on show, the crotch of her lace panties was now coming into view.

"*A couple of thou a week,*" stuttered Pip. The swell of her breasts almost stopped his breath. "*Pocket money that's all.*"

Pip no longer resembled a piece of snot in Maureen's eyes. She had found a diamond in a sea of pebbles.

He watched her down another drink, too quick for his liking. His wallet couldn't stand the strain of another screwdriver. His eyes searched the hall for a friendly face, one that had mug written all over it. He spied Steven, Elsie's and Bert's son.

"*Excuse me for a minute. Have to go to the bogs. Don't go away.*"

Maureen had no intention of straying. Her ship had come in. One of its sailors had docked, and in her port.

"*How's the auld belly aff fer spots, Stevie?*" asked Pip, scratching his head as he spoke and picking up courage for the next question. "*By th' way, how are ye aff money-wise?*"

"*Why? Are ye givin' any away?*" asked Steven, his lips twisted in a sickly grin, for he knew that the day Pip gave money away the Pope would become a Free Presbyterian.

"*No, I'm askin' for a loan, face-ache.*"

"*Clear off, skiver! Ye never paid me back the fiver ye borrowed last week. An' if yer askin' for money ye should be more polite. Some people can get their faces re-arranged for less!"*

"*Ah, come on,*" pleaded Pip. "*I'm on a pramise the night.*"

"*On a pramise! Get on yer bike, dunny. The only pramise ye deserve is another bump on that misshapen snout af yours to keep th' other one company.*"

"*Tell ye what,*" implored Pip. "*Lend me a ten spot an' I'll pay ye back with interest.*"

"*Look here, Richard Craniun. Don't give me all that bullshit about interest. I want paid back with money, filthy lucre, nat interest. The only interest I have is in the size of my bank balance, which is rapidly goin' downhill as it turns into alcohol for the benefit of your sex drive.*"

"*Fer Christ's sake, Friars,*" hissed Pip at the same time glancing in Maureen's direction in case she took off. "*Think of yer auld mate in his hour of great need,*" he pleaded.

"*By god, yer need must be bad if it's for that ugly lukin' tart sittin' at the bar. Seein' as yer that desperate I'll take pity on ye for she's a face on her that wud turn a hat-blooded male into a faggot. An' by the luk af her she's riddled wi' th' clap. Then again, yer nat that fussy, are ye, dunny?*"

Steven dug deep into his trouser pocket and extracted a crumpled ten pound note and waved it under Pip's nose.

"*Here, ye horny get, take it. But remember, I want the ten pounds plus a fiver interest next dole cheque, or yer dead meat.*" He held up his right arm as if cocking a gun just to get his message over.

"*Take it easy, there. No need to go all Arnie Schwarzenegger on me.*" As if he could, for Steven was only five feet eight and build like a kipper. He went around with Ian, his mate, who was six feet six, built like a brick shit-house and a head with wall-to-wall bone for brains.

"*Remember, I'll be back, as the man himself wud say.*"

"*Yer a saint, Friars, a saint. I'll remember ye in me prayers at mass on Sunday.*"

"*Fuck aff! I don't want no taig prayin' for my benefit. An' remember, if I don't get that money back you'll be run out of Ballyhornet quicker than I cud shove me boot up a pervert's arsehole!*"

"*My sentiments entirely,*" answered Pip, punching the air with his fist in triumph.

Steven turned and craned his neck to look at his mate.

"*See that dunny guy? If he doesn't give me that money back I'll cut his crystals aff wi' a blunt knife an' he'll be talkin' in a high-pitched voice for the rest of his natural. An' he'll be crawlin' on all fours, fer he'll have no kneecaps.*"

He reached into his pocket to extract a tenner for a round of drinks. It was empty. To his horror he realised he had handed Pip two ten pound notes that had got wrapped round each other.

Grabbing his mate Ian by the arm he raced through the crowd on the dance floor. Ian was the hard man of Ballyhornet and a weekend was not complete unless he landed someone in the casualty department of the Belfast City Hospital.

"*Do ye want this one killed or badly maimed?*" He asked Steven as he flexed his muscles.

"*For Christ's sake, don't kill it. Just knock the crap out af it.*

Ye can kill it after I get me money back."

They got caught up in the middle of the mayhem but this did not stop Steven yelling, "*Hey dunny! Give me back that tenner, ye skivver.*"

No one took a blind bit of notice of Steven and his muscle-bound mate. They continued with their flaying of arms and legs, which angered Ian. He started punching at random and a couple of poor buggers caught a right hook up the fid. They were so drugged they did not feel a thing, and dropped to the floor.

"*Watch it, Ian me auld mate,*" cried Steven. "*Don't use up yer energy on that lat. Keep yer strength fer Dunlap. I want to see that pipsqueak beg fer mercy. I've had him up to here.*" Steven grabbed Ian by the collar with his left hand and hit his forehead with the side of his right hand to get his point over.

Ian looked down at Steven and grunted. "*Don't worry, Stevie. These fists are made af iron.*"

"*So's yer friggin' head, poker face. Where were ye when they were makin' the planet of th' apes?*" Steven punched him in the chest with frustration, then cried out in pain as he nursed his knuckles. "*What the hell have ye under that shirt? Iron pecs? Yiv effin near broke me hand, Ye big … Ye big … Ah, take that stupid look off yer bake. It's that ugly ye cud take it for a crap, now get yer big kebs over to the bar.*"

Back at the bar Maureen had ordered another drink at Pip's expense. Joe gave him the thumbs-up sign, which meant all was well. Pip saw Steven jumping up and down in the crowd waving his arms wildly in the air. He waved back. It was only as he was paying for the drink that he noticed the extra tenner in his hand.

Lucky days, thought Pip. Not a bit of wonder Friars is throwing a pink fit, that stupid twat has just paid for a carry out. He peered over at Steven and Ian, and realising they were not bidding him the time of day, decided he had to plan an escape. After paying the barman, Pip grabbed "lips, legs and lycra" by the wrist and headed towards the exit.

"*I haven't finished me drink yet.*"

"*Never mind that nye. There's a party up at me mates. Fancy goin' for a bit, I mean a while?*" Pip corrected his *faux pas.*

"*What's yer hurry, lover boy? Can't ye wait five minutes?*"

He looked across the dance floor. "*No!*" came the high-pitched reply.

He pulled Maureen behind a curtain that separated the dance floor from the toilets, shoved her against the wall and, as a ploy, kissed her passionately on the lips. Her eyes closed and she gave herself freely to his advances, his lips were soft and warm and she melted in his arms. As he kissed her he watched Steven and the ape disappear out the exit door, their faces contorted with rage. He came up for air, took a deep breath and, before Maureen could utter a word, got stuck back in with a tonsil tickler.

"*Oh, Paul, yer a quick mover. I like a man who doesn't hang about.*"

"*I'm hangin' about alright, but nat fer too long.*" Pip answered under his breath.

"*Another two minutes an' the coast will be clear.*"

"*What did ye say, Paul?*"

"*I said, another two minutes an' we'll go, dear.*"

Maureen took this as a sign he wanted to get warmed up before leaving. She threw her arms around him and examined his tonsils with her tongue.

Pip momentarily forgot about Steven and his brutish mate, returning her ardour he moved his hands up and down her thighs.

She showed no restraint and he moved up higher. She sighed and he cupped her breast in his right hand. She rubbed her leg up and down the inside of his. He started to bite her earlobe and he could feel the heat of her breath on his neck. Normally he would have got a slap up the face for being so forward within an hour of meeting a girl. She gave in to his roaming hands so readily that Pip knew he was not only on a promise. He was on a dead cert. He was in the mood and he felt around for his packet of three.

"All right let's go nye. At least we wont have to shout over the noise."

Maureen was almost hyperventilating with passion. After opening her handbag and applying some lipstick from her make-up case she nibbled his ear and almost dragged him outside.

Jesus H. Christ, thought Pip, this one's beggin' for it like a bitch in heat. He rattled the car keys in his pocket. The realisation that he didn't have a car to fit the keys into hit him in the guts. Ploy number two came into operation.

"I'm afraid we'll have to take a taxi. The car's in getting an oil change!" Maureen believed him and followed him like a bitch in heat.

He craned his neck to make sure the coast was clear before waving down a taxi. If Steven and Ian caught him now they would rearrange his face and borrow a *Black and Decker* to drill holes in his kneecaps and it wouldn't be to let the air in!

As the taxi sped off he could see their two figures thumping the air with their fists.

"That was a close shave," declared Pip, wiping the sweat off his brow.

"What did you say, Paul?"

"I said, I think those two were giving us a wave."

"What two?"

"Never mind," answered Pip, as he pinned her to the seat and planted a smacker on her lips. Time enough to worry about tomorrow when tomorrow comes. He came up for air to tell the driver where he wanted dropped off.

The same taxi driver that had earlier taken Pip to the Starlight gave a knowing smile. He had dropped off a couple of "auld tarts" at that address about an hour ago. It was going to be a hot time at the hoe-down alright. He peered into his driving mirror at the writhing bodies in the back seat of his taxi and mouthed. "Good on ye lad, give 'er one fer me, an' I don't care how polite ye are about it!"

4

Peggy in a drunken stupor was not a pretty sight. On the other hand, Peggy was not a pretty sight when sober. Her tall, angular frame resembled a marionette and her arms hung from her broad bony shoulders as if they had been sewn on with string. Her long legs did not grow gracefully from her hips but appeared to have been stuck on the sides of her pelvic bone as an afterthought. She had feet that would have looked more at home on a man while her features looked as if, well, let's just say when heads were being handed out and God asked her what kind she would prefer, she mistook the word "head" for "bed" and asked for a big soft one. In other words, it looked well slept in.

The evening was still young but already she lay sprawled on the settee, legs apart, exposing what was normally hidden from view to everyone accept her husband and gynaecologist. She had removed her knickers earlier on in the evening after wetting them when she failed to make it to the loo in time. Her bladder had been weakened with years of alcohol abuse. Her head lolled from side to side, the slabbers tripping from her gin-numbed lips. Rab had to listen to her call him the mother of all whoremasters to ever grace the world. This latest tirade of abuse was nothing new to Rab. Over the years he had become impervious to his wife's insults. For the past decade he had been impotent through ill health, rendering him unable to rise to the occasion. His happy-go-lucky nature that once used to irritate his spouse was now an escape from the reality that stared him in the face.

"Wud ye take a luk at that! What th' hell wud ye do wi' it?" Rab summoned Elsie and Bert over to the chair he was sitting in so they could witness the sight.

Bert pulled on his cigarette and inhaled deeply. As he tried to stifle the urge to break into laughter he choked on his spit. This scenario was nothing new to him or Elsie. In fact Peggy's private parts were quite familiar to Bert. It was not the first time he had to help Rab put her to bed naked after a skinful of drink. She had the habit of stripping off when inebriated. Performing the Dance of the Seven Veils as Salome when she wanted Rab's head on a platter for not performing his marital duties was one of her party tricks.

"I suppose we may take her up the stairs before Sharon comes home." Bert managed to voice this through lips wrapped round a cigarette butt and a haze of smoke that was bringing tears to his eyes. "Come on, Rab, give us a haun." He hitched up his trousers, spat on his hands, smoothed back what little bit of hair he had left on his cranium and braced himself for the task that lay ahead.

"Never min' Sharon, she's scarin' the bloody dog," said Rab as he prized himself from his comfy armchair. Brandy their pet rotweiller was cowering behind the settee for he knew he would get a kick up the arse from his master's size-eleven boot if he got in the way of the struggle of getting Peggy up the stairs to bed. Brandy's tail was tucked firmly between his legs and the poor crathur was trembling with fear.

"Christ you wouldnae know whether to pluck it, stuff it or put it in the china cabinet. It's no Sharon Stone all th' while, is it? Come on Bert, you grab an arm an' a leg an' I'll grab the other two. Let's get it out af sight afore we all throw up.

Christ almighty it shud be pickled in formaldehyde in some scientist's laboratory. At layste ye cud carry out tests on it."

Rab slid her on to the floor by pulling on her feet. She was so limp it took hardly any effort. She hit the floor like a rag doll, and returned into the land of the living for a few seconds.

"Come along, Major, letshh get it over wi ..." Peggy grabbed Bert by his shirt collar with her scrawny hand and pulled him towards her before conking out again.

"What's she bloody on about, Rab. Let's get it over with. An' who's the Major?"

"Don't ask, just don't ask, Bert. Ye know Peggy. She talks a lat af shite when she's blootered."

Peggy was carried up the stairs like an old mattress and fifteen minutes later Rab was fighting for breath in the kitchen. His daily asthma attacks were becoming resistant to the stronger medication his doctor had prescribed, but after a few heavy intakes of breath at the open door of the kitchen plus a couple of sucks on his spray and he was once again the jovial giant everyone knew and loved. He was a bit of a con man, up to all the tricks of the day when it came to robbing the rich to feed the poor. To those unfortunate enough to have to kow-tow to self-opinionated pip squeaks who looked down on the unemployed as second-class citizens, he was a saviour and protector. A turkey for the price of a chicken, or a tin of paint at a quarter of the normal price, would be delivered to one's back door by means of a sleight of hand at the supermarket. A two pound price tag taken off a chicken and stuck on a twelve pound turkey could easily slip through the check-out when the teller was up to her eyeballs. This was put to a halt when some "bastard af a boffin", to use Rab's words, invented the bar code. Unfortunately, Rab failed to notice this change and was nabbed by the manager outside the supermarket. He spent three months in jail, and half the residents of Hetherington Green had to make do with chicken instead of a large free range turkey for Christmas that year.

Rab resembled a genial genie of the lamp, his wicket yet mischievous smile coupled with a glint in his good eye was almost hypnotic, while his bad eye, injured when his hunting rifle backfired on a duck hunt, remained almost closed. When Rab laughed he guffawed, his belly shook and his shoulders made attacks on his ear lobes. Having been born to farming parents he was a lover of nature. He knew the names of all plants, shrubs and trees, and could identify any bird by its song. He loved all God's creatures except one. He didn't give a damn whether it was a prized feline worth thousands or a mangy moggy, but if a cat as much as crossed his path it was a gonner, extinct, post pussy, never to be seen again. One minute pissing on his doorstep, the next wrapped in a sheet up to its neck and held between Rab's knees, its neck stretched six inches longer than when it had stalked the tiles the previous night, then buried it in his back garden. Many a time he threatened his wife Peggy with the same fate if she didn't stop exposing a certain part of her anatomy. Yet, in a strange way he had a love-hate relationship with her. He loved to hate her.

"A penny for yer thoughts, Rab," said Elsie as she handed him a mug of tea poured from a large teapot that had seen better days. Life centred round the teapot in Peggy's kitchen. She spent the better part of the day huddled over a cuppa as she tried to fend off her hangover.

Rab was staring into space, the glint in his eye almost exploded with the wicked thought that had just crossed his mind. He thumped the kitchen table with the palm of his hand and yelled, "Goddamit! I've got it."

"Got what?" screeched Elsie, jumping off her seat with fright at Rab's sudden outburst.

"I'm goin' to dae somethin' terrible on that wum'n afore th' night's out, even if it kills me." He was so excited he knocked the mug of tea out of Elsie's hand as he made a bee-line for the stairs.

"Bert, get up off your arse and see what that man's up to. If I know Rab he's liable to slit her throat an' tell the police she fell on the knife."

"Ach Elsie, catch yourself on. Sure he's only actin' the cod. You get carried away with yerself, readin' Agatha Christie books an' *Tales of the Unexpected*. Sometimes I think there's wee men in yer head hammerin' at yer brains."

"At least my brains are in my head and not between my legs. Bert sneaked up behind Elsie, nuzzling his chin that felt like coarse sandpaper against her cheek. He grabbed her by the bum and whispered in her ear. "Yer dead right. Come on home an' we'll have an early night. I'll soon show ye where me brains are. I've a quare touch of the Tipperary toothache the night Elsie. A year's abstinence between a bit of the other is far too long for any maun with a healthy sex drive."

Elsie looked at his feet. Sure enough his toes were beginning to turn upwards. She slapped him on the ear and threatened him with Sarah's cure for over-sexed men. Instant castration. He winched, and covered his crotch as his toes returned to their normal position.

The back door opened and slammed shut so hard the glass pane almost shattered.

"See thon big lad that lives next door to yousens. He's a dork." Sharon had come home early from the disco in a drugged frenzy. "I saw him borrow money off your Steven the night, and do ye know somethin'? The wee frigger wouldn't even buy me a *Coca Cola*. If I were yousens I'd tell his da he's goin' out with some auld tart that's riddled with disease." She put a disc of Take That on the hi-fi and started to dance like a Tazmanian She Devil.

"Stop actin' the maggot will you for God's sake. Your eyes are sittin' out like organ stops. By the look of things you've had more than *Coca-Cola* the night. Your da's up the wall with your ma's drinkin' without you resortin' to drugs. Come on home with us till ye calm down."

Elsie turned the hi-fi off and ushered Sharon out the front door, yelled goodnight to Rab who was still upstairs, grabbed Bert by the scruff of the neck and threatened him with a skite up the gub if he even *thought* of removing his pyjama bottoms when he got into bed.

Bert lit up another cigarette and farted.

"Don't be so bloody ignorant," retorted Elsie. "At least *try* an' act like a gentleman, even if you don't sound or look like one."

"Well," answered Bert in a sarcastic voice, "If I'm nat gettin' me oats I might as well get a bit of pleasure, even if it's only clearin' me throat."

"God, you're disgustin. That's one thing my family didn't do, was pass wind in front of people. We were raised better," Elsie answered as she pinched her nose and ran up wind to avoid the aftermath of Bert's eruption.

"*What?* Am I hearin' right?. Who was the one that whistled the tune of the National Anthem through his bum for a party piece?" choked Bert through a fit of the smoker's cough. "You wud have thought yer da's arsehole was made of elastic."

"He did not!" answered Elsie indignantly.

"He bloody did", quipped Bert.

Elsie voiced her disgust and warned, "Don't you dare do that in bed for yer rotten."

"Ah shut up, it might make yer hair curl. Save me a fortune in perms it will." Bert bounced up the estate as if he were on springs, exaggerating his bandy legs. "An' anyway, it wuz only a wee fartlet."

They were no sooner through the door when the phone rang.

"Is that you, Elsie? This flamin' gate is rattlin' against my bedroom wall, I can't get to sleep."

Sarah's voice pierced her daughter's ears and Elsie had the urge to throw the phone against the wall. For the umpteenth time that week Elsie had to listen to the saga of the gate. Of all the gates in the history of man, heaven's gates, hell's gates, park gates, cemetery gates, prison gates, Watergate, even the gates of Buckingham Palace, none could have caused the havoc that Sarah's gate was causing in Ballyhornet.

"Take a sleeping pill, mother."

"Sleepin' pills are no use, it would take tea laced with arsenic to rid yer head of the clatter over in this hell hole."

Elsie cupped her forehead in the palm of her hand and thought to herself, I wonder if it's still legal to buy arsenic. We could always get her cremated before anyone gets wind of foul play. She was so deep in thought she forgot she was on the phone.

"Are you still there? I can't hear ye. These bloody contraptions. I hate speakin' when ye can't see who yer speakin' to." Sarah shook the receiver a couple of times then slapped it in the palm of her hand as if to rid it of any gremlins that had taken residence without her permission.

"I'm still here mother. The only way I'll escape without notice is if the aliens take me off for experimentation. And for someone who hates the phone, you're never off the bloody thing."

"Aliens, what are ye on about? Now you've made me forget what I rang for."

"The gate, ma. The flamin' gate! What do you want me to do about it at twelve o'clock at night?"

"Could ye give that wee crathur Percy a ring. He seems to have some clout with the housin' office."

"Not at midnight he doesn't! For heaven's sake, will you let that man have his sleep."

"Do you think he sleeps with his wig on?" Sarah enquired.

Elsie lost her rag. "What has Percy's wig got to do with your gate beatin' against the wall, for heaven's sake?"

"I just thought if he had it on he could take a wee run over on his bike to have a geek to see where the rattle's comin' from."

"Ma, just take another sleepin' pill. I'm off to bed." Elsie slammed the receiver back on to its rest and screamed, "*When in blue blazes am I goin' to get peace from that cursed gate?*"

"Make us a cup of tay, Elsie," piped Bert as if he had just come home from a hard day's work.

"Shove a tea-bag in a mug and make one yourself, that is if the effort won't kill you liftin' your backside off that seat."

"Sharon will make me one, won't ye. Use up a bit of the energy from whatever it was ye took the night."

Sharon was too busy jumping up and down to hear Bert's request and he asked his wife once again to make him a drop of tea. Before Elsie had time to answer the phone rang again.

"*Yes?*" Elsie yelled down the line.

"The phone went dead," whined Sarah.

"The phone did not go dead. I hung up."

"Ye don't care, do ye? Ye would let me take sleepin' pills till they came out of me lugholes. Oh aye, why don't ye just put me in a home an' let that be th' end of it."

The idea of Sarah tucked away in a home was a thought that often crossed Elsie's mind, but there wasn't a home in Ireland that would take her. Too healthy for a nursing home, you have to be sick or senile, was the response. Or, too poor for a residential home, cost an arm and a leg to stay in one of those. There was only one other alternative, the twilight home for the mentally bewildered. But Sarah was neither mentally ill or bewildered. Bad tempered and lizard-tongued maybe, but not quite ripe for the men in white coats.

"No-one wants you in a home," lied Elsie.

"Ach sure, I'm ready for the knacker's yard anyway." Sarah had gone all maudlin, her voice had turned into a whine again and one would have easily been taken in by the ploy.

"When Bert comes over in the mornin' to take my bin out will ye tell 'im Duck's Disease up the stairs put a beg of rubbish in it and would he remove it. There's beer bottles in it an' I don't want the bin men thinkin' I drink like thon other auld pockle in the flat above me."

"Ma, did you ring about the gate, Percy's wig or your wheelie bin? Anyway, I'm sure the bin men are not interested in your rubbish. Another thing, the bin men don't come until Monday. Tomorrow's Sunday."

"The gate, the ruddy gate. Will ye not take heed? If it doesn't stop bengin' agin this wall I'll take a hatchet till it." The whine had now taken on the tone of a demented gospel preacher.

"*Right! Right!* Say no more. The gate shall be *removed!* Bert is on his way over with the screwdriver." Elsie had just about had her fill of her yap of a mother. Once more she slammed the phone down, and instructed Bert to get his backside over to the flats and remove the gate.

Elsie closed the door and went into the living room. Sharon was still bouncing around like a red setter which made Elsie light in the head. She threw herself on the settee with fatigue, and realised that tomorrow was Sunday. Her daughter and son-in-law would be round with their two children for dinner. What was she thinking about, it was already tomorrow, half-past-two in the morning. At seven-thirty she would be up again, cleaning the house, laying the dinner table and sweating over a hot stove. Five hours sleep to regain her energy. Not much rest that Saturday. The walk back and forth to the shops, trailing her bag on wheels through the snow, had affected the varicose veins in her legs and they felt as if they were filled with lead. She rubbed her legs and visualised her five grandchildren. She loved them dearly but like all children they were boisterous. Charlotte and Mark would be making their usual demands for ice lollies and crisps. She had remembered to buy white ice lollies for raspberry ones had left a stain on her carpet the previous week. Nothing would remove the stain. She'd felt angry but would not let it show. Grannies were not to show anger in front of their grandchildren. They were for hugging and cuddling up to their big fat bosoms for a nap and not for smacking, as Sarah would have you believe. How she would have welcomed a Sunday off that week, to read the papers in peace and make do with a light lunch instead of roast beef, roast potatoes and an assortment of vegetables.

"Oh God", she exclaimed out loud. "I forgot to put the jellies down, the weans will go mad."

She raced into the kitchen to put the kettle on. As she waited for it to boil she looked around her small kitchen and sighed, "Maybe some day I will get two matching taps and a nice stainless steel sink. Maybe even a couple of those nice grey-and-white cupboards on the wall, the ones with lead glass windows to show off my bits of china and teapot collection. Her tiredness made her feel all maudlin and she thought of Tom, a childhood sweetheart. He had cared more for her than she had for him. His father had owned a successful furniture business. If she had married him she more than likely would have been the proud owner of a fully-fitted kitchen and all the modern gadgets. But Tom, like the rest of her past, had disappeared into oblivion, a memory that had been wiped from her mind by her interfering mother. She toyed with the memory of Tom. What was his second name? Anderson, that's what it was. Anderson. Tom Anderson. He had a shock of red hair and freckles. The freckles had put her off him, but what a body. At the age of seventeen he had shoulders like Sylvester Stallone, only he was a lot taller. What was his pet name for her? She scratched her head and thought hard. Valentine, because of her heart shaped face. *My Funny Valentine* he used to sing to her, but she never appreciated it then. How she wished to be able to go back in time. She mused on the idea of trying to trace him, but forty odd years had passed. He probably looked like Bert now with a ginger band of hair round the back of his head and sore teeth. Anyway, he was most likely married with half-a-dozen children and a larger-than-life wife who would beat the bake off you.

The kettle clicked itself off bringing her back to reality. She poured the hot water over the squares of jelly and as they melted she thought of her daughter Sandra and son-in-law James. Sandra was very gentle, like herself, but James was a strict father. His constant shouting at the children made her uneasy. He reminded her of her own father.

"It's freezin' out there." Bert stood shivering at the back door, and, forgetting to kick the snow of his shoes, he made his way into the kitchen. A puddle of water formed at his feet, making the wretched place look worse than it was and Elsie threw the mop in his direction.

"Wipe that or you'll be slapped tonight instead of tomorrow."

"What are ye on about now? If it isn't one thing it's th' other. Which brings to mind, a bit of th' other would fairly warm me up the night."

"Stop talkin' like that in front of Sharon. You don't want to put her off men for life do you? Scarin' a child at her age into thinkin' all men turn out like you."

"Tell her to go home, she luks all right nye. From what I hear she cud learn ye a thing or two about the art of sex herself."

"Sharon, you'd better go now, your da will be in bed."

"I seen that lad next door go into the house with a quare bit of stuff hangin' on till his arm. They are both poleaxed, by the luk of the way they were fallin' all over the place."

Elsie ignored her and asked Bert, "Did you remove the gate?".

"Aye, I put it round the back. If the housin' executive doesn't want it it'll do our back garden."

He let out a cry and, putting his hand up to his cheek, hollered, "Me bloody teeth have started with that cold whizzin' round me, give us a couple of aspirin for goodness sake."

"Get them yourself. I'm off to bed."

"Ach Elsie, have ye not got an ounce of mercy in ye?"

"*Not a bit,*" lied Elsie as she climbed the stairs. Her heart felt heavy. She had a lot of compassion and wore her heart on her sleeve. But why could she not show some of it to her mother ...?

5

At number ten Peggy's snoring reverberated around the front bedroom like a pack of pigs being led to the market. Rab stood at the bedroom door, his large frame blocking out the landing light except for a small shaft on Peggy's face. He gazed upon his wife's mannish features, and felt like throwing up.

"God curse ye, ye ugly auld cow," he uttered under his breath.

"I've had some scares in me day, even nabbed by the polis, an' locked up fer three months, but nathin' scares me as bad as the sight af yer ugly auld bake bathed in a low light." He stepped back from the bed and in the darkness could make out her body outlined under the blankets. He pulled back the bed clothes, revealing her body spreadeagled on the crumpled sheet. "How in Gods name did *she* get a fancy man? He must either be blind or mental," he muttered to himself.

Peggy did indeed have "a bit on the side", an old Etonian army officer, who had been given an honourable discharge after losing the sight of an eye, had taken a shine to her. Heaven knows what he seen in Peggy out of the other eye. There could only be one explanation. He must have been half blind in that eye or else half got.

In fact, it was her profusion of pubic hair that turned him on. When he had first laid eyes on it he declared his approval in Sergeant Major fashion by stroking his handle-bar moustache and yelling, "My God, old gal, let the dog see the rabbit. A short-back-and-sides would not go amiss on a thatch such as that!"

She boasted to Rab of her extra-marital activities, in the vain hope of making him jealous. Rab just laughed, for it saved him the energy and effort of love-making. He nicknamed him "Major Bolsover" to the annoyance of his wife and the amusement of his mates. Peggy was Rab's second wife, his first wife having died of cancer in her twenties. That happy marriage had been cruelly cut short before they had the chance to have a family. He married Peggy "on the rebound" on his thirtieth birthday, a birthday present he could, in retrospect, have done without. His sexual prowess was at its peak and Peggy was a more than willing partner. He often remarked to his friends, "Me brains must have been in me balls at the time. I didn't luk at the mantelpiece when I wuz stoking the fire."

Twelve years later their daughter, Sharon, was born, a difficult birth for both Peggy and Rab. She had grown to enormous proportions during pregnancy and resembled a giraffe about to drop triplets. Her gangly arms and legs looked ridiculous attached to her elongated body, with its grossly swollen abdomen that rested between her legs when she sat, legs parted. Peggy did not believe in over exerting herself in her *enciente* condition. Not that she ever exerted herself when in any other condition other than engaging in the joys of sex. The pangs of labour did not endear her to her husband, who was being called all the lop-eyed bastards under the sun at the height of each contraction. Rab had to duck every object not fixed to the walls, floor and table tops, as they flew through the air. Each seemed to make contact with his head or body, and he had ached for weeks.

He vowed to never again get his wife in that condition and abstained from sex, using his bad back as an excuse. His health had gone downhill rapidly, and at the age of fifty-seven, he was now resigned to a sexless sham of a marriage and a medicine cabinet full to the brim with pills, potions and sprays for his weakened heart and lungs.

He scratched his chin in deep thought as he took in the awful sight that lay before him. He was bent on revenge at his wife's antics earlier in the night but couldn't make up his mind what to do to her. It huz tae be samethin' drastic. Oan the other haun, nat fatal, he thought. He remembered the night he had left her on the hard shoulder of the M1 as pissed as a newt. The police had brought her home at two o'clock in the morning covered in a blanket. Rab had removed most of her clothes and she was shivering and blue with the cold.

"Ye bastard!" She had spat out the words, covering his face with spit in the process.

"Now Mrs Kirk, that's enough of that. No point in using bad language." The police officer had taken a note book from his top pocket and proceeded to ask Rab a few questions.

"Were you on the M1 with your wife earlier on tonight, Mr Kirk?"

"No", he had replied, not moving a muscle except for a twitch in his bad eye.

"She says you were, and that you threw her out of the car, sir."

"Peggy, hae ye been tellin' porkies again? Ye know ye can't keep pretendin' I don't care fer ye. Ye know, afficer, I had tae get her admitted tae the mental home oan two occasions tae get dried out. She kept turnin' up in th' oddest af places. She goes out wi' other men ye know, it's her mind. She gets drunk an' thinks she's Ursula Andress, or in her case Ursula Undress. I've nay control what-so-ever wi' her. In ways I feel sorry fer 'it'."

"It's a serious offence to sit on the hard shoulder of a motorway, Mr Kirk. Someone will be brought to court over this."

"Well, if ye fin' the maun that did it let me know, fer he deserves a medal fer takin' her out. He can hae that wan I huv in the bedside drawer up the stairs."

They could find no evidence to prove that Rab had done it, so he had got off the hook. No second chances. This time it had to be legal. He carefully covered her nakedness with the blanket and tiptoed into the bathroom for a pee. As he stood at the toilet a pink-and-white tube of cream on the bathroom window-sill caught his attention. At first he thought it was a tube of toothpaste. Lifting it he saw the name *Immac* written in bold letters. Then he noticed the words printed below. *Hair removing cream* or words to that effect.

He scratched his head in deep thought, and then the answer hit him. It must belong to Sharon, she's quite hairless. Her legs are anyway, and under her oxters. Another thought flashed through his brain. By Jaysus, that's it! Remove his wife's pride an' joy, the only flamin' thing she huz that attracts that auld geezer wi' th' wan eye.

He almost had an asthma attack with the prospect of removing Peggy's one and only asset. Then the tears started to roll down his cheeks and he had to bite down hard with his teeth to stop himself from laughing out loud. He dropped to his knees and beat the floor with his fists. Lord God, forgive me! but it huz tae be done he thought. If I die tomorrow this little act will give St Peter a bit af a laugh when he reads out me sins, even if he huz tae send me down tae auld Nick at th' end af it. He pulled himself up by leaning on the bathtub, and after wiping the tears from his eyes and inhaling a few puffs of his *Ventolin* spray, he read the instructions: *Apply evenly and leave for five to six minutes before removing with cool water*. He failed to notice the warning: *Before applying, test on a small area of skin for sensitivity*. Not that this would have stopped him. He tiptoed across the landing, cursing the creaky floorboards.

"Shut up will ye," he hissed, as if the floorboards would obey. He continued his journey until he stood beside the bed. He carefully pulled the blanket back. He need not have worried. Peggy was not only four sheets to the wind, she was almost comatose. Peggy's long legs would not do as they were told. As soon as he had one leg in place, bent upwards and out, it collapsed as he tried to get the other one to respond to the same treatment. In the end he stuffed a pillow under her backside and climbed on to the bed. He sat himself down between her legs and held them apart at the knees with his feet. Peggy started to mouth obscenities in her inebriated stupor and Rab almost fainted with fright. If she woke up now she might get the notion he had got his sex drive back, an that would be a fate worse than death itself. He needn't have worried for a loud snore told him she was still well and truly out of it. From his position it was difficult to reach his intended target and he had to stretch his arm to the limit to apply the cream to his wife's thatch of thick black pubic hair. He plastered it on as if he were building a brick wall, now and then coming up for a breath of air. It smelled like burning rubber and he almost had second thoughts for it had said red rose fragrance on the box.

Maybe it's gone aff, he thought. Ah, what the hell. In fer a penny, in fer a poun'. Better keep it on fer ten minutes though, tae get through that lat.

He gently pulled her legs down into a flat position, covered her up and crept out of the room, then washed his hands in the bathroom and made his way downstairs.

Rab forgot time was ticking by, and twenty minutes and a cup of tea later decided to get on with the job of cleaning up the missus. Armed with a bowl of water he sat himself down between Peggy's splayed legs. He leant over and pulled at a piece of the profusion to see if it was ripe for removing. A clump came away in his fingers and he gagged, for it felt revolting. He proceeded to wipe her down with a piece of cotton wool that he had dipped in the bowl of water. The hair came away like black slime. It took ten minutes to finish the job and he felt worn out but exhilarated. He sat back to admire his work but gasped at the sight that faced him.

"It luked better covered up," he said out loud, for the flaming space between her legs had turned a livid red, and swollen to boot. "By Christ, she's goin' tae be sore in the mornin', fer I'm sure I kep that oan tae long." He started to laugh again, only this time out of nervousness. "She luks like a purple-arsed baboon, begod." As he covered her up and tucked her in for the night he comforted himself, thinking, Ach sure it wuz only a bit af a geg!

Getting rid of the evidence soon took the smile of his face. The cursed hair would not flush down the toilet. He had to bombard it with clumps of toilet tissue to rid the pan of traces of the revolting slimy mess. He breathed a sigh of relief after about ten minutes and retired to bed.

About three o'clock in the morning Sharon opened the front door and slammed it shut again behind her. The effect of the Ecstacy tablet she had taken earlier had worn off and she was ready for bed. The noise aroused Peggy from her alcohol-induced slumber and she started lashing about the bed. Rab, who couldn't get to sleep for thinking about what he had done to his wife earlier on, lay as still as a mouse for fear of waking her. He didn't want to ruin the second part of his cruel plan before the morning. After mumbling something about feeling a bit sore around the crotch she fell fast asleep, her snoring taking on a new resonance. With every snore the headboard of the bed vibrated against the wall.

At precisely half-past-seven in the morning Rab tiptoed down the stairs, made himself a cup of tea, sat back in the easy chair beside the roaring fire and waited patiently for the sound of creaking floorboards, a sign that Peggy's bladder had reached bursting point.

The heat of the fire had put him into a doze, and had Peggy not hit her toe on the beside table and screamed he would almost certainly have missed his chance to make his next move.

"Jaysus, she's up!" Rab jumped up from his chair and made a beeline towards the bottom of the stairs. He cupped his hand round his ear, held his breath and braced himself, for he knew all hell would break out any second.

A shriek similar to that of the banshee echoed round the house.

"It's worked! It's bloody worked", tittered Rab as he ran towards the kitchen. "Now tae put plan number two inta action." He opened the back door and raced down the back garden and hid behind the bird shed.

Ten seconds later the back door opened. There stood Peggy, stark bollock naked, screaming her head off and at the same time examining her now bald and badly swollen genitalia.

"Are you down thur at them auld birds, Rab?" she yelled out loud. "Will ye hae a luk tae see if they are moultin' fer I think I've caught some terrible disease fram them mouldy friggin' pigeons af yurs. Did ye wash yer hauns last night before ye gat inta bed?"

Don't tell me sh' actually thinks I touched it, he thought. She knows I wouldne touch it wi' a barge pole, never min' me haun.

Rab could hardly contain his amusement at the sight of his wife.

"What's wrang wi ye, wuman?" he asked, holding his hanky up to his face in a bid to hide his tears of laughter. "Get yoursel' in outa the cold afore ye die af frostbite."

Peggy jumped back into the kitchen and hid behind the door. She peeped her head round the corner and ushered Rab in with a wave of her bony hand. "Com'n in a that will ye an have a luk. I don't know whether tae go tae the dactor or call in the vet. I'm awful sore down thur".

"Down whur?"

"Down the fuckin' pub." She grabbed him by the scruff of the neck and pushed his face towards her groin. "Down thur, ye gormless git! Where the friggin' hell did ye think I meant! Did ye touch me last night after workin' wi' them friggin' birds?"

Rab closed his eyes for it looked bad enough from a distance, never mind close up. "I wouldnae touch it wi a pair of tweezers, niver min' me hauns, wuman dear. Ye must hae caught a dose af the mange fram that moth eaten moggy ye cuddled."

"I never cuddled any auld moggy!"

"Then ye must 'ave caught it fram that anchient sergeant major ye cavort aroun' wi. You've only gone an' caught a dose af the clap. Now stop yer whingin' an' gurnin'."

"Don't you say a word af this tae no-one, or I'll lace yer tay wi' weedkiller ye ugly bastard."

"I'm away fer the papers. Hae a cup af tay an' calm down."

Rab sauntered down the street to Elsie and Bert's, to tell all. This was too good a story to let slip by without a laugh. Elsie had just put the Sunday roast in the oven when Rab let himself in by the back door.

"You're out early today Rab".

"Where's Bert? Get 'im in here quick afore I tell ye what happened tae Peggy." Rab was jumping around like a herring on a hot griddle with excitement.

"Bert! Rab wants you for a minute", shouted Elsie.

"Will ye wait till I've finished, I'm on the toilet."

"Well nick it. Anyway, yer only readin' the papers".

"Give us a minute, for God's sake. I'm in the middle of a crossword."

"This is goin' tae take more than a minute," Rab informed Elsie, still jumping around as if his pants were on fire.

Bert ambled into the kitchen, lit up a cigarette and inhaled deeply. As usual it made him cough and Elsie gave off to him for plugherin' all over the trifle she had just sat on the kitchen bench.

"Niver min' the bloody trifle. When ye hear me out you'll niver ate rabbit again, fer it will remind ye af hare pie, as in h.a.i.r."

"Your an auld blether", said Elsie, after Rab had told them. "You can't believe a word that passes your lips, Robert Kirk. Sure *Immac* would burn you down there. It's for removing the hairs of your legs."

Rab winked at Bert and answered with a mischievous grin on his face. "Aye, I know that nye. The auld cow's hoppin' about the house as if 'er arse wuz on fire."

"Here, tell me this and tell me no more. Does she really think she has some awful disease?" asked Bert.

"Aye, she does that alright, nat a hair left on the ould fan tiddle. I laughed that much the tears ran down me legs. It wud have made a hen laugh." He started into a fit of uncontrollable laughter, forcing a double dose of his asthma spray.

"Are ye all right, Rab, for ye don't look in too fine af shape the day?" Bert was worried that the man was going to have a heart attack in front of him.

"Aye, I feel finer than the hair on a baby's bum. A good bit af craic is better than all th' auld drugs ye can lay yer hauns on," tittered Rab.

"You wouldn't think it the way you're suckin' on that spray."

"Ah give over gripin', Friars. Com'n roun' tae the house an' see fer yersel' if ye don't believe me."

"She's hardly goin' to let me luk at it, is she?"

Rab laughed again. "For frig sake, Bert, she wud let the vicar see it fer a battle af gin. Put yer shoe's on yer kebs an' come on roun' wi' me. I only ask ye tae promise me wan thing. That is, don't let on I taule ye or she'll skin me alive."

The three of them traipsed round to Rab's and slipped in by the back door unnoticed by Peggy. She was standing in the living-room with her skirt up round her waist, peering down her knickers and muttering to herself, "If that randy auld bastard of a Brit has given me the clap I'll deball him wi' two coal breek!"

It was only when the dog yelped as Rab gave it a kick up the backside that she came to her senses. Letting down her skirt she composed herself by knocking back a couple of *Valium* with the remains of some gin that had been left in her glass from the night before.

She shouted out, "Is that you, Rab?"

"Aye it's me alright, Elsie an' Bert hae come up fer a wee drap af tay. Do ye want a cup?"

"I'll have a cup in me haun, fer I've a hat-pat in the oven."

Rab scratched his head and turned to Elsie, "What the hell's gates has a hat-pat gat to dae wi' a cup af tay?"

His country brogue made Elsie laugh, for it was completely unlike the broad Ulster dialect of the rest of the Ballyhornet residents.

Elsie shrugged her shoulders and, with a display of the hands, answered, "You've got me there, Rab."

"I've a bit af fresh bap in the bread bin if ye want it with yer tay, an' thur's a few slices af corned beef in the fridge if me boyo thur hasn't wrapped his gub roun' it." Peggy informed Bert and Elsie, who were now sitting at the kitchen table looking anywhere but at Peggy. They felt as if they were the guilty party of the terrible trick Rab had played on her during the night. They almost wished he hadn't have told them.

Rab kicked Bert on the ankle and winked with his good eye.

"It's a caule day Bert. You'd sure miss yer fur coat if ye had wan all the while." He glanced in Peggy's direction but Peggy was holding her composure rightly. "I read in the *Sunday World* some auld geezer is skinnin' pussies tae make fur gloves."

Peggy's back was to the table, her hands had tightened round the handle of the teapot. For one awful moment Rab had visions of it connecting with the side of his head and he ducked. She swung round, teapot in hand and, with a look that would have soured milk hissed, "I think I fed that bit af bap to the pigeons an' the corned beef is a bit green roun' the edges, just like the luk on Bert's bake, Rab!"

"It's ah, it's ah ..."

"It's what, Bert?" asked Peggy slapping the teapot down hard on the table. It was her turn to kick Rab on the shin for she had an idea he had something to do with her dilemma.

"I think Bert's tryin' tae say he's only after his breakfast."

"Has the cat gat his tongue?" asked Peggy.

"I hope it hasne fer it cud hae been wan af the wans that wuz skinned." At this point Rab made a bee-line for the stairs. He had to get out of the kitchen before he exploded with suppressed laughter.

"Excuse me a moment will ye. I hae t' get a towel fram the hatpress."

"Aye sure, Peggy, we'll go on home nye anyway," answered Bert and Elsie at the same time. They felt nervous for when Rab and Peggy started playing tricks on each other anyone within a half mile radius was in danger. It was not unknown for the contents of the knife drawer to be used as darts in these situations.

"Oh no ye won't", screeched Peggy. "Rab wud be quite angry if I let ye go without a cuppa. God knows what revenge th' auld blirt wud think up." She poured out their tea and instructed them to drink it before it went cold.

Elsie hissed out of the side of her mouth at Bert, "Do as your bloody told," spilling half the contents of her cup with nerves as she put it to her lips.

Peggy fled into the hall and up the stairs closely followed by Rab. She yanked him into the bedrom by the scruff of the neck and stared him in the face. "Ye taule them didn't ye, ye gormless big hallion. They thought they wud come up fer a bit af a geek, fer a laugh at my expense."

"I did nat, they know nathin'. What wud I be doin' tellin' them about you havin' the clap?"

"I do *nat* hae the *clap!*"

"All right then, maybe it's *nat* the *clap*. But, by Christ, it just didn't moult wi' the caule."

"I *know* you had somethin' to do wi' it. It's very funny thur's nay sign af it in the bed, and I know it wuz all there when I went."

"When ye went tae bed last night ye didn't know ye had a hair on yer head niver min' a hair anywhere else. Now get down them stairs an' try tae act normal in front af yer guests. Even though ye don't luk it!"

"I'll get ye back, Rab Kirk, if it's the last thing I do. Mark my words: *I'll get ye back should I commit murder to do it.*"

"Will don't dae it till we hae our tay", laughed Rab.

The back door slammed shut as Bert and Elsie fled to safety.

6

Sunday, 25 February

Sunday morning in Ballyhornet estate could best be described as "leave me in peace and let me die day". Hangovers from a night at the pub or even a night at home in front of the television with a carry-out were being slept off.

Shaun could not afford a drink of a Saturday. His pockets were usually emptied of cash by his offspring before he had a chance to even contemplate a night at the pub. His only escape from the family was spending Sunday mornings attending to his beloved car. While his sons and daughters lay wallowing in their pits, he usually washed and polished his BMW, not content until it looked in pristine colookin'ndition.

The snow that had fallen the previous night had turned to sleet.

Shaun sat in his well-worn armchair and stared forlornly out of the window. He had read the papers and looked up the following week's television programmes in the supplement to the *People*.

"Soaps! Nathin' but bloody soaps," he said. "They're nat content with showin' them every other damned night, they have to repeat the blasted things the next day. Christ almighty, are they nat content wi' fillin' us all wi' the thoughts of suicide after each flamin' episode without makin' us watch them all over again?" He spat out these words as if they had left a bitter taste in his mouth.

"No-one ties ye to yer seat an' threatens ye wi' the death penalty for nat watchin'. Ye can lift yer arse of the chair an' walk away, ye know." Jacinta shouted from the kitchen. The kitchen was getting more like home to her these days as she spent most of her time in it. She fed the washing machine another load of jeans and pressed the boil-wash button. The thought of how she was going to get them dry on such a day almost made her weep.

"Why shud I have to leave the comfort of me own home so bloody television producers can vomit out stories about homosexuals an' Aids? If it's nat that, it's weemen buryin' their husbands in the back yard an' oul lads having it away wi' young bits of skirt. That thing that luked like a cow lukin' over a wall sent us all up the wall, moanin' about why she did her auld lad in fer months."

"I don't blame her for bumpin' him aff. All men shud be put agin a wall an' shot after they have past their prime, an' you're only jealous ye can't get a dolly bird yerself. Why are ye nat out cleaning the car anyway?"

"It's effin wet out there. Are ye blind or daft? Jealousy! Who in the name af Christ wud be jealous af men havin' it aff with mutton dressed as lamb? Half of those auld dolls have taken at least ten years aff their age. An' don't for heaven's sake accuse me of bein' jealous of bloody poofs. An' before ye even think of burying me in the yard remember yer no spring chicken yerself. Who else wud ye get to take on that lat up the stairs? I sired the friggin' stickin' plasters. Nat that I enjoyed it that much fer it cost me the price af a twenty-pound Provident cheque fer the three minutes that it tuk to start their journey inta this world."

"God forgive ye, Shaun Dunlop. I gave myself too freely, that's why we have the 'bloody stickin' plasters' as you so eloquently put it. An' anyway, it only tuk one minute if ye want to be fussy about time."

"Well, I suppose I did get it free an' gratis on th' odd occasion. You an' yer staunch Roman Catholic upbringing. No contraceptives. No contraceptives an' no sex. Sex was for procreation as the priest wud say at mass on Sunday, an' you bloody well heeded him. The same auld lad wud jump on a cracked windie."

"May God forgive ye fer a second time today," retorted Jacinta who had now started to peel the potatoes for dinner. "Father O'Dowd is a saint. He warned me about hangin' aroun' wi' you. Have you been to confession at anytime with him? For if ye have whatever ye taule him must have made a lastin' impression for he gives me the most unusual luks of a Sunday mornin'."

Shaun cringed at the thought of Father O'Dowd. He shuddered and called him all the bad names of the day into himself, the deaf old bastard being one of the kinder handles. Only last month he had went to confess his sins and, being in a hurry, had gone to Father O'Dowd as his queue was the shortest. It was only after he had sat his backside in the confessional that he realised the flaming man was as deaf as a post. It had started all right.

"Bless me father for I have sinned. It has been two months since my last confession." Normally he only went every six months so he thought he would have got a slap on the back and a "God bless you my son" for being so pious. Alas, this was not to be.

"Speak up whoever you are!" The outline of Father O'Dowd's profile was pressed against the screen, his hand cupped round his ear.

Shaun had gone over his "Bless me Father" bit all over again, a little louder. After the fifth attempt the old priest had finally managed to get Shaun's drift.

"Two months. Two months! Did ye say two months? That's far too long a gap in between confession. Two months ye say?" He had heard that all right, so had the rest of the parishioners who were waiting in the chapel. Unknown to Shaun they had decided to move closer to Father O'Dowd's confessional for a bit of an eavesdrop.

This set off a chain reaction between the priest and Shaun. The louder Shaun replied the louder Father O'Dowd asked him his sins.

"Ye stole what!"

"It wuz only a few nails, Father."

"A few nails lead to a couple of hundred, then before ye know it the nails will lead to a hammer, then a saw, then a couple of planks of wood. It will only be a matter of time before ye steal a house!"

"But they were only fer an' old woman's gate."

"Who do you hate? Do you not know that's a sin as well?"

Shaun had gritted his teeth and clenched his fist. "Shut up, ye pious auld bastard." He had muttered under his breath.

"Did ye say something there my son?" His head was nearly coming through the grill. Shaun had peeped out the door to be met by a sea of faces, all turned in his direction. He was trapped; now he had started he would have to finish. He had a mind to clonk the old priest on the side of his head with his fist and knock him out. May God forgive me he thought to himself, echoing the words of his wife: I'll have to go to confession to confess my confession of plotting a mugging in a confessional. He had laughed at his last thought.

"Do I hear a titter of laughter in there?"

"No, Father, I choked on me spit."

"You choked who?"

"I choked no-one."

"Ye choked Noel? Do ye mean to tell me ye committed murder?"

Shaun could hear the shuffle of bums on pews, the gathering masses had decided to come a little closer. This confession was hotting up.

"Speak up lad! did ye kill the man?"

Shaun had no other choice he had to shout to be heard. "I choked no-one Father." Although the thought of murder was getting stronger by the second, he decided to change the subject and get on to some menial sins. "I refused to do the dishes fer the wife."

"You don't mean to tell me you cheated on the wife?"

"I didn't say that, but sometimes I think af it." Shaun rubbed his temple and resigned himself to the fact that he might as well take what was coming to him.

"You had sexual thoughts as well, sins against the flesh. You've stolen, you've murdered, you've cheated on the wife. I don't want to hear more. In fact I want you to go straight to the altar and say fifty Our Fathers and one hundred Hail Marys. And what's more, you will attend mass every day for the next month to repent your sins."

"But ..."

"What are ye saying now, lad? I know who you are, ye know. I will hear no more. Be off with you and may the Lord forgive you your sins. Show in the next parishioner on the way out." No-one went into the confessional when he came out. As he passed the stations of the cross, head bowed in shame, he heard the muted whispers, "Does the man nat know Father O'Dowd only hears children's an' old people's confessions.

Anything more sinful than stealing an apple is a mortal sin to O'Dowd these days. As fer the old, well, half of them have forgotten what sins are."

Shaun had not set foot inside St Mary's from that day. In fact the very name Father O'Dowd sent shivers up his spine and he had come to the conclusion, seeing he knew so much about sins, Father o'Dowd must be guilty of each and every one. Especially sins of the flesh, for he seemed to know quite a lot about them.

Jacinta looked at the kitchen clock and, realising the last mass of the morning would be starting any minute, left the potatoes she had been peeling, put on her boots and coat, wrapped a scarf round her neck and informed her husband she would light a few candles for his soul.

"The man's deaf, is that nat penance enough. He's a saint, is Father O'Dowd. Nat a dirty thought in his mind."

"Get away a this, woman. What do ye think him an' that housekeeper af his gets up to? She's rubbin' more than his candlesticks with Duraglit. In fact, see the next time ye go till confession, tell him I'm nat gettin' me conjugal rights. Even the bloody bishop gets more than I do an' they've the bloody gaul to tell ye aff fer thinkin' about it."

"That's it! I will listen no longer to yer filthy tongue. I'm off to mass to pray to the Lord to have mercy on yer soul when ye die."

"Aye, an' when yer there say a prayer that some af them upstairs get work. Sorry, did I say a four-letter word there."

The front door slammed shut so hard it almost fell off its hinges.

"Lift the bloody dur aff the footpath will ye," yelled Shaun out of the window at Jacinta, who was wrapping her scarf tightly round her head in an effort to keep the cold from nipping her ears.

Moses the dog got up from the rug in front of the fire and turned full circle. It had farted and the shock had made it chase its own arse. It looked at Shaun as if he were the culprit and gave a doggy huff before arranging its hairy self back into position. It rested its head on its paws and stared at Shaun through bloodshot eyes.

Shaun stared back.

Moses did not like humans staring him in the eye and he changed position. He shuffled without lifting its body off the rug so his backside now stared Shaun in the face.

Typical, thought Shaun. Feed the bastard an' it shows ye its arse in return. Mind you, I feed the rest of the scroungers in this house and the only time I see them is when their arses are goin' out the front dur to the pub! He got up from the comfort of his chair and looked out the window. The sleet had turned to icy rain, his beloved car looked as forlorn as he felt, parked as it was between two filth-infested lorries. The little bit of hair left on his head stuck out untidily round his ears, the knees of his well-worn trousers sat out like balloons, while the top of his backside mooned over the drooping waistband. He wore a short-sleeved shirt summer and winter in the vain hope of proving to his offspring that central heating was not needed. Many a time he nearly froze to death on a winter's day trying to make his point. What the poor man was really trying to say was, central heating costs money.

All of a sudden he felt cold, and glanced at the fire.

"The bitch never put any coal on the fire before she went out. She's as bad as the rest of them, takes me fer granted she does.

I'll teach her a lesson, I'll let the bloody fire go out." He plonked himself back in the armchair and, to help him think, he beat out the rhythm of the theme tune to the *Lone Ranger* on the threadbare armrest with his finger tips.

Moses shifted position once more and growled in Shaun's direction.

"What's up, mutt, am I disturbin' yer beauty sleep?" He kicked the dog up the backside and it scurried off into the kitchen to get out of his master's road.

"Is yer centre piece sore? Nye ye *will* have something to growl about, ye screggy lukin' mongrel."

He felt pleased at himself with this little act of aggression. Pity he couldn't give that lot up the stairs the same treatment.

He had heard in a film once the line, "You're a pain in the arse of humanity" which reminded him of his family and he often made this remark to his brood. Not that they cared a fiddler's fart. It ran off them like water off a ducks back.

He shivered with the cold, almost giving in and banking up the fire but reneged at the last minute.

"Why the hell shud I?" He asked himself, I'll put on a jumper an' clean the inside of the car instead. Nye, where did I put the keys? He scratched his head in deep thought, like Detective Columbo, and paced the living room and kitchen without success.

He thought of his son Pip lying in his bed and remembered lending them to him the previous night. He looked at his watch. Twelve o'clock. Why were his brood not up watching Little House on the Prairie? They might pick up a couple of hints on how to behave as a family. He pictured the O'Hare family, who lived in the next street. The da acted like Mr Ingles, with his mealy-mouthed manner, but his kids would give you the skitters they were that sanctimonious.

Nah! thought Shaun. At least *my* affspring are nat all brainy bastards who think they are somebody they aren't.

Shaun stopped halfway up the stairs, realising he had forgotten his *News of the World*.

Might as well have a bit af a read on th' toilet. He enjoyed clucking on the toilet of a Sunday morning with a good read, and retracing his steps he lifted the newspaper off the settee.

Shud I wake that lat up first? At least I'll nat be interrupted fer a while if I do, no bengin' on th' dur when I'm concentrating about what the Bishop gets up to in th' vestry. Ever since his run-in with Father O'Dowd he had had an unhealthy attitude towards the sex lives of the clergy. He changed his mind and sprinted up the stairs to waken his brood.

"Hey you three. Get up out af yer pits." He knocked the boys bedroom door and shouted. "Pip, Kevin, Declan. Will ye scrape the beds aff yer backs an' get yer lazy backsides down these stairs.

It's three o'clock. Do ye want to lie there till th'marra?" He always added a few hours onto the time of day, he hoped this ploy would work, but it never did.

There was no response, so he decided to enter his son's flea-pit at the risk of being overcome by the aroma of smelly feet and week-old Chinese takeaways. Four lumps in the shape of bodies lay prone in two double beds. He scratched his head and prayed he was not going prematurely senile. At the last head count he could have sworn he had three sons and not four. Had his brain gone AWOL without his knowledge?

One of the lads passed wind in the bed at the right a blonde head rose from its pillow in the bed on the left and a groggy voice said, "Put a cork in it will ye, fer yer ratten."

The smell of stale booze and the remains of garlic laced take-aways made his eyes water. His stomach turned with the stink of the place and he opened the bedroom window to the hilt.

"That's one awful bloody mornin'." Lynus, Dickie McGrath's son, was wheeling spare car-parts in an old pram past Shaun's house and stopped below the bedroom window for a chat. He was soaked to the skin in his navy overalls that were held together with an assortment of safety pins. And his Doc Martin boots had seen better days. An old woollen balaclava covered his head but did nothing to disguise his face, which was covered in acne and blackheads. Him and his da were worth a mint, their scrap metal business had taken over from his da's rag-and-bone trade and every penny went into the bank for a rainy day. The rainy days had come and gone but the hunger was hanging out of Dickie. The two of them resembled vagrants, except for Saturday night when they dressed up like dog's dinners for a night at the King Williams Arms.

"This auld pram is knackered. It saw me an' me brothers though the first years aff our lives alright, but I think it's time it went out to graze."

His two brothers, Joe and Jimbo, had emigrated to Australia to join Dickie's brother who was doing well in the antiques business. Dickie saw no difference between antiques and scrap metal. Sure, it was all second hand at the end of the day.

"What's wrong with the van, Lynus?" Shaun asked.

"Dickie's away to the scrap-yard to pick up an engine fer Cyril's Cortina. Why th' hell he holds on to that car af his is a mystery, sure the big end is about to give in," answered Lynas.

"That friggin' poof? It's a mystery to me why *his* big end hasn't gone, never mine that rust bucket he drives" voiced Shaun.

They both burst out laughing.

"Here you, big lad," joked Lynus in a girly voice, as he stood with his left hand on his hip, while the right one sat out like the handle of a teapot. "Don't knock it till yiv tried it. Cyril an' I are in love, did ye nat know that?"

Shaun pictured Cyril and his woolly hair swanning over Lynus as he squeezed his pimples and blackheads, and his stomach turned.

"Take yeurself aff by the hand before I vomit, fer Christ's sake," Shaun answered with a look of disgust.

"I'm only jokin', I'd rather be covered in pig shit."

Before Lynus positioned himself for another go at the pram he saw Percy Thorndyke head towards the pensioners' flats. He put the brake on with his foot and lent himself against Shaun's wall.

"Shaun", said Lynus, "what dae ye think Percy's up tae on a Sunday mornin' all business-like? His wee arse is makin' buttons he's that sprightly, an' 'is wig is all ship shape an' freshly laundered by th' luk aff it."

"God knows, it's nat for the benefit of the residents, for there isn't one under eighty years of age over there," answered Shaun.

"It luks as if there's a meetin' goin' on, fer I heard Elsie and Bert say they were goin' over later, as I passed thur dur."

"Sure it's probably that blasted gate Sarah Cruickshank is on about. One minute it's on, the next it's aff again."

"Dae ye see the size af 'is umbrella? He must hiv got plannin' permission, for that it's that wide. It's bloody well nigh six fut wide! It wud keep a futball team dry. Then again I suppose it keeps thon wig from blowin' aff in the wind. He's a wan fer th' weemen is wee Percy. Wee dogs hae big tails, an' all that crap. Well, good luck till him, that's what I say, if it keeps ye young lukin'. Christ Almighty, if that's the case I must luk ninety fer I can't get a dog tae bark at me. Do ye know, Shaun, I can't fer the life af me think why. Maybe I shud carry a gamp like Percy. Gamp an' camp, do ye get it Shaun? Ah, never mine, although I don't have any doubts about Percy's sexual preference. As I said before, he's a maun fer the weemen."

Shaun glanced at the wretched-looking face in front of him. "No, an' I don't know either, Lynus" he lied. He bit down on his knuckles in a bid to quell the urge to laugh out loud.

"Like it's nat that I don't wash or anything. I shower once a week an' use that deodorant – what dae ye call it nye?" He scratched his head and smelt under his armpits for a clue. "Phew! Whatever it is isn't workin', fer I smell like a wrestler's jock-strap even if I dae admit tae it. Ach, I know nye. It's thon wan ye splash all over, *Thug*, or somethin' that goes by that handle."

"Do ye mean *Brut*?"

"Who's a brute?" asked Lynus indignantly.

"I said, do ye mean *Brut*" laughed Shaun, "*Brut*, the aftershave?"

"Ach, I know ye did Shaun. Sure I know it's called *Brut*. Sometimes I don't know shit fram sugar, so me da says anyway. One thing I do know wud surprise ye."

"What's that?"

"Do ye remember Elvis?"

"Who doesn't? Sure thon wife af mine goes mad over him. Goes all goofy-eyed when she hears him singin'. I wish she'd make love till me the way she makes love till that record player when she plays his songs."

"Well *he* wore *Brut* an' the weemen went wild over him. Nat many people know that, as yer maun Caine wud say."

"I suppose that means I can die happy nye after that bit of useless information," Shaun replied, turning his eyes towards heaven with disbelief.

Lynus struck an Elvis pose and curled his upper lip. "Ah, huh huh. Yeah man, can't ye see the resemblance?"

"Not really, Lynus. For a start Elvis wuz good lukin'. An' he didn't wear boiled boots, he wore nice white ones an' a jump suit studded with jewels, nat a boiler suit studded with safety pins!"

"Ah, but he might have before he became famous".

"No harm till ye Lynus, he wud still have luked better than you if he wuz covered with boils from the Black Plague".

"Yer no bloody oil paintin' yerself, Shaun Dunlop!"

"Clear aff."

"Nat before ye tell me why I can't get a woman when I smell like Elvis."

"If ye were drippin' wi' diamonds ye still wudn't get a woman. Now frig aff! Luk I've no time ..."

"I'm only havin' ye on," bantered Lynus. "Dae ye think I'd be pushin' this pram if I luked like Elvis? I'd be havin' it away wi' every bit af skirt fram here till Kerry."

Giving Shaun a two-fingered salute, he said, "I'm away aff, fer my nose is drippin' wi' the cold. Before I go, did I tell ye there's an Elvis look-a-like competition on at the King William's Arms next Saturday? Do ye fancy goin'?"

"I do nat, never liked the man. I don't intend watchin' a load of eejits makin' fools af themselves. Anyway, I can't foresee many turnin' up. They're an ugly lat round here."

"Well, I expect a lat. Ye cud say, there will be a plethora af Elvii marchin' towards the pub come Saturday night. Must get me jumpsuit out af the cleaners." He lifted the brake of the pram up with his right foot, and with his head bowed and back braced for the slog he headed towards home.

"See ye, Shaun. Give the wife a kiss fer me, will ye. Fine lukin' woman, yer Jacinta. Me da always said he wud huv married her if you hadnae came on the scene."

Shaun thought of his idle brood and wished Dickie had married Jacinta. He too would have been worth a fortune by now. As the sayin goes, "When you've reared a family, you've spent a fortune!"

"Will ye close that bloody windie, da. It wud freeze the goolies aff a snowman." Kevin, his middle son, had wrapped the duvet tightly round his neck and was looking bleary eyed at Shaun.

Shaun closed the window, not because his son told him to but because he didn't want to let the neighbours hear him giving his brood a rollicking.

"Get the fuck up, ye lazy bastards. And that goes for the rest of you scumbegs. Nye, get out af yer pits or I'll throw a bucket af water over the lat af ye!"

"Watch yer language, da. There's a girl in here." A small, muffled voice could be heard coming from under the duvet of Kevin's bed.

Shaun stopped in his tracks and yelled, "What do ye mean there's a girl in here? Are ye tryin' to make me go all ga-ga so ye can get snatterin' on in yer pits?"

Declan, who shared the double bed with Kevin decided to get his oar in. He peered over the top of his duvet, and wiped his eyes with the back of his hand and repeated, "There's a girl in Pip's bed", then pulled the duvet back up over his head and sighed as if it were quite normal to have a girl sleeping amongst three men.

"Get the hell up will ye an' stap festerin' in yer beds. If there's a girl in here she must have no morals like yerselves." Shaun stared at Pip's single bed. *Was* the other lump in the bed a female form? He was in the process of pulling the covers back when a blonde head shot up followed by a naked pair of boobs. After the initial shock of seeing a pair of perk 36 double D's with nipples like hat pegs attached peeping straight at him, he managed to find his voice.

"Who the hell are you?"

"I suppose I cud say the same till you! I assume you are Paul's dad, Mr O'Leary. Am I right?" She pulled the covers up to her neck and in doing so she covered her breasts, but exposed Pip's head in the process. "Paul didn't tell me you lived with him."

"Paul? Who the frig's Paul?"

"Your son, Paul, Mr O'Leary. He brought me back with him last night. He told me he shared a house with his brothers," said Maureen sheepishly.

Her mascara had run and she looked a ghostly apparition. Pip awoke to the frightening sight of his da's face. It was puce with rage. He knew he was going to be called something worse than a shitehawk. He hit the top of his head on the headboard and cried out in pain. "Oh shit! Eh, da, this is, er ... Maureen." He rubbed the top of his bonce, and with a sickly grin tried his best to explain.

"It wuz too late fer her to go home ..."

"What the ..." Shaun was stuck for words.

By now Kevin and Declan were sitting up in bed, grinning like two scarecrows. With hair on end and eyes the colour of rubies from the previous night's drinking, they both chided, "Come on mucker, try an' talk yerself out af this mess. Let's hear ye tell daddy all about it."

"Ah fuck up!"

"Daddy, did you hear that?" said Declan in a childish voice. "He cursed. You'll have to beat his bum with the back of mammy's hair brush fer being a naughty boy!"

"You two, eff up! This house is nat a bordello. If that runt Pip wants to sow his wild oats it will have be somewhere other than under my nose."

"Who's Pip?" asked Maureen.

"Belt up, fer Christ's sake, will ye?" snarled Pip. "Let me do the talkin' here."

Shaun felt as if he were in a bad dream. Voices were coming from all directions and not one of them was making any sense.

"Hey! Hey, Pip, me auld mucker. You've overstepped yer mark this time. Should have sneaked her out before me da an' ma got up this mornin', like ye usually do." Kevin felt ecstatic at his younger brother being caught out. He was grinning like a Cheshire cat from ear to ear.

"Get a life, will ye? Maybe I'm nat just as crafty as some people I cud mention. Last Saturday night ye had two bits af crumpet in here, an' auld baldy there didn't know a thing about it. Fuck aye, luk after yerself. Ye can hump all night an' I'm kept awake, but let auld Pip here get his oats an' ye have to make a meal aff it."

"Paul, who's Pip?" Maureen tried to get heard once more but was cut to the quick by Shaun.

"Who the hell's gates are *you*, never mind Pip or Paul or whoever that shit thinks he is! This is *my* house, Mr Shaun Dunlop's house to be precise. I don't know what crap that eejit has fed ye, but he hasn't two pennies to rub together, never min' own a house!"

"Steady yer head, da, an' keep the noise down. My fuckin' head's splittin'" Pip pleaded, fearing he had overstepped his mark.

"Luk you! An' listen to what I have to say. Get that harlot out aff this house before yer ma gets back fram chapel."

"I'm nat a harlot, whatever that is!" retorted Maureen.

Maureen jumped out of the bed, her nakedness startling Shaun. Not since before his wife had given birth to five kids had he seen such a perfect body. For a second he almost forgot about his son's indiscretions. It didn't help when she started jumping up and down with frustration and her boobs shook like two perfectly moulded jellies. All the males in the room fell quiet at the sight, until the bedroom door opened and Siobhan and her sister burst in. Now the whole family was witness to the escapade.

"What are ye all gazin' at like eegits. Have ye never seen a naked woman before?"

Maureen had jumped on Pip's bed and she had him by the throat. His eyes almost flew out of their sockets as he gasped for air.

"Ye told me ye were in double glazin'. Ye told me you had yer own home. Ye told me ..."

"He told ye a bunch of lies. Surely to God ye didn't fall for the oldest trick in the book, did ye? He's a waster af the first degree," Shaun informed her.

"He tuk my virginity!"

"I tuk *what!?*" Pip couldn't believe what had come out of her lips." I think the Parachute Regiment took that back to the barracks when the IRA called the ceasefire an' didn't give ye it back when they ended it."

"How bloody dare ye accuse me aff bein' easy t' get," shrieked Maureen. "You raped me last night!"

"Catch yerself on. Raped, ye opened yer legs that quick I thought ye had dislocated yer hips in the process."

Pip managed to pry her hands from around his throat and wrapping a sheet round his naked body he swung his legs out of the bed. He held his head in his hands and cursed himself for not getting rid of her earlier.

By now everyone was at each others throats. Pip's two sisters were protesting about being woken up. His brothers were yelling at Pip to get out of the way so they could get a better view of Maureen's body. And Shaun was busy with his shitehawk speech.

Maureen lit off the bed like a scalded cat and raced to the bathroom.

"Where the hell does she think she's goin' in the nude?" Shaun hollered.

"Me thinks she is slightly sick, da, fer I can hear her bokin' down the echo chamber!" answered Kevin in a devilish tone.

Shaun gazed out the bedroom window. Holy God, Jacinta was on her way up the street. Mass must have ended early.

"Get her bloody out, fer Christ's sake! Yer ma's comin'. She'll be all pious an' drippin' wi' holy water. Ye know what she's like, especially if auld Father O'Dowd's been sayin' the mass. Oh, Jaysus! She'll blame all this on me. For heaven's sake, get her out quick."

Shaun was beside himself with panic. He leapt into Pip's bed, in a bid for shelter, throwing him off the end as he did so, and buried his head under the duvet. His muffled voice pleaded, "Get her out! Get her out!"

It was too late.

"Who's that naked woman in the bathroom?" The bedroom door framed a very agitated Jacinta who stood pointing towards the sound of vomiting.

"Well, it's nat me or Mary," Siobhan informed her mother.

"I can see that! An' as far as I can make out it's nat th' dog!" shrieked Jacinta who had by now spied Shaun's feet sticking out from the duvet.

"I know those feet! Only Shaun Dunlop would wear socks with more holes than sock. Get out from under there, me boyo, or I'll cut the feet clean aff ye. *Do you hear me? Get out!*" She trailed the duvet off Shaun, who lay curled up like a fly caught in a web.

"It's that bastard Pip, Jacinta. He's the culprit." Shaun's eyes were sitting out of his head like the hat pegs that were attached to Maureen's boobs. He hoped his wife didn't think he had a woman to play around with whenever she was at mass.

"He had her in his bed all night, the wee sh…"

"Fer Christ's sake, don't say it, da", whined Pip. I'm nat in the mood t' listen till ye …"

"I'll say it for him. *Shitehawk!* Now I've sinned my soul, ye wee, ye wee. Ah, sod off!" Jacinta hit Shaun round the ear. She was about to give Pip the same treatment when Maureen ran past, almost knocking her for six.

"Get out af my way woman! An' who th' hell are *you* anyway? I suppose yer the mother af that lat. The mother af that lyin' bastard Pip, who calls himself Paul when he wants to get away with molestin' young girls. An' I suppose yer the wife af that pervert who couldn't keep his eyes aff my body. If I were you I'd get that lat seen to by a shrink."

On went the lacy pants, on went the *Wonderbra* followed by the lycra dress that Pip had earlier ripped off in a frenzy of lust. She grabbed her coat and shoes and after calling Pip a bastard she fled out of the room.

Jacinta had come home from the tranquillity of chapel to a house of bedlam. She was almost speechless. "Jesus, Mary an' Joseph," she blessed herself, before adding, "What is this house comin' till? I leave for an hour an' all hell breaks loose."

Shaun turned on his brood and gave then another rollicking, in more hushed tones. "See what yes have done nye. Yer mother will go all menopausal an' I'll get the balls chewed aff me. She'll think I aided an' abetted in all this bloody carry on. *Mein Gott im Himmel!* If you lat don't tell her the right story of all this I'll be made into mincemeat by the lash of her tongue. As for you, arsehole, get yer bags packed an' clear aff before I ram my boot up yer ... Ah, never mind. Just, just do as I tell ye."

"Aye, da, I will try to remember *you* were a saint when ye were young," answered Pip sarcastically.

"Don't tempt me! Don't fuckin' tempt me," hissed Shaun, as he waved his fist at his errant son.

"Go on, da, hit it, hit it!" egged Pip, jutting out his chin.

SLAP! Pip's lights went out as Maureen turned the corner of Hetherington Green, her high heels going from under her as she slipped in the melting snow.

7

Councillor Thorndyke arrived after Sarah had bent his ear on the phone for half an hour jabbering on about the gate. He had tried to explain that Sunday was a day of rest and would she not wait until Monday morning. He could not get the housing office to open up on a Sunday, even if it was for Sarah Cruickshank's benefit.

He would have been better off keeping his trap shut, for Sarah had threatened to expose his sordid sex life if he didn't shift his backside over to Hetherington Green, pronto.

He had broken the world record in getting dressed and slapping his hairpiece on his bald pate, for it had only taken him one minute instead of his usual thirty. He prayed to God to calm the wind outside to a gentle breeze for fear of losing it. Holding his opened umbrella upright in one hand while gripping his hat with the other to anchor it on his head left him feeling unbalanced, and he found it hard to keep his feet from going from beneath him as he slipped and skidded his way in the icy snow to the old crone's abode. He would have taken his car had he not have left it at the hotel the night before, after downing half a bottle of his favourite tipple.

After ordering him to leave his umbrella outside the door and to wipe his feet before entering, Sarah continued her barrage of insults as she ushered him into her flat.

"She'll still be thur when ye get back, Percy." The old witch knew. He wondered if she had a crystal ball, a black cat and a broom. The sarcasm made him shudder. He knew his only day of rest, was not going to be a happy one.

"You will have to excuse the state of this auld flat, if the council did something about it instead of sitting on their big fat behinds drinkin' tea an' coffee, it might look better."

He took his life in his hands by answering back. "It's a pity you couldn't get someone to give it a lick of paint, Mrs Cruickshank, it might brighten you up a wee bit"

"It's a pity ye couldn't move the damn thing to a better district Mr Thorndyke!"

Bereft of words, he shrunk another four inches into the settee. Sarah guldered at him for skulking like a schoolchild and he found himself sitting bolt upright, staring rigidly, straight ahead.

Elsie tentatively opened the living room door in her mother's flat, closed it quietly behind her and gasped at the sight.

It was as near to a scene from a murder re-enactment as one could get. The face of the man on the settee had the pallor of a wax dummy. For a brief moment she thought her mother had poisoned and stuffed Councillor Thorndyke and she stopped dead in her tracks. He was sitting bolt upright, hat firmly ensconced on his head and staring into space with eyes that appeared glazed by the extinction of life. Elsie breathed a sigh of relief when he turned his head stiffly in her direction and gave her a sickly smile before cowering like a chastised child. She and Bert had just come down from Rab's house when her mother had summoned her over by telephone.

Bert shuffled in behind Elsie and peered over her shoulder at the Councillor, who by now was nervously biting his nails. Then Sarah lifted her newspaper, rolled it up, bent forward and slapped Councillor Thorndyke on the wrist. "That's one dirty habit ye have there. How ye ever made a councillor is a mystery, for ye wud turn the guts of people, atin' at yer nails as if they were a rack of ribs!"

Elsie and Bert were affronted at Sarah's abrupt reprimand. Elsie blushed while Bert inhaled on his cigarette. They stood rooted to the spot with embarrassment.

"Will ye come on in an' stop gawpin' like two big overgrown glipes," continued Sarah, making Councillor Thorndyke jump. He coughed politely into his fist and, holding onto his wig with his left hand, while removing his hat with the other, he stood up to greet Bert and Elsie.

"Will ye sit down man! An' stop yer jumpin' up as if yer rear end was on fire, for yer makin' me head light." Councillor Thorndyke sat down quicker than he had stood up. Her settee groaned under him and Sarah tut-tutted. "Will ye min' how ye sit on that settee I can't afford another one."

Elsie scurried over to the settee and tried to comfort the poor man by smiling affably and offering him a cup of tea by way of consolation.

"I'll have a wee cup in my hand if you don't mind," answered the Councillor meekly. The man was afraid to say no for fear of Sarah accusing him of being too high and mighty to drink from her cups.

"You'll have it in a saucer, like everyone else," Sarah yapped back at him in a sarcastic tone. Elsie glared at her mother.

"The man knows what ye mean. He's not senile."

Sarah huffed, and sitting back in her chair muttered under her breath, "You could have fooled me. He looks well ravaged, a bit green around the gills and too much of him turned up for feet."

Percy played with the rim of his sports hat, stroked the small feathers stuck in the band and stared nervously at the floor, his eyes trying to take in the pattern on the carpet as way of distraction.

Sarah sneezed and twisted in her chair to retrieve a tissue from the box on the table behind her.

Councillor Thorndyke jumped up from his seat, strode across the room grabbed Bert by his hand, and pumped it up and down. He invited him to sit down beside him, thinking that another male would protect him from the wrath of Sarah's tongue. He should have known better.

"And just where do you think you're goin' till, Percy me lad? Sit back down on that seat an' stop twitterin' about, yer makin' my head light."

Percy obeyed, placed his hat on the arm of the settee and perched himself on the edge of the cushion.

Elsie busied herself in Sarah's small kitchen. She sorted through the cupboard for four cheery cups and saucers. The crockery that sat on the bench beside the sink had seen better days. The cups didn't match the saucers and Elsie was fussy when it came to offering tea and sympathy.

Sarah levered herself out of her chair and tottered over to Bert.

"Did you get my newspapers this mornin', cleghorn?" Her bony finger dug into his shoulder. He rubbed it and winched with the pain.

"Aye, they are over in the house," said he, massaging his aching joint.

"An' what bloody use will that do me? Do ye think I'm clairvoyant or somethin'? Ye daft eejit."

"Don't be so vitriolic, ma." Elsie shouted from the kitchen. Being bitter-tongued does not suit the elderly, it only gets peoples dander's up. Instead of feeling sorry for you it will only serve one thing. They will talk about you all the more, and I don't mean in a nice way."

"Ah, get away wi' ye. Put that tea out an' come in here till we talk over this blasted gate. If it blattered against the wall of Percy's bedroom he would soon get it seen till. Then again he might be too busy to hear it!" She glared in Councillor Thorndyke's direction and added, "If ye know what I mean Percy?"

Percy blushed to the roots of his wig and the sweat glistened on his brow. "I'm sure I don't know what you mean Mrs Cruickshank!"

Sarah laughed menacingly, then squinted and drew her mouth up like a purse on a draw string. "Ah shut up and have a titter of wit. Sure there isn't a female safe within spitting distance of ye. Not a bit a' wonder ye haven't a hair on yer head. What is it they say about men who like the weemen? The hornier the man the less hair he'll have on his pate!"

"I have hair, Mrs Cruickshank. This wee hairpiece is only to make it look thicker. I suffer from an under-active thyroid and it thins out now and then."

"Ye suffer from baldness, maun dear. Sure yer hair started to wave goodbye about twenty-five years ago. Do ye glue that on?

Now don't try to tell me you weave it in with the rest of yer hair, for there's more hair on that bit of bacon rind I have in the fridge."

"Hhhhmmm," Councillor Thorndyke cleared his throat and straightened his hairpiece, for it had started to slip with the sweat that was forming on his head. "I notice, Mr Friars, you're a bit follically challenged yourself," he gave a little titter and patted Bert on the head as if suggesting Bert was engaging in extra-marital activity himself.

"Fiddlesticks!" screeched Sarah. "The weemen that go with you must be hard up, but by God you'd have to be desperate to go with *that!*" she observed with a nod towards Bert, who just sucked on his cigarette and rubbed his jaw, for his teeth were still giving him pain.

"Are you still at the bowls, Mr Friars?"

"Aye, but sure it's nat the same indoors. I'd rather play outdoors in the summer. Do ye nat fancy a wee game yerself, Percy?"

"He's too busy bowlin' maidens over than bowlin' balls on the green," remarked Sarah, taking the cup of tea Elsie had brought in.

"Give them two crathurs a slice of that fruit-cake, Elsie. Not the one in the tin, the one in the fridge. I put it in there to keep it fresh, for it was goin' a bit stale."

"You can't give a stale ca..."

"Never bother yourself, Mrs Friars," Councillor Thorndyke interrupted with a wave of the hand, "I'll be havin' my dinner soon anyway."

"Settle yerself, for God's sake, it will put hairs on the soles of yer feet. Anyway, we have this little matter of the gate to discuss yet."

He gingerly lifted a piece of cake from the plate Elsie offered him and put it on his saucer, giving it the once over for bluemould.

"*Eat it!*" snapped Sarah.

He slowly lifted it to his mouth and nibbled round the edges seductively.

"I said *eat* it, not make *love* till it!"

For a moment his mind thought back to the previous night when he and Annie had romped between the sheets. She had perfect breasts for a woman of her age. They were still as pert as a twenty-year-old's and not pendulous as one would have thought for a middle aged woman of ample proportions.

His thoughts of Annie's mammeries made him blush. It had not gone unnoticed and he was soon brought back to earth with a bang. Sarah was watching his every move with a disgusted look on her withered face.

"Don't be so bloody finnicky and pernickity. You weren't so fussy when yer ma an' da left ye in shitty nappies as a baby. When they sneaked off to the pub to get blootered on a Friday night. Your ma even fed ye from an old beer bottle with a tit on it."

Now it was Elsie's turn to blush. "You mean teat ma, not tit. Tit as in bird while teat as in bottle."

"Teat, tit, same flamin' thing. I'm sure there's no difference to our Percy. An' I'll be jiggered if his ma knew the difference."

"Did you know my mother and father?" He asked this question as if it had been an honour to have known his parents. The man would have been better bitting off his tongue.

"Aye, indeed I did. We used to have a quare laugh at yer auld man. Auld Thornydick we used to call him. A bit like yerself he was. A wee man for th' weemen. The only difference was he had one at home, unlike yours truly. It's funny ye never married, Percy. I suppose ye were put off marriage when yer ma left yer da for the insurance man."

Sarah tittered at the thoughts of Percy's da. Her and her mates used to follow him at night when he left his house. His wife was oblivious to his wee bits on the side, as he was ignorant of her dalliances with those content to be paid behind the door. Percy's da didn't reckon on Sarah and her chums having a wee jook when he had a bit of nookie up the alley behind her house.

'God, thon man should have been born a rabbit', she thought to herself.

"You're a terrible woman, Mrs Cruickshank. One for the craic, you might say."

"Aye, an' your da was one for the other kind.

"That's enough mother. Your too old to be talkin' filth," chastised Elsie.

"Ah, get away wi' ye. I'm only havin' a banter wi' the wee crathur."

Percy squirmed and shrank another four inches. He tried to change the subject. "Are you going anywhere for your holidays this year, Bert?"

"Aye, the wife wants to go to Tenerife for some ungodly reason. Bloody foreigners. I suppose we'll spend the fortnight on the bogs wi' the runs. Ye can't drink the water there ye know, it's full a' germs," Bert informed Percy as if he was an expert on foreign travels.

"If we get a summer like last year, Mr Friars, you won't want to go away."

"Well nye, Percy, the wife thinks she's missin' somethin', nat gettin' abroad like."

"Never min' bloody holidays!" Sarah beat the arm of her chair with her fist to get attention. "Get that flamin' gate seen till or I'll be goin' away in the head, never min' on me holidays."

"Do you really need a gate?" asked Percy. Was this ever the wrong statement to pass a man's lips? Sarah's wee legs went a mile a minute trying to gain balance as she rose from her seat. Her face had taken on the look of the devil and she hirpled towards Percy. Her nose almost made contact with his as she hollered, "Do you really need thon head of yours? God …" said she, "I've a good min' till knock it clean off yer shoulders. Maun dear, did ye ever see th' dirt that gathers in thon hall at night? An' I don't mean dirt aff th' groun'. I mean human dirt, the kind that has arms an' legs an' pisses up the walls!" She hit the arm of the settee, just missing Percy's head as she brought it down, and Percy grabbed his wig for the force of her fist had brought on a down draught.

"Will ye get a titter of wit, ma. Your actin' like a demented ape, and at your age. I thought you had no energy? There's enough strength in that arm of yours to break concrete slabs!" Elsie tried to pry her mother away from Percy. His wig had gone askew and he looked a sorry sight.

"Well, he has no right askin' me if I really need a gate. It's not only for me ye know, it will benefit all the people in the flats. That auld prune face Nesbit up above put a rug in the hall last week an' some culprit nicked it. It was most likely that Rab one for he wud steal the eye out of yer head an' come back for the lashes."

"And what would Rab do with a bit of carpet that has seen better days?"

"What does he do with anythin' he plunders? He's that sneaked he cud walk up the road on razor blades."

"That's blind prejudice. You don't know half of the good turns he does for people."

"I do more for people wi' me eyes shut."

"Don't tell me you are thinkin' of other people now? And don't go wallowing in self pity, 'cos it doesn't suit ye."

"Don't get maggoty wi' me. You're still not too big for me till hit." She lifted her hand to slap Elsie, but pulled back. "In my day …"

"Yes, we all know mother, in your day. But it's not your day now so calm down."

"If I'd have spoke to my mother like that I wud have been the dirtiest word in her mouth." She removed a hanky from her apron pocket and tried in vain to force a tear from her eye.

Percy gazed heavenwards in supplication. His morning had started out quiet calmly. Annie had brought him breakfast in bed, and if Sarah hadn't phoned he would be cavorting under the sheets with his beloved. Now he felt as if he had landed in bedlam.

"You're gettin' too mixed up with that scumbeg an' his whore, our Elsie."

"Such profane language on a Sunday, Mrs Cruickshank!"

"Ah, shut yer pious gob or I'll slap it!" screeched Sarah. She threw him a sly look, then her mouth drew up into a wee smile. She loved to take the hand out of people now and then.

"This is desperate, Elsie. I'm away over home to read the papers an' take a couple of asprins for me teeth." Bert had found his tongue but as usual he tried to take the easy way out: vanish at the first hint of trouble.

"You'll stay where you are, Albert Friars. You've no consideration for anyone apart from yerself." Elsie pushed him back down onto the settee and sat down beside him, threatening him with a good slap on the back of the hand for disobeying her. He retorted by calling her a head bin.

"Our Elsie is not a head bin. On the other hand she must have been at one time – she married you! And all men are selfish and inconsiderate. They don't even have the decency to die at the right moment. Take my brother, Jack for instance. He went an' died in the middle of the night an' got us all out of our beds.

If that wasn't bad enough he had to die on the toilet! The police had to be called out, for they thought he had been murdered. Then the doctor had to pronounce the man dead while he sat cluckin' on the loo. The neighbours all stood glarin' like Brown's cows on the landin', an' to make matters worse he wasn't wearin' any clothes. There he was naked as the day he was born with toilet roll stuck till his arse an' the toilet not flushed."

Percy, Bert and Elsie were silent, speechless and bewildered. Where was this story leading to? "My husband, God rest him, had the decency to give notice before dyin', he had his nice maroon pyjamas on, an' he had soaked his dentures an' shaved. I felt proud when the doctor pronounced him dead, he looked like a man that was well looked-after and not an' old reprobate that sat in the pub all night before poppin' his clogs. Which reminds me, I must go to the toilet. I'm wettin' meself."

She pockled into the bedroom that led to the bathroom, then came back for a roll of toilet tissue that she had planted under the kitchen sink. "Mustn't forget this, for I would only have to get one of yousens to bring it in to me. Could someone unstick the glue, they're the divil till get started off, ye cud pick at it for ages"

The sound of piddling came forth from her mother's toilet. Elsie hightailed it over to the bedroom door that separated the toilet from the living room and slammed it shut. It didn't drown out the noise and she apologised to Percy for her mother's ignorance.

"I heard that!" Her mother was shouting. "No need to apologise for nature's call. I'm sure the son of Thornydick will not be offended by the tinkle of pee." The usual burst of flatulence followed and Elsie felt like climbing up the leg of her knickers with humiliation.

A steady *thump, thump, thump* could be heard over the noise and for a second Elsie thought her mother had collapsed and was knocking on the toilet wall for aid. "Oh my God, Bert, go in an' see if she's fallen!"

The words were no sooner out of her mouth when Sarah's voice once more echoed from the confines of the toilet. "Will ye stap batin' that ball off the wall, ye wee skitters, or I'll ram my boot up yer arse!"

Sarah hadn't fallen, much to Bert's relief. He didn't fancy the idea of trying to lift his mother-in-law up from the floor while her knickers dangled off the ends of her scrawny feet. A couple of kids had been playing ball games against the wall of the flats and Sarah was not amused. She emerged from the bedroom with a face on her that would have soured milk.

"Now do ye see what I'm gettin' at, Mr Thorndyke. Or Councillor to be precise. Could you put up wi' that racket?"

I'd rather put up with that racket than your narkin' Sarah Cruickshank, thought Percy.

The doorbell rang.

"Will ye get that, Elsie. Me hip is playin' me up."

Elsie went to see who it was. It was Rab Kirk. This was all Elsie needed.

Sarah peered towards the door through squinted eyes and muttered, "I suppose he'll be up to no good, probably on the tap for money."

"Rab doesn't borrow money, ma."

"No, I dae nat," Rab poked his head round the door and rounded on her, his wit as sharp as a knife. "I steal it!"

"An' I'm sure yer not jokin' either," Sarah shot back, just as sharply.

"I wuz over at yer house Bert, fer shelter fram that wuman aff mine. Seein' as no-wan answered I thought y'ed be here. Jaysus but she's hoppin' mad, 'er auld fan tiddle is givin' 'er jip. She's plannin' all sorts tae get 'er oan back. Can I come in fer a wean o minutes till she settles down?"

Rab's eyes were twinkling, he was in his element. Another trick on Peggy, another notch in the barrel of his hunting rifle.

"Aye come in, but don't let on to my ma what you done for she's no sense of humour," hissed Elsie in a whisper.

He ambled into the flat as only an auld country man can. No need to hurry, just take life at a slow pace, that was Rab's motto.

"Ach hello, Percy, me auld mucker. Are ye nat shaftin' this mornin'? Err, excuse me, Mrs Cruickshank, but I'm sure ye know wut shaftin' is?" His eyes twinkled even brighter as he thought about it. "Ieeee mean, diggin' th' garden like, ye know, the shaft aff a spade an' all that."

He guffawed and his shoulders went up and down like pistons.

"I know rightly what ye mean. Ye have a mind like a sewer," answered Sarah as she twisted her face in disgust at Rab.

"Ohh nye, it takes wan till know wan. The arse af the pat an' all that crap," jibbed Rab. Echoing one of his wife's sayings.

"Will ye tell him to leave my flat, Elsie! He wasn't invited."

Elsie decided to ignore her mother. "Do ye want a cup of tea an' a piece of cake, Rab?" asked Elsie, wiping the sweat off her brow with her mothers dish cloth.

"Aye, I suppose it will fill a hole in me tooth."

"Don't mention teeth," cried Bert. "I'm gettin' this lat removed as soon as the dentist opens the marra."

"Indeed you are not. You're bad enough lookin' without gettin' your teeth removed," Elsie said to Bert.

"By Jaysus, ye'll be able tae give someone a nasty suck when ye dae that, Bert," chided Rab.

"I'll have to go back on the bottle."

"As long as ye don't hae tae go back oan the tit! Oan the other haun, it's nat such a bad idea, eh Bert!" He glanced at Percy and added, "There's a maun there who wud gi' 'is eye teeth tae hae the honour."

Percy laughed uneasily. Sarah rounded on her daughter. "See, he said tit an' ye didn't chastise him."

Percy tried to cool the situation by adding, "I'm only here on business, Rab. Council work, ye know. We all have to do our bit in times of need, isn't that right Mrs Cruickshank?"

"Is that so Percy, me lado? We all hae tae do our bit, and I think you've done enough bits in yer time." Rab was bleeding the conversation to the hilt, and enjoying every last bit of the situation. "I take it it's the gate that brings ye out in the caule? Jaysus, that wuman will nat be content till she barricades the flats in like the pace line. On the other haun she cud be doin' the neighbours a service, it'll keep the tick men out."

"There's no tick men comin' to my place. I pay on the nail. I never got anything on the never-never in me life."

"You should write a book, ma, for you tell more stories than Hans Christian Anderson. You spent your time hidin' behind the door when the insurance man called. The only time you paid him was when you thought my da was goin' to kick the bucket. And that was only to make sure his policy was in order."

"I told you off yesterday for talkin' ill of your father. Don't you do it again or I'll wash yer mouth out with soap."

"Look, do you want me to call back tomorrow?" asked Percy. "You seem to be at sixes and sevens today. A wee bit annoyed about things, if you don't mind me saying so."

"You're goin' nowhere until ye promise to do somethin' wi' that ruddy gate. Have ye no say at all in the housing office?" asked Sarah with a supercilious smile imprinted on her wrinkled face.

"Well, I do have some clout. I didn't get made a Councillor for the good of my health, you know."

"Well, why don't ye put it to use an' do something for the good of the neighbourhood."

"And what exactly do you think this gate will achieve? You know, Mrs Cruickshank, it can be opened. There will be no lock on it." He had joined the fingers of his two hands together as if in prayer and had tilted his head to the side in thought. His wig slipped a little further and Rab could not let this opportunity go unnoticed.

"Hey Else! Dae ye think we're goin' tae see another auld mangy puss take a walk the day?" He nodded his head in Percy's direction and winked with his good eye.

Elsie blushed to the roots of her hair, she felt so flustered. She shoved another piece of cake in Rab's direction and hissed, "Will you be quiet, Rab, my nerves are shattered as it is without you makin' silly remarks."

"Well, some people shud make sure their pussies don't wander. He shud hae stuck it oan wi' a bit af superglue," answered Rab out of the side of his mouth and winked at Elsie who was that flustered the sweat was dripping off the end of her nose.

Bert's teeth were that sore he couldn't care what they were talking about. Percy was so engrossed in thinking he was going to say to the housing office and Sarah about the gate keeping people out that they had let Rab's remarks go unanswered.

"If we put a padlock on it only those with keys will be able to get in," suggested Sarah.

"Well, that poses the question of how the postman and binmen will get in, Mrs Cruickshank, not to mention doctors and such."

"Bert could keep a lookout for them," voiced Elsie.

Bert shot her a shocked look but it went unheeded.

"Well, I suppose it's worth a try." Percy glanced at his watch and suggested a meeting of the residents of the flats would be a good idea. He wanted out and this was as good an excuse as any to make an escape.

Elsie realised it was nearly half-past-one, Her daughter would be up any minute with the children. She agreed with Percy and he relaxed.

Reprieve at last. He stood up, straightened his hairpiece and slapped his hat on his head.

"Now, wait a minute thur. When will ye be back for this so-called meetin'?" asked Sarah.

"Let's say Tuesday at three o'clock, Mrs Cruickshank."

"We won't *say* it, we will *mean* and *do* it," Sarah rammed her words home with a wave of her fist.

"It *can* be done, it *shud* be done, it *shall* be done ... on Tuesday!" said Rab through fits of laughter, the tears flying out of his eyes.

"I bid you adieu, Mrs Cruickshank." Percy straightened his hat and made a bee-line towards the door.

"See the man to the door, Elsie."

The door was already open. Percy was wasting no time getting out of the madhouse. He fled as if the Hound of the Baskervilles was on his tail, forgetting his umbrella in the rush. And his wee feet hardly touched the ground as he ran towards the safety of his home.

"Can he not say cheerio like anybody else?" asked Sarah.

Rab dunted Bert in the ribs. "Here Bert, I bet he's away back for a wee poke at Annie Webster. A wee bit af corkin' gets ye goin' just as much as a bit af mischief, eh Bert."

"I don't know how you wud know. Th' only corkin' you do is when ye make home-made wine." Bert reminded Rab of his inability to perform his marital duties.

"Ach sure, Bert, thur's more till life than ballin' an' bowlin', if ye know wut I mean, only that siren af a wife af mine wud disagree." He took a few puffs of his inhaler.

"I suppose yer right, Rab." He watched as Rab put his inhaler in his trouser pocket. "There's more to life than ballin' an' bowlin' alright, like havin' yer health for a start."

"I'll wash these few dishes before I go home, ma. Do you want to come over later on for a bite to eat? It will save you cookin' somethin'." Through it all she still thought of her mother's welfare. Now she felt guilty again as usual after visiting her mother.

"No! I wont go over. But take them two over with ye. For Christ's sake, don't leave them wi' me. Little and Large wouldn't be in it. You wouldn't know which one was the stooge for they're both gormless lukin."

Elsie said a silent prayer. Lord, please! Please give me the strength to resist the urge to commit murder, and remove the thoughts of suicide from my mind! She gave Bert and Rab a nod and told them to get their skates on. "Come on you two! Men are worse than children, but then again, not quiet as bad as some I could mention!" She looked in her mother's direction and shook her head. "Not quite as bad as some!"

8

"Did ye ever hear anything like that in all your life?" asked Elsie.

"Like what?" Bert had been reading his newspaper and felt annoyed at being interrupted. "One minute yer busy doin' somethin', then out af the blue ye ask a silly bloody question. Just like the other day when ye asked me if space men really existed."

"*Her!* over there. Talkin' about her uncle snuffin' it on the toilet."

Elsie was busy preparing the dining-room table for the onslaught of adults and children who were about to arrive starving with hunger and ready to eat anything that sat still for more than five minutes. She plonked the salt and pepper pots in the centre with such ferocity they almost shattered and Bert told her to get a grip of herself.

"Why don't ye get a hold of *yourself?*" she answered. Ye sat there like mum's chance and let me cringe with embarrassment in front of that man, Percy. 'Dying without thought for anyone'. I never heard the likes. I'm sure her uncle didn't die on purpose. He didn't say, 'I think I'll just empty me bowels here an' then I think I'll just croak it so the neighbours can have a wake.' I'm sure he had other arrangements made for the weekend."

"I'm sure he had," answered Bert. "Like downin' a battle af rum an' a couple af dozen cans of beer fer a start. Unlike yer ma, I heard he wuz fond af the auld fire water. He cud have pissed fer Ulster after a night out of a Saturday. If yer ma hud any sense she'd keep her gub shut about drunkards. Thur are plenty af them in 'er own family."

"Hae till agree wi' ye there Bert," chimed Rab.

Elsie went back to her small kitchen and opened the oven door. The heat made her back off and she lifted a drying cloth and waved it too and fro, then proceeded to baste the roast that was just about beginning to crisp.

"Another ten minutes will see that done nicely," said she, closing the door quickly before seeing to the vegetables. "I remember the minister callin' to give his condolences the night before her uncle was buried as if it were yesterday. In fact, I will never forget it. There she was, sitting all prim, as if butter wouldn't melt in her mouth, gabbin' on about how nice-natured the man had been and all the time lying through her eye teeth. She hadn't a good word to say about the man when he was alive. The minister looked like a gentleman an' spoke with a polite but not put-on voice, while her gob almost turned inside out with the effort of trying to put on the politeness. The man saw through it but was too polite to make any remarks. We all sat starin' at each other being stuck for words for we hardly knew her uncle Jack. Then the minister was stuck for words. He made comments about how he had enjoyed his time in Donegal when he had been a cleric there a few years earlier just to fill time. Of course, what does Sarah ask the man. 'Did ye ever meet Daniel O' Donnell?' We ended off talkin' about Kincashlagh an' the merits of Daniel an' how nice he was to his mother. Then she goes an' informs the man of how she would be honoured to meet Daniel. He tried to tell her he didn't know him but would she listen? No, she damn well wouldn't. She nattered until the poor man had to make a hasty retreat. Not a flamin' word about uncle Jack passing on to pastures new. No, she was more interested in what Daniel did for his mother and if she appreciated it. If Daniel had a mother like her he would have done her in by now, and would be singin' about Donegal in jail for his supper. I was affronted an' that's no lie."

"Aye, she'd be a quare craic at a wake all the while, wud our Sarah. It's a pity she cudn't be at 'er oan funeral," joked Rab. "Then agin she will be at it!" He thought for a moment before continuing. "I'll tell ye what. I'll stick me haun up her ass an' work 'er mouth fram the inside fer a laugh. That's if I'm nat gone afore her, of coorse." He mimicked a ventriloquist and his dummy as if he were playing to the gallery. Then he scratched his head and stood deep in thought. You could almost see the thoughts tumbling round in his good eye like clothes in a tumble dryer.

"What's goin' round in that head of yours now, Rab Kirk?" Elsie asked.

"Did ye know men die fram the head down an' weemen die from the feet up?"

"Well, I never! Who th' hell did ye hear that bit of useless information from?" enquired Elsie.

"Well, it makes sense! The last bit aff a wuman tae die wud be her tongue, whereas a maun wud try his best tae block out the sight af his wife polishing the insurance policies as soon as passible."

"Rab Kirk, you haven't an ounce of respect for the livin' or the dyin', do you know that? You an' my ma are tarred with the one brush." Elsie was busy wiping the sweat off her face with her grandchild's nappy, that she kept for such emergencies, as she hopped from kitchen to dining room. She knew James liked his dinner on the table when he arrived.

Rab guffawed and tittered, "Ach nye, Elsie, who else wud gi' ye a laugh? Auld Albert thur wud gi' ye the willies, he's that mournful. Fer Christ's sake, man dear, gi' us a laugh instead aff runnin' aroun' rubbin' yer bake."

"Me jaws are sendin' me inta rickets wi' agony. Will ye give us a couple of tablets to ease th' pain of me teeth, Elsie?"

"Ye must be in some pain, min' ye, for yer bake's screwed up like a billy goat's balls," Rab laughed at his own choice of words to describe Bert.

Elsie plundered the medicine cabinet above the counter in the kitchen. The only tablets she could lay her hands on were two *Paracodal* that had laid dormant for months under a crepe bandage. She tore the silver wrapping off and exposed the contents to a terrified Bert.

"I'm nat swallowin' those! They're the size af saucers," Bert exclaimed with a worried look.

"Well, bend down an' we'll dae it the French way an shove them up yer arse," joked Rab.

Even Elsie laughed, for Bert thought Rab had meant it and he backed up against the kitchen wall as if protecting his rearend from impending doom.

"Catch yerself on. You dissolve them an' drink it. God, but your one eejit Bert Friars. I should do as Rab says an' ram them up yer bum for badness." Elsie dropped the tablets in a drop of water and shoved the glass in Bert's hands. The pain had him trembling and he almost lost grip of the glass. "Drop that an' I will make ye get the hoover out for I don't want any of thon children pickin' up bits of glass with their feet. An' wait until they dissolve properly, or you'll be moanin' about them stickin' in your throat."

"Ah, give over grippin'. Yer tongue's that long ye cud lift the broken bits up wi' the end of it. Yer gettin' just like yer ma. Yap! yap! yap! That's all ye ever do. If yer nat careful yer tongue will stick to the roof af yer mouth wi' cramp."

The phone rang in the hall.

"I'm not answerin' that!" Elsie stood defiant. "I bet you all the tea in China that's my ma."

"Well, I'm nat!" said Bert just as defiantly. "When she gets me on that phone she won't let me aff, and how do ye know it's yer ma anyway? It could be yer sister."

"Oh, it's her alright. I know the ring."

"Sufferin' Moses! She knows the ring. Did ye ever hear anything like it in yer life, Rab?"

"Well, it does hae a certain resonance till it, like the bell that wud summon ye tae Satan's parlour."

The three of them stared at the phone as if it was an alien that had just landed from outer space. It rang and rang and rang, then stopped. The silence was more deafening than the phone ringing. They all began to whisper as if the phone could hear and then all three jumped when it rang again. They made a bee-line for safety in the kitchen and shut the door on the offending noise, as if that would make it go away. But it did not go away. Whoever was on the other end was not going to give up until someone answered, should they have to hold on for a week of Sundays.

"I'll answer the bloody thing," said Rab girding his loins. You would have thought he was John Wayne going out to face Big Chief Sitting Bull at the Battle of the Big Horn.

Elsie pinned him to the wall.

"Indeed you won't, for you'll make some wisecrack, an' you know rightly she has no sense of humour." She remembered the phone call the previous night, when she had pretended to be from the morgue. Her mother had eaten the gob off her for doing that.

Rab's breathing became laboured as he gasped for breath and Bert had to pry her hands from his throat.

"For heaven's, sake Elsie. The man can't breathe. Let go of his gizzard!"

Elsie released her grip and apologised. "God, I'm sorry Rab, but you know what effect that woman has on me."

"Will ye answer the bloody thing!" The argument over who should answer the phone started all over again.

Rab lifted the receiver. "The Friar's residence. Butler speakin'. The master aff the house is haundlin' the maid, an' the maid is made up tae' say the least."

"Is that you, Rab Kirk?" It was Helen, Elsie's younger sister, the one who had fled to Ballymena to escape her cranky mother.

She had recognised Rab's country brogue and wit. "What were you all doin', havin' an orgy? It took you a hell of a while to answer."

"Ach Helen, me auld sex machine. Are ye still gettin' enough af th' rumpy pumpy? We wud hae been if you hud been here, I know yer a wan fer a bit af th' other, ye auld tart," joked Rab.

"Have a titter of wit, Rab. One good shag an' you'd be carted off to the Royal Victoria for a heart by-pass."

"Give me that phone!" demanded Elsie, relieved on hearing it was her sister and not her mother. She started on Helen almost before she had freed Rab of the handset. "Helen, somethin' will have to be done with that mother of ours. For I can take no more!"

"Slow down, Elsie. I'm not goin' to run away." Only Elsie was too wound up to slow down.

"She had poor Percy held captive this mornin'."

"Percy who?"

"Wee Percy Thorndyke. Ye know who I'm talkin' about now? The wee councillor for our area, for heaven's sake!"

"Aye, I know who he is. Didn't he get the swimmers opened up on a Sunday?"

"The same man, Helen. Well, when I arrived over the poor crathur was almost hyperventilatin' with fear. She called his da 'Old Thornydick'. She made fun of his wig. She accused him of being a sex pervert. She told him off for being meely mouthed. She told him there was more of him turned up for feet. She started on Bert. She started on Rab. She ..."

"Hold on there, Elsie, calm down. Did you not tell her off?"

"Would you tell her off?"

"Well ..."

"Exactly, Helen! You would have sat there an' said nothin'. You and Isobel will have to do your bit, even if it's only to take her up for a few days to give me a break."

"Alec wouldn't have her, Elsie!" proclaimed Helen. "If she deigned to grace this door he would tell her where to go. He's done it before." Helen went on about how her husband Alec had run her up the street by the scruff of the neck and threw her on a bus home after she tried to tell him how good a husband Helen's father had been; that he himself was nothing other than a time waster and a lazy bastard for taking a week off work with the cold. 'My husband never took a day off work', she had voiced in a most bitter manner. Alec had reminded her, 'Your husband couldn't bear to be at home on his own for a whole week in your presence, and anyway he was so mean he wouldn't have taken a week off work. In those days you never got paid for being off sick. He would have worked through an attack of the heebie-jeebies.' It would have been alright Elsie if she hadn't have called him a bastard. He hates that word, and he had reminded her of the fact he had a mother and father, an' a better mother than she ever was at that."

"She has called Bert worse names than that, Helen."

"But Bert can turn himself off Elsie."

"He's not a flamin' radio Helen! He doesn't have an off an' on switch on the back of his head."

"But he's easier goin' than my Alec."

"He may well be easy goin', but he's not impervious to insults."

"Give Isobel a call then. Get her an' Liam to take her for a while." Helen was sorry she had rung Elsie now. Her blood pressure had risen to stroke level at the very thought of her mother being planted on her, even if it was only for a few days. In fact, she was so taken aback she had forgotten what she had rung about.

"Isobel an' Liam! Sure those two are that busy gallivanting all over the world they don't have time to bless themselves, never mind putting their arses in a cramp to take mother for a few days. Isobel would take a buckle in her eye if you even reminded her she had a mother."

Elsie's front door opened and in paraded her daughter, son-in-law and two grandchildren. She told them to sit in the living room until she came off the phone. She mouthed the name Helen to her daughter and pointed at the receiver. Her daughter knew what she meant. Her mother appeared flushed. There must be a bit of a flap in the family; she guessed it was about her gran.

"They can't be anywhere this time of the year, February is not a good month to go anywhere apart from bed." Helen was trying desperately to pass the buck onto her sister Isobel, but Elsie held the trump card.

"You are invited to a meeting on Tuesday!"

"What meeting! Is it being held in the gospel hall by Pastor Ellis? If it is I will be down, for I love that man. He fairly gets the adrenalin goin'. Him and the Reverend Paisley are great at the auld no-Popery business."

"No it isn't! An' you'll better not let Isobel hear you talkin' like that, her being married to a Catholic."

"I know Elsie, isn't it awful. Our own sister turnin' into a traitor. I don't know about you but I haven't been able to live it down these past twenty-seven years, especially now I'm livin' in Ballymena. They're all Paisley mad in this *private* development."

"I think Helen, we should put the past twenty-seven years behind us now an' get on with living. When the Troubles started you were cursing the Reverend Ian in an' out of hell along with the mouth pieces on the other side of the fence. Your Alec was lucky to be in a job remember, and not out on the streets fightin' and throwin' petrol bombs."

"Are you trying to tell me Bert was out of work? He had a good job himself, ye know, why you didn't put it to good use and buy your own home was something Alec and I could not fathom."

Elsie's dander was up now alright. Who the hell did her sister think she was? Private, indeed! Was Ballyhornet a ghetto? She gazed out the side window of her door and eyed the surrounding area. It wasn't exactly a ghetto, more like a recycling estate for well-used townies. Her sister might live in a *private* development with her town-reared husband but as the saying goes, you can take the man out of the town but you can't take the townie out of the man. He had brought her down to his standard and turned her into a bigot. At least Elsie still remembered where she had been reared, in the country alongside both religions, and she respected both.

No, Helen, it's not in the gospel hall, it's in mother's! We're goin' to talk over this problem of where mother goes to stay for a few days to give me and Bert a rest." She lied deliberately. She felt scundered at Helen's hints of Ballymena being better than the estate of Ballyhornet. She could sweat it out until Tuesday for being so uppity and snobbish.

"Well, it will have to be Isobel's."

"Will it, Helen? Well, we will just see. But I daresay Liam will object to a Protestant breathing his Catholic Lurgan air for a few days!"

"Ah, but will Isobel? Remember, Elsie, she's still one of us!"

"Do you mean a Cruickshank or a Protestant, Helen?". asked Elsie sarcastically.

"Both!" screeched Helen, before replacing the receiver back on its hook.

"Grrrrrr... !" Elsie slapped the handset back on its base. "That Helen one needs a good slappin' round the lugs. How the hell Alec puts up with her is a mystery to all. She's too like my ma, that's her fault. Just like her she thinks she's better than anyone else. Private development in Ballymena me backside. They have housin' estates there too, ye know. Her in the arsehole of Ballymena and Isobel in the arsehole of Lurgan an' me stuck in the middle like a fairy. I might as well be a fairy for my legs are worn down to the size of fairies runnin' after that thing across the road. I was the forgotten one in the family by *her*. Now she depends on me for every whim an' fancy. Well, I'm not goin' to let it go on much longer. I must remember to ring Isobel after dinner."

"Hae you money in the bank or are ye goin' mad?" asked Rab who had been listening to her ramblings from the kitchen. "Hae you been listenin' till yerself? It's nat like you tae get in tae a state like that, girl. Calm down, afore ye take an attack of the brain. God ye don't want tae end aff in the loony bin nye, do ye? Ye might end aff sharin' a room wi' Peggy whenever I sign her in fer a wee haliday."

"Do you know, Rab? I sometimes think I'd be better off tucked away in the mental home."

"Dae ye hae a death wish, woman? Wan week wi' Peggy wud hae ye jumpin' out af a windie fer pace." Rab tried to cheer her up with talk of cats and the mange, but Elsie was too depressed for even Rab's gift of the gab.

She walked slowly, head bent in despair, into the dining room, pulled a chair out from the table and sat down heavily, letting the tears roll down her cheeks. In her mind she had thought the tears would wash away all the bad thoughts. The teardrops rolled down her nose and over her mouth. She could taste the salty fluid as it as it trickled in between her lips and wiped it off with her tongue.

Charlotte, her granddaughter, put her small arms round her neck and asked. "What's wrong nannie? Is your wee tummy sore?" She rubbed Elsie's tummy, rotund with middle-age spread and in her childish voice offered her own solution to the problem.

"Put a hot water bottle on your tummy nan. That's what *my* mummy does when I feel sick." This made Elsie's tears fall even faster, now they were dripping off her chin and onto her apron. She gave in to her pride and wailed.

"Why! Why! Why, does it always fall on me to sort out other people's troubles? God knows I can't even sort out my own. I want to go line-dancing in cowboy boots with a friend. I want to go to a slimming club to get back my shape, I want to ..."

"Ye want yer head examined," exclaimed Bert, turning his eyes back in his head at his wife's outburst.

"*I want to live a little, for heaven's sake!*" she screamed. She hadn't noticed Sandra, James, Bert, Rab and little James enter the room. They all stood staring at her. She felt stupid now and turned towards the window to hide her tears.

Bert, breaking the habit of a lifetime, came to life. He put his arm round her shoulder and asked, "Would ye like a wee cup of tea?"

"Why, do you want a cup? I'll make one now," she sobbed in between sniffs.

"Good heavens, Bert. Yer nat afferin' tae make us a cup are ye?" It was Rab's turn. "Heavens tae Betsy, the maun hus lost all pride in hisel'. Wut's come over ye Bert? Ye hav'ne been at Peggy's *Valium*, huv ye?"

"Well, it's just this once like. I'm nat goin' to make a habit of it."

Sandra burst in at this point. "My da's made tea before today Rab. Sure he's always doin' wee things for me ma." Sandra could see no wrong in her dad. Being easygoing like him she could not abide others poking fun at his expense.

"I know he is Sandra, I'm only jestin'. God even *I* make tay fer Peggy, an' that's more out af a guilt complex than out af politeness. Auld age softens th' edges aff hard youth. Ye cud say youth wuz wasted oan the young. I know; my boyhood days were nathin' but wastage. I wasted me strength oan wine an' bad weemen. I hud me health an' didn't appreciate it wan bit. Af coorse I threw mesel' about a lot an' the weemen appreciated it, even if I say so mesel'."

Elsie bucked herself up. She had the dinner to put out. She dismissed the offer of a cup of tea and headed towards the kitchen. "Will you stay for a bite, Rab? There's plenty here for us all."

Rab excepted without persuasion. His wife could take a rain check. If Rab had his way the rain could check in every day.

"Hunger's mother ye are," gasped Bert. "Do ye ever say no?"

"No! There I said it, so shut yer gub an' get yer finger out fer I'm starvin'."

After dinner, when the dishes were washed and the children were watered, Bert dozed in the armchair. His toothache had eased. Young Mark was busy gazing at the hairs up his nose and pulling at his ears while Charlotte drew a face on his bald head with a felt tip pen. Bert snored like a well-fed pig and Charlotte giggled as she drew, while young Mark sat mesmerized on his granda's bony knees. With each snore his nose hair popped out, but not long enough for the child to grab it.

James peered at Elsie. If he got her off guard, he would slap his son on the legs for being so naughty, only he knew his mother-in-law would slap Bert for letting him do it and the children would start crying at the sight of their granda being hit. They hadn't forgotten the Sunday Bert got slapped for doing nothing to stop their father when he had slapped Charlotte for being fractious. Elsie had warned him of the same fate if he ever sat back and left the children to the heat of their father's wrath, and they were very protective towards their granda ever since.

Steven had come down from his room with his dishes. He didn't eat with the rest of the family as his friend Ian usually called at dinner time on a Sunday. And Ian was not exactly "family material". He grunted something inaudible at Elsie. He was trying to say "How are you Mrs Friars" but it sounded like "Horarye, Missus Frirs'. He appeared to be in one hell of a mood today, and he clicked his knuckles as he squeezed them in his fist. Steven wasn't very friendly either, for some reason. He kept opening the front door and gazing furtively up and down the street. He was muttering under his breath, "I'll kill that bastard Dunlop. I'll fuckin' wring his screggy neck with me bare hands fer stealin' that tenner. I'll make a wallet out of his ball beg, the friggin' wee shit."

Bert came back to the land of the living. "What's up with our Steven, Elsie? I hope he's not botherin' ye for money or anything, for we haven't gat it."

"Oh, go back to sleep, will ye!" Elsie pleaded. She had been enjoying the peace. She told Steven off for cursing but it fell on deaf ears, and the last she saw of her son he was making a bee-line for next door with Ian in tow.

The cursed phone rang again. She was sure it was her mother this time.

"Sit there Elsie." Bert didn't speak out of concern. He had remembered the charade that had taken place earlier and he couldn't stand the prospect of a repeat. He ambled out to the hall.

"Hello," said Bert in a depressed tone as he lifted the handset.

He held it about six inches from his ear in case Sarah screeched down the line.

"Is Elsie there, Bert?"

Bert breathed a sigh of relief. "Thank goodness it's you, Isobel. We're bein' tortured today by yer mother."

"I know all about it. I've just been on the phone to Helen." He could hear her lighting up a cigarette and he knew Elsie was in for an ear-bending conversation.

"Elsie, it's yer other sister," shouted Bert, and holding his hand over the mouthpiece, told Elsie that she seemed none too happy.

"And she'll be even less happy by the time I've finished talkin' to her." Elsie relieved Bert of the phone. "Hello, Isobel! Bert tells me you've heard the newsflash from Helen."

"Do you mean the meetin' on Tuesday?"

"Indeed I do! If I were you I'd take a couple of tranquillisers before comin' up."

"Surely it wont be that bad?"

"No! It will be worse than bad. It will be deadly."

"Who else is comin'?"

"Well now, apart from Bert, Helen an' myself, there'll be all the other residents of the flats, a fire brigade officer, a policeman, the postman, and Percy of course, plus an assortment of curious onlookers, I dare say! We're tryin' to get one of the doctors from the health centre but that depends on who's sitting in surgery that afternoon. If auld Dr McNulty is free we may forget it, for he doesn't like old people. Someone told me he had been heard giving a talk on euthanasia the other week. So I'm sure an' certain an eighty-nine-year old's problems will not be high on his agenda. He'll probably come armed with a lethal injection!"

"God have mercy on your soul our Elsie, she's not as bad as that!" Liam's Catholic background must have rubbed off on Isobel for she had started coming out with very "Catholic" sayings recently." What's it all about anyway Elsie? Helen said it was about takin' her in for a couple of weeks."

"We have to take turns in looking after her. You get '*it*' every third weekend," lied Elsie once more.

"Jesus, Mary an' Joseph!" exclaimed Isobel. "Liam will have a fit!"

"Liam will have to *be* fit for she expects to be lifted an' laid, ye know. If sh' had her own way she would have you wiping her backside after she craps."

"What's the fire brigade an' the police got to do with it all? Surely we are not going to be arrested or burnt at th' stake for not havin' it?"

"Between you an' me an' the wall it's about the gate. Only don't go tellin' Helen, for she'll not turn up."

"Holy Mother of God, thank you! Do you mean we don't have to take her week about after all?" sighed Isobel with relief.

"Well ... not for a while anyway. But if she gets any worse we will have to do it."

"We could get her put in a home!"

"Isobel! Do you realise how much a nursing home costs? Nearly four hundred pounds a week!" answered Elsie, her breath catching in her throat at the idea. "An' the family has to pay some of it now with all these cut backs on the National Health."

"Bugger that idea." Isobel had lost all traces of religion at Elsie's statement. "The auld cat will just have to suffer in silence. After all, she's lucky to reach the age she is. All I hear lately is young people dying of cancer. An' your hearts in your mouth with all this auld Aids goin' about. Every time our young Patrick goes out his da makes sure he has condoms in his trouser pocket. Could you imagine our da doin' that with his sons? His mind was that dirty he examined yer knickers when ye came home at night. At least my Liam recognises his responsibilities. He knows what's what when it comes to the young of today."

"Now, Isobel. Liam knew what was what when we were young. He didn't go into the chemist like Bert an' come out with a toothbrush or a packet of razar blades."

Isobel laughed heartily. "Ach sure, Elsie, we all knew what was what. We just hadn't the wit to keep our legs crossed. That's why half of our generation was pregnant when we got married. The young of today think we were sex maniacs. We got up to no more than they do, only we hadn't the preventatives or the wit they have nowadays."

Listen Isobel, I must go now. Rab is up an' so is Sandra an' th' kids. I'll see you on Tuesday afternoon. An' remember, not a word to Helen."

"My lips are sealed Elsie. Bye for now."

"Hey Elsie, why dae men always wear ginger wigs? Bert here wants tae know."

"I do nat, why would I want to know a thing like that for?"

"Shush a minute Bert. I just want tae cheer Elsie up a bit," hissed Rab.

Elsie had just made a cup of tea to waken herself up when Rab stumped her with this brain-teaser.

"I'm sure I don't know Rab. Why, do you?"

"Well I've come tae the conclusion that's where all the auld ginger toms that disappear go tae! They end aff as hairpieces an' sold till eejits like Percy. That wig aff his reminds me aff an' auld puss I poisoned nat too long ago."

Rab sat splayed on the settee, hands clasped and rotating his thumbs. He sucked on his teeth as he pondered his next remark.

"That wuz a nice bit af meat Else, tender as a virgins tit if ye don't min' me sayin' so. It must hae been easy fer you till ate Bert wi' thon sore teeth af yer's, ye cud hae sucked it anyway seein' it wuz that tender."

Bert hollered out loud and held his cheek.

"God Curse ye Rab. Did ye have to mention teeth? Nye they have started hurtin' again."

Rab looked at his watch. "Only another seventeen hours an' the dentist will be open Bert!"

The phone jangled on the hook. This time it *was* Elsie's mother.

"Hello mother, now how did I know it was *you!*"

9

Monday, 26 February

If Sunday in Ballyhornet was "leave me alone and let me die, day", Monday could well have been labelled "I wish to God I had have died yesterday, day".

There is always a feeling of impending doom on Mondays. Maybe the shenanigans of the weekend come back to haunt the devious and mischievous, or else the beginning of a new week suggests a whole new meaning to the word "boring". Nothing seems to happen on a Monday. The postman only ever seems to deliver bills or reams of useless advertisements.

If the world were to come to an end, it would most likely be on a Monday. Long before the postman arrived. About three o'clock in the morning, to be precise. After the Sunday lyings-in to sleep off Saturday night's boozing, the Sunday afternoon nap to sleep off the effects of dinner and the Sunday night doze in front of the television, out of boredom, people's natural alarm clock's are knocked completely out of sync. And so we find ourselves lying awake in the middle of the night, with nothing other than our own thoughts for company.

Pip was no exception. Mind you, he hadn't surfaced at all on the Sunday, except for an untimely call around four o'clock in the afternoon, and that was only for ten minutes. He had tossed and turned in his bed, much to his brothers annoyance. At one point his bare backside was shoved so far up in the air Kevin was on the point of sticking his tin whistle up his rectum. Declan had thrown a beer can at him which had made contact with the back of his head. Mind you, it was just as well it had been empty or Pip would have seen stars for the second time in twenty-four hours. He had just about recovered from being clocked on the chin by his irate father for giving back cheek. God knows that had embarrassed him. His brothers had torn the arse out of it with snide remarks about getting thumped for being humped. Kevin had gone one better. He had got out of bed and poured the stale contents of a beer can over his head and rubbed his face in a mouldy Chinese take-away before telling him to fuckin' lie still or die.

Pip had had to get up, change his bedclothes and have a shower. Once up he had torn the house apart looking for money to pay back Steven Friars his ten pounds. Him and his burly mate had threatened him on Sunday afternoon with all sorts of torture if he didn't come up with the money by eleven o'clock Monday morning, castration being one of the more painful. If they were in a compassionate mood they would do it with a sharp instrument, although Monday was not their favourite day either, and the job would most likely be carried out with a blunt instrument, without anaesthetic and without mercy. He had taken apart the suite in the living room, plundered all the drawers and cupboards in the house and emptied out the pockets of his da's working clothes that hung in the kitchen. All he had managed to accumulate was seventy-six pence in five and ten-pence pieces and a one-pence coin that had tried to escape out of a hole in his da's trouser pocket. He had contemplated suicide as way of escape, but thought better of it when the voice of Father Cunningham rattled round his head. Hadn't he said something about burning in hell for committing suicide? He had gone on and on about it at mass on his last visit, that being about two years previously. He couldn't even bear his mouth being burnt with hot soup, never mind the fires of hell licking round his ass for eternity.

He caressed his scrotum and shuddered. "Well boys, you have been two good friends but like the ways of all man it looks like we'll soon be parted. But we did have some good times all the while, didn't we lads!"

The cold made him shiver. One of the dying embers in the grate came back to life. The orange flame lapped itself round the bit of cinder, then died as quickly as it had come to life as if winking at him and mocking his nakedness.

He pushed his long fringe of damp hair back with open fingers and smiled peevishly. Maybe he could do a runner before the light of dawn. He tip-toed over to the window, pulled back the curtain and peered into the darkness of the winter's night. He shuddered at the sight that met his eyes. The snow had melted to a brown slush and the bushes in the garden appeared to be dripping blood from their leafless stems. A cat was stalking the walls of the flats opposite.

Christ it looks like the dark side of the moon out there, or the waitin' room to hell he thought. No, I don't think I'll bother runnin' away this mornin. If the worst comes to the worst I'll give Steven me suede jacket for the tenner. Jaysus, that's a terrible dear price to pay for a mangy drink an' a shag. I love that auld coat. It doesn't make ye luk gypie like the leather coats that ye get in the market for a few fivers.

He snitched one of his ma's *Mogadon* from the medicine cabinet and hightailed it back to his pit.

∞ ∞ ∞ ∞ ∞

Elsie came back from the shops, entered the living room and screamed. She fled out the front door at three times the speed she had entered and thirty seconds later lay prostrate on her mother's settee.

"God ma! I've just had an awful shock. Will ye give me a drink of water an' one of your nerve tablets?" she was trembling from head to foot.

"*What's wrang wi' ye woman? Has Bert gone an' died on ye?*" Sarah had taken a laxative the previous night and was stuck to the loo. The conversation was conducted by shouting from toilet to living room.

"*Christ ma, that would have been better compared to th' shock that I've just witnessed over in my house!*" Elsie got up and shakily poured herself a glass of water from the kitchen tap, unscrewed the top of her mothers pill bottle and tipped a *Librium* into her hand.

"*It's terrible, ma, indescribable, to say th' least.*" She popped the capsule into her mouth and took a swig from the glass. "*It's just lyin' there, like something from ... from* Tales from the Crypt"

"*Wait a minute till I pull me knickers up. I don't understan' what yer talkin' about. Stay there till I come out.*"

"*Don't worry, I don't intend goin' anywhere after clappin' eyes on somethin' only ever seen in horror films.*"

She went back to the settee and plonked herself down. A hot flush crept up her neck. She lifted the *Daily Mirror* and fanned herself with a swift flick of the wrist.

Her mother teetered unsteadily. The laxative had left her feeling weak and she faltered at the bedroom door.

"In the name of heaven woman' dear, what is it? Yer always in some sort of a lather. Help us over till me chair for God's sake, before I fall down."

Elsie went to her mother's aid and led her to her seat.

"Have you ever seen a black hole?"

"I don't even know what a black hole is, never min' see one, why?"

"That's what's over in my house!" answered Elsie.

Has the floor fell in? You'd better ring the housin' office an' get it filled in quick."

"It would take more than the housin' office to fill in this hole. It's terrible, ma. It's lyin' there on the settee without shame, uncovered and bleedin'."

"You're talkin' in riddles, Elsie. Will ye talk sense, what the hell is it?"

"Bert's mouth!"

"Bert's mouth! I know it's bad, but it's not *that* bad as to make ye go inta a fit. Are ye sure it's his mouth?"

"Aye, Bert's gob. The gormless git has got all his teeth removed in one go. God ma, it would scare the daylights right out of you. I wouldn't mind, but he could at least cover his face with a towel or somethin' and what do you mean, am I sure it's his mouth, I know a mouth when I see one."

"Did ye not ask him to cover it up?"

"I didn't stay long enough to ask him anything. One look an' I was off. All I saw was this wee head lyin' on my nice fluffy cushion with a mouth on it like th' opening of the Grand Canyon. Only there's light shinin' in the Grand Canyon, an' ye don't have to sleep with it."

"Well they were givin' him jip ye know, he's been atin' them auld painkillers all week."

"He could have taken it gently. Have them removed in bits and pieces instead of *en masse*."

"Well ye know, sometimes it's better to have them all removed at once."

"But he could have had false one's made before gettin' them out. That way the dentist could have stuck them in right away without havin' to wait six weeks."

"It's better to let the gums harden an' shrink first. They only wobble roun' yer mouth if ye get them in to soon. That's what happened till me an' I can't wear mine at all"

"Better to wobble than to have none at all. Ma, go over an' have a look at him. He'd turn your guts." Elsie was almost in tears by now and there was a hysterical tone to her voice. "Lets face it, you've a thirty year start on Bert."

"I'm not haulin' meself over there in this weather. I'll take yer word for it. There's one consolation, Elsie."

"What's that?" squealed Elsie.

"He wont be able to drive ye crazy chompin' on that peanut brittle he's so found of. He'll have to stick to jelly babies in future!"

The phone rang and she jumped. For a second she thought it was her ma and realising she was with her mother she relaxed and sighed with relief. Sarah answered it, then passed it over to Elsie.

"It's Bert. He wants to speak till ye."

"Oh no! I can't. I can't speak to a man with no teeth!"

"Here, take it! Ye have till face up till it some time." Sarah slapped the phone in Elsie's hand and pockled into the kitchen to wet the tea.

"What do you want?" squealed Elsie down the phone.

"Elthie, haf ye any athpirin? me teef are killin' me."

"You mean your gums are killin' ye. Ye have no teeth."

"Ah, thut up an lithen will ye, haf ye no merthy in ye? Me mouf is achin', th' injecthins wore off an' me gums are th,th,throbbin'. God, that wuz hard to thay wif no teef, Elthie."

"Why did you do it, Bert? Could you not have given me notice before disfigerin' yourself like that?"

"Dithfigerin' me arthe. Will ye come over an' get me thome tableths?"

"They're in the kitchen cupboard. Get them yourself. And don't let

Steven see you with no teeth. A young lad like that is easily shocked. He takes the headstaggers every time he gets a toothache. He'll imagine himself with no teeth an' commit suicide."

"He's seen me already. What will I ate for me lunch? I'm thtarven."

"Do you mean to say our Steven has been subjected to that awful sight?"

"Aye."

"Jaysus! Now you'll have driven him from his own home. You can't expect a young lad to look at your bake all day. What if he wants to bring a girl home? You'll just have to get used to things you can suck or drink through a straw. I'm stayin' here with my Ma until you get fitted with false ones. And I dare say Steven will not be home either."

"That'll be weekth away Elthie."

"Too bloody bad, Bert! You should have thought of that before takin' your teeth in your own hands."

"There's a bit of a comothon goin' on outside Dunlopths next door. I think our Stefen hath somethin' to do wif it for I can hear his voith."

"Well you keep your face indoors. You don't want to scare the neighbours."

"Ah, go an' thite!"

"The same to you!" Elsie hung up and told her mother she would sleep on her settee for six weeks.

"Don't be daft woman. Go home to your own bed. Just tell him to turn his face till the wall."

"That's all very well, but what do I do during the day?"

"Make sure you're sitting behind him!"

"I'll make him wear a bag over his head. One of them terrorist balaclavas would do. I wonder where I could get one." Elsie pondered for a while, then came up with the bright idea of asking the *UVF* for the loan of one.

Her mother shot her a look of disgust at mentioning the UVF in her presence. "I remember when the Ulster Volunteer Force was a proper army, when they went to fight in the war like proper soldiers and not like rats from the sewers. In fact, my uncles fought with them and won medals for bravery, not like the scum of today who aren't fit to wipe the arses of the brave men who honoured its good name."

"I'm only jokin' ma. No-one would let on they were in it. I'll just cut two eye-holes out of my canvas shoppin' bag an' put that over his head."

Sarah poured out two cups of tea, put two cream doughnuts on a plate and shouted for Elsie's assistance.

"Will ye carry this in fer I can't manage it. I'm that shaky nowadays I'm liable to spill it. God but it's awful to grow old. I never thought I would end off like this. I worked right up until I was sixty, pressing trousers and opening seams all day, from half past eight until five o'clock. I wouldn't have seen you in my way. The bosses were sorry to see me go. And I wouldn't have left only your father fell ill and needed me at home. I wish I had have stayed with him when he wuz dyin'." She added wistfully, "but the nurses told me to go home. I should have known the time wuz near. They had put him in the side room to die. He died like a dog ye know, gaspin' for air an' grabbin' at life. The last word he uttered was 'Sarah'. He must have been trying to tell me something."

She lifted his photograph off the fireplace and ran her finger over his face. He wuz a fine lookin' man, your da. That's where you get your young looks from, ye know. He still had all his own hair. Mind you, his teeth were false, but he carried them off well, good shaped mouth and jawline. Not all frayed at the lips or haggard in the jowls like some people. Ach anee an' anee, as my mother used to say when she wuz troubled, sure the time flies an' not a one has time till ask ye if you're feelin' alright or are ye dyin'."

Elsie felt a lump rise in her throat. Her mother either made her feel like committing murder or else she had her feeling like a louse for not doing enough for her. No in-between. Feelings swaying from anger to pity. Not love. Love had no place in Elsie's heart for her mother. She felt guilty about this but was unable to force it into her heart. Every time the feeling of love tried to break through her mother would cut her to the bone and the barrier would only get higher and thicker.

She swallowed the lump and started to read the newspaper. The weak winter sun had come out again just as it had done on the Saturday morning. With a feeling of deja vu she grabbed the opportunity to help her see the print.

She only looked up once and said, "Well I'm sure I don't know what I'll be like if I reach your age, for I couldn't go out to work an' I'm only fifty-seven." She said this to try to make her mother feel better but her mother was too engrossed in her father's photograph to hear. In a strange yet relieved way she was glad.

ꝏ ꝏ ꝏ ꝏ ꝏ

"Your bake doesn't appear to be havin' a good day, Dunlop!"

Steven was leaning against the door frame of Pip's front door. Pip had offered him his suede jacket as security until he received his dole money on Thursday. He would then be in a position to redeem it with interest. Steven had refused on principal as he already owned a similar coat. Pip's mouth was gaping, being lost for excuses and his eyes were popping in his head. His chin had dropped to his chest, and he resembled a depressed camel that had just had its balls bricked. He was already depressed at being dragged out of his bed at the ungodly time of midday; his brothers were still in their pits, snoring like wart hogs, while his sisters were looking forward to *Neighbours* at half-past-one. They were still in their night clothes and feeling the draught from the open door.

"Will ye shut that friggin' door, big lad," his sister Siobhan yelled from the comfort of the living room.

"Ian an' his side kick Steven are havin' a bit of a con-fab with yer wee brother. Will ye belt up!" snapped Pip.

"Go an' play tig with a bus," screeched his sister through a mouthful of *Shredded Wheat*.

"Hell roast ye! Ye've just spat *Shredded Wheat* all over me dressin' gown," his other sister rebuked Siobhan. "You'll han' wash this, for it's silk an' won't go in the washin' machine." Silk dressing gowns and on the dole. Their parents were out at work slaving to keep them up in the custom they had got used too over the years, work being as alien to their brood as Dracula sunbathing in Ibiza.

"Bloody sisters, who'd have em?" retorted Pip.

"Will ye listen to me. I want my bloody money back!" snarled Steven.

"It's caule standin' out here, I'm ball freezed," shivered Pip.

"Your lucky ye still have yer balls to freeze."

Pip gulped as he felt his scrotum shrink with fear and his testicles ascend into the safety of his lower belly.

"Sure ye know fine rightly Steve, me auld mucker. You will get it back no sweat," Pip pleaded, almost sweating blood at the imagined pain that would accompany this awful act of savagery. He protected his groin with crossed hands, kept his ass well back and bent his legs at the knees for added protection. Make the target harder to get at and he just might have a fighting chance if Steven made a sudden surge forward.

"You can always be fitted for a suit by Jean Paul Gaultier. I hear he makes skirts instead of trousers, just the thing for a man with nathin' to hide, if ye get my drift, scum beg." He pushed Ian towards Pip, Ian took this as a signal to get stuck into Pip and he pulled his fist back in readiness to give the lad an upper cut to the chin.

"Get back! Get bloody back ye big hallion." He shoved Ian in the chest with all the energy he could muster but only managed to ruffle his shirt. "Keep him sweet for a wee while longer. He just might get a flash of inspiration an' pull a tenner from thin air Ye never know, he could be playin' for time." He glared at Ian, his anger rising by the second.

"What the hell do you have for breakfast, iron bollox? Four *Shredded Wheat* mixed with concrete followed by a cup of liquid lead?"

"At least I don't use an elastic band as a chest expander. Auld skinny ribs there cud do with a bit of body buildin'," hissed Ian.

"Aye, an' he cud do with a bit aff face rearrangin' an' all. Which remin's me, hear anythin' more about yer claim, big lad? A few gran' wud fairly pay aff yer debts to society," said Steven.

"Money isn't everythin', lads," answered Pip.

"No! It's nat everythin'. But it's better than a kick in the teeth. An' my boot is just beggin' for exercise," threatened Steven.

"It's only a bloody tenner extra than I already owe ye."

"Can ye nat get it off yer da? he's workin' an' so's yer ma."

"He needs his money for that car of his. It's his pride an' joy so it is. I can't ask him for it, I just can't, can I nye ?" Pip implored.

"Emmm, I just wonder what he wud do to you if he saw that scratch along the side of it, scum beg."

"What scratch?"

"The one he'll find tomorrow mornin' if we don't get that money." Steven was trying another tactic.

"Ah no lads. That's cruel. Me da never done youse no harm now. No need to make him suffer. Do you know how much a re-spray costs?" Pip pleaded, but it fell on deaf ears.

"More than a fuckin' tenner, so get beggin', or start prayin'." Steven hissed like a cobra about to strike and pointed his fingers at him Mafia-style, knuckle clenched with forefinger and little pinkie pointing directly at Pip's eyes. "The next time I do that they'll connect with yer eyeballs an' you'll be wearin' battle battoms fer glasses."

"Fer Christ's sake, ye wud think it wuz the national debt or somethin'. Whatever happened to all this love-thy-neighbour mallarky?"

"Luk here, face-ache, a mother cudn't love a bake like yours, niver min' the friggin' neighbours." He pulled Ian over to his side by the collar of his coat and slapped him round the ear.

"What did ye do that fer, Stevie? I done nathin' on ye. Me ma loves me, so she does."

"Was I talkin' about you? Was I?" Steven hit him round the other ear for being so thick. Ian just rubbed his ears and grunted. Steven's voice became high pitched with temper. "See big Ian here? He cud bate ye till pulp an' spread ye all over th' estate if the notion tuk him."

"Are yer underpants too tight, Stevie? Ye soun' like one af the Bee Gees, the wan wi' the buck teeth," queried Ian, the man with no brain.

"They've all gat buck teeth."

"Fuck up Dunlop, or you'll soun' like someone who's lost his bollox in the Louisiana swamplands. Crocodile bait, *Get it?* Was it worth all the trouble eh? Was thon auld tart good value fer money? She'd better have been, min' ye, for it'll be the last shag you'll ever have. Ye wont have the full equipment till go pullin' broads after Ian an' me's finished wi' ye."

Pip reflected on his night of passion on Saturday-night-come-Sunday-morning. Was Maureen worth all this hassle? Well, she did know what was what as far as sex was concerned. She had a few tricks up her sleeve that had been alien to Pip, all right. And, if Pip had learned a thing or two, it most certainly *had* been worth it. There weren't many of the auld sex positions left to be written into his book, but by heavens she knew her business. She had a tongue on her like a lizard, lips that were not only for talking and hands that could work wonders on the auld brewer's droop. He pondered for as long as he could, thus enabling him to think up a reply to Steven's question. Yes, she was most definitely worth ten quid. You wouldn't get that service for under fifty quid anywhere else. Why the hell did he tell her lies? She would come in very handy at the weekends.

"Well, one has to admit the lassy was more than adequate when it came to the crux of the matter, she knew what, ahemm, what to, ahemm, to do, to do when one, when one ahemm, started to get down to a bit of the, of the, of the old … ," he held his hands, Prince Charles fashion, and fidgeted about most annoyingly.

"Luk, fuck face! Less of that auld Hugh Whatsisname jargon. Take the marlies out aff yer gob an' talk English, will ye, or I'll knock the shit clean out af ye."

Steven was beginning to feel very annoyed with Pip, for this conversation was going nowhere quickly. "Jaysus, only the other week ye were actin' all John Travolta out of *Pulp Fiction*. Now, since hirin' out *Four Weddin's an a fuckin' Funeral* ye got that poofy haircut an' yer gubs turning, itself inside out wi' politeness. Now, spit those marlies out this minute before I knock them out wi' me fist. Anyway, it doesn't suit that neb of yer's. If ye had huv been aroun' in Hitler's Germany ye wud most definitely not have been picked for his youth movement."

"Well now Steven, my old pal, one would think one was jealous. And it's Northern Irish my dear boy, not English that comes out of my mouth."

"Fuck up!" Steven's fist was about to connect with Pip's chin when the handsome Lynus passed by.

"Hiya, lads! I hope yer practisin' fer Saturday night?" Lynus pulled an Elvis stance before continuing. "A huh huh, I'm all shook up ... yehhh."

He straightened up and sauntered up Pip's path to his door.

"That wuz good wuzn't it? Just a wee bit more practice wi' the lip curl an' I'll slay em down at the club." He peered at the three lads and concluded by the look of sheer hatred imprinted on Ian's and Steven's faces that they were not exactly having a friendly tete-a-tete. He ignored what he saw and continued, "I'm nat that bad am a? There's wurse like, a lat wurse, even if I do say so meself. Ye shud see that auld poof up the street. He tried to sing *Love Me Tender* right in me gub he did. Me! I ask ye, do I luk like a poof?"

The lads forgot about their squabble for a while, they were that stunned.

"Nah, nat really Lynus." The trio of voices were in such unison they could have passed for the Beverly Sisters. Even Pip forgot to keep up his Hugh Grant image and slouched against the door frame like a hoodlum. He took a butt from behind his ear and lit it up with a match found hidden in his jeans pocket. Exhaling slowly, he eyed Lynus up and down and suggested the man should "polish up his act a little or change his aftershave".

"I know I'm too manly lukin' to be effeminate like, but what about the Elvis bit. Luk if I dye me hair wi' black boot palish an slap on a wee bit aff fake tan wud ye think I wuz in wi' a chance like?" asked Lynus with a worried look. Earlier on in the morning when he had practised in front of his bedroom mirror he had himself convinced of his Elvis likeness.

"Ye fall down on both points, Lynus," answered Pip.

"Ah here nye, lads, I know I'm nat as young an' pretty as I used till be, but then again neither wuz auld Elvis near th' end."

"Ye have to admit Elvis wuz a hell aff a lot better lukin' than you," said Pip. "I know he isn't my cup of tea, I'm more yer Van Morrison sort of guy, but when I luk at you an' compare ye till the photos me ma has of Elvis, I wud say Elvis wins by a long chalk, no harm till ye an' all that." Pip laughed.

"Huh, we all can't be in the prime aff our lives ye know, but when I'm all spruced up I don't luk that bad. There's a few weemen in this estate wud be glad to get thur mitts on me. I'm nat on the dole like you lat."

"Dream on, Lynus," said Steven, raging by now at getting interrupted in the middle of a good auld battle. "If I were you I'd go back to that hypnotist an' get brought back outa that trance yer in."

"What hypnotist? I niver saw no hypnotist!" answered Lynus indignantly.

"Well, ye shud see one," challenged Steven, "to get the wee men outa yer head. Now, clear aff!"

"I'm aff, I'm aff. just keep yer hair on before ye keek yerself."

Lynus shuffled up the path and, stopping at the gate, turned round. "You ain't nathin' but a houn' dog, crappin' all th' time." He clasped his hands behind his neck and thrust his pelvis towards the them before heading down the street, laughing at his own cleverness.

"Buck eejit!" muttered Ian. "He shud put a bolt through his neck an' enter a Frankenstein-monster-look-a-like competition. He'd have no trouble comin' first in *that*."

"Yer one till talk Boris Karloff! Did ye ever have a good luk at *yerself?* Now, where were we before that head bin came along. Fuck me, now he's ruined everything. I can't be serious after lukin' at that. Hugh Grant, Elvis, Van Morrison, it's like bloody *Stars In Yer Eyes* night. The next thing ye know we'll have wee Percy Thorndyke over actin' Elton John wi' thon wig af his. Jaysus, but I'm browned aff." Steven stuck his hands in his trouser pockets and effed and blinded.

"*Hey, Steven!*" Elsie had left her mother's, albeit unwillingly, as the thoughts of Bert's toothless mouth had her stomach turning. "*Are ye comin' in for your lunch?"*

Steven sighed deeply. "Ah shit! See you Dunny, ye must have been touched by angels fer ye've the luck aff the devil!"

"That's effin' Irish, Friars! Yer ma must have been touched on the nut wi' a brick when she had ye – an Irish brick aff the Sinn Fein office!"

Ian bounced forward, fists at the ready. "Do ye want me till duff 'im up nye Stevie. He's insulted me an' all wi' that remark. He's a Fenian bastard alright. Luk, 'is eyes are that close he cud see through a crack in a wall with his two eyes at the wan time."

"Leave it Ian. He can wait. He's only a small fish in a big pond. We're big fish in a small pond. In fact me auld mucker, he's only a maggot." He cocked his nose at Pip before warning him that he would be on his doorstep on Thursday morning, waiting on the postman.

"Ah, my old bean," jibbed Pip, once more falling into his Hugh Grant image. "You will have to be up early to catch me on the hop. Because I will be hopping it down to the old dole office this week to collect my little wad of notes. I have been summoned by no-one other than the head of social services himself."

"What ye friggin' mean is, ye owe them more than ye owe me. You just make sure ye have that money or I'll report ye fer doin' the double at Christmas in the Starlight bar."

"And I, my dear man, will report you to the law for sellin' stolen drinkie poos over the same festive season! And for takin' drugs."

"I do nat take drugs!" Steven grabbed Pip by the scruff of the neck and gave him a head butt, an Irish kiss.

"You take me to the fair, Friars. That wasn't Kali sucker in thon wrap."

"What wrap?"

"Well, it wasn't yer ma's fur wrap, wuz it? The one Hugh slipped into yer haun outside the bogs," answered Pip as he nonchalantly flicked his cigarette butt into the garden.

"That was fer Ian."

"Don't give me all that flannel. It wud take five wraps to get into that brain of his."

"Was that a compliment, Stevie?" asked Ian.

"Aye, it was that all right," answered Steven sarcastically.

"Just as big a compliment as tellin' you ye have a face like a gorilla," laughed Pip.

"*Steven, did you hear me?*" yelled Elsie out of her front window.

"Now run along. Mater is calling for you. You don't want to miss your lunch, do you, my dear man."

Pip fled into his house and slammed the front door shut, leaving Steven and his burly sidekick gobsmacked.

"*Aye I'm comin', ma!*" He turned to Ian. "I hope that auld lad af mine has gone up till his bed. The sight of that bake af his will do my head in completely. I thought *you* were brute ugly till I clapped eyes on my auld lad's fid earlier on. You luk like Elvis compared to *that!*"

"I taule ye I wasn't that bad lukin', didn't I Stevie?"

"Ah, belt up, an' go home till yer ugly ma."

"Right Stevie, see ye later."

Nat if I see you first, thought Steven.

10

Tuesday, 27 February

Elsie had spent a restless night. Every time she fell into a doze Bert turned his face from the wall and breathed in her face. The smell of stale blood had sickened her, not to mention the sight of his gaping mouth. She had turned her back on her husband and stared towards the window praying for daylight. She had been praying for a long time now, since half-past-five to be precise.

She had given up trying to escape into a dream world, because each time she dozed off her dreams turned to nightmares. She felt herself falling into dark bottomless pits where dentists lurked in crevices. Open wide now, Mrs Friars. This won't hurt at all. Men in white coats held instruments of torture to her face, while long bony fingers tore at her mouth in an effort to pry it open. No-one could hear her screams, while her legs felt as heavy as lead and worked in slow motion as she tried to run from her tormentors.

It was now half-past-seven. Daylight was still a good hour away. Should she get up now and eat her breakfast before Bert awoke and asked for something that could slide easily down his throat? She was not given the chance to make a decision. The phone in the hall jangled her nerves as it sprang into life. The ringing made her heart beat faster. What was on the old crone's mind this morning? She assumed it would most likely be to find out if she was going to the shops. Her assumption was spot on.

"What time are ye goin' to the Co-op?"

Elsie sat on the last step of the stairs, phone in hand. Her body felt limp, her eyes somewhere in the back of her head through lack of sleep.

"I need milk, I need bread, I need toilet rolls, I need ..."

I need a good night's sleep, thought Elsie.

"Ma, it's only half-past-seven. Do you think the shops stay open all night?" She felt like crying and almost dropped the phone with fatigue. "Do you ever sleep, ma? You never miss a trick during the day, you ring at midnight, then your on the blower first thing in the mornin'." She held her head in her free hand to ease the throb in the side of it. She could feel a migraine coming on as she saw flashes of light flash in front of her tired eyes. Elsie had never suffered from migraines until recently. Now she never seemed to want for one.

"At my age yer afraid to sleep in case ye don't wake up," snapped Sarah. Elsie held the phone at arm's length, Sarah's harsh voice was making her headache even worse. "You could find me dead one of these mornin's," added Sarah looking for sympathy.

"Hope springs eternal," said Elsie under her breath, but her mother had heard.

"God forgive ye woman, at least you can have a sleep without the worry of not wakin' up."

I wouldn't worry if I never woke up, thought Elsie. "Ma, I go to the shops every mornin'. Why do you get me out of my bed to ask me the same flamin' question every day in life?"

"Is Bert's mouth all right?"

"Bert's mouth is havin' a ball. I'm the one that's sufferin'. It gaped at me all night."

"Good God ma, do I not deserve a bit of human kindness to be thrown my way for a change. Bert's mouth is tantamount to mental torture, are you aware of that? There should be a law that calls for hangin' when husbands get their teeth removed without the wife's permission."

"Don't be so daft. Put him in the other room an' you'll get a bit af pase at night to sleep."

"I can't put him in the other room. It's full of junk."

"Well then, one more piece won't make a difference. Throw him in it an' put cotton wool in yer ears!"

Elsie closed her eyes and tried to imagine what sleep felt like. Her mothers voice just went on and on and on. Her mind wandered to the afternoon, when her sisters would be coming for the dreaded meeting. Should she get something in for a cup of tea? Ah, bugger the lot of them, they can go to hell, or else go to the cafe in the shoppin' precinct. She came back to the land of the living and told her mother that she would be going to the shops as usual. After all, there is life after teeth removal.

"Will ye call over then before ye go?"

"Right, right, ma."

"Don't keep saying right. It's annoyin' me."

"*Right!*" Elsie replaced the receiver and wearily made her way to the kitchen. She no sooner had the kettle on when Bert appeared from behind her as if he had been spirited down the stairs. She hadn't heard him get up and she jumped with fright. She always seemed to be jumping with fright these days, maybe a visit to the doctor might be a good idea. To get something to calm her ravaged nerves.

"You must have come down those stairs like a flat-footed ferret, I never even heard ye."

"Haf ye put the kettle on Elthie?"

"Hide your bake, Bert Friars! Go into the other room an' stoke up the fire, or else go back to bed".

"Me mouf's still sore, Elthie. Jaysus, I thought the pain wud eathe after gettin' all me teef out. It's bloody wourth."

"You're not kiddin' it's bloody worse! It was painful enough lookin' at yer gub when you had teeth but it's flamin' awful now you don't have a bar in the grate." Elsie held the drying cloth up to her eyes to help block out the sight, hightailed it up the stairs and locked herself in the bathroom, refusing to come out until he wrapped something round his mouth.

"That's the sympafy ye get in this houth. Did ye want me to suffer for ever wif sore teef?" He rummaged through the kitchen cupboards in search of sustenance, something soft and mushy. He found a packet of porridge, put a pot of water on the cooker to boil and added a few cups of the oats and a pinch of salt and stirred it with a wooden spoon until it thickened.

Ten minutes later Elsie crept down the stairs and went into the living room. The sight that met her eyes was stomach churning. Bert sat on the settee, with a baby's nappy wrapped round his neck slurping porridge.

"I left thome for you an' Stefen in the pot."

"Jaysus, you are the spittin' image of bloody Steptoe sittin' there. Do you honestly think Steven will ate that slop? And cover your mouth when he gets up or I'll fill it with *Polyfilla*."

"Get us some *Parathetamol* when ye go till the shaps will ye?"

"Look, spit them out an' I'll sort them. I can hardly understand a word you're sayin'. I don't suppose they would sell me some arsenic?" said Elsie.

"Arthenic me arthe, give me head pase, will ye?" He continued slurping, the porridge dribbling down his chin. "First it wuz arthenic fer yer ma. Nye it's arthenic fer me. Ye must haf arthenic on the brain."

Elsie put on her coat over her nightdress, put some clothes in a bag and fled over to her mother's. The snow had almost melted in the grass that separated the flats from the houses.

The postman passed as she scurried out the gate.

"There's a letter here for Bert, Elsie."

"Give us a look, Jimmy. Ach, just put it through the letter-box it looks like it's important. What does it say on the back? From Arbuckle, Arbuthnot and O'Neill, Solicitors. Must be about his claim."

"Another one. That makes four in the one street. I suppose this is yer holiday money?" He laughed out loud. "Well I guess there's a severe epidemic of whiplash goin' around."

"Nothin' to do with me Jimmy, but I will say one thing: Bert has done himself an awful injury without goin' out in a car. His bake looks as if it has gone through a windscreen."

Jimmy looked perplexed but carried on with his business of delivering letters. Nothing surprised him in Ballyhornet.

"Here there's one for yer ma. Take it over. Ye might as well save me the journey." She keeps yakkin' fer hours on end, then I'm late home an' the wife chews the bake aff me fer another couple, until I'm blue in the fid.

"Do ye think ye could cram any more people into this auld flat?" asked Sarah in a sardonic tone. "Ye shud have hired the City Hall an' a brass band for entertainment."

"It's all for your benefit, ma," answered Elsie, dunting her mother with her elbow.

"Watch me auld arm will ye? There's no meat on it till take a punch like that." Sarah rubbed the top of her arm and gave her daughter a withering look. "Anyway it's nat *all* for my benefit. Her upstairs will reap the rewards as well; she'll be able to get drunk without being interrupted by childer rappin' on her dur. An' him out of the Parachute regiment, the one who doesn't know his arse from Joe McKibben's, will be able to sleep in his bed at nights without worryin' who's goin' to steal his tartles off the washin' line."

"Who the hell's Joe McKibben, ma?" asked Elsie.

"No-one *you* know. Now, shut up till I listen to what's goin' on." Sarah sat like the Queen Mother on her throne surveying her minions. In her mind people were only put on this earth to be her slaves and jump to her every need. She cocked her ear to get a better listen and squinted as if ready to do battle with anyone who said anything to her disliking.

Helen and Alec had arrived from Ballymena in their red Ford *Escort*, the interior of which smelled of car freshener, and not a sweetie paper in sight. The ashtrays were devoid of cigarette butts, the back seat littered with velvet cushions and a toy dog sat strategically placed in the shelf by the rear window, its head nodding as if in approval of its surroundings. Helen had breezed into her mother's flat dressed from head to toe in Marks & Spencer's best and the finest Italian footwear that money could buy. Alec, dressed to please his brusque wife in perfectly creased trousers and Pringle sweater, put the steering wheel lock on, plus the car alarm, double-checked the doors and scanned the surrounding area for undesirables before following in her footsteps. He dressed to suit his wife, but it didn't always work out. On this occasion he had but on his brown shoes instead of the black ones, to match his blue sweater and she had reprimanded him. This made him nervous. He sniffed on entering the flat and coughed, an outward sign of his nerves, rubbed his hands together and tried to show concern for his mother-in law's plight. His wife told him to shut up and sit down and he obeyed, just as their poodle Petra would have done.

Isobel and Liam arrived about ten minutes later in their racing-green

Rover. It smelled of stale cigarettes, was littered not only with sweetie papers but overflowed with empty *Coca Cola* cans and old newspapers. A cluster of teddy bears won from a teddy bear machine in Portrush lay carelessly scattered on the rear window ledge, and a sticker proclaiming "This is only the runaround, the Rolls is getting an oil change" was stuck to the rear window. Liam had turned the key in the central locking system after Isobel had warned him about the natives of Ballyhornet feeling restless when a strange car sat for more that ten minutes unattended. Liam, being careless with his possessions as well as his appearance, was dressed in clothes that a charity shop would have refused. Isobel, like Helen, also wore Marks & Spencer, but not as carefully matched as her sister. Her shoes, on the other hand, were from Shoe Express and badly worn at the heel from driving. Liam did not believe in chauffeuring his wife about like Alec. Liam was too bloody lazy. He had brought a half dozen cans of beer along to quench his thirst and had warned Isobel of his intention of letting her drive home. Alec, on the other hand, had to be content with a cup of tea to lubricate the tonsils. Isobel did not make as grandiose an entrance as her Ballymena sister. She slipped in almost unnoticed apart from her sister Helen giving her the once over. She flirted with Bert and batted her eyelids at Alec, a sure sign of desperation. Elsie asked her if she had lost her eyesight, and did she not feel scared at the sight of Bert with no teeth.

"I do not!" said she. "Liam looks worse after a skinful of Guinness after a GAA match when he has removed his partial dental plate in case he chokes in his sleep."

Helen turned up her nose in disgust. Her sister's mention of the GAA almost had her running to Pastor Ellis for solace. Isobel needed a good talking too to save her from the clutches of the Catholic church and the demon drink.

"Nothing in this world could equal the sight of a toothless Bert, not even the rearend of a monkey's arse," Elsie had answered indignantly.

"A, thut up, Elthie! Let Ithobel come over here an' I'll give her a big thloppy kith." Isobel laughed when Elsie told Bert to go back over to the house and hide his cavernous gob, preferably in the gas oven after turning it on.

"I told you not to come over here today, Bert Friars. That's not a face to be showing in public, it's a face that should be locked in the wardrobe, along with your fancy bowlin' clothes."

Percy had arrived before Elsie's sisters. Along with a policeman from the local station, a fire officer had agreed to attend plus the neighbours, who really only came in for a bit of a neb, it being new light out of an old moon to be asked into Sarah's domain. They couldn't give a fiddlers fart if the Highland Light Infantry passed through the flats on night manoeuvres. As far as they were concerned the only person they needed protection from was Sarah herself.

The room was buzzing with conversation now. Sarah became quite agitated at not being able to be heard over the din and to distinguish one conversation from the other. She slapped the arm of her chair with the palm of her hand.

"Will ye talk one at a time, if ye don't mind. My head's light tryin' to make sense out of any of this auld carry on."

Silence prevailed as everyone stared in Sarah's direction. She glared back, steel blue eyes challenging everybody in her small living room to even hint at breaking the silence, never mind have the audacity or temerity to talk without her permission.

The silence was broken by Rab. He whispered something in Bert's ear. Sarah glared in his direction like Queen Victoria, she was not amused. Rab grabbed Bert by the elbow and shepherded him towards the hallway for privacy.

"Did ye get a letter fram the solicitor this mornin', Bert?"

"Aye, did you?"

Rab closed the door to the living room so no-one could hear.

"Aye, an so did Peggy. Luk here Bert," said he peering over his shoulder. "Don't go sayin' anythin' tae anyone in thur, careless talk an' all that shit. What wuz it they said durin' the war, loose lips sink ships. This is wan ship we don't want sunk." He ushered him out into hallway of the flats before continuing. "Hae ye seen Lynus about? He shud hae gat wan an' all. Whit did yer's say anyway?"

"It just thaid an appointment had been made for me to attend the big dactor for an examinathon nexth week."

"Same here. Well we all hae tae get our story right. By the luk af things we cud be in the money by May if we're lucky. It only takes a few months after the big dactor sees ye."

Rab's chest started to heave. The excitement made his breathing laboured and he used his ventolin spray like it was going out of fashion.

"Tee-he, Bert. They say whiplash claims are nae worth at least three-an'-a-half gran', Jaysus, Bert, that's seven gran' between me an' Peggy alone."

"Don't forget Andy an' Roy. They have to get a couple aff hundred for goin' witnesshh."

"Ach, I know that. That's only wee buns, Bert."

"What's that glipe of a husband of yours doin' out there? Get him in here till we get this meetin' underway," demanded Sarah.

Elsie dragged Bert in from the hallway, chastising him as she did so.

"Don't you go gallavantin' off again like that. I need a bit of support in here. What's that Rab one up to anyway? No good, I suppose. I hope he's not leadin' you astray. He's caused enough trouble this weekend without you gettin' us into any more."

She remembered the letter the postman had for Bert that morning.

"What was in that letter ye got? I hope to God you're not in trouble. You're not goin' to court with that *face*."

"Ach, it's only about my whi..."

Rab tapped the side of his nose with his finger and mouthed the words loose lips.

"Right Rab, I won't mention a ..." Bert almost let the cat out of the bag, his lips were that loose, especially now he had no teeth to give them support.

Elsie had now got the drift of what was in the letter. "Shut up, will ye? We don't want Percy or the neighbours hearin'. And don't forget there's a policeman in here," hissed Elsie through gritted teeth, a smile beaming through a hot flush. "Right ma, we're all here. Let's get started."

"Aahhmmm!" Percy cleared his throat before starting. "Now, let's take the minutes of the meeting." He proceeded to open his large diary, rummaged in his briefcase for a pen and coughed nervously.

"Get on with it!" snapped Sarah. "An' stop futterin' about. We're not here for a holiday, but God knows I've come to the conclusion your life's one big holiday, Percy, for ye seem to do nothin' but flit around houses an' attend meetin's."

"Bear with me for a moment, Mrs Cruickshank," implored Percy.

"Your ma didn't bear with yer da long, did she? Ten years, that's how long it lasted before she ran off with the butcher, or was it the insurance man."

"Mother!" shrieked Helen.

"What are ye motherin' about? I'm entitled to an opinion if nothing else."

"You have the right to an opinion, but you have no right to blabber it to the world," scolded Helen.

"Ach, you give me the nyerps! Who in hell's gates do ye think ye are? Livin' in a babby dish of a house among self-made snobs who used to run aroun' without an arse in their trousers an knickers made out of flour begs".

"Me and Alec bettered ourselves. We could have stayed in that wee house in the Shankill Road only Alec wanted the boys to grow up in more salubrious surroundings. The clean air was better for Andrew's health, his chest being a bit on the wheezy side."

"He takes that after his da. Us Cruickshanks had good chests an' strong constitutions. Good breedin' an' always well fed. Thon one ye married was reared on the scrapin's of tin, that's why he had to retire early from his work," rebuked Sarah.

"My Alec retired because he made provision for an early retirement," Helen answered indignantly.

"And so did Liam!" Isobel got her say in at this point, for she knew her mother would start on her and Liam at some time.

Elsie looked forlornly at Bert, who had enough insurance to just about pay for her and his own funerals and sighed. "Th' only bit of land we'll own is a bit six feet by three in Roselawn Cemetery. As for makin' provision for early retirement, well, providing we live that long he'll make sure he signs on every fortnight until he receives his pension!"

The room had gone that quiet you could have heard someone change their mind as Sarah's daughters private business was spat out for all to hear. This did not go unnoticed by Sarah.

"Take that supercilious luk of yer gubs. There's not one of ye's has a bit of pride in yous, so close yer gapin' gubs an' listen to what Percy has come about. And you three *Golden Girls*, sit there an' shut up."

"Right, Sophie!" joked Rab.

"Just you give over. Did I ask for your opinion, Robert Kirk? Let Percy have *his* say for that's why we're all here starin' like bug-eyed eegits," reprimanded Sarah. "An' what the hell are you doin' up here th' day anyway. Nobody invited ye. Up nebbin' as usual."

"I care about ye, Mrs Cruickshank. Nat everyone in this room can say the same. Anyway, yer beauty is drawin' me like a duck till water. If ye were married till that auld heg aff mine ye'd sit in shit in a piggery for a bita pase."

"Carry on, Percy. Ignore that auld waster."

"Thank you, Mrs Cruickshanks," proffered Percy. He felt important now Sarah had given him her attention. "Well now, let's see. The minutes of the meeting." He looked round the small room to see who could act as secretary, and clapping his eyes on Bert, asked in a pleading manner, "Will you take the notes, Bert?"

"Aye, all right then. If ye tell me what till do like," answered a bewildered Bert.

"Just write down what the people suggest and the time the meeting started and the time it ended." He gave Bert a strange look, one that said, "Are ye some sort of idiot not to know a thing as simple as that."

Bert ceremoniously opened the book and held the pen in a writing position. With the look of a wise old owl, he cleared his throat and stated out loud as he wrote, "Aahhmmm. It's three thirty five prethiselly."

A round of applause reverberated round the room.

"Jaysus, Bert, ye said that like an auld pro. I think Percy thur is in danger af losin' his jab if ye keep up wi' thon line af patter," bantered Rab.

"Ah, thut up, Kirk! Do I have to enter that, Perthy?"

"*No Bert!*" Percy almost lost his balance on Sarah's settee as he shot forwards and put his hand over the page of the book that Bert was hovering over with the pen. As he did so his wig slipped ever so slightly and he patted the back of it so it sat flat with the rest of his hair. A slight snigger came from Rab's direction and a very nervous Percy snapped back through gritted teeth, "Now as we are all aware, this is not a pleasure trip. No time for frivolities or pernicious backchat."

"God but you'd make the middle an' two ends of a quare fella wi' all that fancy talk. Just talk English an' get on wi' it!" snapped Sarah.

"If you'll give me half a chance, Mrs Cruickshank, I'll do just that! But on the other hand if you keep interrupting I will have to bring the meeting to a close!" reprimanded Percy, taking his life in his hands.

"Was that a veiled threat, Percy me laddo?" hissed Sarah. "Ye know I can talk fancy as well. I could cut the cooter off ye wi' one word. Thorny ..."

"That's enough, ma!" Elsie held her hand over her mother's mouth and apologised to Percy.

Sarah pried her daughters hand from her mouth. "Ah, give over, our Elsie! An' don't do that again, ye nearly smothered me. Sure I'm only havin' a bit a craic wi' Mr Thorndyke. No need to get all hysterical. God, wud ye look at Constable McCabe there. He nearly took a buckle in his eye. He thought ye were goin' to kill me in front of his eyes." Sarah laughed at the look on the policeman's face. "Cheer up man, ye look like death warmed up."

"Well now Mrs Cruickshank, you're not often a witness to a murder at such close proximity," the policeman exclaimed. "I didn't think I was here to keep the peace. I was under the impression this meeting was about a gate being erected, an' nat the Berlin Wall."

"Has that to go down, Perthy?" Bert sat poised with the pen once more.

"*No, it hasn't!* Mrs Cruickshank! Can I command your attention, *Please!*" Percy was on his feet and demanding that he be heard.

"Ah, keep yer hair on!" Sarah held her own hand to her mouth now, her little *lapus linguae* had caused a fit of the giggles, which in turn made her want to pee and she struggled out of her chair and towards the toilet.

Percy glared at the people in the room in turn, defying them to join in Sarah's laughter. His wig had slipped slightly over his forehead, unnoticed by himself in his temper, but not by anyone else. A sea of faces stared in Percy's direction, each willing his wig to slip off. Not a word was spoken. Indeed there wasn't a word to describe the atmosphere in Sarah's little flat. The tinkle of pee hitting porcelain broke the silence followed by the usual burst of flatulence, at which point Percy threw his head back and tut-tutted in disgust, giving his wig cause to slip a little further down his forehead. A slight gasp passed from each and everyone's lips, followed by a sharp intake of breath. Will it? Wont it? The entire roomful of people were silently putting bets on that the councillor's hairpiece would escape right down his face and land on the floor.

Percy casually pushed his wig back on his head as if this was an everyday occurrence. Unknown to himself it sat slightly askew and he looked a sorry sight. He kept on staring with baleful eyes at the roomful of people, defying them to even contemplate laughing at his expense, knowing rightly that his wig was the cause of all the mirth.

Rab had to use his inhaler as he had become quiet breathless, trying not to laugh. The fire officer and the policeman lit up cigarettes and inhaled deeply to calm their ravaged nerves. Alec asked Liam in hushed tones if he wanted to go outside for a drag of his feg, only to be put in his place by his wife who shot him a look of disgust at contaminating himself with the smell of cigarette smoke. Liam offered him a beer instead, but just as he was about to accept a can, Helen slapped him on the back of the head and reminded him of the drinking and driving laws. Liam opened his can and the hiss of the ring pull as it peeled back was almost deafening in the deathly silence that was slowly casting a shroud over the tiny flat. Bert's toothless mouth drooled. A cool beer would slip down his throat nicely and he snitched a can from the pack that sat at Liam's feet and slurped the contents. The coolness eased his sore gums and he groaned as if in the throws of an orgasm, breaking the silence.

"Help yourself," said Liam sarcastically.

"I justht did," answered Bert with a toothless grin, the amber fluid dribbling down his chin.

The eye's of the auld doll from up the stairs almost popped out at the sight of alcohol in the old crone's flat and the wee legs of the old soldier from the Parachute regiment almost buckled with fright when Sarah hirpled in from the toilet and glared at him as if he had escaped from the lunatic asylum.

The three sisters escaped into the kitchen to put the kettle on and to have a chin wag.

"It's all right for you two," said Elsie. "How would yous like to have *that* day in an' day out? And on top of everything Bert went an' disfigured himself without even askin' me if I could stomach the sight."

"Well now, Elsie," answered Helen, "he was no Greek God when he *had* teeth!"

"Come to think on it, Liam is no Adonis either. Did ye ever lay eyes on such a beg of regs in all your life?" remarked Isobel.

Elsie thought for a moment before answering. "At least yous can escape for a while, go for a jaunt in the car or have yer dinner out in a nice restaurant. Bert can't even afford a tandem to take me on the rear seat to the park."

"Remember, Elsie, when you used to go cycling round the Lake District?," said Helen as she lent on her elbows on the counter of the sink and rested her chin in her cupped hands.

Elsie's eyes misted over. "Aye, indeed I do! Indeed I do. God, do ye know? If Bert knew the boys I could have had then. An' the muscles in their legs with cyclin', an' their wee tight bums that could have cracked nuts. God, but they were gorgeous," recalled Elsie wistfully.

"Ach sure Elsie, maybe now their wee tight arses are all hangy an' their gubs all toothless. Ye just wouldn't know now, would ye?" surmised Isobel.

Helen agreed with a sigh. "Ach sure, none of them are oil paintin's when they reach fifty."

"You mean sixty!" said Isobel, nodding her head in the direction of the living room.

"Well, Liam's not sixty yet," Helen butted in. "He might look it, but there's still a bit of life left in th' old dog yet. Can I tell him I'm in the menopause? *No!* He still wants his oats twice a month. Do men ever stop thinkin' about sex? He ogles anything that wears a skirt. Sometimes I think he even fancies wee Billy Burns, an' he only wears a kilt in th' Orange Lodge on the Twelfth."

"Well, we all know he is highly sexed," said Isobel.

"And how do you know that, our Isobel?" asked Helen with a worried expression. "I wouldn't exactly say two times a month was over the top."

"Well now Helen, that wasn't a stick of rock he had in his trouser pocket when Bert showed him those pornographic photos the other week."

The peals of laughter alerted Sarah, who pottered into the kitchen to see what all the tittering was about, interrupting their little tete-a-tete. "I hope yous three aren't thinkin' of makin' tea for that lot! This is not Sarah's self service cafe ye know."

"No ma, we're wettin' our own whistles. We're dyin' with drooth," answered all three at once.

"Well, come on out of here. I want to get this bloody meetin' over before I die. At eighty-nine ye can't hang about." Sarah summoned them with a wave of her bony hand and blattered unsteadily on her bunioned feet into the living room where Percy was almost puce with frustration.

"Maybe we should put this meeting off until a more suitable day, Mrs Cruickshank. We don't appear to be getting anywhere with this one." Percy had a look of defeat emblazoned on his face. He was hoping Sarah would agree but he was to be disappointed.

"*No!* We will battle this out once an' for all. An' I wish you would stop hoppin' about as if your arse was on fire, Percy."

If wishes were horses, beggars would ride, thought Percy, and if that was the case I would have a whole stable full.

"I wish you would settle down and listen, instead of gabbling, Mrs Cruickshank," he added with a slight tremor in his voice.

"I will, I will. Just tell me what yer plans are for this blasted gate."

"Will I write down what yer goin' to thay now?" asked a bemused Bert.

"All right, Bert. You can write whatever the hell you like," answered Percy in an exasperated tone.

"I only asked," Bert added forlornly.

"I'm sorry, Bert. But never in my life have I attended a meeting such as this." Percy pleaded with his eyes at the sea of faces. The sea of faces merged into one as they came up with idea after idea that Bert registered religiously in the red book.

"This is like *This is yer Life,* Perthy. Will this be handed to thome unthespectin' crathur by Michael Aspel?" joked Bert.

Percy pretended he hadn't heard Bert's ridiculous remark.

"Well now, we have all come to the one conclusion. *I* will get a new gate erected with a locking bolt on it. *You* will all have a key to gain access and the same one will let you exit. Now, that means keeping your keys in a safe part of your person."

"That'll be in Sarah's knickers," joked Rab. "No-one's been in those for donkeys. It wud take a braver maun thun Captain Kirk tae boldly go where nay maun hus gone afore to explore the mysteries aff the deep in them auld bloomers," he added. The rest of the people in the room agreed merrily, but their mirth was cut short when Sarah gave them a look that would have wiped the smile off the Mona Liza. "Only jokin' Mrs Cruickshank. I'm only jokin'. Put it down yer shift. If someone tries tae steal it they'll get a thrill."

"Nobody will get a thrill outa me," huffed Sarah.

By Jaysus they won't. Ye wudne get the time o' day outa you, thought Rab.

"Right! That's it then. We will try out this plan of action. Are we all in agreement?" pleaded Percy hoping no-one would change their mind.

"We're all in agreement!" shouted a choir of voices, except for the fire brigade man, who was worried about the escape route should a fire arise. He was promptly told his worries were groundless as the side door would be kept open in case of such an emergency. No-one stopped to think that the children could then also get in by that entrance, as well as undesirables.

Percy wondered if they had a brain cell between them, but decided to keep his mouth shut for the time being. That problem could wait for another day, when he had recovered from today's experience.

With a flick of the wrist and a flourish of the pen, Bert wrote down. "*The minutes of the meeting ended at four thirty five precisely*," then sighed with relief. "Christ! I think I'll thtick till me bowls of a Thaturday. All this writin' buthiness wud thend ye mad."

Percy straightened his wig and started on the subject of bowling, much to Bert's delight.

"Will you be having a game of bowls tonight, Mr Friars?"

"Indoors, Perthy. Nat the thame, as I told ye before. I with April wuth here to get out on the green," Bert said, a statement that did not go unnoticed by Rab.

"I wish April wuz here tae I got inta her drawers," joked Rab.

Sarah puckered her lips in disgust and threw him a look of contempt.

Her eyes narrowed further when Liam answered, "Who do ye think yer kiddin' Rab. There's no lead in yer pencil. Ye cudn't get a hard-on if ye sprayed yer willy wi' plaster af paris."

This did not go down too well with Percy who, rebuking the filthy-minded individuals with a wave of his hand, and inquired of Bert the rules of the game. Bert gladly enlightened him, as he loved nothing better than a good natter about bowling.

"You could say bowls was your bailiwick, Mr Friars?"

"I don't know about it bein' my bailiwick, whatever that is, but it's th' only interetht I have nye, Perthy. Would you nat try a wee game, Perthy."

"I did a few times, but really I'm only a fairweather supporter, Mr Friars."

"Well I suppothe it is better in the thummer months."

At this point Percy gave up the ghost of a chance of holding a sensible conversation. He gathered up his bits and pieces, bade all farewell, and scarpered out the front door without a backward glance, for fear of Sarah nabbing him for another bit of backchat.

"The wee geezer's forgot his hat." Liam held Percy's hat up for all to see and then moved towards the door.

"I'll run after him an' give it to him."

"Sit where ye are!" scolded Sarah. "I'll hold it here in the flat. He'll have to come an' collect it. I'll use it as bait for another day, just in case he doesn't get that gate on quick enough for my liking."

"That's an awful thing to do, ma. His wig might blow off in the wind without it. How would you like people to play tricks on you?" Elsie fired back.

"Ah, get away with ye, an don't try to tell your granny how to suck eggs. Awful indeed, it's nathin' till the way you're treatin' that man of yours for gettin' his teeth removed."

The neighbours, the policeman and the fire officer followed in Percy's footsteps while the going was good, all wondering why they had been summoned in the first place.

Are you comin' over for your dinner, ma?" Elsie asked, "Bert will help you over."

"No, I'm just goin' to sit here an' watch the TV. I'm exhausted after all that auld fuss."

"That's alright then. Give us a ring if you need anything."

Isobel and Helen looked at Elsie as if she wasn't right in the head.

"Did you ever hear anything like that in your life, Helen? She's a glutton for punishment. *She is ye know, she is!*"

"I know she is Isobel, but think what it would be like if mother lived beside one of us!"

"For Christ's sake, let's get out of here before our Elsie comes to her senses!"

"Alec get your arse off that seat. Th' Escort needs washed!"

"Liam, get a move on. There's someone eyeing up yer car!"

"I havn't finished me beer, Isobel," whinged Liam.

"Well leave it with Bert. It will cool his gums."

Bert grinned from ear to ear, his chin almost hitting his nose. "Thanks Ithobel. You're a wee thaint."

"She's as bad as a wet weekend. She would ruin your happiness," retorted Liam.

"No, she wouldn't. Helen would do that," said Alec in whispered tones. He peered over his shoulder to make sure his wife hadn't heard. His life wouldn't have been worth living if she had.

"Cheerio, mother, Isobel an' I are off home!" shouted Helen as the two sisters and their husbands left the flat.

"We'll talk to you on the phone, Elsie!"

Of that I have no doubt thought Elsie. Sometimes I wish the bloody thing had never been invented. At least I would get a lie in of a morning, and not have to arrange flamin' meetin's.

11

Wednesday, 28 February

The "green wine gum" spluttered its way through the streets of Ballyhornet, exhaust fumes throwing out enough carbon monoxide to almost poison the residents. It backfired three times on reaching Hetherington Green and a few choice words had been thrown its way by the string-vested one and his wife, who were heading towards the shops for their daily fix of cigarettes. They were sharing the dregs of a butt and had cheek to give off to Ernie that his exhaust fumes were a hazard to their health. Ernie was laughing at the idea that the fumes from his van were the cause of their coughs and he put his boot to the floor.

The vested one shook a fist at Ernie. "Do ye remember what I told ye to do wi' yer horn on Saturday? Well I'll stick thon van up yer jacksie to keep it company if ye don't get thon exhaust fixed!"

"Ah, belt up! An while yer over at the shaps get thon auld butcher to get his eyes tested or else change his dog."

"Bastard!"

"An' the same till you, o' vested one! Why don't ye get him till knit ye a new wan wi' the string he ties his meat with while yer there."

"Was he referring to me, Billy, wi' thon remark about the butcher gettin' his eyes tested? See if he was I'll run up thon street an bate the bake af him." The vested one's wife rolled her sleeves up, ready to do battle.

Her husband grabbed her by the arm and dragged her up the street, protesting. "Fer Christ's sake woman, will ye come on a that. Ye finished that last cigarette an' I'm dyin' fer another dreg."

"Oh aye, ye'd die fer a feg but ye wudn't stan' up fer yer wife!"

He looked at her out of the side of his eye. "At least ye get a bit af enjoyment out af a feg."

"I wud say *yer* the bastard, an' nat Ernie!" hissed his wife.

Ernie blasted his horn and continued his journey, whistling as he went. He took all cuts as compliments, being used to dealing with the public. He came to a halt outside Peggy's, on seeing the mistress of the house wave him down with her long bony hand. He put the gear stick into reverse and turned off the engine, his hand brake having given up the ghost months back. He hopped from his driving seat and proceeded to open the back doors of the van.

"What happened till ye on Monday Peggy, were ye sick?"

"I suppose ye cud say that Ernie. I wuz feelin' the caule a bit more than usual." Peggy peered at Ernie suspiciously. Did he know anything about her little mishap?

"It's bloody colder nye the snows melted. Thurs a wind that wud blow the cooter aff ye." A cat skulked at the wheel of his van and he shooed it off by giving it a good boot up the rear end." Mangy auld gits. Your Rab isn't doin' his jab properly. That's the first moggy I've seen in ages."

Peggy's face turned a livid red, for she was sure Rab had been tittle-tattling.

"Are ye havin' a hat flush thur, Peggy? My auld missus is always fannin' herself these days. It must be awful t' be a wuman mine ye. She even says her hair isn't sittin' right. I taule her the hairs on her chin were sittin' lovely. Do all weemen get hairy when they reach fifty, Peggy? I wudn't be surprised to see hairs on her chest. Af coorse I wouldn't know, nat feelin' that romantic towards her these days. Are ye still gettin' a wee flutter yoursel' nye Peggy, apart fram thinkin' about Tom Cruise? Ye were quare an' hat lukin' th' other mornin', almost at boilin' point, if ye don't min' me sayin'."

"Listen Ernie, I'm nat in no mood till joke the day," snapped Peggy.

"Keep yer hair on! Keep yer bloody hair on, girl. If ye keep that up ye'll end aff wearin' a wig like wee Percy."

He knows! The get bloody knows, she thought to herself. I'll kill that flamin' Robert Kirk. I'll think af a way. No sweat. His days are numbered.

"What wud ye like fer yer dinner the day, Peggy? What about a wee drap af stew fer a change!"

"Very funny, Ernie. Did ye ever think af goin' inta comedy fer a livin'? Wi' a face like yours ye wudne hae to tell jokes. Just stare at th' audience like."

"Christ, yer sharp the day alright, Peg. Somethin's neggin' at ye fer yer auld brain's firin' on all of its three cells."

"Yer bloody mouth is firin' on all cylinders. Nye get yer wee arse inta gear an' weigh me a stone af them spuds ye saule me on Saturday."

"Were they all right! Ye don't want th' Egyptian ones the day fer a change?"

"Frig aff! Ye'll hae tae wait till I win the lottery before I buy those."

"Carrots, onions, parsnips, the same as usual then?"

"Aye, an' a couple af pounds af those nice apples an' a beg af those wee oranges."

"Havin' a party, Peggy?"

"Cheeky bugger! You min' yer business an' I'll min' mine. Now, how much dae I owe ye? I've no time till stan' banterin' in this weather."

"That'll be seven pounds and twenty-five pence, Peggy. Make it a roun' seven. I'm feelin' generous the day."

"Oh, me eyesight! That's a shackin' price, Ernie. Ye cud have gat a week's groceries fer that twenty years ago."

"Well Peggy, we have come a long way since then ye know. Even the price af dulse hus gone up." He asked for his money. Peggy shoved it in his hand and he popped it into his shoulder bag. He nodded his ginger head in the direction of the Friar's house and enquired.

"Why's Bert standin' all cowboy like wi' a hanky roun' 'is gub? Hus he joined the country an' western club up the road, or hus he takin' up robbin' in daylight?"

"Luk here, Ernie, I don't give a fiddlers damn if he's joined the Christmas rhymers. He gat 'is hoofs out on Monday mornin' an' Elsie made 'im cover up 'is bake till he gets 'is false one's in, an' no harm till ye

I wud huv done the same. I can't stan' a man wi' lips frayed at th' edges."

"Well I niver. Auld Bert is gettin' fitted wi' false teeth." Ernie rubbed his chin in thought "Do ye think it'll improve him any, like? Is he goin' through a midlife crisis or somethin'?" he enquired his head tilted to the side.

"Midlife! If he's in midlife he'll live till a hundred an' twenty," exploded Peggy.

"Catch yerself on Ernie, the maun's sixty if he's a day."

"I see your Rab's there wi' him, an here comes Lynus wi' a few other cronies in tow." He hesitated for a couple of seconds to see what was going on.

"Here Peg, take a luk at that! They've all disappeared inta Bert's house. Maybe they're plannin' a heist on the bank."

"Maybe they're plannin' tae rob yoursel', Ernie. If I were you I'd get a move on." Peggy dunted Ernie in the ribs with her bony elbow.

Ernie winched with the pain, then recommended she got corks fitted to her elbows for the protection of others before he climbed back into his van.

"Nye, we're all in agreement then? Hae ye gat yer stories all tied up nice an' tightly. We don't want some buck eejit ballsin' up the whole sheebang by drappin' a spanner in the works."

Rab was holding centre court, trying to act out the part of judge and jury.

"Do ye think we stan' a chance, like? I hope th' insurance company doesn't smell a rat or nathin'," said Harry, the driver of the hired car that had hit Rab's old banger.

"Ye'll be as happy as a pig in shit, I tell ye," wheezed Rab. "Sure Andy an' Roy were witness tae the whole incident."

"Ah, but they weren't, Rab!" whined Harry.

"Aye, *we* effin' know that, slabber mouth! But the bloody insurance company does'nae. Fer Christ's sake, will someone hit him oan the back af the head wi' a blunt abject."

Rab felt a twinge in his chest and slipped one of his wee heart tablets under his tongue. "Luk bugger lugs! Andy an' Roy were standin' at the bus stop, mindin' their own business when you in yer hired car came along the road. A dog ran out fram no-where an' the next thing ye knew yer fut slipped aff the brake onto th' accelerator an' ye rammed inta the back aff mine. They witnessed the whole bloody thing. Are ye stupid or what?"

"There wuz no dog, Rab. An' will they twig on I hired the car just till crash it".

"I know there wuz no bloody dog. Neither were there two bloody witnesses. But the flamin' insurance company doesn't know that either. An' how the hell were you till know ye were goin' tae crash in the hired car! Now *I* know ye were goin' till crash, but *they* don't. An' they can't prove it, can they? I hope tae fuck ye don't get oan like this in front aff the solicitor. Ye gat it right the first time. Fer Christ's sake don't go changin' yer bloody story at this late date."

"Alright! Alright Rab! Me nerves are just goin' till pot." Harry sat wiping the sweat off his brow with a hanky that was covered in oil, and lifted his oil-stained face. "What if we lose, will I be out aff pocket like?"

"How the fuck can ye lose? Ye were fully comp, fer Christ's sake!" bellowed Rab.

"Aye, I know that alright. But do ye think they'll buy the lot aff us claimin' fer whiplash. Like, there's four aff us fram the one street claimin', ye must remember." He shifted uneasily in his chair. "Doe's that nat luk a teeny weeny bit suspicious, like?"

"An yer car, Rab, wuz ready fer the scrapheap, an auld rutht bucket. Even if I do thay tho, Rab," remarked the toothless Bert.

"Don't you start, Friars, fer God's sake! Jaysus, all you hae to say is ye were a passenger in my car," spat Rab.

"But I ..."

"But I what? You were goin' till say ye jumped in after the crash there, weren't ye? Ye stupid twat! Why don't ye go the whole hog an' tell the solicitor no-wan wuz in the bloody car, nat even the bloody driver, an that wuz me!" Rab raged sarcastically.

"No-one *wath* in the car, Rab. Remember, we weren't even in th' vithinity," lisped Bert.

"Why the hell dae ye think we're payin' Andy an' Roy till go witness? Don't you go actin' the maggot, fer cryin' out loud. Jaysus, but yer all gormless. Luk here, just listen till me. I was travelling up the road – at normal speed, min' ye don't ferget. I went to turn right. The car behind, that's Harry nye, was comin' up. A dog ran out an' Harry braked. The next thing he knew his fut had slipped aff the brake an' hit th' accelerator an' he shot forwards an' hit me slap on the back af th' car full force. Me, Peggy, Lynus an' Bert were in the car, two witnesses – that's Andy an' Roy sittin' there – saw the whole bloody thing. Nye there wuz no-one else about, so there are no other flamin' witnesses tae go agin us. Is that clear till yes, ar dae I have tae go over it till I'm blue in the bake?"

Rab rummaged in his coat pocket to get his *Ventolin* spray. He had to give himself a double dose, he was so winded after this tirade.

"Right then, Rab. So we all get three-and-a-half thousand quid, an' Andy an' Roy here get a hundred each fer witnessin' somethin that niver happened, like?" asked Harry.

"Got it in wan, Harry. Only it mightn't be three-an'-a-half thousand. It cud be only fifteen hundred or on the other haun it cud be five gran'. Ye just don't know nye. Nye will ye wipe that stupid luk aff yer bake till we get our symptoms right."

Rab continued to detail the symptoms of whiplash to all in the room. He suggested they make another visit to their doctors for more medication, and that they wear their neck braces at all times until they received the money from the insurance company.

"An' another thing. Vary yer symptoms a bit. Don't all say 'Me neck won't turn roun' like gormless gits'. Make up a few headaches an' stiff backs an' such. An' don't go walkin' in wi' a limp an' say yer necks sore, fer Christ's sake."

"Will I get the same money even though I wuz drivin' the hired car?" asked a worried Harry.

"Dae ye think these are made outa crystal?" answered a highly agitated Rab holding onto his crotch. "Holy Jaysus, they're flesh an blood like yer oan, only sametimes I think ye hae nan fer yer actin' like a big girl's blouse. Af coorse ye will. Nye fuck up or clear aff," answered a weary Rab.

"Did ye give Peggy the gen on all this, Rab?" inquired Lynus.

"Don't worry about Peggy, Lynus. She's done this afore, so she's nat as green as you lat," Rab informed Lynus, his bad eye twitching with a slight touch of nerves.

"Are you nat a wee bit dilatory about lyin' Rab, after spendin' a bit af time locked up once yersel' like?" Lynus inquired, a worried expression imprinted on his face.

"Nat at all, it wuz wee buns. Nathin till dae all day but laze aroun'. The flamin' jails here are like hotels. Anyway, nane aff us will be goin' till jail, so haule yer tongue ye excuse fer a beezum."

"What's a beezum,Rab?" asked Lynus.

"A thing ye brush the flur wi'. It huz a head like yersel' Lynus, tied together wi' string so it won't fall apart."

"How long do ye think it'll be before we get the money Rab?" inquired Harry.

"As I said before, me balls aren't crystal or I wud take up fortune tellin'. But I wud say we'll be in Tenerife by August, me auld mucker, an' I'll hae a wee car an' all," answered Rab rubbing his hands together.

"As quick as that?" said a delighted Lynus.

"As quick as a hare in a greyhoun' race Lynus, so start packin' yer begs wi' suntan lotion."

"Andy an' me won't get far wi' a hundred quid," huffed Roy.

"Ye'd travel a hell aff a lat less wi'out it," joked Rab.

"The Devil finds work for idle hands alright."

Sarah was staring out of her kitchen window. She had spotted the six men leave her daughter's house and had described them as being a shifty-looking lot, especially Rab.

"I don't like thon man one bit."

"What man?" Elsie shifted herself from her mother's settee and made her way to the kitchen window for a look.

"Thon Rab one. I don't like him one bit. His eyebrows are joined together, a sign he was born till hang."

"Who told ye that bit of nonsense? That's superstition," said her daughter belligerently.

"The Kray's eyebrows were close knit An they were no saints!" Her mother was also in a fighting mood this morning. "I can see through thon man like a sheet of glass, he's that transparent. No substance or backbone, just a big pockle of dung. What th' hell are they all doin' stuck up each others bums so early in the mornin'? Up to some kind of mischief, no doubt."

"It's half past eleven, for heaven's sake, Ma! It's not exactly the dawn of day. Give over will ye? An' stop lookin' out of that window."

"I was just havin' a wee jook to see if they're comin' wi' the gate."

"Ma! It'll be at least next week before they come with the gate. They have to make the ruddy thing first. Give them time," Elsie pleaded, adding, "I hope they don't ask for the old one. Bert is goin' to use it for our back garden to keep the kids from runnin' over his rhubarb later on."

"See! You're givin' off about the kids as well. I'm not the only one who's moanin' aroun' here." Sarah waved her finger at Elsie as if reprimanding a child. "You can be cranky yourself when it suits ye."

"I'm not cranky. The kids can run about in my garden anytime they like except when Bert's rhubarb is growin'. We like a bit to keep our bowels regular, that's all."

"Ach, *Bonamint* will do that!" snapped Sarah.

"*Bonamint* binds you up, ma. It's a known fact that too many laxatives make the bowels sluggish."

"Poppycock!"

"They do!"

"Go an' flah will ye!"

"What does flah mean, ma?"

I don't know, just do it!"

Elsie was mystified as to what her mother was referring to. Was flah Irish for the 'F' word?

"Did ye see Joan Collins on the TV yesterday, ma, she looks well for her age mind ye."

"Facelift!" screeched Sarah.

"She has not had a face lift."

"Thon one's had more face lifts than husbands!"

"Your thinkin' of Elizabeth Taylor, ma. She's had quite a few husbands. I think it was eight at the last count."

"I'm not bloody senile yet. It was Joan Collins I tell ye!"

"Well she says she's had no face lifts."

"That's like me sayin' I've had no run-ins wi' that auld doll up th' stairs. Look, if thon woman stood near a fire she'd melt."

"Do you ever have a conversation where you don't run anyone down ma? You run everybody down, even wee Percy, an' he would do no-one a bit of harm."

"Well, ye wouldn't give it the kiss of life if it died. God knows what ye'd pick up with all them weemen he goes about with. I wouldn't be surprised if he has had a fling wi' thon Peggy one, skinny Lizzie from the bone yard. She'd carve a sausage for dinner before she'd buy a bit of dacent meat."

"I don't think Peggy's feelin' too well this week so don't go nyamerin' at her in the street." Elsie thought she'd warn her mother away from starting any arguments with Peggy, just in case she thought Elsie was talking about her behind her back.

"What's wrong with her now? God knows what that headcase doesn't have isn't worth talkin' about. The doctors must have run out of illnesses on that woman."

"Just keep out of her road, that's all. Do you hear me?"

"Aye, sure what th' hell would I be doin' talkin till the likes of her anyway," said Sarah, her face screwed up as if she had drunk a glassful of vinegar.

"I'm away over home. I'd rather look at Bert's toothless gub than listen to you runnin' all and sundry down."

"Away you go then. Ye can take a drop of that soup in the pot over for the crathur. It's about to go off anyway."

Elsie was beaten once more; her mother had shown a kindly streak by offering her soup. Only Sarah could do a thing like that, make Elsie feel guilty. Before she went out the door she lifted her mothers shopping list and felt like crying an ocean of tears.

Peggy had put the kettle on for a cup of tea. She sat huddled in front of an old electric fire in the kitchen planning revenge on her errant husband. She knew in her heart he had done the dreaded deed on Saturday night, but how had he done it. She had broken out in small blisters down below. Surely to God he hadn't used a blow torch! Knowing Rab, he would go to any lengths to have a bit of a laugh at her expense. Hadn't he left her outside one of her men friends house stark naked and inebriated in the middle of winter. Rapped the door he did and left her leaning drunk against the door-frame like a spectre, and the man living beside a graveyard! The awful thing was, his wife was in at the time and she collapsed with fright!

The doctor had to be called out to sedate her and the police took Peggy home wrapped in a policeman's overcoat. By a stroke of luck the man was a policeman himself and had managed to get out of that sticky situation by bribing fellow officers with a twenty pound note each. They let on to his wife that the woman had escaped from the psychiatric hospital but heaven knows what the doctor thought. Mind you, they all knew Peggy. Even the doctor who was sick to the gills with her visits to the surgery. Needless to say, that was the end of that amour with the nymphomaniac of Ballyhornet!

The kettle started to whistle and Peggy jumped. God, how her nerves were on edge. She turned down the gas under the kettle and wet the tea. Before pouring herself out a mug of the hot brew she popped two *Valium* in her mouth and washed them down with a drink of water. She grimaced at the taste of the water. The only way she could suffer the taste of water was when it was mixed with gin, but the green bottle stood empty on the windowsill of the kitchen, teasing her. She poured tea into her large mug and cupped it in her hands to warm them. She shook her slippers off her huge feet and wiggled her long toes in front of the bars of the electric fire. After a few minutes she felt warmer and her nerves settled. The silence enveloped her and she could almost hear her brain tick over with ideas of how to commit the perfect murder. What about weed-killer? Didn't Rab keep some of that in his garden shed? No. Too easily traced. What about changing his heart tablets with her *Canderel* sweeteners, No. His heart tablets had no taste. What about scaring the shit out of him? His heart was that weak he would die on the spot! How? She had almost fallen into a doze when the idea hit her between the eyes. Make him fall ass over tit! His heavy frame could not take the strain of falling and his heart would give in. No need to hide the body under the patio like the unsuspecting crathur in *Brookside*. It would look like he died from natural causes. And if he didn't die, well, nothing would be lost anyway. At least she would have tried, and that was better than not trying at all.

Voices coming from the back garden interrupted her murderous thoughts. Slipping on her carpet slippers she got up from her chair and peered out the kitchen window.

Rab was leaning on the fence that separated them from old Maggie Johnson next door. Him and Maggie appeared to be deep in conversation. From where Peggy was standing it looked like Maggie was in a bit of a state. She was pointing her finger in all directions and holding her chest with the her free hand. What th' hells goin' on there, thought Peggy. I hope thon Rab one hasn't told her some auld cock an' bull story about break-ins on lonely widows just to scare the livin' daylights out af her. That man is a menace till society he is. I may go out an' see what's goin' on.

"Pussy! Wit pussy, Maggie?"

Peggy almost fell over herself in her haste to get down the garden. She thought her husband was telling Maggie Johnson about her disappearing pubic hair. She was getting herself ready to slap him round the ear when she spied Rab's wellington-covered foot stuck in a bucket. Why th' hells blazes is he standin' wi' his fut in a bucket' thought she in bewilderment.

"My Tiddles has disappeared, Rab. You didn't see him, did ye, in yer travels?" asked a worried-looking Maggie.

"Nye, Mrs Johnson. If I saw your Tiddles I wud make sure he came till no harm, ye know that Maggie. God knows I hae a saft spat fer cats. I just love then till *death*," he emphasised the last word.

"Rab Kirk," hissed Peggy behind his back, making sure Maggie couldn't hear. "What are you doin' wi' thon cat in the bucket?"

"I'm drownin' the effin' bleeder," said he, through gritted teeth. "Now fuck off inta th' house afore auld Maggie here cottons oan."

"What did ye say, Rab?" asked Maggie, who was slightly deaf.

"I said I'll feed it if I fin' it, Maggie."

"Ach, I know ye will, Rab. Sure I know ye love all Gods creatures. Ye've only till luk at the way ye fuss after them birds af yers."

"I dae that alright, Maggie." Tiddles struggled a bit, Rab thrust his boot deeper into the bucket and the moggy splashed around like a demented rat.

"Stap that, Robert Kirk. "Yer a wicked get, dae ye know that?" Peggy was trying to shove Rab so he would lose his footing on the cat, but his bulky frame wouldn't budge.

"Frig aff, woman, will ye! Givus another minute, an' th' effer will be a goner." He hissed out of the corner of his mouth.

"I'd be lost wi'out thon wee cat af mine, Rab. I just love the wee dear."

"So dae I, Maggie. I pray till God it turns up fer me heart cries out till ye in yer grief," answered Rab, his face as solemn as a funeral parlour's assistant, except for the twitch in his bad eye. "I wudnae like to think af that wee crathur sufferin' for the lack af love, or even dyin' af thirst fer that matter."

"Do ye think whoever finds him will give him a wee drink, Rab?"

"Nye Maggie, I wouldnae see the wee soul want fer a drap af water ye know that!"

"God, Rab, but yer a saint. I know my pussy's in safe hands when you're about. I'll go up the street an' see if I can find him."

"You dae that Maggie, an' I'll fin' a nice wee cosy bed fer him in the mean time."

"Yer a lop-eyed bastard, do ye know that?" exclaimed Peggy, once Maggie was out of earshot. "Let thet cat go, dae ye hear me, or I swear I'll have yer guts fer garters."

"Ye can use cat gut, fer th' flamin' things dead!" laughed Rab as he stared into the bucket. "Now get me the spade till I bury the fuckin' thing afore auld Johnson gets back."

"Get it yerself, ye ugly bastard!"

"Nye Peggy, don't go all lovey dovey oan me. I know ye love till use bad language when yer sexually aroused," Rab chided.

"Fuck aff!" yelled Peggy, as she fled up the garden into the safety of her warm kitchen.

"Jaysus, but yer beautiful when yer angry, dae ye know that? Fer a wee second there I cud huv jumped oan ye wi' lust." Rab could hardly control his laboured breathing as he made his way to the garden shed to get the spade. He wheezed and spluttered as he searched for the tools for his grizzly task. Finding a good sharp spade, he eyed his garden for a spot that didn't already harbour a dead cat. Not an easy task as there were more mounds than a family of moles could have made. He spied an even spot under the lilac tree and started to dig. He dropped the cat into the hole and hastily covered it up.

Peggy could barely control the urge to lift the carving knife out of the kitchen drawer and stab him between the shoulder blades. She could always bury him beside the cat!.

"I can't find him, Rab." Maggie had returned from her search. "Will ye keep a good eye out fer him?"

That's a geg, thought Rab. "I hae only gat wan good eye, but I'll keep it out alright Maggie."

"Oh, I am sorry Rab. No offence meant."

“Nae offence taken, Maggie. I’ll hae a wee jook up the street after I’ve finished plantin’ these daffodils an’ tulips!” He scratched his head as he thought up a good answer. “In fact I think I’ll plant a wee pussy willow instead.”

“Yer a saint, Rab do ye know that?” said Maggie.

“Aye, an I think I’ll give the pussy willow a wee name. I’ll call it *Tiddles*, just fer you Maggie.”

“May God bless ye, Rab, May God bless ye.”

“An God bless yer wee pussy. I suppose he’s just havin’ a wee rest under the shade af a tree.”

“There’s nat many leaves on the tree’s this time af the year, Rab, to give him shade.”

“Well now Maggie, it won’t be long afore there’s leaves oan this tree wi’ the lawn feed I use!”

“An’ what’s that, Rab?”

“Well Maggie, I don’t believe in usin’ auld artificial shit. I use nathin’ but the best.”

“Like what?”

“Now that wud be lettin’ the cat out af the bag, Maggie. Us gardeners hae our oan secrets.”

12

Saturday, 23 March

"Ye know Elsie, I can't for the life of me see why Alec and I had to be at that meetin' the other Tuesday."

Elsie was sitting at the bottom of the stairs, near the telephone, the receiver stuck to her ear, listening to her sister Helen natter, a welcome change from her mother and the relief could be heard in her voice.

"Well, I was fed up to the eye teeth havin' to see to that woman on me own, Helen."

"But, were me and Alec *really* needed?" asked Helen.

Elsie sighed, "It wasn't a case of being *needed*. I just wanted you to see what I have to suffer day in an' day out. My nerves are shattered, between Bert an' his teeth, me ma's gate, an' now poor auld Percy. How my heart goes out to that poor wee man. I saw him yesterday at the shops and he looks as if he's aged by twenty years."

"Well now Elsie, he should stay out of the kitchen if he can't stand the heat."

"What's that suppose to mean?" asked Elsie.

"He shouldn't have become a councillor."

"I'm sure he didn't envisage the likes of my ma bein' on his agenda, Helen."

"Well now Elsie, who would? She's a law onto herself is our mother."

"There should be a law that forbids women like her to have children," retorted Elsie.

"Then we wouldn't be here, Elsie."

"That mightn't be such a bad thing, Helen. What we never knew we would never have missed. I believe in reincarnation anyway. We would have been born to other parents, and God knows they could not have been any worse than the one's we had, and still have, at least one of them anyway."

"What religion are you now Elsie?" asked Helen in an exasperated tone. "It was only last week you were a Jehovah's Witness."

"Nothin', I made up one."

Helen massaged her brow before continuing, and yelled at her husband. "Alec, will you dissolve me two headache pills? I can feel a New Age religion being born." Returning to her sister she asked, "Elsie, tell me do, how can ye make up a religion?"

"Well, I've gone off all the others. There's no excitement in them. There was a programme on the TV the other night about some sect, I've forgotten their name, who swear they have been regressed back in time. One woman had been Anne Boleyn in King Henry's reign. Her throat is always sore and she shivers at the sight of anything that's sharp."

"My throat is always sore. As for sharp instruments, well, Alec won't let me near one in case I behead him in a temper fit."

"But this woman takes to her bed with a headache every May the nineteenth," Elsie's voice had raised two octaves as she relayed this tale to her sister.

"Elsie, I take to my bed every other day with a headache! But I don't think I'm Anne Boleyn. Have you been smoking funny cigarettes lately or eating mushrooms from the forest up the road?"

"But May the nineteenth, don't ye see? That was the date Anne Boleyn lost her head." Elsie was beginning to sound like Miss Marple on a murder mission.

"I'm beginning to wonder if *you* haven't lost your head. For goodness sake, don't go telling the doctor this or he'll get you committed to the mental home."

"I'm not losing my head. I'm only making up a religion to suit my needs."

"I think you need your head examined. Anyway, if you believe in reincarnation it doesn't necessarily mean you'll come back as human being. You could come back as an animal or, even worse, a neighbour of our mother."

"God, that's worse than burnin' in hell, Helen. Never mind me, I'm just feeling a bit fanciful at the minute. Whenever I feel down I go into a dreamworld to keep me sane."

"Do you ever wonder how we turned out to be so sane?" asked Helen capriciously.

"And what makes you think we're sane, Helen?"

"Well, none of us has ended up in the mental ward – yet!"

"Give me time Helen, just give me a little more time. I can feel a nervous breakdown breathin' down me neck. It was only yesterday I imagined ... no ... I didn't imagine ... I did hear voices coming from the washin' machine."

"Voices from the washin' machine! Elsie, me thinks you are havin' me on."

"No, Helen! I'm speakin' in dead earnest. As I was loadin' the wretched thing it told me to shove Bert's *Calvin Klein* underpants up his backside."

"Don't tell me Bert wears *Calvin Kleins!* That's more hilarious than tellin' me the washin' machine spoke to you, for heaven's sake," laughed Helen hysterically.

"There's more sex appeal in a potato than Bert. Surely to God he doesn't romp about in *Calvin Kleins* with thon bandy legs of his. For God's sake, tell me he doesn't before I wet myself laughin'."

"Indeed he does. He loves himself, ye know. God knows no-one else does, apart from those auld dolls at the bowlin' club who rally round him like he was Liam Neeson or some other film star, so he might as well. He prances round the house in his sexy drawers an' white bowlin' socks with a diamond pattern up the sides."

"Even now? When he has no teeth?"

"Yes Helen, even now! He humps around in his underpants grinnin' from ear to ear with that toothless gub of his. I ask you, would you say it was cruel of me to deny him sex?"

"I would say it was cruel of him to ask for sex. Is he a vampire or somethin'. Can he not see his reflection in the mirror?"inquired Helen, almost struck dumb by her sister's last remark.

"The strange thing is, Helen, why do all the auld dolls at the bowlin' club thinks he's the bee's knees? They clamour for his attention at the annual dance. They even have a draw to see who gets the next dance with it."

"Do you mean the blue cauliflower brigade?"

"The blue cauliflower brigade, Helen? What's that, when you're writin' home?"

"Did you ever have a look at those women who play bowls? They all have wee tight perms and their hair dyed blue. Hence the heads resemble blue cauliflowers. They sit in their tweed skirts with their legs wide open showin' off their thermals, then they cross their arms under their enormous bosoms as if they were two melons slung in a hammock. The men get all excited as they imagine they're witnessing older versions of Samantha Fox. Then the auld dolls sit and talk in hushed tones as they watch the men bowl, more often than not about sex, as really they are all inverted sex maniacs. They probably only ever had sex with their husbands to have the one child to take the bad look of them. Well, one child proves to the neighbours their husbands can actually rise to the occasion, if you get my meaning. Half of them were lucky to get a man, they're that horsy lookin'. An' I'm sure they didn't look any better when they were young. Whenever a bowl kisses the jack they jump up and down an' wiggle about that much you would swear they were having an orgasm. It's the only thrill they ever get, as they are usually widows on the lookout for a man."

Elsie could do nothing but laugh at her sister's outburst, but was brought down to earth by a sudden thought.

"Do you know, Helen, you could have hit the nail on the head. That Bert one only comes alive when he goes to the bowls. Slaps on the aftershave, and he goes into a rage when his whites aren't properly ironed. His bloody wardrobe is full of bowlin' gear. If he was invited to a weddin' he'd have to go in his whites, and the only funerals he attends are those of departed bowlers."

"Need I say anymore, Elsie? When he gets his new teeth he'll have to be grounded for his own safety," joked Helen.

"That's *why* he got the bloody things removed! To make the ugly gob more attractive with a new set of pearlies."

"Do you not think it would take more than a new set of teeth to turn Bert into a sex object?" Helen burst out laughing again.

"I heard all that, Elthie. Yer mind's warped, it is. Me mouf wuz killin' me, that's why I gat them out." Bert had come down from the toilet, where he had heard Elsie's side of the conversation, his face puce with rage.

"He's gone all irritated now, Helen. I think we've hurt his feelin's, God love him."

"Ah, go to hell!" bellowed Bert, farting as he passed his wife on the stairs.

"Did you hear that?" exclaimed Elsie. "The ugly gets just parped and then told me to go to hell."

"Aye I did, Elsie. If I were you I'd hide his balls ... er ... bowls, that is."

"It wuth only a wee body cough," retorted Bert.

"I think you were right the first time, I should hide his balls. Somewhere apart from the comfort of his *Calvin Kleins* which are probably hummin' from that outburst of flatulence. Which reminds me. Bert!" yelled Elsie, "will ye wrap that scarf round your mouth. It reminds me of your arsehole!"

Helen's squeals of laughter echoed from the receiver. Bert skulked into the kitchen and poured himself out a cup of tea. He passed Elsie on the stairs as he made his way into the living room, cup in hand, and gave his wife a rude gesture with the fingers of his free hand. Elsie laughed too. For a few minutes her mind had been diverted from her mother, but not for long.

"Here, what are we goin' to do with that woman? No jokin', she is goin' to be quite a handful in a few years time."

"She's quite a handful now, Helen. What am I goin' to do if she dies on me?"

"Bury her!"

"I know that! I mean, what am I goin' to do with her body before they bury her?"

"Christ Almighty, *I* don't want it! Alec wouldn't have it in the house for a start. And Petra would have a doggy breakdown at the sight of a rickle of bones lyin' in a coffin."

"Well, we don't expect him to eat her, for heaven's sake, Helen! He could have a wee lick but he doesn't have to make a meal of her," joked Elsie. Her nerves started to jangle at the thought of her mother lying in her coffin for all to view.

"You two are thtark ravin' mad! If ye cud hear yourselves ye wud thwear ye were in the nut houth." Bert lisped through toothless gums from the living room.

"Well now, I'm not havin' her here! I wouldn't be able to sleep for the duration. Her spirit would be earthbound, I know it!" Elsie shouted back.

"I thought ye believed in reincarnation a couple of minutes ago. Will ye make up yer bloody mind, woman! The woman's nat even dead yet, tho thut up will yes. Anyway she'll outlive the lat af us. We'll be laid out in *her* flat for the neighbours to view *us*."

"He could be right ye know, Elsie. That woman has no intentions of departing this earth before she has us all round the bend."

"Oh here Helen, I'm off to get a cup of tea to calm my ravaged nerves. I'll give you a ring when the gate arrives."

"Do you really think that's necessary, Elsie! Have we to come and admire it or somethin'?"

"You might have to come to help me hold her down. If it isn't right she is goin' to have kittens an' wee Percy will be in danger of gettin' his wig rammed up his rectum."

"Oh heavens, Elsie, I think I have to go to the toilet. Me bowels are playin' up again. Cheerio."

Elsie replaced the receiver, shook her head with frustration and ambled into the kitchen. It's funny how the mention of my ma can end a good conversation an' empty a room, she thought as she poured her tea. It can't *all* be my imagination. I never saw a roomful of people disappear as quickly as I did at that meetin'. I must give Isobel a call to see how things are over in Lurgan.

The thought of phoning her sister had no sooner entered her mind the doorbell rang.

"Will ye get that, Bert?"

"I'm nat dressed yet. Get it yerself," growled Bert.

"Jaysus, but you're one lazy baste... Ach, Isobel, come on in. I'm glad to see you. I was just about to give you a call on the phone."

Isobel stepped into the hallway and shushed her sister's welcome away with a wave of the hand.

"Sorry, Elsie, I don't mean to be rude but my nerves are away with it."

"Nat yer's as well? I've never met a family so preoccupied wif nerves in all me life."

"Ah, shut up, Bert. Your that easy goin' ye don't have a nerve in your body to go bad."

She turned her attention to her sister again. "What's wrong, Isobel?"

"That bloody mother of ours! She has been on the phone no less than four times this mornin'. She says you've taken your phone off the hook for badness." Isobel went straight into her sister's kitchen as usual and put the kettle on. As she went about the task of milking and sugaring a mug she rambled on about how she was going to annihilate her mother with one of her own support stockings."

"And if *that* doesn't work I'll slit her scrawny neck with a razor. Where's the coffee, Elsie? Oh, it's alright. I've found it. Here, put a spoonful in that mug while I put on a bit of toast. I haven't had a bite to eat since last night. Where's the bread? Never mind, I've found that too. Does she ever sleep? She was able to tell me what time everyone in the street came in at last night. Even those who didn't come home at all. Where's the butter? It's alright, Elsie, don't bother lookin', I've found it. How's Bert's mouth? Is it any better?"

Elsie's head felt light as she watched her sister race round the kitchen like a whirling dervish.

"What's all the racket about in here?" Bert stood at the kitchen door, watching his sister-in-law with amusement. "Are ye makin' me a cup, sexthy drawers, for I'll have one even though I've already had a cup af tea."

"It's auld fan tiddle across the road. She's been on the phone six times this mornin' with an update as to what the people of Ballyhornet get up to."

"Now Isobel, you're exaggerating again. You're only after tellin' me it was four times," reprimanded Elsie with a wave of her finger.

"Well it felt like *ten* times. And not only that, I had to tell that auld nosey parker Adams off for shovin' his neb in my affairs."

"Who's Adams?" asked Elsie.

"Ach, he's a wee know-all. He's a one-man neighbourhood watch. He had the bare-faced cheek to take ten thousand pounds off the price of my house. He takes a pleasure in gloating about our house not selling as quickly as the ones beside him. I informed him of the fact our house was detached and his was only a semi. Would he admit to my house being bigger than his? No! He harped on an' on an' on."

"Just like yerself, eh, Ithobel. Jaythus, I'm away back into the other room to get me head showered. There's a black-an'-white film on the television."

"Ye pay for a colour television licence and he watches black-an'-white movies. I sometimes wonder if he has senile dementia." Elsie threw her head back in dismay.

"Did you take the phone off the hook, Elsie?"

"I did not! I was on the phone to our Sandra for nearly an hour an' then Helen rang. She's been tryin' to get through when it was engaged."

"I think I'm goin' mad, Elsie. Liam is convinced of this. In fact he told me I was just like my mother and that he was goin' to leave me if I don't change my ways." She poured the water into her cup and stirred vigorously. The toaster popped out her slice of toast. She buttered it and then proceeded to crunch her way through it. "I told him to bugger off himself. He wont get another eejit to wash his rugby kit twice a week. Do you know, I go through a mountain of washing powder to get that auld muck off his kit. An' he scrapes all that filthy muck off his boots over the kitchen floor as if it was an honour to wipe up after him."

"Has no-one made an offer on your house yet, Isobel?"

"Not a one. In fact no-one has come to view it. We're goin' to take the sign down before it takes root an' extend the kitchen. Make it more country home in decor. Put a pine table in and an Aga cooker, an' then put a wee conservatory on the back for me an' Liam to sit in of a summer evenin'."

"I thought you were goin' to leave Liam a few moments ago."

"An' have to split the proceedings of the house? Ye must be jokin'."

"You were the one that said it, not me, Isobel."

"Ach, don't take any heed of me. My head's that far up me bum I don't know me arse from me elbow."

"Your language is gettin' worse Isobel. You must be attending too many GAA meetin's with Liam," rebuked Elsie who blushed after doing so, as rebuking others was not in her nature.

"I'll have to curb it in front of Helen an' Alec. They're disgusted with me marrying a Taig, without resorting to the language of the Falls Road."

"It's more like the lingo of Ballyhornet. The Falls Road people are more polite than this lot. I wish I had a house to sell to get to hell out of here." Elsie's eyes misted over. "All I have to look forward to is a Saturday night up at Rab an' Peggy's house, an' that usually ends off in disaster."

Isobel started on the subject of her mother once more.

That one across the road is still goin' on about her nippin' ankle. That ulcer of hers is no more than a pin prick. The way she goes on you would think it was the size of a volcano. As for her bunions, I told her to rub an onion on them."

"Rub an onion on your bunion! That sounds almost poetic. Where did ye hear that remedy?"

"The television doctor on *This Morning* said it was an old wives tale that worked," Isobel explained. "That woman will make medical history! Eighty-nine an' hardly a pain or ache. Do ye think we could organise a murder weekend in that hotel in Dublin? We could really murder me ma an' no-one would be the wiser. Blame it on the chef or somethin'. It's the only way we're goin' to get rid of her, ye know."

"Well, she does have some redeeming characteristics, even if you do have to search deeply for them."

"Like what? You're only playin' devil's advocate, Elsie. I bet you can't think of *one* off th' top of your head. Come on, our Elsie, tell me one good turn that woman's done for any of us." Isobel stood in a defiant manner, her right hand splayed on her hip, the other waving in Elsie's direction.

"Isobel, please don't try to intimidate me. I'm the one who takes the brunt of everyone's bad moods in this family, an' quite frankly I'm ready to run off. Then who'll look after mother? I'm sure it wont be you *or* Helen." She retrieved a hanky from her apron pocket and blew her nose in a bid to quell the flow of tears from her eyes that were now smarting with the effort of holding them back.

"I'm not intimidating you," replied Isobel in her own defence.

"Indeed you are. I'm fed up being an Aunt Sally to all my family." Elsie could be just as defensive when riled.

Isobel stopped talking and looked at her sister, realising she had gone too far and offered to take her to Marks & Spencers to do her shopping by way of apology.

Elsie cried in earnest and ran from the kitchen. The tears blinded her as she fled up the stairs and locked herself in the bathroom. She had no money to spend, so what was the use of wasting her energy going to Marks & Spencers in the first place.

ꝏ ꝏ ꝏ ꝏ ꝏ

Rab had gone out on the blatter. He had decided to visit Sir Robert Townsley and his exotic birds. The feathered variety. Sir Robert was a confirmed bachelor. He spent his money on whiskey and birds of paradise. He lived in an old rambling red-brick house surrounded by five acres of land. Magnificent trees and overgrown rhododendron bushes ringed the land, hiding it from the prying eyes of the lower classes.

As Rab was more country than Belfast, plus a tad on the eccentric side, he was welcomed into the fold of the Townsley family. Sir Robert's mother had been a second cousin twice removed of Queen Victoria. The family had lived in Fermanagh in the late nineteenth century but had moved nearer Belfast when Sir Robert's father became director of a large merchant bank.

Sir Robert had been an only child reared by nannies and privately tutored. When his parents died he had inherited his father's title and become somewhat of a recluse. No-one was quite sure of its the title's validity, but it was never questioned. He sometimes employed Rab to take care of his precious birds when he decided to venture off to warmer climates in the winter. He received a pittance for this task, but would gladly have done the job for free and non-gratis. Sir Robert had just returned from a safari in Africa and a new delivery of exotic birds was expected any day. Rab made sure no cats ever got roaming on Sir Robert's land. If anyone was wanted for this task Rab would have been first in line, for his three favourite pastimes were looking after birds, killing cats and, the most important of all, getting shot of his wife for a few hours. Utter bliss.

Sir Robert called Rab "Bob". Having the same handle as himself he preferred "Bob" to "Rab". Bob sounded more refined, while Rab sounded Scottish. Sir Robert used Rab during the grouse shooting season when he donned a kilt to stalk the grounds of his estate, trying to convince himself that he was at Balmoral as a guest of the Queen.

Rab himself could be described as classless. He could mix with the upper and lower classes on equal terms, his country brogue masking his origins. The locals were used to seeing him roam the streets with his shotgun slung across his back. Even though the Troubles should have been a deterrent to this practice, the police turned a blind eye to this blatant display. Anyone else would have been arrested.

"How's the better half, Bob?" enquired Sir Robert. He had never met Peggy but from Rab's happy-go-lucky demeanour he had assumed he was happily married.

Rab laughed. "The better hauf? Jaysus, if thon wife af mine is the better hauf I must be bloody bad. I must bring her up tae meet ye Sir Robert, but I'll gae ye a warnin'. I'd down a couple af whiskies tae settle yer nerves if I were you afore ye meet it, fer she'd scare the livin' daylights out af a ghoul."

"Any good at the old rumpy pumpy, Bob? Does she keep you happy in that department? That's the main thing. A good filly is worth its weight in gold."

"Well, she does luk like a horse at times," joked Rab.

~~~~~

Major Bolsover had decided to visit the stable when he spotted Rab leave the estate to visit Sir Robert Townsley. Peggy had been pouring herself a mug of tea when she spied the Major climbing over her garden fence.

He appeared decidedly frustrated, his cheeks crimson with lust. He weaved his way up the garden. After peering right, left and behind him to see if the coast was clear, he tentatively opened the back door and slithered into Peggy's kitchen, quickly shutting the door behind him.

"Are we alone, my dear old gel. Is young Sharon out? Lord I do so hope she is, my dearest darling Peg." He stroked his handlebar mustache between finger and thumb, his bloodshot eyes searching the house for signs of Peggy's daughter.

Peggy jumped. In her shocked state she had let her mug overflow with scalding hot tea. The tea had run over the kitchen counter and dripped onto her feet. She knew the Major was not making a social call. By the look on his face he was feeling more than a trifle randy, and the horny auld git was going to be in for one hell of a surprise when he found out Peggy's finest feature had gone AWOL.

"Up the stairs, old bean! The galloping Major is ready for a good old mount." He slapped Peggy on the bottom and pinched her cheek which
~~~~~

was as flushed as his own, but not out of sexual frenzy – more out of panic at what his reaction would be when he clapped eyes on her bald and blistered genitalia.

"Nat nye, Major! Th' auld buck will be back soon." She tried to push him towards the back door but he refused to budge. "Will ye get out fer God's sake! Come back in few months time." She knew or rather hoped her thatch would have grown back by then.

"Come! Come, old gel. It's not like you, Peg old thing, to turn down a romp between the sheets. Anyway your old man is carrying his gun. He's most likely away to Sir Robert's. If I know Robert he'll have the old whiskey bottle out and the two of them will be half sozzled by now. Old Percy here is raring to break loose from his moorings, and I don't mean jolly old Councillor Thorndyke."

Peggy gazed down at the Major's crotch, Percy was indeed ready for action by the look of the bulge in his cavalry twills. She wondered if he would notice the absence of feathers round the nest. She shuddered. Yes, he would definitely notice. He liked to savour the sight before making the final attack. As far as the rest of her was concerned she could but a bag over her head. It wasn't her facial beauty that turned him on.

He thrust his loins in her direction. "You see what I mean, old gel. Get up those stairs before I gather you up in my arms and carry you up." Wishful thinking on his part. The weight of Peggy would have given him a coronary.

"No! No Major! I'm afraid I will hae to decline yer affer this mornin'. I'm beginnin' tae feel a wee bit guilty doin' this behin' Rab's back." She cursed Rab under her breath. She had been feeling horny herself for the past week; now the frigging auld bugger had ruined her chances of being laid for ages.

"Desist? You mean to say you are turning down a bit of the other? Good heavens old bean, you will not desist my offer! You haven't taken a vow of abstinence since our last rendezvous, my darling. Please! Don't tell me you have, my heart will break," said he in a throaty voice, as his cheeks twitched with nervous tics.

"Nooo! It's nathin' as drastic, Major. It's just that ..."

"Get them off, Peg! I can wait no longer." He lunged at Peggy and pulled down her knickers before she had time to defend herself. He grabbed her between the legs, then a stifled cry of alarm escaped from his lips.

"My God, Peg, It's as bald as a coot! Whatever happened old gel?" He pulled his hand back as if it had been burnt. His face dropped and his ardour froze.

"I think I've caught somethin' aff Rab's birds. Will ye mine if it's bald?"

"Will I mind! Indeed I will, I will certainly mind. Be off with you woman. I will away, for I will not go near it for fear of catching whatever it is you caught." He rushed to the sink and gave his hand a good wash under the running tap, as if he had been contaminated with some dreadful disease, then opened the back door and fled as if the hound of the Baskervilles was at his heels.

Peggy watched him as he jumped the fence. She cursed Rab in and out of hell. Lifting a framed photograph of her husband off the windowsill she peered at it and yelled, "God curse ye, if it's the last thing I dae it will be tae commit murder. Yer days are numbered, Robert Kirk, yer days are numbered!"

She hitched up her knickers and lit a cigarette, popped a couple of *Valium* with a slug from her gin bottle, and let her wicked thoughts weave a plan.

∞ ∞ ∞ ∞ ∞

Pip was standing outside his front door puffing on a joint he had hidden, for an emergency, in a shoebox in his wardrobe. Tonight was such an emergency. He had no money to go out boozing and he felt depressed. The joint did nothing other than heighten his feelings of loneliness and he stood staring into space. The clomp of feet brought him back to his senses and he straightened himself and peered into the darkness. In the night light he saw the outline of an Elvis look-a-like complete with guitar come down the street. As the figure closed in he recognised the acne covered face of Lynus.

"What's wrang wi' ye, young lad? Yer standin' thur like the Hunchback af Notre Dame."

"Ach, I'm sufferin' from PMT, Lynus," answered a depressed Pip.

"Get away a this. Only weemen suffer fram that."

"Nat this type, Lynus. It stands for pre-mental torture."

"Pre-mental torture? Why's that then?"

"I have to sit in on Saturday night. Paid back the money I owed Friars next door. The wee shite tuk every last penny I hud. I hope he chokes on his drink the night. Imagine a virile young stud as meself havin' to sit in on a Saturday night without the comfort of a sexy bit af stuff to satisfy me needs."

"That's terrible, Pip. He tuk the lat, ye say?" Lynus dandered up Pip's path and asked for a dreg.

Pip handed Lynus the joint that was almost down to the cardboard tip. "Aye, he tuk the fuckin' lat, left me without the price af a pint, on a Saturday of all nights."

"Whatever happened till yer Hugh Grant image Pip? Did the marlies drap outa yer gub then?"

"Ach, that wuz only a passin' fad. Anyway, it's no use talkin' polite when ye haven't two pennies till rub together."

"Come on out wi' me Pip. I'll buy ye a few fer auld times."

Pip stared at Lynus and straightened up at the sight. "What the fuck have ye on! An' what's that ye huv plastered on yer bloody hair?"

"Dae ye like it?" Lynus burled round to show off his outfit to full effect. "I sat up all last night sewin' on the sequins."

"It's yer flamin' overalls, Lynus!"

"Aye, but I bleached them, an' they came up a lovely light blue. I put a wee bit af velvet inta the battem af the legs till turn them inta flares like. Dae ye nat think I made a good jab af them then?"

Pip felt sorry for him. "Ach, I suppose yer doin' no-one any harm, Lynus. Nat like some I cud mention." He nodded his head in the direction of next door and cursed, "Fuckin' wee runt. Him an' his friggin' sidekick Godzilla."

"Dae ye like my *piece af resistance?*" Lynus pointed to his belt. He had covered it with bits of old toilet chain he had found in his da's scrapyard and draped them loosely over his hips, Elvis-style.

"Do ye nat mean piece de resistance, Lynus? Ye might have removed the handles af the chains before ye put them roun' yer waist. It luks bloody rediculous"

"Same thing, Pip, me auld mucker. Anyway the handles hold the chain down."

"An what about the barnet?"

"I dyed it with black boot polish an splashed meself all over wi' Brut so I wud smell like the maun himself."

"Yer in danger af turnin' inta a narcissus, Lynus."

"Is that nat a flower?"

"That's a narcis... Ah, niver mine, Lynus. I don't want till addle yer brain."

"It's hard till swallie, min' ye."

"What is?" asked Pip.

"Him next dur takin' all yer money." Lynus held his head to the side in thought. "Like, his ma an' da are real nice people. They dae everythin' fer thon ma af hers over in the flat. I see Bert wheelin' out her bin every week wi'out fail. An' the cheek she gives the maun." He straightened up, all five foot six of him, and thrust out his puny chest. "If I wuz that maun I'd shove it."

"Lynus, if you were Bert you'd do what that auld bat tells ye. Ye haven't the balls to say no to anyone."

"Aye, I suppose yer right. Nobody's perfect."

"In that case call me Nobody," joked Pip.

Lynus thought about this answer for about ten seconds before the penny dropped. "See you Pip, you take me till the fair wi' yer wit. Come on get on yer Saturday gear. We're goin' till the pub."

"Giv'us a minute, Lynus. I think I'll take ye up on that, if ye don't mine." Pip disappeared into the house while Lynus practised his hip swaying and lip curling.

"*Hurry up there Pip, I think I've gat it. By God, I've gat it. Get yer arse in gear afore it wears aff!*" yelled Lynus.

"*Call me a taxi, will ye?*" Pip shouted back.

"*Yer a taxi. Nye shift yer wee arse,*" bellowed Lynus as he strummed his tuneless three stringed guitar.

∞ ∞ ∞ ∞ ∞

A glut of Elvii had arrived at the King Williams Arms. The fancy dress shop must have done a roaring trade that day. Every other male was attired in white jump suit and black duck-tailed wig, each one strutting his stuff and talking in an Ulster-stroke-Memphis drawl.

Cyril minced towards Pip and Lynus, dressed from head to toe in imitation gold lame, his black poodle hair hidden beneath his mother's light brown wig.

"Ach, hello Lynus. An' hello to you too, Pip," he tapped the two lads on the chest with the middle finger of his limp hand before standing back to admire Lynus's outfit. "Well, well, what do we have here? Mmm, a bit crass, if ye don't mind me saying so, Lynus. Nat a lat af imagination went into *that*, ah, *creation*." He glanced at the belt that Lynus had made. A slight smile formed on his tightly-drawn lips and he started to finger the chains. "Nice touch, chains. Pity about the rest. Yer nat into bondage Lynus, by any chance?"

Lynus jumped back as if he had been poked by a cattle prod.

"Frig aff, ye turd burglar!" he waved his fist at Cyril and threatened him with all sorts of torture.

Cyril puckered his lips. "Pramises, pramises, that's all I get these days. I hope ye mean all that, Lynus? Especially the bit about the snooker cue!"

"Ferget that bit. You'd only enjoy it."

"Nye, nye, Lynus. Ye can't go back on a pramise."

"Come on, Pip. Lets get a drink. That dickhead's gettin up my neb he's that queer. He's that bent he cud kiss his own arse.

Pip forlornly followed Lynus to the bar.

"Luks like thur's a new barman on the night," Lynus cupped his mouth with his hands and yelled, "*Hey mucker! Throw a couple af pints this way, will ye?*"

"*Hang on thur lovies. I won't be a wee tick.*"

Lynus cupped his head in his hands and sighed loudly, "As Victor Meldrew wud say Pip, 'I don't believe it, I don't bloody believe it'. It's a bloody queer servin' behin' the bar! They are all over the friggin' place, like flies round a cow pat. Since all this come out af the closet business, half the flamin' nation's turned into poofs."

"Nye, Lynus. Don't jump till conclusions. He might not be a poof," reprimanded Pip.

"Af coorse he's a bloody arse bandit! Just luk at th' hack af it! Who else but a poof wud call another maun lovey, I ask ye? An his hair all blow dried. I bet that's nat th' only blow job he's had th' day by the luk on his fid."

"Aye, right enough. Well Lynus me auld mucker, just keep yer arse to the wall an' ye might get out wi' yer bum intact."

After the tenth rendition of "American Trilogy" in the space of thirty minutes, Pip was almost ready for the men in white to carry him off.

"Does nobody in this buildin' know anythin' other than that flamin' anthem. What about a wee rendition af "Jailhouse Rock" or "Moody Blue" fer a change. One more 'glory, glory, hallelujah' an I'm aff. Cud they nat have had a wet T-shirt competition instead, Lynus?"

"I don't think Elvis ever did that, Pip. He sweated a lat on stage, like but he was wearin' his jump suit an nat a T-shirt."

"Jaysus, but yer thick, man." Pip was ready to clock Lynus on the dial when his name was called over the microphone.

"I'll slay em, Pip. I bet ye don't know what I'm goin' till sing."

"Surprise me, Lynus!"

"One two, one two, one, two, three," Lynus was hitting the mike with the palm of his hand.

"Get on wi' it, fer frig sake."

The audience was becoming impatient. A bottle missed Lynus's ear by a fraction of an inch. He turned to the compere and threatened to walk off the stage if he was hassled.

"It's yer prerogative mate." The compere was just about to lighten Lynus of the mike when Lynus told him to bugger aff. A very obese woman waddled up to the stage and gave Lynus a wallop round the ear.

"Watch yer mouth, big lad thon's my husband yer talkin' till."

"Who threatened *him* if he didn't turn up fer yer weddin' missus, King Kong?"

Whack! The compere's wife came back with an upper cut to the chin. Lynus reeled. He saw stars, but decided the show must go on for the sake of Elvis's memory. It would take more than a double whammie round the head to stop Lynus from imitating his hero.

Pip nursed his head in his hands. God, how embarrassing. He eyed the bar for familiar faces. Please God, don't let anyone I know see me here with thon eejit. I wish I'd stayed in the house with me da, he silently prayed.

Lynus struck an Elvis pose, left leg bent, right leg splayed to the side. With head slightly bent and arm stretched in the air he strangled Elvis's "Hurt".

"Iyeaaammmm hhhuuu-a-rrt, tae think that ye lied till me. Iyeaaammmm hhhuu-a-rrttt way-a-aayyy down deep inside af meee..."

"We're hurt listenin' till ye," yelled the audience, but Lynus was well and truly in another dimension.

Bottles whizzed past his head. Undaunted, he carried on to the end.

"I willl nevvverrr evvverr hhhuuu-a-rrrt yewwwahh, yeesss yewwwahh, ahhh hahhh, ahhhh hahhhh..." He was down on his knees by now. The audience was also down on their knees, laughing. He left the stage to a barrage of slow handclaps and high-pitched whistles.

Pip's head was now flat on the bar, his hands clasping his ears tightly to drown out the noise, and also to hide his face.

"They loved me, Pip! Dae ye hear them, they're goin' wild fer more."

"What did ye say? Wild fer more?" He lifted his head off the bar and steadied himself on his elbows, kept his head down low and glared up at the eejit who had trailed him out for the night. "I don't think so Lynus, me auld mate. I wud be more inclined to say they were goin' wild for yer hide. If I were you I'd get to hell outa here before they skin ye alive."

"Listen! Listen! They're callin' out the winner's name. Be quiet will ye, till I hear if I've won".

"Don't haule yer breath Lynus. Ye cud die waitin' for yer name to be called, ye know."

"Shut up an' listen will ye!"

"Don't tell me to shut up. It wud have been more fittin' for you till shut yer gub. That wuz bloody woeful."

The compere removed the card from the gold envelope. "The winner is ..."

"Get on with it!" yelled the impatient audience.

"The winner is ... Cyril Thompson."

"I don't believe it! He cudn't have won. *It's a fix. It's a fix!*" yelled Lynus over the applause.

"He bloody has. An' how the hell is it a fix?" asked Pip.

"Did ye nat see who handed the bloody envelope to the compere?"

"No."

"It wuz the bloody barman! Can't ye see? It's Cyril's boyfriend. Luk at the way he's lukin' at auld woolly head. His bake's all lit up an' he's winkin' at him."

Pip could see the barman fawning over Cyril as he handed him the prize. He presented him with an Elvis mirror, and as they held it up in front of them, Cyril kissed the barman on the cheek. Pip could see this as he leant over the bar to grab a bottle of vodka that the barman had left on the counter. He slipped the bottle down beside his feet, before agreeing with Lynus. "An' I thought he fancied you, Lynus. I'm sure yer gutted. I know ye were dyin' till get suckin' the boils aff his neck."

"Don't make me vamit, Dunlap." Lynus got up off his stool and made his way towards the stage. "Here, big lad! This competition was a fuckin' fix. He doesn't even luk like Elvis. His wig is light brown, an' Elvis's hair wuz black. An' another thing. Frank Sinatra sung 'My Way', nat Elvis."

"I beg your pardon, Mr McGrath. Elvis *did* sing 'My Way'," said the compere, who was standing in front of Cyril. Cyril was skulking behind him for safety.

"Indeed he did, lovey," lisped the barman who jumped up from behind Cyril. He too was skulking in case Lynus clocked *him* as well. "And another thing, Elvis's hair was light brown before he became famous. He dyed it when he went into the movie scene."

"Don't you call me lovey, ye fruit. I'll knock yer melt in along wi' thon other shirt lifter. Cyril wud have done it my way if I cud make a maun outa him, but that's impassable."

Lynus jumped on to the stage and before you could say "Graceland" a full-scale fracas had erupted. Lynus had Cyril pinned to the floor by straddling his backside and twisting his arms up his back. He jumped off when he realised the man was enjoying it. Cyril's wig had fallen off and the black boot polish was melting all over Lynus's face.

A comedian in the audience remarked, "It's the black an' white minstrel show nye, fer frig sake. Come on lads, let's join in. 'Oh, de Campdown ladies sing dis song, doo dah, doo dah!' Come on lads, sing along there. 'Oh, de Campdown ladies sing dis song ..."

All the people, men and women, were now on their feet clapping and stamping their feet.

"*Order! Order! Can we have some order please?*" the compere was now yelling.

"I'll have a double!" quipped Pip.

"An' we'll have whiskeys all roun'," yelled the other patrons.

The police arrived at that moment. Pip grabbed Lynus by the scruff of the neck. "Let's get to hell outa here, big lad. I don't want to get into any trouble with the polis till me claim comes up."

"Haule on there Pip, I'm goin' till knock the shit outa that gold-covered woolly-headed po..."

Pip threw Lynus out through the side door of the bar and told him to run like the hammers. "Let's just say, Elvis has left the buildin', Lynus. With a bit of luck we just might get away unnoticed by the law."

They arrived in Hetherington Green gasping for breath.

"Thank Christ we weren't arrested. That's all I wud need at this time," sighed Pip. "Don't bother askin' me out for a drink again, Lynus. I can't afford it."

"I paid fer it, Pip," replied a dishevelled, blackened Elvis.

"Oh, fer Christ's sake get a life. McGrath! In fact get a brain instead!" He saw Lynus did not have the bottle of vodka he had nicked and slapped him on the head.

"Ah frig it, I forgot me vodka over the head af ye." He peered at his hand as it felt slimy. He thought it was blood, but the smell of polish invaded his nostrils. "An' that bloody boot polish is mingin'. Go an' wash it aff."

"Do ye fancy comin' out wi' me next week, Pip?"

"I wudn't go out wi' ye if ye pissed vodka. Nye fuck aff!"

"Right! Right! I'm away home. But I still say I shud have won that contest. No-body else thought of singin' 'Hurt'."

"I think that was the straw that broke the camel's back, seein' as they all felt hurt listenin' till ye."

13

Wednesday, 29 March

"Do ye know somethin', Rab?"

"I know quiet a few things, Bert. But me mine's al'us open till new enlightenment. If ye hae a wee bit af interestin' tittle tattle I'll oblige ye by lendin' ye me ear."

"My neck *is* thore, ye know!" Bert's head was peeking from above a surgical collar. "I *think* I have done mythelf a bit af an injury."

"How's that then? Did ye get a bita whiplash lukin' at thon blonde thing we passed comin' up the road?" quipped Rab.

"Fer Jaysus sake, don't come out wi' any wisecracks like that when yer in wi' the dactor. Ye *think* ye've done yersel' an' injury! Ye *have* done yersel' an injury. Ye've had a whiplash, maun dear, an' don't forget it."

Rab, Lynus and Bert were sitting in the waiting room of a large redbricked residence off the Lisburn Road. A Mr Kildare had summoned them for an examination, on the instructions of their solicitor. Peggy had refused to attend. She had been in a bad mood since the major had run out of her kitchen. Rab was worried about her claim, and hoped she could get another examination so his plans would not be destroyed.

Bert ruminated through the well-thumbed copies of the *National Geographic* that lay scattered on the small table. Now he was feeling testy at not being able to light up a cigarette to calm his nerves.

"Ye wud think they'd let ye thmoke in plathes like these, Rab! They're bound till know yer nerves wud be thyattered waitin' till see a mithter. It's nat like yer ordinary everyday dactor now, is it?" Bert shifted uneasily in his hard plastic chair and pulled at his surgical collar. He wished he was pulling on a fag instead.

"Christ Rab, it wud give ye the willies thittin' here. Did ye see the luk on that auld doll's bake at the rethepthion desk? She luked at us as if we were three bits of dog crap thtuck till th' heel af her winter boots." He scratched the top of his head in thought "I bet that auld doll owns a Pekinese fer her bake's th' image af one. I bet ye she doesn't luk at her dog like that when she lifts its turds up af the lawn after it thites. Aye, I bet ye a poun' she feeds it on the best af mate an' all. I bet ye that ugly auld biddy feeds it thteak while I have till ate thausiges."

He peered at a picture on the wall. "See that Rab, do ye think that's a real oil paintin'? I bet it is, fer these mithters are loaded. They spend years tryin' to get the handle af dacter in front af thur names an' then they go private till earn more. Then they go back to mithter. The worlds upside down, if ye ask me." He rubbed the side of his neck and winced. "I tell ye Rab, my neckth achin' so it is."

"Will ye give over grippin', Friars! Ye hae yersel' that worked up, ye hae yersel' convinced ye hae whiplash. If I were you I'd get yer arse fitted wi' teeth fer yer talkin' a lat af crap. An stap sayin' 'I bet'! Dae ye think yer in Las Vegas!"

"Luk Rab, if I thay me necks thore it's thor. Anyway, I won't be lyin' when I go in then, will I?"

"Well if it eases yer conscience any, tell the dactor it's sore. But ye can't pull the wool over my eyes, ye know." Rab's good eye glistened. "Think on it Bert, a couple af months fram nye an' we'll be laughin' all the way till the bank."

Bert brightened up at the idea of pocketing a couple of thousand quid, beamed a toothless grin at his two mates and rubbed his hands with glee.

"Nye, don't luk so bloody cheerful when ye go in till be examined, fer Christ's sake, or ye'll give the game away." Rab crossed his legs and huffed.

"An' try yer best till keep yer bake shut! Ye cud cause mental damage tae a person wi' a gub like that."

"Aye alright! Don't get yer knickers in a twitht."

The waiting room door opened without warning.

"Mr Albert Friars, Mr Kildare will see you now. Follow me please". The Pekinese-faced receptionist held the door open for Bert who jumped up on his bandy legs with a look in Rab's direction, terror imprinted on his face.

As the receptionist glanced at Bert's file, Rab gave him a thumbs-up gesture, which did nothing to dispel his fear. He followed her clutching his cap as if he were about to face the gallows.

"Well Lynus, are ye all set?" Rab started on Lynus. "Where's yer bloody collar? Hae ye nat the wit till wear it the day?" He guldered, then realising walls have ears lowered his voice. "Are ye a half wit, maun dear? Jaysus, I'm only noticin' it nye. Did ye lave it in the back sate af the car?" He made a movement as if he were about to get up to retrieve it for him when Lynus told him to sit back down.

"I cudn't be bathered wearin' that auld thing. It hurts yer flamin' neck. In fact, it wud give ye bloody whiplash if ye didn't have it in the first place".

Rab hit his forehead with the palm of his hand in frustration. "Bloody hell maun, hae you no brains at all?" He realised his voice had risen again and he put his hand over his mouth as if to shut himself up. "Where's me spray, for God's sake." He plundered his coat pocket as he tried to suppress his cough, then started to gasp for air.

Lynus got up off his seat, lifted a magazine and waved it too and fro. "Breathe easy there, boy, take deep slow breaths."

Rab found his spray and gulped down a good few puffs before telling Lynus where to go. "Will ye fuck aff, or I'll ram that bloody magazine up yer rectum! An' don't tell a hen how tae suck eggs. I've had this asthma longer than you've had bum fluff. I know all about deep breaths. If I sucked any deeper I'd suck them chairs up af the flur."

"Rectum, nearly killed 'im," joked Lynus. It took a lot to ruffle Lynus, the threat of a magazine disappearing up his backside was no great risk. "Come on nye, Rab. I'm nat as daft as I'm stupid lukin'."

"Your both stupid lukin' an' daft!" Rab informed him. "How are ye goin' tae explain why yer nat wearin' yer callar?"

"Easy Rab! I'll just tell 'im it hurts me when I wear it."

"Well, just don't come moanin' till me if ye don't get paid out," spat Rab.

Lynus started futtering about the waiting room. He noticed the chairs were screwed to the floor. "Are they screwed down so no-one will steal them, Rab? Who the hell wud want till steal those, eh?"

"People like you an' me, Lynus." Rab lifted a *National Geographic* and thumbed through the pages. "Dae ye see the tits oan this Lynus!"

"What's that, Rab? Tits! Are there naked weemen in that book?" He pounced, but Rab held the magazine to his chest so Lynus couldn't see.

"Get away wi' ye. You're not seein' it. You'll only get all horny an' I wouldne know wit tae dae wi' ye."

Lynus wrestled with Rab, trying to pry the magazine from his hands.

"Come on Rab, let's see them! Are they big one's?" He flushed and Rab laughed.

"Aye Lynus, they're a quare set af milkers alright." He quickly shoved the pages under his backside and refused to budge.

Lynus tried to push Rab off his chair. "Will ye lift yer arse, Kirk? Come on, let me see before that auld biddy comes back in."

"Will ye belt up if I let ye see them?" asked Rab.

"I'll sit here an' be as quiet as a church mouse so ah will. I havn't seen a dacent pair af tits fer ages."

Rab lifted his behind off the seat and showed Lynus the photograph.

"It's a bloody cow! Hell roast ye, gettin' me all worked up like that over a cow's tits." Lynus huffed like a child who had been sent to bed early and slumped in his chair.

"Did I say it wuz a woman, Lynus? I only said dae ye see the tits oan this. Yer mind's warped. Thank God I'm nat a sex maniac like yersel'. An' don't slump. Ye can't slump with whiplash, it's a physical impossibility, Ye hae to sit up straight like. If anybody shud be slumpin' it shud be me."

"Why's that Rab?"

"I've a touch af the dingle berries."

"What th' hell's that, when your writtin' home?".

"Piles!" Rab lifted his right hip to ease the pain in his backside. "There's nathin' as bad as a dose af the piles. Ye can't get comfort nae matter what way ye sit."

"It cud be worse, Ye know, ye cud be a busted boot like Cyril! An' piles wud be an awful hindrance till yer love life. An' another thing, if ye were a busted boot ye cudn't get a maun till fancy ye wi' a bake like yer's, Rab."

Just then the door opened and Bert walked in with a spring in his step. He closed the door gently behind him and nudged Lynus, "Here, thon dacter's a gentlemaun. He taule me to take it easy for the nextht couple af months, nat till stretch meself in case I did any more damage. He swallied it hook line an' thinker. Ye'll be alright I tell ye. He even said he hud it 'imself, whiplash that is."

"An' I take it ye'll take 'im at 'is word, Friars. Nat lift anythin' heavier than a glass af beer till yer lips," grizzled Rab. He felt scundered with the two eejits that sat before him. "If the two af yes hud brains ye wud be dangerous. Ye won't be able tae throw the bowls then, I take it?"

"Oh Gawd!" cried Bert, "an' I've a match on Thaturday afternoon."

"Don't be bloody daft. Ye haven't gat whiplash ye eejit."

"Oh aye, that's right, Rab. I forgot. Jaysus, I even had meself convinthed there fer a moment."

"God keep me sane!" beseeched Rab.

"Robert Kirk, Mr Kildare is ready for you now." The receptionist interrupted.

∞ ∞ ∞ ∞ ∞

Back in Hetherington Green, Peggy had dragged her drink-and-drug ridden body over to the green wine-gum.

"Nye Ernie, jusshht give me me usual." She slapped a tenner on the floor of the van and swayed too and fro like a reed in water.

"Don't tell me yer plastered at this time of the mornin,' Peggy? It's only gone half past ten. An' by the luk af ye, yer still on them auld happy pills. Where th' hell do ye get them fram? Ye cudn't be gettin' them all fram the dacter, th' amount *ye* swallie." Ernie knew Peggy had a seedy supplier tucked away in some dirty flat in Ballyhornet, but didn't know who. He didn't really want to know either. The less he knew about drug dealers the better. That way he was in no threat of being kneecapped for grassing.

"I've been snattered since Saturday night Ernie. Nye shut ... hic ... shut ... hic ... shut yer gub an' weigh me a stone af them spuds. The chape ones min' ye or I'll slap ye inta next week."

"It wont be long till May. Ye'll be able till get Irish an' Spanish spuds then. Nat as dear as the Egyptian ones," Ernie informed her, thinking he was doing her a favour.

"What th' hell do ye expect me to do nye. The Riverdanshe!"

"The Riverdance! What's that when yer writin' home?"

Peggy inhaled deeply then exhaled in Ernie's face. Ernie was very nearly overcome by gin fumes as Peggy blew the answer in his face. "The effen Riverdanshe. That thing they done at th' Eurovishion Song Contesht. All feet they wur. God but thon wee man knew how till dance, an' he wuz gorgeous wi' thon wee tight ass of his."

"Ach, I know nye, Peggy. It wuz a mixture af Irish an' Spanish an' such."

Do ye want me till do a wee bit af it fer ye, Ernie?" Peggy tried to tap her big feet but she teetered slightly with the drink.

"Hang on there, Peggy. I don't want ye to start an earthquake wi' thon feet af yours."

"I can do it, ye know."

"I'll take yer word for it if ye don't min' Peggy."

"I can, ye know! I can do th' Riverdanshe, no sweat."

"Ye can show me on Saturday mornin' Peggy. I'm in a bit af a hurry the day."

"Well get yer finger out an' serve me me bloody vegetables, ye snatter."

Ernie duly did what he was told. As he handed Peggy her change he glanced towards the pensioners' flats. "What's goin' on over at Sarah's, Peggy?"

Peggy tried to focus on the flats. This made her even more unsteady on her feet and Ernie had to help her to her house for she was in danger of falling flat on her face.

"Will that make ye happy, missus?" A burly workman had erected a new gate outside of the flats. "The wind won't blatter that about, I can tell ye."

"Th' only time I will feel happy is when I win the lottery an' get out of this God forsaken place, whatever they call ye," replied a flustered Sarah.

"Billy to all me mates, missus, an' this here is Harry," Billy said pointing towards his workmate.

"*When* ye win th' lottery! Nat *if* ye win it, missus. Ye must be qaure an' sure af yerself. Nat a lat af people your age are as positive. Take Harry here. He isn't even sure af gettin' his dinner the night when he gets home. His missus taule him she felt like runnin' aff."

"That's the trouble with you youngsters today. There won't be many more silver weddin' anniversaries celebrated. In my day ye stayed with your man through thick an' thin until death parted ye." Sarah tottered over to inspect the gate. "My man could have made anything out of wood, ye know," said she wistfully. "If he saw the wood in thon gate he would have pan cracked." Her tone had changed now to one of anger as she gazed at the two men. They couldn't hammer a nail in straight, never mind carve the finest of wood into a work of art. A picture of her husband's work flashed before her eyes: she compared it to the shoddy workmanship that passed as a wooden gate and grizzled with anger.

"He would use nothin' but the best of wood. Pine, rosewood, mahogany, you name it. He knew the lot by smell alone." She put her nose to the gate and sniffed. "Is thon gate made out of mahogany?" she asked, as if she had inherited her husband's skill of sniffing.

"Ye must be jokin, missus! Mahogany? Th' Housin' Executive doesn't even know what mahogany is, never min' make gates out af it." He laughed as he asked his mate if he had heard what Sarah had just said. "Did ye hear that, Harry?"

"Aye Billy, I suppose ye cud say it wuz bastard mahogany!"

"That's terrible language, young lad, to use in front of a woman," chastised Sarah. "Not a bit of wonder your wife wants to run off if that's the way ye talk to her. An' I take it ye talk in front of your childer in thon auld way an' all."

"The kids talk to *me* in thon auld way, missus," Harry informed her.

"I could well believe it. An' don't keep callin' me missus. I have a name ye know. It's Mrs Cruickshank to you."

"Well Mrs Cruickshank, you wouldn't be puttin' the kettle on by any chance? It's time for our elevenses," asked a parched Billy.

"Indeed I'm not! Here, tell me this an' tell me no more. Have ye enough keys to go round all of us in here to open that gate? I'm too old to limbo dance under it."

"We have a key for ye all plus a few spares in case any go missin', missus ... err ... sorry, I meant Mrs Cruickshank."

"Well, ye'll better hand them round for I'm not. I'm not a prison warden ye know, although God knows it's like livin' in a blinkin' prison in here." Sarah's voice softened for a moment, through all her sharpness she had a soft spot in her heart. "Ach, come on in lads. I'll make ye a cup of scald, for it's a caule auld day the day."

"Yer a wee darlin', Mrs Cruickshank. Just wait a wee minute here till we gather up our bits an' pieces an' we'll be in."

Sarah hightailed it into the flat and lifted the phone. "Hey Elsie, come on over will ye. I've invited two men in for tea."

"You've done *what*, mother? Invited who to tea?" Elsie choked.

"Do you know these men?"

"Ach, never mine. Just get over here an' help me make the tea for them."

"I suppose it's them two men who put on the gate?"

"How do you know?" asked Sarah belligerently.

"Don't get ratty now, mother. I saw them put it up from my livin' room window. You should be careful who you invite into your home, ye might be raped."

"Get away with ye, woman dear. Who th' hell would want to have their way with a woman of my age?" screeched Sarah.

"It's goin' on a lot now ye know, rapin' old women. There's some dirty gets runnin' around nowadays. I'm not jokin', mother. Ye should be more careful. And I can't for the life of me work out your logic. You won't let your neighbours in, yet you'd let strangers in your home without battin' an eyelid."

"They are comin' in now, Elsie. Will ye come over?" pleaded Sarah who felt a bit panicky now she thought about her hasty invitation.

Elsie detected the fear in her mother's voice. "Oh, alright. But don't do it again," reprimanded Elsie.

Sarah replaced the receiver, but told the two men her daughter was on the way over as a precaution. Her heart was pounding as she told them not to shut the front door.

"Don't bother makin' anything to eat. We've brought our own sandwiches with us," Billy told her.

"Take the weight of your feet there. Sit yourselves down on the settee.

Here have a wee look at the *Mirror* there while I wet the tea." She shoved the newspaper into Billy's hand and hirpled into the kitchen. She peered out of her kitchen window to see if her daughter was on her way. Thank heavens she's on her way over, she thought as she spied her daughter walking towards the gate. She composed herself now she felt relief at the sight of her daughter.

Elsie pushed the gate but it didn't budge. She looked at it this way and that but could she gain entrance? The bolt was on the other side and there was no gap in which to put her hand through. Even if she had her hand through the bolt was held shut with a large padlock that was locked.

Her mind started to play tricks on her. She felt scared and anxious. Her mother might have been an old targe, but your mother's your mother, when all's said and done. Who were these men? Elsie had never seen them before. They could be new on the job, a couple of wasters who only worked when the notion took them. She wondered if the side door was unlocked and she raced round the perimeter of the flats. Sweat broke on her brow as she turned the handle. The door didn't budge.

She rapped on the window of the door and screamed "Mum! mum, let me in . Are ye alright?"

Bert turned the corner in a cloud of cigarette smoke. She yelled at him.

"Will you bloomin' well come over here, Bert. Me ma's locked in the flat with two strange men!"

Bert flicked his cigarette butt on the ground and quickened his step. "What in the name of heavens is she doin' wif two men in the flat?"

"I'm sure she's not bloody ravagin' them! Good God man, will ye help me push this door in, me nerves are shattered."

"Is that you, Elsie?" Her mother's shrill voice echoed from behind the door.

"Of course it's bloody me!" screamed Elsie. "Are ye alright?"

"Of course I'm alright! What are ye nyamerin' about? Wait a minute till I get me key." Elsie fell against the door with relief.

A few seconds later Sarah opened the door beaming from ear to ear. "What's all the fuss about? Come on in. These two lads are a weg. They've got me in stitches. They think I'm a great wee woman for me age an' they say I don't look a day over seventy."

"That's just great, ma! I feel as if I've passed my first century with worry over you. Don't you ever do that on me again or I'll put a stop to

Bert comin' over to attend till your feet."

"Ah shut up woman, an' get in there. These two are better lookin' than thon thing ye married. Play your cards right an' ye might get a night out with one of them."

"Do you know somethin'? You're not worth worryin' about. You've gave me a hot flush now, Bert will have to go to the shops now over th' head of you an' your shenanigans. Flirtin' with young men at your age, an' you have the cheek to talk about degenerates. You're actin' like a floozy yourself ye ... ye ... God, I could knock ye into next week ye have me that worked up. I don't want a night out with anyone, never mind a strange man, thank you very much. One man is enough to handle at my age. An' don't you dare try to get me a date. I'm a married woman, an' not a loose floozy!"

Bert shimmied up beside Elsie. "Is yer ma alright?"

"Aye, by the look of her she is. Now hop off home. I'm away in to see what she's doin' with these men."

"Huh, no doubt she'll be actin' the wee hard-done-by pensioner. In between sendin' them roun' the bend wi' thon sharp tongue af hers." Bert shrugged his shoulders and cupped another cigarette in his hand to shield it from the wind as he tried unsuccessfully to light it.

"Get you home with thon face of your's, Bert Friars. You will speak when spoken to. An' just at this moment I'm speakin' till people with teeth, so tittle along home on those two kebs of yours an' give me head peace," hissed Sarah. She grabbed Elsie by the arm and trailed her into the hallway of the flats. "Get in there an' pour yourself out a cup of tea. He can make his own over in the house," she glared at Bert, and slammed the door in his face.

They were in Sarah's living room for less than five minutes when Billy started to flirt with Elsie. He undressed her with his eyes and Elsie felt very vulnerable and very fat. Had she been twenty years younger and three stone lighter she might have felt flattered, but not now.

Sarah, never missed a trick, realised her invitation might not have been such a good idea. She conveyed to Elsie, through tightened eyes and lips, that she should go into the kitchen. Then she squared her shoulders and waved a bony finger at the two men, "The two of ye's, get to hell out of here before I bury me boot!"

Billy and Harry lit from the settee as if a charge of electricity had shot up from the cushions on which they had been sitting. "Haule on there, missus. We didn't ask to come in here, ye know. You invited us in. What did we do anyway?" asked Billy.

"Your peeper's are just that wee bit wanderin' for my likin'. So push off." Sarah tried to herd them out the door but her scrawny arms failed her and she asked Elsie to give her a hand. Elsie was embarrassed. She knew the men would talk about the silly, overweight granny who lived in Hetherington Green. The one who imagined young lads like them would even consider making a pass at her.

"See that, our Elsie! There's life in th' auld dog yet. I'll protect ye from dirty minded rascals such as them."

"Mother, I am free an' over eighteen, for Christ's sake! Will ye just keep your nose out of my business for five minutes, please. I could have handled those two on my own. Do you not realise you have only made me out to be over-imaginative, overweight, and over-the-hill!"

"Aren't ye glad I'm here till protect ye, then?" Sarah felt pleased with herself. She had her daughter where she wanted her now, under her thumb; for a few hours, at least.

Elsie plonked herself onto the settee. Out of bad comes good, she thought, at least it got her away from Bert's ugly gob for a while.

ꝏ ꝏ ꝏ ꝏ ꝏ

A bulky, unmistakably male figure lurched up the street.

It stopped in its tracks when a cat ran in front of it and the figure became quite animated its arms reached out, the hands clenched. "Get th' hell outa here, ye mangy auld flea-ridden, randy, slanty-eyed, sleeked ... bastard!"

The cat stopped and glared indignantly at the figure before it ran up the street and slunk under a hedge.

"Don't worry. I'll get ye. Ye can hide but ye can't stay hidden forever, ye know!" The figure continued it's homeward journey.

Five minutes later it retrieved keys from a coat pocket and opened the door.

"What the ... Jaysus help me!" Rab tripped over the sill of the doorstep as he entered. The shock of it made him reel. He balanced himself with his free hand on the bannister of the stairs, the other hand was wrapped firmly round a fish supper that he had bought for his lunch. He tried to make it up the hall, the colour drained from his face.

Peggy had witnessed this from a chair in the kitchen. She pitched him a resentful look, then closed her eyes and pretended to be asleep.

Rab sighed and his laboured breathing eased.

She's that out af it she wouldne know if Worl' War Three hud started he thought to himself. But Peggy never missed a trick.

That cud have finished him aff, a fall like that. I must keep that in min'. She opened her eyes and pretended to yawn. She unfolded her arms and called out, "Is that you Rab?"

"Aye, it's me handsome sel', so it is."

"Handsome me arse!" She removed a cigarette from its packet and placed it between her lips, then toyed with her cigarette lighter.

A couple of seconds passed before Rab enquired in his breathless voice, "Are ye nat goin' till light that, Peggy?

Peggy's mind was on other things. She drummed out a rhythm with her fingers on the arm of her chair.

"Well, there ye are. An' wherever ye, are ye won't be anywhere else." Rab came up with one of his stupid sayings and pulled Peggy out of her dreamworld. Peggy's thoughts were usually devious and Rab felt worried. He clicked his fingers in front of her face. "Will ye wake up, woman? Ye luk like a fart in a trance. Anywan in there? Rab callin', Rab callin. Come in, Peggy. Come in, Peggy. Over an' out."

Peggy started "Oh it is you? Fer a minute I thought I wuz seein' things!"

"Nah it's nat! It's the men in white till take ye away," answered Rab sarcastically. "Then again, it cud be a figment af yer imagination. Yer brain's are that addled I wudne be surprised if ye saw rabbits dressed in tap hats." He spied four empty gin bottles lined across the window sill and burst into song.

"Four green battles sittin' oan the wall, if wan green battle shud accidently fall ..." He lifted one and dropped in into the bin before continuing, "... there'd be three green battles sittin' oan the wall ..."

"Stap that, Rab Kirk!"

"Three green battles ..."

"*Shut up, ye bastard!*"

"As I've often said before, you're beautiful when yer angry, dae ye know that, Peg?"

"I taule ye to shut up. Nye do as yer bid!"

Rab kissed her on the cheek before sitting down. "Pour us a cup af tay there, Peggy. No sugar, I'm oan a diet this week."

"Pour it out yersef. Are ye crippled or somethin?" She lit her cigarette and blew the smoke in his face.

He spluttered as he unwrapped his fish supper. "Keep yer cancer sticks till yerself. If I wanted to kill meself I'd get it over quick like, instead af gamblin' wi' thon things." He sniffed the air. "Is thon stew I can smell. Are we havin' a change the day?"

Peggy rose from her chair and slapped him on the face. Winching, he held his jaw and asked her what he had done to deserve it.

"Ye were bloody born, that's why."

His face stung, and his temper rose.

How dare that ugly auld bitch slap me, an' me a big strappin' maun. Who the bloody hell does she think she is, he thought. He gazed round the untidy kitchen. Potato peelings, carrot scrapings and onion skins lay in the sink. Half empty mugs of tea littered the counter tops and he felt ashamed that his friends were witness to this every time they called. His eyes lit on the gin bottles.

"Af all the gin joints in the world I hud tae walk intae yers! Whoever thought up that line must have hud you in min'. Humphrey Bogart wudne have asked Sam tae play it again if you hud have been the woman oan his min'. He'd have paid him till stap playin'." Rab didn't often show his anger. Today he could have happily murdered his wife and buried her beside the cats in the back yard.

He ate his fish supper, then went out of the house to get a bit of air into his lungs. He headed towards Sir Robert's, where he stayed until bedtime.

Rab was upstairs in bed, asleep. Daughter Sharon had been staying with her new boyfriend since the weekend. She had told her parents she was staying with a friend though Peggy couldn't really care where she was staying as long as she was out of the house. Rab had given up on his wayward daughter when he realised she was following in her mothers footsteps. He couldn't handle another Peggy-in-the-making.

Peggy was busy with the screwdriver. She had unscrewed the brass stoop at the front door. She screwed down a thick strip of wood in its place, then carefully screwed the stoop back into position on top. She went outside the door and proceeded to walk in and out the door. Her foot caught in the risen stoop three times out of four and she could hardly contain her excitement.

"It works! It bloody works!" She jumped up and down on the spot until a neighbour passed by and gave her a funny look. She blushed as she composed herself. Just make sure to hang a loose garment over the bannister. That way her husband would have nothing to help curtail his fall. She made this mental note before closing the door. She had to push it hard against the frame to make it close tightly. Then she shot the bolt over into its holder.

The thing is, he'd better nat use the front dur till get out. It has to be used tae get in. I'll tell him the catch is broke an' he'll have tae use the back dur instead she thought. She stealthily tip-toed up the hall and placed the screwdriver back under the sink in the kitchen. She felt euphoric.

Peggy gazed at Rab as he slept, just as he had gazed down at her on that fateful Saturday night. His asthma spray and heart pills sat on his bedside table. They reminded her how his ill health had contributed to his impotence. She screwed up her face, then spat on the floor. The bedclothes were pushed down to his waist to ease his laboured breathing. Her eyes followed the contours of his upper body. He still had the muscular build of a man used to heavy work. His large chest, although slightly barrelled by the effects of asthma, was framed by two strong arms that lay by his sides. Her gaze moved up to his face. She tried to look with her heart instead of her eyes. His rugged face looked almost handsome with his eyes closed. His sleeping medication had relaxed his features. His large manly lips were set in a slight smile, except when he had to open them to take in air. His bad eye looked normal in his relaxed state.

She wondered how he had looked when he was young, before the accident with the gun. My, but he must have been a handsome big man all the while. Thon first wife af his must have had the best af him. Did he hold her in them strong arms af his an' make love to her with the strength of Samson? Did he satisfy her needs? Did she have to go an' fin' satisfaction fram other men? Somehow I don't think so, by the luk af that body he must hae been quite an athlete in the bedroom.'

Peggy's needs had been satisfied in the early years. Her heart quickened as she remembered those times, before his health had started to go downhill. She had nothing to complain about then.

Her thoughts were interrupted when he gave a loud gasp and turned over on to his side. Her brain took over the work of her heart.

"That's right. Turn yer back on me again, matey. You've broken my heart fer the last time with yer lies an' pranks. I may nat be a ravin' beauty but I dae have feelin's," she hissed through gritted teeth. Did he not realise how degraded she felt after she let dirty-minded old men paw her as if she were a piece of meat? How filthy she felt when they dressed quickly and fled out her door as if staying one minute longer would stain them. He had no idea how her body ached for him, to feel his strong arms hold her. Undressing, she slipped into bed beside him. She stroked his back with her hand, she hoped he might miraculously turn round but he just grunted at the disturbance. She pulled her hand back as if she had been burnt and cursed his name.

14

Thursday, 28th March

"Don't use the front dur!" The voice sounded as if it were coming from the bowels of hell as it echoed round the house.

Rab stopped dead in his tracks. His wife had scared the crap out of him with her deep throated husky command. He had just finished his breakfast of stewed tea and burnt toast. The toast had given him heartburn and now his wife had almost given him a heart attack.

"Christ Almighty, woman, don't give me ears a batterin' at this time af the mornin'. Anyway I'm nat goin' tae open the dur. I'm only goin' up tae the toilet fer a pee." He rubbed his chest and it made him rift. "Thank God till get that up. The acid wuz burnin' holes in me throat."

"Ye'll hae till wait. I'm washin' meself."

"I can't wait! Me bladder's burstin'," Rab yelled back.

"Is yer auld prostrate away wi' it nye? There's nat much af ye left, is thur?"

"Thur's enough af me left tae haule me together fer another ween o years," snapped Rab.

"Well, take yerself in haun an' go an' pee behin' the birdhouse." An' go out the back dur. Th' front dur lock needs fixin'. I asked Jimmy over the road till hae a luk at it."

"Ye'd think I wuz bloody haunless! I'll luk at it meself."

"Don't you dare, Rab Kirk! When you fix a thing it's flamin' nat worth a damn afterwards."

Peggy started to panic. She cut short her ablutions, but before heading downstairs to prevent her husband opening the front door, popped her false teeth into a glass of *Sterident* to soak.

Rab studied his wife as she stood before him. "My God, you an' Friars wud make a fine pair af bookends, or a couple af gargoyles. I've seen better lukin' cows' arseholes than yer bake. Has yer fancy maun tuk a likin' tae shaggin' weemen wi' bovine features?" Peggy tried to connect his head with her large fist.

Rab ducked, and her fist hit the wall. She yelped with pain and kicked him on the shin.

"Ye effin' bleeder!" spat Peggy, before adding, "Did ye ever find out who yer da wuz?"

"Oh, the wit's sharp the day alright. Hae ye been watchin' funny films again. What's wrang wi' the word 'bastard'. Is plain speakin' nat good enough fer ye nye. Dae ye hae tae spake in riddles?" He rubbed his shin.

"Nye who's talkin' in riddles?" asked Peggy before she kicked his other shin. "That'll keep th' other wan company ... bastard!"

Rab limped out the back door then turned and limped back into the kitchen.

"I'll piss over Maggie's wall! The sight af a strange willy might make her day. Af coorse yer no stranger till strange willies yerself like, are ye? Ye must hae seen some specimens in yer day, eh Peggy!" A milk bottle missed his head by inches. "Oh ho, me girl ye, yer aim is nat as good as it was. It must be the auld drink. Hae ye a wee touch af the shakes nye?"

"Fuck aff!"

"That's what I like till hear, sweet nathin's comin' forth fram me loved wan's own fair lips," chided Rab. "It makes ye feel good af a mornin', it does."

Peggy threw another bottle. Rab ducked and it smashed on the ground at his feet.

"Hell roast ye! Will ye nat staun still. Get to hell outa here or I'll poison those bloody birds af yours. Ye think more af them than ye dae af me." She slammed the door shut and turned the key. "Nye yer out, stay out, An' don't come home without a wooden overcoat."

"Jaysus! I get a bollockin' because I wanted a pee. I dread to think what I'd get if I wanted a crap." He shouted at his wife.

"Ye gat a bollockin' because ye woke up. Now clear aff!"

Rab peed behind his birdhouse. He watched the steam rise from the flow.

"By God I needed that. It wuz near boilin' point I held it in that long." He adjusted himself before entering the shed to feed his pigeons, budgies and Love birds. "You're the only birds in my life nye, at least ye don't yap back."

He cleaned out the droppings before pulling up the zip of his heavy anorak, then closed the shed door behind him, sidled up the side of his house and headed towards Sir Robert's house.

Peggy watched from her living-room window as he turned the corner. She unbolted the front door and left it slightly ajar. She wrapped a blanket round her shoulders to keep out the draught and waited. She had plenty of time.

"Answer that!" Elsie tucked her feet up underneath herself on the settee. "I can't take another phone-call from that women the day."

"I'm nat antherin' it! I'm readin' the paper," retorted Bert.

"Indeed you will!" Elsie had come up for air to give Bert his orders.

"I will nat!"

"You will!"

"Will nat!"

"Will!"

"Nat!"

"Oh for goodness sake, Bert, get up off your lazy arse an' answer th phone will ye?"

"Nah! It's your ma nat mine."

"Well, thank God it is. Your ma's been dead for ten years!"

"Then what th' hell are ye moanin for?" Bert rubbed his chin as he thought. "Mind you Elthie, you wud enjoy nyammerin' till the dead. What with all this spiritualism lark yer inta these days. Have ye changed yer min' about becomin' a Jehovah's Witneth again?"

"You get better hymns to sing in the Spiritual meetin's. All jolly an' guitars an' hand clappin'. Not all organs an' dull tunes. An' with a bit of luck ye might get a message from th' other side."

"Well, that thounds like a methage from across the road." Bert nodded his head in the direction of the hall." You had better anther that Elthie, she's nat goin' till give up till ye do."

Elsie fortified herself with some coffee and made her way to the phone.

"What is it now? Do ye want to run down another few people before dinner time? Good heavens, I've had it up to the oxters with your moanin'." She was ready for another verbal attack when a frightened voice answered her.

"Is Bert in? I'm sorry to interrupt ye, but it's Jimmy from the bowls." Elsie put her hand over the mouthpiece. "It's not me ma, Bert. It's Jimmy. I think I've scared the wits clean out of him." She quietly cursed her mother for making her look an idiot again.

Bert took the phone off her. He tried to make an excuse for his wife's behaviour, only the more he tried, the more foolish he sounded. When he finished, he found Elsie crying in the kitchen.

"What are ye gurnin' about nye, Elthie? I explained all to Jimmy. He underthstands. He has the thame problems with his ma, an' she's ninety-theven!"

Elsie wailed even louder. "Ninety-seven? That means that auld battle axe over there could outlive me!"

"Heavens Elthie, yer a hell fer exaggeratin' at times. Is there nat a religion fer people with overactive brains? See if there wuz, you'd be the head af it!"

"I'm not over reactin'! You know that woman's been on the phone four times since we got out of bed. We're gettin' a news update on that gate an average of twelve times a day now."

The words were no sooner out of Elsie's mouth when the phone rang again.

"Who was on the phone! I couldn't get through. I could be lyin' here dead an' you'd be on the phone," screeched Sarah.

"If ye were dead mother, ye would *not* be tryin' to telephone me, ye would *not* be in the position to telephone *anybody*."

"You don't need to shout! I'm not deaf ye know," snapped Sarah.

"No ma, you're *not* deaf, you're *not* blind, you're *not* ill, you're just *old.*" Elsie's tether was getting shorter by the second. Bert passed and she slapped him on the ear.

Bert held his ear."What wuz that for?"

"It was either you or me ma. I couldn't very well slap her now, could I?"

Bert threw a strange look in Elsie's direction. "Jaysus, but yer nuts. Yer all a brick thort of a hudfull in your family. One's man mad and th' other one's just inthane!"

"Did you hear him, ma?"

"I did indeed. I'll come over there an' cut the cooter off him if he ever comes out with anything like that again."

Elsie closed her eyes and cocked her nose in the air.

"Go ahead, suck up to yer ma nye I've inthulted yer family. By God! Talk about pullin' rank whenever ye hear the truth." Bert lifted the morning paper and tucked it under his arm. "I'm away up till the loo for a read. It's the only plathe in this houthe where a man can get a bita pathe."

"What do ye want anyway, ma?"

I must ring the doctor. Me head feels all light. I keep fallin' over I'm that dizzy, an' me auld ankles nippin' again."

"*Right!* I would do that. Give the doctor a ring an' send *him* loco!"

"Do ye think Doctor Wright would come out to see me?"

"Whoever's on duty will come out. An' what's so special about Doctor Wright anyway?"

"He's thorough. He gives ye a good examination all over. He doesn't give your heart a wee listen an' then fly out the door."

"He'll hardly examine your heart if it's your ears or ankle that's ailin' ye."

"How do ye know my heart's alright? It could very well be goin' into heart failure. No-one would think of askin' me how I feel lately anyway."

"No-one needs to ask you how you're feelin'. Ye telephone often enough to keep us all up-to-date on your complaints. Ma, you're eighty-nine! Bert was at a funeral th' other week of a bowler. He collapsed in the kitchen an' died on the way to the hospital, an' he was only my age."

"I suppose he drank an' smoked! I've led a healthy life, so I don't see any reason to die." Sarah started to giggle. "The last time Doctor Wright came out he looked up me passage."

"What did he look up your passage for?" asked Elsie.

"What th' hell do ye think he looked up it for? To find his stethoscope!"

"What was his stethoscope doin' up your hall?"

"Nat up that passage! Me back passage. I felt all embarrassed, but sure you're only a bit of meat to these boys."

"You sound as if ye got a thrill or somethin' the way you're gigglin'. I'm sure he didn't get one anyway." I hope you had your good knickers on an' not those auld pink things with the loose elastic."

"Look here Elsie, I might be old but I'm not in me dotage yet. Of course I had on me good knickers. I keep them ready just in case he wants to have another wee jook up it."

"It's not the bloody Grand Canyon, for heaven's sake, ma. I'm quite sure he's not out on a sight-seein' trip. He examines you up your rectum for a reason, not to practice his yodellin'."

"I don't like that word 'rectum'. It doesn't sound nice," scolded Sarah.

"It sounds better than passage. A passage is a place that leads to another."

"Same thing! My passage leads to all kinds of places."

"Like what!"

"Me innards an such."

"Oh, for goodness sake, ma. Will you put the phone down. I'm just havin' a cup of coffee an' a sandwich. Now you've turned me guts."

"*Right!* I'm puttin' it down nye."

A couple of seconds passed and there was still no sound.

"Have you put it down yet?" asked Elsie.

"Yes!"

"Mother, I think the next time Doctor Wright looks up your bum he should shine a strong light up it to see if your brain's still workin'."

Sarah tut-tutted, and slammed the receiver down.

ꝏ ꝏ ꝏ ꝏ ꝏ

Bernard the milkman sailed up Hetherington Green in his milk-float, late as usual. He whistled and the milk bottles rattled in their crates. Bernard was as easy-go-lucky as Bert, but that's were the resemblance ended. He was tall and willowy, with a long gaunt face. His black moustache his only redeeming feature as it helped disguise his empty expression. Bernard could carry eight milk bottles at a time, an asset to a man with his job. He had an extra bottle tucked down at the side of his seat. This bottle was not filled with the juice of the cow; it was green and filled with the juice of the juniper berry.

Bernard had been filled with lust since the weekend. His wife had left after finding him in bed with the Avon lady. The door bell was not the only ding-dong in *her* life. The saying, "Ding dong, it's the Avon lady", had become something of a joke in Ballyhornet, after Bernard's wife had been seen chasing her through the streets wearing nothing more than body oil.

Bernard had a list of desperate women who would drop their knickers as a way of paying for a fortnight's milk and eggs. His wages were very low some weeks! Peggy was on his list of willing females, far down it, but on it. Hence the gin. Well, he had to make some sort of gesture for services rendered.

Bernard slipped round the back, gin bottle hidden from view.

Peggy had dozed off in her armchair and failed to hear the timid knock on the back door.

He knew she was in for he could see the back of her head through the window. It lolled from side to side. He also knew Rab was out. He had spotted him entering the gates of Sir Robert's as he passed on his rounds. Planting the gin bottle on the back step, he jumped up and down and waved his arms about in the hope of disturbing Peggy.

"What's up wi' you, Bernard? Ye luk like ye've caught a dose af somethin'. Crabs or somethin' else that itches." Maggie next door had been hanging out her washing.

Bernard stood rigid with shock then jumped to the side, crab-like, to hide the bottle from view with his long legs.

"I'm practicin' me aerobics! Have till keep yerself fit nye, Maggie."

"In Peggy's back yard?"

Bernard searched for an answer. His eye's lit on Rab's shed, "Iieeyah, I wuz just havin' a wee peek at Rab's birds. They're nice wee things all the while – love birds an' such ..." He laughed nervously. "Yer cat doesn't go for them at all, Maggie?"

"Ach, Bernard, my wee pussy disappeared a while back so it did."

A tear formed. She wiped it away with the corner of her apron and praised Rab for the concern he had shown to her in her grief.

"Thon Rab is a quare nice big man. He wuz that worried about its safety he dug up his garden till see if any auld waster had killed it an' buried it. He taule me there wuz no sign af it so I tuk him at his word. He's a man af his word, is Rab. If he says he'll do a thing fer ye, he does it. He taule me my pussy wud nat go thirsty. That's why he left that bucket af water there, just in case it wasn't dead. See what I mean? That bucket has stayed there day in an' day out. Nye I'm away in to take a powder, fer me head it's splittin'. You'll excuse me if I don't stand around till keep ye company, like." She shuffled into her kitchen and closed the door.

Bernard sighed deeply. "Phew! That wuz a close shave. Nye, let's see." He cupped his hands and peered through Peggy's window. She was still there, snoring away. "God, curse ye, woman, will ye open the dur."

He was down on his knees hissing through the keyhole, but Peggy slept on. He lifted the gin bottle and, head bent, headed back to his milk float. As he passed the front door his heart leapt. It was open. Peggy must have known I wuz on my way, he thought. Sure she cud smell sex from a mile away, cud our Peg! He tucked the bottle under his arm and rubbed his hands together.

Peggy's slumber was shattered by the sound of a scream, followed by an earth-shattering bump. Then silence. She couldn't move, her heart started to palpitate and she listened and waited. Finally, she lifted her bum off the chair. She tentatively made her way to the kitchen door. She listened again. Still no sound. Everything started to happen in slow motion.

"Oh my God! I can't luk'. I didn't mean it, Rab. Wake up will ye, fer God's sake! See if he's only lettin' on, I'll kill 'im.' Oh Jaysus, where's me gin."

She flip-flopped over to the sink, lifted the bottle off the window ledge and gulped down a few measures, then she braced herself and headed towards the hall.

"What the ..." She peered down at the body and gulped. "It's nat bloody Rab! Unless he's grown a moustache in two hours I wud say that's another maun."

She bent down and tapped Bernard on the arm. He didn't even flinch. Turning his head to the side she noticed a large red bump on the front of it. His nose was bloody and two false teeth were protruding from his mouth. The green gin bottle was still tucked firmly under an arm that was trapped underneath him. She yelled so loud that a passing neighbour ran to her aid.

"Is it Rab, Peggy? Call the dactor quick!" Mrs O'Kane, from three doors up, had joined Peggy. She blessed herself and cried out, "Holy Mother af God, is he dead?"

"It's nat Rab, Mrs O'Kane. It's the milkman! And I don't think he's dead."

"Well I'm goin' till whisper th' act of contrition in his ear just in case. It'll do no harm anyway."

"But he's nat Catholic!" Peggy pushed her away, but Mrs O'Kane had her rosary out and was determined to get this man into heaven whatever religious persuasion he inclined towards.

Lynus rushed through the open door at that minute.

"Peggy, the wee brats are robbin' Bernard's milk float! Where th' hell is he?"

"He's down here," pointed Peggy.

Lynus gazed down at the lifeless body.

"Holy shit! Huz he been shat?"

"Don't be so bloody wet! He just trip ..." Peggy remembered hiring the door stoop the previous night. How many years did a body get for murder these days?

"Were ye goin' till say tripped?" Lynus looked out of the corner of his eye at Peggy. "Nye, how wud he trip in the hall?" His eyes narrowed with suspicion.

A wee lad no older than seven stood at Peggy's door. "Heh missus, thank the milkman for all that nice milk an' them eggs. An tell him we tuk his moneybeg as well," then he took off like a whippet.

A police car pulled up. The policemen had seen the young lad running away from Peggy's house, followed by an irrate Lynus, and wondered what was going on. Two policemen got out of the car and ambled up Peggy's driveway.

"Well, well, what have we got here then?" The bigger of the two stood over Bernard's still form. "Someone have an accident then?"

"It's the milkman," answered a breathless Lynus, who had returned from his chase.

"The milkman? Started to deliver gin now, I see." The policeman extracted the gin bottle from under Bernard's arm and examined it.

Bernard groaned. Peggy breathed a sigh of relief. Mrs O'Kane pocketed her rosary annoyed. She loved a good death, one that required a quick act of contrition in the earlug. The policeman started to ask questions. Peggy flip-flopped her way down the hall to the kitchen. She lifted a bottle of pills unscrewed the top and deftly tipped three *Valium* into her shaking hand.

"Will somewan givus a drink. I think I'm goin' till faint," she shouted back.

"That means three fingers af gin, afficer!" Rab had slipped in unnoticed in the furore. "Peggy here alus washes her wee helpers down wi' gin, she can't stan' the taste af water. Water tae Peggy is th' equivilant af daylight till Dracula."

"And who are you?" asked one of the policemen.

"Who am I? Nye, that's a good question, afficer! I have a qaure strang feelin' I shud be the wan lyin' oan that flur."

"Mr ... em?"

"Kirk! Robert Kirk, the husband af this here lunatic." He nodded in Peggy's direction.

The policeman took a small note-book from his pocket and raised his pen.

"Now, Mr Kirk. It seems to me there's a bit of scullduggery goin' on here."

"Aye, afficer. Get yer pen well oiled there, fer ye never know what ye might hae tae write down afore the day's out."

Rab made himself comfortable in Peggy's armchair. Peggy threw him a dirty look, and he jumped up from the chair.

"Oh, I am sorry, Peggy. Did I take yer seat? Sit yersel' down there. Take the weight af yer feet afore the nice policemaun runs ye outa the house.

Peggy thrust her face towards Rab and hissed, "Fuck up, ye bastard! What brought ye back anyway? Did Sir Robert count his birds an' fine a couple missin'?"

"Ye never complained afore, whenever ye had pheasant fer Sunday dinner, did ye?"

The police officer interrupted their argument. "If you don't mind, Mr an' Mrs Kirk, there's an injured party in here."

"'Party' is the right word, afficer. If all had gone till plan my wife here wud be havin' a ball up the stairs right nye. In fact I wud go so far as till say she wud have been havin' a couple af balls, wi' a bita the auld John Thomas as an extra bonus."

Rab heard groaning behind him. and he turned round. Lynus and the other policeman were holding Bernard. His face was ashen except for the huge red bump on his head, and the blood that was running out of his nose and down his blue coat.

"Here, sit yerself down, Bernard." Mrs O'Kane had pulled a chair out from the kitchen table. "Jesus, Mary an' Joseph! What did ye do till yerself?"

"I don't know!" he cried. "One minute I wuz standin' at the door, the next thing I know is I'm covered in blood an' achin' all over."

"Why where you standin' at the door Mr Um ...?" asked the policeman, getting ready to take notes.

"Lowry, me name's Lowry."

"I'll start again. Why were you stand ..."

"I wuz deliverin' milk."

"You didn't let me finish, Mr Lowry. But seein' as your able to mind-read I'll ask the next question, that's if you don't already know it."

"He knows it alright. He just doesnae want till answer it," spat Rab.

"Let me do the questioning, Mr Kirk." The policeman snapped back.

"Tell him Bernard, tell the nice policeman why ye were deliverin' gin till the missus." Rab looked him in the eye. He was enjoying seeing him squirm.

"Gin! Do you mean to say you weren't delivering milk to this woman?"

"Nat exactly, officer."

"What do you mean, 'Not exactly'. You were either delivering milk or you weren't. Which one was it?"

"Alright! I wasn't."

A hush fell over the small gathering of people.

"I wuz hopin' Mrs Kirk wud do me a sexual favour."

A gasp escaped from Mrs O'Kane's lips. She blessed herself and took her rosary out of her pocket.

"A sexual favour? In return for what?" asked a puzzled policeman.

"A battle af gin."

Mrs O'Kane started to finger her beads.

"If I were you I'd put those beads away, missus. By the time ye hear what goes on in this house they'll go on fire, the way yer rubbin' them through yer hauns."

"Are you aware of your wife selling her body for gin, Mr Kirk?"

"Indeed I am, afficer. My wife wud sell her body fer a pramise af a battle af gin. An' many a time she huz. Sometimes I feel sorry fer her, fer nye an' then the bleeders give her water in gin battles an' bugger aff."

The policeman could hardly believe his ears. "If you don't mind me askin', Mr Kirk, do you not mind your wife sleepin' with other men?"

"Oh she doesnae sleep wi' them, she has sex. I *sleep* with her, the rest have *sex* wi' her."

The policeman turned his attention back to Bernard. "So you get sex for the price of a bottle of gin, then Mr Lowry?"

"I need a dacter, officer. I need my head luked at till see if it's alright." Bernard felt the bump on his head.

"Aye, indeed ye do. Only it's nat a dacter ye need tae see. It's a shrink, or a clairvoyant that reads bumps," laughed Rab.

Will someone send fer one quick! I can feel me life's blood drainin' outa meself."

"Hold on a minute there, Mr Lowry." The policeman sat down, facing Bernard, and scratched his head. "Do ye deliver a lot of gin in this estate?"

"No, just to Peggy."

"Just to Peggy. Ah nye, that's just as well. For a minute there I wuz goin' to ask to see your licence for sellin' alcohol."

"Luk, officer. Can't we just forget this wee incident. My missus wud sell her soul till the divil fer a battle af gin. Yer lucky yer able till go home at the end af the day an' put you're feet up. I'm afraid till put me feet up, I hae to keep oan the move whenever thon woman's conscious. I hae to keep wan step ahead af thon headcase. If I rest on me laurels, I'm in grave danger af bein' bumped aff."

"You're sayin' it was attempted murder, Mr Kirk?" enquired the policeman, pen poised.

"I'm sayin' nathin! An' somehow or other I don't think Mr Lowry will be sayin' anymore either, will ye Bernard?"

"What th..." Bernard tried to defend himself, but Rab had the last word.

"I hear yer nat makin' much money these days, while the men af th' estate are findin' themselves a wee bit better aff money-wise, this past while back!" said Rab in a threatening manner.

"I ... I ... think I fell over me own feet, officer. In fact, I think I walked into th' wrong house. Is this number twelve Hetherington Green?"

"Nah, Bernard. It's number ten. An' somehow or other I don't think Maggie's pussy drinks gin, in fact, Maggie's pussy isn't drinkin' at all nye, Bernard, me auld son," chided Rab.

"Is that why ...?" Bernard put his hand to his lips to silence himself.

Rab tapped the side of his nose, warning Bernard to keep his mouth shut. "What were ye goin' till say Bernard?"

"Nathin', Rab. Nathin'."

Rab turned to the policeman. "I think th' incident is closed, afficer. No-one is pressin' charges."

"Thank God for that! I don't fancy writin' a report on this one. I want to finish early the day. Come on, let's get back to the station. I'm dyin' for a cuppa."

"He nearly died for a bita th' other, said Rab, pointing at Bernard. He reached into his coat pocket for his inhaler. "I'm dyin' tryin' till avoid it. In fact, afficer, some af these days I might just snuff it tryin' tae escape Peggy's clutches."

"Are you nat too well, Mr Kirk?"

"Let's just say there's no point in plannin' a garden. I'll hardly live tae see it grow."

"That bad, Mr Kirk?"

"Aye, afficer. I stick till beddin' plants, nye." Rab looked over at his wife. "She sticks till beddin' men."

The police officer followed Rab's gaze and shook his head. "Well it takes all sorts." He pocketed his notebook and winked at his fellow officer. "Come on, lad. Let's get out of here."

The two policemen left the house climbed back into their car and drove off.

"What about my effin milk float? It's been stripped bare."

"Too bad Barney, too bloody bad," hissed Rab through gritted teeth. "Nye ladies an' gentlemen, ye can all go home. The party's over fer the day." He glared at Peggy. "As fer you, missus, ye can plan a new way tae do away wi' yer auld man. I'm here till stay for another wee while! So take yer gin battle an' lie down afore ye fall down."

15

Friday, 29 March

Dr McNulty had dressed in a hurry. A telephone call from a distressed female pensioner had interrupted his breakfast. He had been sitting in his dressing gown eating his boiled eggs and buttered soldiers and reading his newspaper when the housekeeper handed him the phone.

Dr McNulty was not known for his sympathetic nature. He had been a doctor for almost forty years now and his own nerves were as bad as the patients that hammered on his surgery door day in and day out for anti-depressants. This old dear sounded beside herself with worry.

He had tried in vain to make sense of the conversation, but the old woman would not let him get a word in edgeways. He managed to scribble down her name and address before she hung up on him.

He was driving through Ballyhornet and glanced at the address he had jotted down. Hetherington Green! God, please not that woman in the flats? Lord help us. I think it is!

He pulled over to the side of the road and turned off the engine. He flicked on the light inside the car, hoping the darkness of the early morning had been playing tricks on his eyes. It was definitely Sarah Cruickshank of Hetherington Green. He cursed himself for not recognising the voice. He toyed with the idea of turning back to his eggs, buttered soldiers and newspaper. He wasn't due in surgery for another hour-and-a-half. He could call to see her in the afternoon. What if she has collapsed? She might have called wolf one time too often. He turned on the engine and sighed. He wound down his window, breathed in the morning air and followed the kerbstones of the footpath very slowly, as if a good blast of air would erase his idea of euthanasia for the over-eighties.

Bernard the milkman, who had decided to get his milkround finished before the men and women of the estate could make snide remarks about his sex life, skidded to a halt beside the doctor's car. He lent over and rolled down his window.

"Hey you! Kerb crawler. Don't ye think it's a bit early in the day till start pickin' up weemen, or have ye been at it all night?"

"Kerb crawler? I will tell you now, my dear man, I am a doctor and doctor's don't kerb crawl."

"Oh aye! Well rumour has it that Jack the Ripper was supposed to have been a dactor, an' he enjoyed the company of the occasional good thing. An' he carved up a few auld dolls inta the bargain."

Bernard lifted his right buttock off his seat and peered into the doctor's car. "Ye don't luk like a dactor. For a start yer shirt's nat buttoned up right an' yer jumpers on inside out. Did the last one rip the clothes af yer back wi' lust?"

Dr McNulty informed Bernard that he did not carve up women, but it fell on deaf ears.

"Luk, mister, I'm partial to a wee bit af th' other myself, but if I were you I'd take a bit af advise fram one that knows. The weemen in this estate that wud give their bodies freely are a bit on the brute ugly side."

"I tell you, I'm a doctor! Look, can't you see the sign on the front of my car? It says 'Doctor on call'."

"It shud say 'Eye Specialist on call'. Half the men in here must have been half blin' or tricked into marrying the things that pass for females in here."

The light off one of the street lamps lit up the side of Bernard's head. Dr McNulty could make out the outline of a huge blueish-purple protuberance on Bernard's temple.

"Have you been in an accident recently?"

"I suppose ye cud say that. That's what ye get fer tryin' to get your oats in this damned place. So forget about feelin' horny. Get yer wee ass outa here pronto, or ye'll end aff wi' a bump wi' a head on th' end af it."

"Here, are ye really a dactor? See if ye are, cud ye have a wee jook at me head an' see if it's alright."

"It wouldn't take a close examination to find that out, my dear man. I can see from here you'll not die in a mental home. It takes brains to have a nervous breakdown. Your brain could fit into an egg-cup." He put his car into gear and made a vain attempt to move on.

Bernard blocked his escape by quickly turning his milk float in front of Dr McNulty's car. He jumped down from the cab of his milk-float, thrust his fist through the open window of the doctor's car and grabbed the man by the collar.

He managed to get his head through the window before Dr McNulty had time to even contemplate winding it up.

"Luk here, bastard features! My brain's firin' on all cylinders. Nye if it's a fight ye want I'm yer maun, but by the puny luk af ye ... hold on a minute, I know that face!" Bernard released his grip on Dr McNulty's collar. Your th' dactor that sent me for a bowel X-ray last year. That wuz bloody uncomfortable, nat to mention degradin'. I don't suppose you've had wan yerself dactor? Ye wudn't be so quick with th' auld pen in writin' till th' haspital fer appointments fer yer patients if ye hud."

"Maybe you will let me get on with my business then, if you don't mind, I have a patient to see." He grabbed Bernard by the wrist and twisted his arm out of the window. "Now move your vehicle so I can be on my way."

Bernard rubbed his wrist. "That's alright then, but ye have till admit ye luked a wee bit suspicious crawlin' along the side af the kerb in that Volvo af yours. Nat many people in here cud afford a car like that. It's well seen you dactors are on a pig's back."

Bernard decided to say no more and thought God knows, I might be in dire need af the maun wan day. He climbed back into his milk float and drove on up the street.

The pensioners' flats beckoned Dr McNulty like an executioner to the gallows. Turning his engine and lights off, he lifted his case and opened the door. He toyed with the idea of driving back home. Sure if the old bat had died he would be of no use anyway. Nevertheless, a moment later he found himself locking his car door and heading wearily towards the gate. Five minutes and ten silent screams later he was still trying to open the gate.

He kicked it, shook it, cursed at it, stood back and prayed at it, but the gate was unrelenting. The light from Sarah's flat teased him with its brightness. Through an opening in the gate he could make out another entrance, a back door.

He went round the front of the flats, accidentally stepping into a large sloppy dog turd in the darkness and he cursed the thing that had deposited it. A further five minutes was spent trying to remove it from his shoe by scraping his foot along the frosted grass.

He stood at the back entrance to the flats. This too was locked and he found himself talking to a door.

"If I had a hatchet you would be firewood. Make no bones about it matey, you would be history. Nothing more than a pile of sticks!"

A man out walking his dog stopped and stared.

Dr McNulty became aware of the man and he tried to explain away his behaviour but it only made matters worse. The man and his dog took off at the speed of light and Dr McNulty yelled after the fleeing man, "Was that your bloody dog that crapped in the grass?"

The man didn't look back as he scarpered up a driveway and let himself and his dog into the house.

Dr McNulty cocked his ear to listen to the voices that were coming from inside.

"There's a flamin' lunatic on the loose out there! By the sounds af him he's straight out af cloud cuckoo land. Tryin' till tell *me* he was a dactor! If ye ask me, he probably thinks he's Henry th' Eighth as well. Standin' talkin' till a dur he wuz, then started howlin' like a banshee. Come away from those curtains, Mary! We don't want him comin' over here till take out his madness on us."

"Ye may stay af that auld drink. Yer nat only seein' pink elephants durin' the night nye, yer hearin' voices as well. I'll be bringin' grapes up till ye when the men in white carry ye aff till th' happy home."

"I tell ye Mary, there's some queer folk aroun' these days. An' one af them is tryin' till talk a door inta openin'. I'm callin' the police!"

Dr McNulty had heard it all, and he felt highly insulted. With a face the length of York Street he made his way to the window of Sarah's flat, and gave it a good rap with his knuckles. The curtains were pulled to the side and a wizened face peered out into the darkness.

"Who's there?"

"Did you call me this morning, Mrs Cruickshank? It's Dr McNulty. I thought you were going to die. What is it that you can't get out?"

"Eh? I can't hear ye. Wait till I open the door."

Sarah fumbled with the keys. It seemed an eternity before she got the door opened. She pottered over the flagstoned yard and stopped about a yard from the gate.

"Who did ye say ye were?"

Dr McNulty closed his eyes and prayed for guidance. "It's the doctor you sent for at the crack of dawn, Mr's Cruickshank."

Sarah started preening her hair like a schoolgirl on her first date. She loved doctors, especially male ones. They were the only people who would let her bend their ears with silly complaints.

She hadn't counted on Dr McNulty calling on her. Nobody bent his ear.

"Well hold on there, doctor." She fiddled with her bunch of keys before adding in a polite voice. "It's most kind of you to leave the comfort of your nice warm home to visit little old me." She laughed coyly.

Sarah fumbled with the lock, the wretched thing refused to yield even though Sarah was cursing it in and out of hell. Now her politeness had left with frustration.

"Ye will have till get me daughter over. There's nothin' else for it. She has a spare key, doctor.

"Your daughter?"

"Aye, she lives over there," Sarah pointed.

He felt the urge to run out throw himself under a bus.

"There are no lights on. Are they not up out of bed yet?"

"I suppose not! I rang her at half past five this mornin, an' she ate th' gob af me for disturbin' her sleep. I told her I was goin' to give you a call but she just taule me to go back till sleep an' slammed the phone down."

"I'm not surprised Mrs Cruickshank. You don't sound as if you're in dire need of a doctor's service, if you don't mind me saying so."

"An' how th' hell would you know? I take it you've no time for th' oule, either?" Sarah reprimanded the man with a wiggle of her finger.

"Go over an' give the door a good blatter, an' yell through the letter box. That'll get them out af their pits. Oh, haule on a minute. I think the gates open nye. I heard the lock click." The gate creaked as she opened it.

"Hear that! Th' housin' office wouldn't even think af oilin' the hinges. I must put a wee drop af me cod liver oil on those, for by Jaysus ye'd die waitin' before a body would put their arse in a cramp to come out till do it for ye."

I wish I had have taken my time coming out, and maybe *you* would have died waiting, Dr McNulty thought as he lifted his case and followed Sarah into her flat.

"Would ye like a cup af tea in yer haun?" asked Sarah as she closed the front door behind her.

Dr McNulty decided to ignore this offer and hurried into Sarah's living room.

"Now, Mrs Cruickshank. What's ailing you? The way you were ranting on the telephone this morning I thought you were dying."

"I very well could be. I was sittin' on the toilet an' I went all dizzy." She looked at the frustration on Dr McNulty's face and added, "A relative of mine died on the toilet ye know!"

"Well, we all have to go sometime, you know."

"Well I don't intend goin' just yet so don't go gettin' any death certificates out af yer wee leather beg."

"Alright Mrs Cruickshank, pull your jumper up so I can get at your chest and back." He examined her chest and lungs, checked her blood pressure, and declared, Do you know? you have the blood pressure of someone half your age, and your heart's as sound as a bell."

"What about me lungs?"

"I wish I had set like them, Mrs Cruickshank."

"Well I've lived a healthy lifestyle. I never smoked or drank an' I never gallivanted about with other men."

He replaced his instruments in his case "Right then, we've ruled out the threat of dying. What else ails, you Mrs Cruickshank?"

"I can't get it out, an' it's nippin'."

Dr McNulty could feel the life drain out of him. "What can you not get out?"

"I sat on the toilet for an hour, an' I couldn't get it out."

It all fell into place.

"You're *constipated!*" he roared. "Do you mean to say you got me out at seven o'clock in the morning because you are *constipated?* Good God woman, take a laxative."

"I did! I did."

"When?"

"An hour ago! I took it an hour ago."

He bowed his head. He thought of the long day ahead of him.

"Mrs Cruickshank, if all my patients called me out for being constipated I would never be at home! When did you last have a bowel movement anyway?"

"Two days ago."

"Two days ago." He sounded as it he were crying. I sometimes don't have a bowel movement for ten days, but I don't worry about it. I go in the end."

"What about the nippin' doctor?" Sarah was going to find some ailment to gain sympathy, even if it meant tying him to the seat until she thought one up.

"It's nipping! Do you mean you have haemorrhoids as well?"

"No! me ankle."

"You have haemorrhoids on your ankle?"

"Don't be so bloody daft! I have an ulcer on me ankle. Haemorrhoids indeed. Do ye think I'm senile or somethin'?"

Sarah removed her stocking. Dr McNulty could just about make out an ulcer the size of a pin-head on her scrawny ankle. He told Sarah that he usually treated ulcers the size of his fist and that she was a very lucky woman to be in such good health at her age.

"Are ye tryin' till tell me I should be dead?"

He was tempted to say yes, but he wrote her out a script for a strong laxative instead.

"Here, take this every night Mrs Cruickshank."

"What is it?"

"It will keep you regular."

"I take porridge every mornin', ye know. That should keep me regular in itself."

"Not really Mrs Cruickshank. It takes a lot more than porridge."

"I eat very well, an' I keep this auld flat as clean as I can. It's hard to make a velvet cloak out af a donkey jacket, but I do me best."

"Would you not put your name down for a Fold?"

"I am not a flamin' horse, Doctor McNulty!"

No, I don't mean that kind of foal. I mean a block of flats with a warden to look after your safety."

"A prison warden? You mean locked in like?"

"Well you're locked in here and it's very dangerous. What if a fire broke out, how would you all get out with the gate and doors locked?"

"Do you know Doctor McNulty, I never thought of that. I must give Percy another wee ring." She rose from her chair, lifted the note pad beside the phone and wrote down, 'Ring Percy'. She felt chuffed. She loved making complaints by the phone.

It was daylight when Dr McNulty left Sarah's flat. He glanced at his watch. Only another half hour to go and he would be writing out sick lines and prescriptions in his surgery at the local health centre.

He shouldn't have taken his eye of the ground for at that moment he trod in another mound of dog excrement. His blood pressure reached stroke level. He scanned the street for the house that harboured the man and his dog.

"Right!" he said, "I am going over to that man's house to make *him* clean my shoe."

Peter answered Dr McNulty's angry rap on the door, then closed the door in the doctor's face.

"For frig sake, Mary, it's that bloody headbin I wuz tellin' ye about."

"Well bolt the bloody dur! Or else set Sheba on 'im." His wife, Mary, made for the kitchen and hid in the broom cupboard.

"Open that door or I'll kick it in!" Dr McNulty was standing on one leg like a flamingo, his soiled shoe held up by its laces in his left hand. "Is this your dog's crap on my shoe?"

"What have we here then?"

Dr McNulty gyrated on his earthbound foot. He found himself face to face with a police officer.

"What the ..."

"I have reason to believe you're annoying the neighbours of this area."

Another policeman joined him. They observed his untidy dress and shook their heads in unison.

"Well, well, well, what do we have here then?" said the first policeman again.

"You've already asked that!" hissed the doctor. "Do you always repeat yourself?"

"Well, well, well, we have a cocky one here, Alf," he said to his partner.

"Well, well, well, aren't we the silly beggars." Dr McNulty mimicked the police man's toady voice.

"Oh ho, Alf! I think we might have an arrest on our hands."

"Well, think again, constable! But I would make sure you have a dog leash in your car before carrying out your job," Dr McNulty told them.

Peter decided to risk an appearance. He felt braver now the law had arrived.

"That's the maun, afficer! He's a bloody menace to society. Runnin' aroun' with his shoe in his hand is he, nye? I suppose he's knockin' th' daylights outa people wi' the heel af it."

"I am running around with my shoe in my hand because it is covered in dog shit! Are you going to wipe it clean?"

"Nah, I am nat! Why shud I wipe it aff? It's nat my shit." The spit ran down Peter's chin as he spat out these words. He ran his arm over his chin and wiped it off with the sleeve of his shirt.

"I know it's not yours, it's your damned dog's."

"How do ye know it's my dog's crap? Does it have it's name carved in it?"

"*No!* But you will have your nose rubbed in it if you don't clean it. I can't go into the surgery with dog mess tripping off my shoes. The patients wouldn't stand for it."

"Nye he's tellin' yousens he's a dactor! Do ye see what I mean afficer? He tried that one on me. Luk at it! Wud you call that regamuffen a dactor? Come on, nye, tell the truth an' shame the devil. Wud you let a maun like that near ye, never mine examine ye?"

Bernard the milkman happened to be passing the house just then. Dr McNulty took the chance to save his good name by hopping towards his float and waving him down.

"Hello there dactor! Have ye hurt yer fut?"

Dr McNulty's face broke into a smile of relief.

"Did you hear that?" He turned on his foot and faced his accusers. "This man will confirm what I already know and you three doubt." He pointed at the men standing at the open door. "Tell them Mr Milkman, tell them I'm a doctor."

"Oh, he's a dactor alright," beamed Bernard. "I bloody hope so anyway, fer he hoked up my rearend with his finger."

"Hey you!" yelled the first policeman. "Haven't I seen your face before?" He rubbed his chin as he tried to put a name to the face. "Ah, hah, nye I remember. Hey Alf, it's nat the milkman. It's the gin man."

"Yer jokin'? Jaysus, this place is like the twilight zone. Queers passin' themselves off as doctors and sex maniacs dressed up as milkmen."

Alf laughed at this and Dr McNulty made the mistake of running up the drive and slapping him over the head with the heel of his shitty shoe.

"Well, well, well, what did we do nye, doctor?" asked policeman number one.

"Well, well, well, officer. It's obvious to all. I hit him on the head with the heel of my shoe. Now take *that!*" Dr McNulty brought his shoe down on the head of the other policeman.

"Hey, Mary! Come out here!" yelled Peter to his wife. "An' bring Sheba with ye. This lunatic has clobbered the policemen over th' heads with his shoe."

"Well, well, well, now, Mr Doggy Man! Seeing as it was your dog that caused all this commotion, you might as well feel the heel of my shoe as well." *Thump*. Dr McNulty went for the triple whammie and hit Peter on the head with his shoe.

"I want that maun arrested forthwith," whimpered Peter as he held his head. He slowly lowered his hand after feeling something sticky on his head. "I'm bloody bleedin'. That nutcase has split me head clean open!"

"Don't worry, me auld bean, he's a dactor He'll stitch it up fer ye," tittered Bernard, enjoying the furore. Yesterday might have been a bad day in his life; today's goings-on were making up for it. It was better than a pantomime. The best part of the whole shebang was that it was free, and offered a front row seat to boot.

Dr McNulty was laughing out loud. His face had taken a crazed look. He jumped up and down. "I don't care any more! I feel free, I feel as if I'm alive for the first time in years." He held out his arms. "Here! Arrest me. Put the cuffs on. Take me to your leader." Then he dropped to his knees and started to sob.

Dr McNulty was led away by the two policemen. They bundled him into the squad car unceremoniously and drove off to the station. Although it was a cold morning the windows were wound down to let the air in and the smell out.

ꝏ ꝏ ꝏ ꝏ ꝏ

"Will Bert collect me prescription?"

"Don't tell me you had the doctor out, ma?" Elsie's brain was trying to make sense of her mother's phone call. She was sounding very perky this morning and when Sarah sounded perky it spelt trouble.

"Indeed I did. An' he's one hell of a nice man. He gave me somethin' for me bowels."

"Well now, mother. Dr Crippen would be hailed as a very nice man if he gave you something for your bowels. You have a bowel fixation. Don't tell me you got the doctor out this mornin'! I thought you were only lettin' on about callin' him out. Who was it anyway?"

"Dr McNulty."

"Dr McNulty?" Elsie could hardly believe her ears. "Did he not do his nut? He hates old people."

"I am not old!"

"If your not old ma, I'm not fat. Now there's no-one in this land who would call me slim, so no way can you say you're in the summer of your life. If your in the summer of your life, I dread to think what age you will live to."

The silence was deafening. When Sarah fell quiet it scared Elsie. The day would not go smoothly.

"Speak up!" screeched Elsie. "I know you're there! I can hear the television in the background."

"You're not very nice to your elders, are ye?" whined Sarah.

"Oh, so you're old now. You have to admit it. If I'm nearing sixty, *you* can't exactly be going into the menopause now can you?"

"Oh be quiet, woman!" Sarah changed the subject.

"He said that gate isn't safe. If a fire broke out we wouldn't have an earthly. He's very worried about me."

I'm sure he is, thought Elsie I'm sure he's losing sleep over this.

"I'm ringin' Percy this mornin'."

"Not again! For heaven's sake, give the man a break. Just keep the gate open for a few weeks. Wait until he gets over the trauma of gettin' that one on."

"Look here my girl, if I want to ring Percy I will ring him."

"Oh, ring whoever you like, ma, I'm away to have a bath." Elsie put the phone down, went up the stairs and started to run the bath water. She had just started to undress when the phone rang again.

Bert answered it this time. "Yith, who ith it?"

Elsie came to the top of the stairs and asked Bert who it was.

"It'th yer ma again."

Elsie told him to tell her she was just getting into the bath.

"Who rang ye?" Bert was engrossed in this telephone call.

Elsie turned the water off and jumped down the stairs three at a time. Something must be wrong.

"The health thentre rang! Why wud the Health Thentre ring you?"

Elsie sidled up beside Bert to listen.

"Dr McNulty's dithapeared! An' why wud they ring you?"

"Give me the phone, Bert!" Elsie grabbed the phone from her husband's hand.

"What have you done with Dr McNulty?"

"I haven't laid a hand on him!"

"Well why are they ringin' you?"

"They rang his home to see why he hadn't turned up and his housekeeper told them he had gone out on a home visit to me."

"Did you let him out again?"

"No! I done him in and buried him in the yard! Of course I let him out, ye stupid woman."

"Did he appear to be in his right mind?"

"What kind of a question's that?"

"Well, you have been known to addle peoples brains with that tongue of yours. Maybe the man threw in the towel an' run off to the hills to get his head showered. Did ye see him drive off?"

"Of course I didn't. I don't neb out the window every second of the day ye know."

"Since when? Your head's always peepin' round the curtains, even through the night."

"I had to run to the toilet after he left. Me laxative started to work an' I just made it in the nick af time. The sweat was lashin' off me in buckets with the cramps. I heard a bit of commotion goin' on over the back, but I think it was that auld lad who owns that flee-ridden mutt. It was barkin' somethin shockin'."

Elsie pulled her curtain to the side and peered out.

"There's a car parked outside the flats. It looks a bit posh to belong to anyone in this estate. Hold on till I go an' have a wee jook at it."

Elsie put on her coat and ventured into the cold April air. On the car window was a sticker which read "Doctor on Call". Now that's suspicious, she mused. She went back into her house and told her mother to hang up, as she had a few inquiries to make.

She went over to Peter and Mary's. "Did you see a doctor this mornin'?"

Peter, jumped backwards with fright. "Jaysus don't tell me it's startin' all over again?"

"What's startin' all over again?" asked Elsie.

"People imaginin' they're dactors, an' people imaginin' they've seen dactors."

"So, what your tryin' to say is, you saw a doctor this mornin'."

"I saw a man who said he was a doctor, but the police tuk him away to th' station in the squad car. If ye ask me he wuz slightly mad. I saw him talkin' till the back dur af the flats earlier on. Then he accused my dog of crappin' all over th' estate."

"My ma's flat door?"

"Well, it wuz the dur that led into yer ma's hall."

"Oh, my God! What has that flamin' woman done now?"

Elsie turned on her heels and headed towards the flats. She was going to wring her mother's neck. This time she had overstepped the mark.

16

Thursday, 18 April

The postman rapped Rab's door instead of putting the letter through his letter box. Rab set down his cup of tea and rose from his chair. He put his head round the kitchen door and froze. The uniformed outline of the postman appeared ominous through the frosted glass. He thought it was the police and he pulled his head back into the kitchen. Peggy's deep throated voice echoed from the bedroom. "Are ye there, Rab? Someone's at the dur."

"Will ye shut up, woman! Keep yer voice down," Rab hissed through cupped hands. He peered round the door again. The figure held a letter. Rab didn't like policemen bearing letters. He never heard of a policeman being the bearer of good news in his life.

The figure rapped the door again. Louder this time.

"Will ye answer that, ye big glipe. It cud be important."

"Hell roast ye! Can ye nat keep yer gub shut woman?" Rab slipped into the hallway to get a better look. He kept his back close to the wall and sidled to the door. He could see the red outline now and he felt relieved that it was only the postman.

"Haule on thur, big lad. Nay need till put the dur in."

Jimmy the postman had put the letter on his clipboard, as if on a tray.

"Yer haliday money m'lord."

Rab looked at the envelope. The names Arbuckle, Arbuthnot & O'Neill were printed in bold letters on the flap.

"Hee, hee, Jimmy, me auld mucker. It luks like me ship's come in early. I wuzn't expectin' till hear fram these geezers fer at least another month.

"He rubbed his hands together before taking the letter. He kissed the envelope, then kissed Jimmy on the cheek.

"Get aff, ye big ape!" Jimmy retrieved a hanky from his pocket and cleaned his cheek with it.

"Th' only time I'd let you gi' me a kiss is when ye win the lattory an' haun me a cheque fer a million poun's. Somehow or other I think whatever's in thon envelope falls well short af the jackpot af ten million quid."

"Right at this minute af time Jimmy, a hundred pounds wud dae me rightly." A worried look spread over his face. "I hope tae Jaysus I've won me bloody claim! Dae ye think it cud be bad news, Jimmy?"

"Well, ye'll niver know till ye open it Rab. I'm nat a singin' telegram ye know. Do ye want me till open it an' sing ye the words like?"

"Spare me th' agony, Jimmy. I've heard yer attempt at singin' on karoake nights. Ye soun' like a cat bein' strangled, an' I'm well versed oan *that* subject." He tilted his head to the side. "Did Friars an' Lynus get wan o' these letters this mornin'?"

"I know Friars gat one. Nye, let's see if thur's wan fer Lynus." He flicked through the letters in his sack. "Aye there is wan fer a Mr L. McGrath alright. It luks like yer all in fer a surprise then. Come on, Rab, put me outa me misery. Open the bloody thing."

"Aye alright, ye nosey wee shite."

"Hurry up will ye? get yer finger out!"

"Haule on, will ye! Me head's up me arse wi' nerves." Rab ripped open the envelope and took out the letter. "It says here. 'Will you kindly ring Mr Arbuthnot at your earliest convenience.' That's all it says. Nathin else. What dae ye think that means, Jimmy?"

"It means, my dear maun, you've till give Mr Arbuthnot a ring. Are ye bloody daft?"

"I don't like the soun' af this, Jimmy. The last time I gat a claim there wuz nay ballsin' about wi' phonecalls. I just received the cheque."

Rab's eyebrows, that almost met in the middle, were now overlapping with worry.

"Ring 'im nye!"

"I've nay bloody phone! It wuz cut aff last week. That's that Peggy wan wi' her gin. Sh' even robbed the flamin' metre bax tae buy it. I had till fix it so it luked like we had been robbed or I'd hae been a guest af her majesty twice in three bloody years."

"Use Friar's. Get on yer bike, maun," Jimmy gazed down at Rab's legs. "An' get on yer trousers as well or ye'll be arrested."

In the excitement of the moment Rab had answered the door in his shirt and underpants. His trousers were drying on the radiator in the kitchen for he had soaked himself trying to fix a washer on the tap earlier in the morning.

"Luk here, Rab, I'm away on I have till deliver the rest af the mail. Some people still have till work fer a livin', believe it or nat."

"Aye alright, Jimmy," answered Rab.

"Will you get af the phone, Elthie. Rab an' I want till ring the solicitor."

"Look ma, I will have to go. Bert wants to use the phone. Right, right, right. I will get you something to stop your running to the toilet. I think Dr McNulty gave you that medicine for badness. I heard you were only to take that in dire circumstances."

Rab, who had called to use her phone, tapped Elsie from behind on the shoulder. "Did you hear about auld Dr McNulty, Elsie?"

"Hear what?"

"He's in the lock-up ward of the mental home."

"The mental home! Dr McNulty in the mental home? Who told ye that?" Elsie's eye's were sitting out like organ stops.

"I never mentioned Dr McNulty our Elsie! Have ye taken leave af yer senses?" Sarah had heard Elsie's side of the conversation. She thought she was speaking to her.

"Will ye shut up, ma!" She turned her attention to Rab again.

"Who told ye that?"

"I have me ways of findin' out these things, ye know."

"What's he doin' in there?" asked Elsie.

"How the hell would I know? No-one tells me anything these days. That auld rat beg up the stairs doesn't even talk till me anymore," ranted Sarah, who still was under the impression Elsie was talking to her.

"I'm talkin' to Rab, ma, will ye haule yer whisht."

"How can ye be talkin' till that glipe when yer talkin till me?"

Elsie slammed the phone down.

"When did he go in?" Elsie turned her full attention to Rab.

"He's been in since th' end af March. Wan o' the male nurses who luks after him wuz tellin' me he is talkin' till the walls an' barkin' like a dog."

"In th' name of ... He was out with my ma about that time. Hold on ... he disappeared without trace after visiting her." Elsie's look of surprise turned to one of shock. "Here, Peter across the road told me he saw him being taken away in a squad car screamin' on the mornin' of the twenty-ninth of March, about half past eight. He was with my ma at eight o'clock, this means *my* mother is responsible for puttin' a doctor away in the head."

"Nye, rumour has it he wuz batin' the heads af two policemen an' a man wi' the heel af his shoe. Bernard witnessed the whole scene, he said the dog shit wuz flyin' an' he wuz down on his knees beggin' till be hauncuffed. An' that's nat all. He's tellin' people he's Jack the Ripper reincarnated."

"Christ! now it all adds up. I rang th health centre for a script for me ma an' they ate the bake af *me!*. Bert, give me my coat from under the stairs I'm goin' over to my ma's to find out exactly what went on that mornin'."

"For heaven's thake thit down. Sure that auld doctor was a nasty auld git anyway. Bernard taule me he thaw him kerb crawlin' aroun' th' ethtate in th' early hours af the mornin'." Bert was standing in his *Calvin Kleins* with a cigarette stuck between his fingers.

"That's how rumours start. If you had a car you'd most likely be kerb crawlin' yourself, Bert Friars."

"What makes ye thay that, Elthie?"

"Well now Bert, it's th' only way you'll ever get a woman, isn't it?" Elsie took in his appearance with a sweep of her eyes and continued "Have you looked in the mirror lately?" She nodded in the direction of the landing "You must have looked in that one at the top of the stairs, for it's cracked!"

Rab intervened. He wanted to make his call to the solicitor.

"Luk here, you two. I have business tae attend till. Quite frankly, I couldn't give a flyin' f... Er, excuse me Elsie, I nearly cursed in frant af ye. I apalagise profusely fer me misconduct. So if you will step aside I will avail mysel' af yer phone an' then be on me merry way." He grabbed Elsie gently by the shoulders and led her into the living room. "Nye, sit yer wee bum down oan that seat an' rest yersel'."

"Hello, Mr Arbuthnot, Robert Kirk here, ye sent me a letter."

Bert shuffled up beside Rab to listen but he could only hear Rab's side of the conversation.

"Three-an'-a-half, ye say?" He gave a thumbs-up sign to Bert. "Well nye, I will hae till think about it, Mr Arbuthnot. Is that their final affer?"

Bert nervously lit another cigarette and breathed down Rab's neck.

Rab moved away. He could feel his asthma coming on.

"Can I take it me wife an' the two passengers will get the same amount?"

Bert was up hovering excitedly over Rab again, his cigarette's smoke making him cough. Rab told him to fuck aff out of the side of his mouth.

"Will ye haule on a minute there, Mr Arbuthnot. There's a pat boilin' over on th' cooker." He put the phone down on the bottom stair and shoved Bert up the hall. "Will ye put that friggin' feg out or I'll ram it up yer arsehole lit end first."

He took a few puffs of his spray before lifting the phone off the stairs.

"Right nye, where were we?"

A couple of minutes passed.

"Thank you very much fer yer precious time, Mr Arbuthnot. I will await yer next letter. An' ye say Mr Friars an' Mr McGrath will be hearin' fram ye in the near future as well? An' af coorse the wife. I almost forgat about her, an' her in agony. God help her, she can hardly walk these days, she's that unsteady oan her feet!" Rab winked at Bert.

Bert now knew all was well and he breathed a sigh of relief. "I will indeed, Mr Arbuthnot. I will give her yer regards. Bye, bye, speak to ye soon, God willin'." Rab replaced the receiver and hit the air with his fist.

"It's good news then?" asked Bert.

"I shud bloody say it is, Bert! We're all on three-an'-a-half gran' as it stauns. He's tryin' till get it upped, well mine anyway. Seein' as I was the driver an' I owned the car I staun' till win another five hundred pounds. What did auld Rab tell ye? I know me business when it comes till claims alright. It wuz quick all the while. That must be a good solicitor. Af coorse he knows his job like, he's nat wan af yer snattery wee skitters only outa law school ye know. Some af these wee blighters are still wet behin' th' ears an' straight af the tit. Get lumbered wi' wan a those an' ye can kiss at least two thou' goodbye."

Bert raced into the living room and kissed Elsie on the cheek.

"Get off, ye toothless wonder! Kiss me again an' I'll stitch that mouth of yours up with a needle an' thread."

"Come on Elthie, give us a big thloppy kith. I'll give ye a wad af notes if ye do."

"Ye can gae *me* a big slappy kiss, Bert, I'm that happy I cud kiss auld Sarah on the bum," Rab thought for a moment before adding, "Er, I take back that remark, I'm nat *that* happy."

"What are we goin' to do with all that money, Bert? Three-an'-a-half thousand! God Bert, I don't think it's right to take it, After all, you weren't really hurt." Elsie started to shake. "Look at me. I'm a nervous wreck! I've never handled that amount of money in one go in my life. I can get that new cooker and that video recorder plus a hi-fi."

"Hang on a minute, Elthie. It's three-an'-a-half thousand, nat three hundred thousand. Just cut out the mental spendin' thur."

"He's right, Elsie. It'll take ye till Tenerife fer a fortnight. Just think about it, nay Sarah fer fourteen whole days. Ye can throw caution till the wind; ye can throw yer tits out in the sun; ye cud drink sangria till it wuz comin' out af yer ears. As lang as ye don't drink the water ye'll be flyin'."

"Who's goin' to look after me Ma?"

"Put her in a home fer a fortnight! I'll run her over till the mental home an' stick her in wi' Dr McNulty. Which remin's me, what am I goin' till dae wi' thon wife af mine in Tenerife? She'll scare th' natives if sh' goes tapless. She'll hae to put thimbles oan her nipples tae stop them scrapin' the groun'."

"I think you'll have till put a beg over her head, Rab! In fact it wud be wiser till put her in a bin beg an' cover her up completely," chided Bert.

"Nye Bert, Peggy thinks she's God's gift till men. An' by the time August comes her pride an' joy will hae grown back to its natural state." Rab had to sit down and slip a heart tablet under his tongue. The excitement had given him a twinge in his chest.

"Jaysus, Rab, you may take it eathy over the next few months or ye won't see Tenerife."

❦ ❦ ❦ ❦ ❦

Next door Pip also had a delivery from the postman. Two letters, in fact. One was welcome the other was not. His dole cheque fell out of one envelope, a job offer from the other. He would have thrown this letter on the fire if his ma had been out. He had only filled in the application form at his da's insistence. Of all the people on the dole, he had to be offered the job of stacking shelves in the local supermarket. This would play havoc with his sex life. How could he explain this at the Starlight on Saturday nights. He couldn't wave his da's BMW keys in front of girls and say he stacked shelves for a living.

"That's great, Pip," stuttered Jacinta. She was stuttering with pride at her son getting offered his first job at the age of twenty. "I knew you'd get a job with a Protestant name. That's why those other four havne't been able to get work."

"Get a grip, Ma! It's only bloody stackin' shelves, for heaven's sake. Nye, if it had have been an affer to train for the post af bank manager I would agree with ye, but a trained monkey could stack bloody shelves."

"It's a start, son. Reg Holdsworth started out stackin' shelves an' look where he ended off."

"Ma, will ye steady yer head. That's a flamin' television programme! Reg Holdsworth is a figment of someone's imagination. Anyway, I'm more yer Curly Watts ... er, forget I said that. I'm more yer Hugh Grant, I am destined for the big time. I'm more yer movie star material. Look, don't let on to me da I got this letter. I'm goin' back till the tech anyway to learn about computers."

Pip had no intention of going to technical college to learn about anything. He had better things to do with his time. Lying horizontal, sleeping or shagging women for starters. Or vertical with a beer in his hand.

"You can go at night Pip, after work."

"You must be jokin', Ma! My brain'll be wrecked with all that auld false lightin' an' piped music. Anyway you have till work late some nights. An' have ye looked at the pay? It's lower than what ye get on the dole."

"No it's not, it's more. An' at least you'll have yer pride."

"Pride! Oh aye, I'll feel real proud in me wee white coat. I always wanted to wear a uniform," he added sarcastically. "An' it won't work out more money. With havin' to pay taxis to get to the bloody place an' buy me dinners I'll be worse off. Jaysus, I can't get me head round this. It's overloadin' me brain."

"*Walk it!* And don't take the Lord's name in vain, please. You know I don't like that talk!"

"You must be jestin', mother. *Me walk!* Do you realise I've gat a bad back?"

"Since when?"

"I didn't like to tell ye, but remember that hidin' I gat?"

"Yes."

"Well, it smashed two of me discs!"

"If you were Pinnochio your nose would be pokin' through the houses on the other side of the street, ye wee liar." Jacinta felt let down. She fell into Shaun's well-worn chair and sobbed.

Pip, who had a soft spot for his mum, felt bad now. "Alright I'll take it ma. Nye, do ye want a wee cup of tea to calm yer nerves."

"God love ye son, I'll light a candle for ye. I knew you wouldn't let me down."

Pip made his mother a cup of tea. As he was pouring it out he thought 'I'll find some way to get the sack, should it bloody kill me!'

~ ~ ~ ~ ~

"Where were you yesterday?" Peggy was standing at the green wine gum, shopping bag in hand.

"I had an awful dose af the flu Peggy. I'm still nat feelin' right, but I can't let me customers down," sniffed Ernie.

"Dose af the flu me arse."

"What's atin' you the day, Peggy? You've a bake on ye that cud kill a maun at ten paces."

"Never you mine. An' don't go sexually assaultin' me wi' yer vegetables."

Ernie looked puzzled. "What in the name af God are you ramblin' on about?"

"Keep yer carrots till yerself. Ye made a lewd gesture to me the other week wi' one."

"Are ye sure ye weren't drunk?"

"Luk here, Ernie Flaherty, if I was capable of makin' it to yer van I wouldn't have been drunk. When I'm drunk I can't even make it to the loo. In fact parts of me disappear when I'm snattered.

"Like what?" Ernie looked at her."What parts af ye disappear?"

"I'm only jokin', Ernie. Nye give me my usual assortment af vegetables an' throw in a couple af hands af bananas."

"The way to a mans heart is through his stomach. That's a true sayin' ye know," said Ernie as he weighed out Peggy's potatoes.

"The way tae a mans heart is through his shirt wi' a ten inch knife, Ernie."

"What has Rab done on ye nye, Peggy?"

"Nathin. I'm just wonderin' how till get me hauns on his money."

"Come into a bit af money then, Peg."

"Nah, it wuz wishful thinkin', Ernie. I found his policies th' other day. Do you know I'd be well aff if that auld lad af mine snuffed it?"

"You weeman are all the same, all heart! My missus is all heart as well. She taule me th' air wud clear me flu. She must think I'm daft. I can feel a bout af pneumonia comin' on." He coughed and spat on the ground, then pointed at the slimy deposit. "Do ye see that? It luks a bad colour to me."

"She probably knows it, Ernie. That's why yer out wi' the van the day. Ye believed her. An' there's nathin' wrang wi' yer spit. I'm an expert on spute. Rab brings up enough af it"

"What th' hell are ye on the day Peggy? Brain pills. Yer nat usually as bright as this af a mornin'."

"Ye cud say they were delivered by post. Seven thousand af them, till be precise."

"You'd better be careful, Peggy, the police are comin' down hard on drugs, nye the Troubles aren't so bad."

"Let's just say I won't be kneecapped, Ernie!"

"I'm very glad till hear that, Peggy. Yer kneecaps are one af yer best features," mumbled Ernie.

Peggy poked him on the chest. "What did ye say there?"

"Here, that's sore. I only said, 'Kneecappin' shud be kept for th' auld creatures that sell them'." He rubbed his chest.

Lynus cupped his mouth with his hands and yelled," Hey Rab! We're in the money eh? I've ordered meself a whole new outfit af summer clobber fram the catalogue."

Rab was on his way down to Sir Robert's, for a bit of peace.

"So ye've heard the news then?"

"Aye Bert! When are we bookin' the tickets?"

"Haule on thur, Lynus. I think yer bein' a trifle premature. This is only April. We hae loads af time till book. Anyway the money's nat in our hauns yet. Ye don't count yer chickens afore they're hatched."

Lynus held on to a gatepost to steady himself. "Don't tell me there cud be a mistake! Cud they take it af us?"

"Well, they cud take a thousand poun's af it if the DHSS fines out about it."

"What for?"

"You're only allowed two thousand five hundred in the bank when yer oan the dole, Lynus."

"I'm nat on the dole!"

"Aye, an' I'm standin' fer the next position of Pope!"

Lynus wiped the sweat off his brow with a piece of oily rag. "But ... I only sign oan in the winter!"

"Well nye, we're inta spring, an' yer still signin' oan fer I saw ye."

"I wuz signin' aff!"

"Once a fortnight?"

"Jaysus Rab, do you mean till say I will have till haun the government one thousand quid? That goes agin my religion, ye know. It's usually th' other way roun', they give an' I receive."

"Th' only answer tae it all, Lynus is tae put it in a swiss bank account!"

"Wud that stap the dole fram gettin' their filthy mitts on it, Rab?"

"I think it wud dae that alright. Th' only prablim is gettin' it over till Switzerland, Lynus."

"Aye. Sure it wud cost almost a thousand quid till go till Switzerland, Rab."

"Post it!"

"Who will I post it to?"

"Address it to th' head of finance af the swiss yodeller's haliday fund!"

The penny finally dropped. "See you, Rab Kirk. The divil will nat be satasfied till he's pokin' ye in th' arse with thon trident af his. Me heart almost stapped batin' fer a while thur. Swiss yodeller's haliday fund! How do ye think them up?"

"Well, it's bein' so cheerful that keeps me goin', Lynus. If I stapped to ponder oan the realities af life I'd commit suicide. Nye, take yerself aff an' order yer safari suit an' thong. Only make sure ye get wan big enough tae haule yer nuts. The monkeys in Tenerife are partial till them."

"There are no monkeys in Tenerife, Rab!"

"Aye Lynus, an you've nae nuts, so ye shud be safe. An' ye know, I wasn't jokin' about that thousand quid. Ye can bank two-an'-a-half but spend the other wan as quick as ye can."

"Luk Rab, that money will go through my hauns as quick as a dose af salts through Sarah Cruickshank's back passage."

~~~~~

Sarah had poor Percy captive again. The man had gone completely to seed. His wig lay redundant on his dressing table beside his trilby hat and his other bits and pieces. He sat facing Sarah, a broken man. His get-up-and-go had got-up-and-gone.

Sarah had made him a cup of tea. The cup rattled on the saucer as he tried to steady his shaking hand, a hand that once deftly signed his name with a flourish of his gold-plated fountain pen. Now he found it difficult even to remember his name at times, never mind sign forms of importance for the Council.

"You look ten times better without thon wig af yours. A man looks better growin' old gracefully. Of course, nye your nat tryin' till hide yer age ye must be findin' it a bit embarrassin' when ye lie about it."

"I never lied about my age, Mrs Cruickshank. I told you I was fifty-five and I was telling the truth."

"If you told the truth the devil would be that ashamed he'd put out the fire's af hell, Mr Thorndyke. Yer that crooked I could clean the S-bend af me toilet with ye." Sarah yanked the cup and saucer from his hand as if the man was going to pocket them and teetered into her kitchen.

"Is your daughter coming over, Mrs Cruickshank?" He prayed she was. At least she would help him make it through the next half hour. Today the gate was being changed *again*. The fire brigade and the police had decided the existing one was a hazard as there was no escape from
~~~~~

fire, apart from the doors, which were always locked. The gate was also locked at all times. He dreaded the arrival of the new gate. He knew what it looked like. Sarah didn't.

"I gave her a ring but I don't know what's up with her the day. Her mind seems to be on other things. She hung up on me three times this mornin'. She's tryin' to say I sent Dr McNulty round the twist. If ye ask me thon auld lad went round the bend years ago. He gave me a prescription for a laxative, an' it was that strong me back passage is on fire I'm passin' that much diarrhoea. I'm slappin' *Lanacane* on it by the tube an' it's nat coolin' it down one wee bit. An' that's only *one* af me ailments. I could write a book on the others."

Percy blushed. He wished he could strike the old bat dumb.

"I hope this gate is not some wee light sticks af wood stuck together with *Superglue*."

"I can assure you it's not light, Mrs Cruickshank!"

"See if it is, you can shove it up yer ..."

The front door opened and Elsie breezed in, much to Percy's relief. His face lit up.

"Take that lecherous look af your face Percy! My daughter is not a loose woman."

Elsie sat down beside Percy and apologised for her mother's failings. "They get crabby in their old age, Mr Thorndyke. I'm sure you understand."

"I'm sure he does. He's almost ready to collect his old age pension himself." Sarah slapped the arm of her chair to ram the statement home.

"You keep that up, ma, an' I'm gettin' you put in a home," snapped Elsie.

"You'll never get me in a home! I'm not sittin' amongst strangers, I'm particular who I sit beside."

"Did you ever stop to think the homes are particular about who they take in. They could refuse to have ye."

Percy looked from one to the other. He felt like a piece of ham sandwiched between two slices of bread.

A rap on the door put a stop to the argument. Elsie answered the door to a beaming Rab.

"God Rab, I told you before not to come over here. You know you only get me ma's dander up."

"Did ye nat here the clank af the gate?"

"How did you get in? The gate was locked."

"It wud take the keys af Belfast Castle tae open *that* gate. Did ye nat hear the men put it on?"

"You couldn't hear a ten-gun salute in here, me ma's givin' it that with her tongue. Poor Percy's ready to join Dr McNulty, his nerves are that shattered."

"Come on out an' hae a wee luk at the new gate, Elsie."

Elsie stepped out into the hallway and peered out the door.

"In th' name of ..." She was rendered speechless.

An iron gate that would have looked more at home on the Berlin Wall had been installed while they had been talking.

"I had tae put me full weight agin it till open it. I think Bert will be actin' as gate master fram nye on. That'll nat blow in the wind. Nat even a hurricane cud shift that thing."

"What's goin' on here?" Sarah hirpled out of her flat to see what was all the talk was about. She gazed in awe, dumbstruck for once.

Percy stood behind her, shaking nervously. "I told you it wasn't made out of light material, Mrs Cruickshank. Nye, before you start, you did say you wanted a strong one."

"Elsie! Get Bert. I want that removed at once!"

"I don't think Bert cud move that, our Sarah. It wud take a five-hundred-pound bomb tae blow it aff." Rab laughed uncontrollably.

"Thurs only wan thing fer it, Mrs Cruickshank. Ye may ring the Provo's up or else hae a chat with yer maun Gerry."

"I'm goin' to ring the Reverend Ian! If I can't be heard loud an' clear in the housin' office, he's the man that can."

"She means that Rab, ye know."

"I'm nat doubtin' a word af it, Elsie. But dae ye know somethin'? I think thon woman cud be the first person oan this earth tae render that maun speechless. Wud ye agree wi' me, Percy me lado?"

"Dae ye know, Percy, life's gran'. The daffodils are comin' up. Thur's yellow wans wi' orange trumpets, an' thur's orange wans wi' yellow trumpets. The pussy willow will soon be in bloom. Peggy will hae a new fur coat. Bert will be able till afford seven sets af choppers, wan set fer every day af the week an' we'll all be in the money. Summer is nat too far away either, I can feel the sun shinin' on me face already." He threw his hands towards the heavens as if embracing the Lord and yelled at the top of his voice. "*Thank you lord. Yer wan hell-af-a-nice crathur. Ye'd make the middle an' two ends af a dacent spud.*

"That's a sin, Robert Kirk. Thankin' God for makin' ye inta a crook. Have ye no principals at all? It's nat the Lord ye shud be thankin', it's the divil himself," reprimanded Sarah.

"Aye Sarah, ye cud be right. Sure it's the divil that has all the good tunes," answered Rab. He took a deep breath, braced himself and walked slowly towards the gate. Stopping a few feet from it he bowed low and tugged his forelock. "Will ye permit me tae pass through yer impressive portal, yer majesty? Yer a grand lukin' specimen all the while. The last time I laid my good eye oan anything as grandiose as yersel' wuz when I wuz hauncuffed an' thrown inta jail!"

"Daft auld eejit," hissed Sarah. "I'm away in to phone the Reverend Ian. If he doesn't help me get the right flamin' gate, I'll ring th' baule Gerry!".

Rab winked at Percy. "She means it ye know. At layste wan good thing might come out af it. They'll hae somethin' in cammon. Maybe they'll start spakin' till each other face till face an nat behin' each other's backs!. An' while they are doin' it we'll be in Tenerife lubricatin' our throats an' lyin' or layin' in the sun." He gave Percy another wink before adding, "If ye know what I mean Percy, me laddo."

He punched the air with his fist and yelled, *Yee-ha, Tenerife, here we come!"*